The Cubic Pea

The Cubic Pea

Tim Morris

JANUS PUBLISHING COMPANY LTD
Cambridge, England

First published in Great Britain 2020
by Janus Publishing Company Ltd
The Studio
High Green
Great Shelford
Cambridge CB22 5EG

www.januspublishing.co.uk

Copyright © Tim Morris 2020
British Library Cataloguing-in-Publication Data
A catalogue record for this book is available from the British Library

ISBN 978-1-85756-913-1

Cover Design: Janus Publishing Company Ltd

Printed and bound in Great Britain

Preface

When a child has a noisy tantrum for no apparent reason in a supermarket aisle, we tend to blame the parents for not being in control. When a stranger ignores our attempts to speak to them in a public situation, we can think them rude and impolite. The explanation for this sort of behaviour may often be Asperger's syndrome, alternatively known as Autistic Spectrum Disorder (ASD). In many cases, this social awkwardness is accompanied by an enhanced ability in other areas. This book is a fictional interpretation of what might be possible if these abilities are given the chance to flourish. In real life, this tends not to happen because of a general lack of knowledge and understanding. Hopefully, after reading this book, you will understand a little more.

Any resemblance to actual persons, living or dead, or actual events is purely coincidental.

For Celia

Chapter One

Dr Alice Selby should have been delighted with her day. Her presentation had been extremely well received and, in the subsequent meeting, funding had been approved for a further three years' research. Her boss was certainly pleased. He'd talked of nothing else on their return journey from Dublin, including submitting her findings for publication in the *Journal of Cancer Genetics*. However, Alice wasn't really listening. She was thinking about Robert. All day long she had been surreptitiously checking her phone and responding as best she could to the various messages. Now all she wanted was to get away from her boss so she could devote her full attention to doing her best to help Robert. Time was tight as their flight back had been delayed and she was now pleased her boss had driven them both to Gatwick despite her living only a few minutes' walk from Redhill station. Alice couldn't help smiling as she thought to herself, if it had been Robert, he would've refused a lift and gone by train instead.

Eventually, they arrived back at Alice's flat. 'Thanks; see you on Friday,' said Alice as she got out of the car, before climbing the stairs to her flat as fast as her court shoes would allow.

Once inside the flat, she kicked off her shoes and curled up on the sofa with her phone. She found the text from William suggesting they meet at the Red Lion in Reigate at 7 p.m. It was now 6.30 p.m. and she hadn't a clue what to wear. She had always thought of William as a bit of a slob in his baggy trousers, worn shirts and tired jumpers. As a consequence, half of her thought, it's only William so it doesn't really matter what I look like, whereas the other half thought, I'm going out in the evening for a change, so I could put something nice on. In the end, she decided on a compromise, replacing her business suit with beige jacket and jeans. As she didn't have time for a shower, she settled for just washing her face, brushing her shoulder-length light-brown hair and reapplying a small amount of make-up, all the time wishing it was Robert she was going to have dinner with.

Although she managed to park easily enough, the traffic along the A25 had slowed her up and she was 5 minutes late entering the pub. William was already sitting at a table in a corner of the restaurant area with a pint of beer in front of him. He waved to her and stood up as she approached. She was surprised to see he was wearing a smart dark-grey jacket, light-grey tailored trousers and an ironed pale-pink shirt. His thinning grey hair had been slicked back and, despite the obvious lines on his round and somewhat podgy face, she thought he'd made more of an effort than she had. He asked her what she would like to drink and then attracted the attention of the waitress, whom he clearly knew, to order her orange juice without ice. The menus were already on the table, but before either of them even thought about food, Alice asked, 'Why does Robert always have to overcomplicate everything? I have to say I've got very mixed feelings about all this.'

'I know,' William replied. 'Most people would have adjusted their plans to suit the client but no, not Robert, he has to insist the client fits in with him. I'm amazed his idea was accepted.'

'So am I but I'm just as bad,' admitted Alice, reaching for a menu. 'I've agreed to do what he asked as well, in spite of not really agreeing with him. I suppose I feel responsible in that I've been banging on about Robert and the others doing something useful. I don't even know how good they are. All three of them talk a good story but I freely admit I don't understand much of the technical side. I was only trying to push them a bit so they got back on their feet and earned some money. This sounds like an ideal job to boost their confidence but I'm already fearful it will have the reverse effect on Robert.'

'Not to mention Simon and Jake,' said William with a smile on his face. 'That's why I thought it would be a good idea for the two of us to have a chat tonight and give us a chance to get to know each other a bit more. It's pretty clear from all the messages flying around today they're going to need our assistance to make any progress with anything.

I should be able to help you a little with the technical stuff but I think you can be confident they know what they're doing on that front. My concern is more about whether they are capable of working well together. How much do you know about Asperger's syndrome?'

'Only what I've read since Robert told me that's the reason he doesn't "do people",' replied Alice, raising two fingers of each hand in the air. 'I know it's something the three of them have in common as that's how they met, through an Asperger's group, and it's why they call themselves Aspies What about you?'

'Similar. I'd heard about it before I met Robert but I've made an effort to find out more about it since. To be politically correct, it's supposed to be called Autistic Spectrum Disorder these days or ASD for short, because of changes in medical opinion and Hans Asperger having Nazi connections. However, for me, the spectrum aspect is the most important factor as that explains why Robert, Simon and Jake are all so different. In fact, I'm far from convinced Simon has Asperger's at all. If he does, I think he can only just be on the end of the spectrum because you can have normal conversations with him about people without him getting upset.

'Jake, on the other hand, is towards the opposite end, the autistic end, as he's obsessed with numbers, doesn't understand how to behave around other people, and demonstrates what books on the subject describe as the classic symptoms. It's Jake I'm most concerned about because he could easily end up like one of those people you occasionally hear about making news headlines. "Man with Asperger's syndrome under arrest for hacking into government intelligence system", or something similar. There's little doubt Jake breaks the law pretty much every day. Robert seems to fall somewhere between Simon and Jake but, given he was diagnosed when he was only six, he's had a lot of help to learn how to deal with people even if he has worked out how to use strategies to suit himself.'

Whilst William was talking, Alice had been playing with a beer mat. 'I'm not sure you're helping me overcome my worries. I suppose I don't like to think of what they do as illegal, even though I realise it often is. They make it sound like such a natural thing to do when they speak of going in or having a look from underneath. I've never heard any of them suggest doing something which sounds like stealing or anything like that.'

'It sounds as though you haven't heard Simon's analogy about robbing a bank.'

'No,' said Alice, sounding shocked, 'what do you mean?'

'It's probably best you hear it from Simon himself. In fact, if you get Simon on his own, I bet he would trust you enough to tell you why he is so security focussed. It's a very sad story and, like most of us, it demonstrates how what happens early in our lives dictates a lot about how we are as adults.'

'I certainly agree with you on that. You don't have to be Asperger's to have had unpleasant experiences in your past,' said Alice, feeling a tear starting to well in her eye. 'Hadn't we better order some food?'

'Sorry,' said William thoughtfully, 'I didn't mean to upset you. From your reaction though, it seems as if we all may have bad experiences bottled up inside us. Maybe that's what brings the five of us together even if we're not prepared to tell each other all the details. Yes, let's order before we get too depressed.'

William called over the waitress. Alice ordered *salade niçoise* and, as she was driving, a glass of tap water. William ordered beefburger and chips with all the trimmings and another pint of beer. Whilst they waited for the food to arrive, Alice continued the conversation. 'So, what else do you know that can help me to understand Robert and Jake more? I'm very wary of Jake. I know he doesn't say much about anything but, when he does, I really don't like the way he talks about some things, especially women.'

'Don't be too hard on Jake. As I said, he didn't have the benefit of knowing about Asperger's until he was an adult. I doubt even you will get his full story. I have pieced together a picture of his early life from the various snippets he has told me and also from what Simon has told me about him. Jake has two brothers, one older and one younger, both of whom are "normal". I don't like using normal as the opposite of Asperger's because I'm not sure anyone is truly normal, but I don't know how else to describe it.'

'I read the opposite of Asperger's is Williams syndrome,' said Alice, 'where people are extremely sociable and struggle to deal with numbers. The difference is Williams syndrome has been linked to a specific chromosome and there is a clear genetic explanation, whereas for Asperger's, there are a number of theories but no clear genetic link, as yet. The majority of people, the normal ones as you put it, fit in between and are classed as being neuro-typical, so that would no doubt include both of us.'

'Being a geneticist, you will understand the science behind it much better than me,' said William. 'In Jake's case, all he knew when he was at school was he was different and didn't really fit in. However, his main problem was at home. He really wanted to make friends and join in with his brothers' games but didn't know how. The more his brothers made fun of his efforts, the more he tried to impress them by doing things like quoting pi to lots of decimal places or reeling off a long list of prime numbers. Not surprisingly, this only made things worse and he ended up getting bullied more at home than he did at school. Fortunately, he had a bedroom of his own and this became his retreat.

'As a way of keeping him quiet, from a very early age, his parents had recognised his love of numbers and bought him calculators and computers for presents. Jake found it easy to understand how computers work. I'm not sure whether he actually thinks in binary or just recognises patterns, but he certainly learnt how higher-level computer languages developed and became a self-taught expert in pretty much every one that he could find. It became an obsession and still is. Nowadays, he seems to search out the most difficult challenges he can find, as if to prove to himself as much as anybody else that he can penetrate any system he chooses. If we don't give him testing things to do, he will continue to find his own and, I fear, one of these days he'll push too far and get caught. Simon does his best to help and protect Jake but Jake won't always let him.

'As for Jake's attitude to women, that also goes back to his brothers. In the same way Jake struggled to make friends with other boys, he struggled even more with girls. Neither of his brothers had any problems when it came to finding girlfriends. Jake became very jealous and spied on his brothers when they were with their girlfriends. His brothers caught him doing this, which led to their teasing and tormenting of him increasing even more. Once he recognised he was never going to be able to get a real girlfriend, he created his own fantasy world based upon fictional characters he came across when watching films and TV, which was his relaxation from his computing activities. As a result he objectifies women. He's mentioned Wonder Woman to me more than once. I suspect he doesn't realise real women have feelings and can be hurt by what he says.'

'I suppose that does put a different perspective on things,' responded Alice. 'I'll try harder with Jake. Interestingly, he now attends our Mad Hatter's tea party, as Robert and Simon call it, on a fairly regular basis.'

'Ah yes,' said William, 'Saturday morning tea with Alice. I've definitely been told all about that. If I didn't have my shop to look after I would be keen to come round to Robert's house on a Saturday morning to experience it for myself. From the way they talk, it sounds like it's become the highlight of the week for all three of them, even Jake.'

'I hadn't realised it meant so much to them. It just seemed to evolve. I admit I kept going back because I was growing to like Robert and I found the scientific discussions quite stimulating. I didn't even see Jake for the first few weeks. He would sneak down to get his tea and take it back up to his room. Then he started to appear sheepishly at the door and now he regularly has his tea with us and has participated more and more in the conversation, although he only speaks when the topic is computing related.' Alice paused and had another sip of her juice. 'I know we've talked a lot about Simon and Jake but the one I really want to talk about is Robert. What do you know about him?'

William rocked back in his chair, laughed loudly but spoke softly. 'You mean apart from the fact you're in love with him?'

'Oh my God!' exclaimed Alice, blushing. 'Is it that obvious?'

'Probably only to me. The only other one who may have noticed is Simon. I'm certain Jake doesn't realise and equally sure Robert doesn't have a clue either.'

'Don't you dare tell him,' said Alice forcefully. 'I don't know how he would take it and it might ruin everything. I don't really understand it myself. How can someone be so infuriating, fascinating and lovable all at the same time?'

Before William could reply, their food arrived. William tucked into his burger as if he hadn't eaten for a week, whereas Alice, although quite hungry, only nibbled at her salad. After swallowing her first mouthful, she blurted out, 'Do you know whether Robert is gay?'

William looked up at her, swallowed his mouthful of food and took a slurp of his beer. 'Are you asking me on the basis that it takes one to know one?'

'Oh, I'm so sorry,' said Alice. 'I didn't mean to embarrass you. I just need to know if I'm wasting my time. I've known Robert for over six months now and I still have no real idea of what he thinks of me. Every time I get close to talking about feelings, he starts to get annoyed and either changes the subject or walks out.'

'Can I suggest we have a bit of a break from conversation and concentrate on our food for a few minutes,' said William calmly, 'but, no, I'm pretty sure Robert isn't gay.'

Alice seemed to accept William's suggestion and went back to eating her salad. They both ate their food in silence with Alice, despite having a smaller plateful, finishing well after William. William restarted the conversation as if there had been no gap at all. 'I've known Robert longer than the rest of you, since he first moved to Redhill almost two years ago now. I've wondered about his sexuality a few times but have never heard him talk that way about anyone, male or female. My conclusion is based upon observing him when customers have entered my shop whilst he's been working with me there. If the customer has been an attractive lady, I've noticed him show some interest if only by an occasional surreptitious glance. I've not noticed him do the same with attractive men and, as you imply, I would be likely to notice that more. It could well be that he's asexual but I suppose my overall conclusion has been he has so many thoughts and ideas going on in his head he hasn't got room for any sexual or romantic ones, plus, like you just said, he's told me countless times, he doesn't "do" people.'

'Well,' said Alice, 'I have my own theory about that. I'm sure being diagnosed so early as an Aspie has helped him to learn various coping strategies and responses but I think it has also worked against him. He's been told for over twenty years, because of Asperger's, he doesn't "do" people. That could well have become a self-fulfilling prophecy and provided him with an easy excuse when faced with situations he doesn't like. I fully accept he doesn't read people's expressions and body language or understand social conventions and that makes things very difficult for him. However, if the motivation is great enough, he can stretch his elastic band, as he puts it, from wherever he is on the spectrum towards "normal", even if he does need a recovery period afterwards. Also, he has a number of people he calls friends albeit, in most cases, they're also likely to be considered geeky, similar to him and with common areas of interest, including, dare I say, yourself.'

'I suppose your theory might well be correct but, as Robert would say, at the moment that is an unproven fact. From my own point of view, I've never considered myself as having Asperger's but, yes, I do regard

Robert as a good friend, in spite of the large age difference between us. However, you are right in that our friendship is very much based on our common interest in machines and how they work. I've lived a fairly lonely life but since meeting Robert and, through him, Simon and Jake, I've been reinvigorated and I really enjoy building computing equipment for them. If there's a way for them to utilise that equipment, along with their special abilities, in a more useful and constructive way, I'm all for it.'

'Well, if it helps,' said Alice warmly, 'they all have a great respect for you. You come up quite a lot in our "tea party" conversations, always positive, and they can be like big kids waiting excitedly for your next new bit of kit. I hope they think of me in a similar way but I've definitely learnt not to expect them to tell me how they feel. As well as getting to know you a bit better this evening, I suppose I'm hoping you might be able to give me some advice based on your own experiences with them, particularly with regard to Robert.'

'Thanks, it does help. It won't surprise you to know all I get back directly from Robert is a dutiful thank you, certainly no other compliments!' replied William. 'Have you ever met Robert's parents? Talking with them helped me understand him a lot better.'

'No. I get the impression he doesn't want me to meet them.'

'I doubt it's that. I suspect it's more to do with Robert not wanting them to find out he's not doing as well as they think he is. When they helped him buy that large house, everything was based around what he needed in order to make his new job a success. When he got fired after just over a year, he told his parents he was going to become a self-employed independent computer consultant. Whilst that was of course true, the reality is just about the only work he's done over the last year has been the various bits and pieces I've put his way. His money is running out but he doesn't want to face up to the consequences of that. I'm sure I don't need to tell you one of Robert's most infuriating aspects is he never admits he's in the wrong. It's always somebody else's fault.'

'Tell me about it,' said Alice. 'Mind you, if that wasn't the case, I probably wouldn't have got to know him in the first place. Has he told you how we met?'

'Yes, but I only have his version,' admitted William. 'He said he accidentally bumped into you in Sainsbury's. He apologised and said that you weren't hurt. Then, on a Saturday morning a few days later, you came across him again when he was in Argos with Simon. You got talking and went back to his place for tea and the tea parties grew from there.'

'Ha,' laughed Alice sarcastically, 'that's just typical of him. Limiting the facts to those that suit him and leaving out the rest. The truth is he knocked me flying in Sainsbury's because he was doing his usual fast walk without too much thought for anyone else. I was standing near the end of a gondola wondering whether I'd got everything I needed for my paella when suddenly I found myself sliding on the floor with enough force I almost crashed into the gondola end at the opposite side of the aisle. He did say sorry, as an automatic type of response, but he did nothing to help me get up. He just stood there looking at me. He muttered something about a trolley used for shelf stacking being in the wrong place and leaving too small a gap for him to get through.

'It was the Sainsbury's lady who'd been stacking the shelf who helped me up and asked me if I was alright. I said yes because that's what you do but my wrist was quite painful where I'd landed on it and I did have a few nasty bruises on my elbow and knees afterwards.

'What really spooked Robert was another man who shouted that he'd seen everything and Robert had been going far too fast. Other shoppers were gathering around and Robert started to look scared. Anyway, just as I thought he was about to burst into tears, he almost threw his basket of shopping onto the ground and stormed out of the shop, walking even faster than he usually does. I was both in shock from the fall and stunned by his reaction.

'The Sainsbury's lady, who's called Jane, was very kind and took me somewhere to sit down and recover. I asked her if she'd seen Robert before. She said yes but he usually came in much later in the day when there were fewer people about. She'd noticed him because he always walked quickly, in that strange style of his and with a rucksack on his back. I felt very cross at his reaction and I did intentionally go into Sainsbury's later than usual the next couple of times in the hope I might come across him and have it out with him. I got to know Jane quite well as I made a point of asking her about Robert but she told me she hadn't seen him since the incident with me. Then, one Saturday morning, I spotted him walking in his usual way on the other side of the road with someone, who I now know to be Simon but at the time seemed like a child, almost running behind him. Before I could cross the road, they disappeared into Argos. I followed them, put my hand on Robert's shoulder and asked him if he remembered me and why he had run away after knocking me over. Robert seemed lost for words so it was Simon who replied, telling me Robert had Asperger's and had been taught to get away from any difficult situation before he made it any worse. I thought it an odd explanation but did soften a bit and suggested maybe we could get a coffee so he could explain properly. Again, it was Simon who answered, saying Robert drank tea not coffee. Robert then did speak and explained they had come to Argos to collect some electronic components but Simon didn't like to be out of the house for very long and they needed to go straight back, so would be having their tea there. It wasn't a proper invitation but, when I found out they lived so close, I suggested I go with them. I knew it was a bit risky but I didn't feel threatened and was so intrigued I couldn't resist. The rest, as they say, is history.'

'I knew it couldn't have been as simple as Robert made out and I'm not surprised he knocked you over. He isn't overly fat but he is 6ft tall and solidly built, whereas you're quite slight and slender.'

'Anyway,' said Alice, 'you were telling me about Robert's parents and how they helped you to understand him.'

'Well, yes they did but it might help you more if I try to put everything in context. Before I do, would you like anything more to eat or drink?'

Alice said she would just have a coffee. William usually had apple pie and custard as dessert but decided it best to settle for just another pint of beer.

As soon as they had their drinks, William began.

'Talking with Robert's parents made me appreciate the significant number of adjustments they'd had to make to their own lives in order to help Robert and to cope with the many issues that arose on a daily basis during his childhood. More than that, it helped me to understand more about my own parents and maybe about parenting in general. I'm not saying being gay and being Asperger's are in any way the same but I do believe there are similarities in perception. Fifty years ago, when I was starting to realise what my own sexuality really meant, Asperger's had not been discovered and the word gay didn't mean what it does now. I knew from a fairly early age I wasn't the same as most other boys and I certainly didn't like taking part in any rough games. Words such as queer and poof were used to taunt me but it was the physical side of the bullying I found most difficult to cope with. I've always been overweight so that didn't help either. I would go home from school and try to hide any injuries from my parents.

'About the same time, my mother had been diagnosed with lung cancer so I didn't want to add to her worries. She found out anyway and did her best to help me and suggest strategies to keep out of the way of the bullies. She told me she'd known for a while that I liked boys rather than girls and she used the word homosexual to describe me. However, whenever my mother and I had a conversation about it, she would always say we mustn't tell my father as he wouldn't understand. Just before she died, shortly before my sixteenth birthday, she made me promise not to let him find out, not to blame him for his views and to look after him when she'd gone. I like to think I kept that promise.

'As a young child, I'd always liked to help my father in his electrical repair shop. I was allowed to dismantle various pieces of equipment that were beyond repair as I wanted to find out how they worked. As we lived above the shop, my mother used to look after the front of the shop, allowing my father to work on repairs in the workshop at the back or to visit customers at their homes. After my mother died, I gradually became more useful. A friend of my mother's, who helped look after her when she was ill, also helped in the shop after my mother's death. In fact, it's her granddaughter, Nancy, who now occasionally helps me. Anyway, my father taught me pretty much all he knew. I used the workshop as a place to hide from the bullies and spent most of my spare time in there.

'I left school at sixteen and worked full time with my father. Technology was changing rapidly and the electronics of control systems were evolving beyond my father's level of knowledge. I, on the other hand, loved the new technology and took every opportunity to understand the latest developments. When the first personal computers such as the Oric and Commodore 64 were brought in for repair, my father turned to me and I became the computer repair expert. I soon started to build my own computers from components rescued from irreparable machines. The reason I'm telling you this is because it became an obsession for me to keep up with and to understand the latest developments, a little like Robert, Simon and Jake with their various obsessions. I also looked after my father by coming to the pub with him, usually this one, and, more importantly, seeing him home safely. I would sit with him and his friends, who also became my friends, even though they were significantly older than me. Drinking lots of beer and getting little exercise didn't help with my weight problem, which is something I've struggled with all my life.

'My father also taught me how to look after the financial side of the business and, when he reached sixty-five, he passed the whole business over to me and retired. He continued to live with me but became something of a couch potato, apart from trips to the pub. He suffered from dementia and eventually had to go into a care home. I visited him regularly, even when he hardly knew who I was. I was sorely tempted to tell him I was gay when he was beyond understanding but I never did. I changed the business into just a computer shop for bespoke machines and repairs.

'One day, about two years ago, Robert came in and asked if I had a rather unusual part as he didn't want to have to wait for an order from China. While we searched for it together, he told me he wanted it for one of his many robotic projects. He was impressed with my workshop and we found we had a great deal in common, including a difficult childhood and an interest in 3D printers. He started to come into the shop on a regular basis. One day I delivered a part to his house and he showed me what he was making. I was extremely impressed and, as you say, the rest is history.

'Most of the time while we were working together we would talk about computers and robotics but there were times when he would open up a little about other aspects of his life. I learned from his parents he would only talk about things like that on a one-to-one basis with people he really trusted but, even then, not if he had to look directly at them. He hated to be told what to do so his parents' strategy was for one of them to plant an idea, possibly whilst Robert was sitting alongside them in the car, and then wait until Robert raised the issue again, often in a way where it came across as Robert's idea in the first place. You might benefit from trying that sort of approach. I also wonder whether you have enough time with just the two of you together, as it seems to me that Simon or Jake are usually around as well.'

Alice thought for a while. 'That's a very good point,' she said. 'Simon is a bit like a limpet but I'm very fond of him and wouldn't want to upset him. Maybe I need to try to manipulate the situation more as

I do tend to get frustrated and then say what I think of Robert to his face, which, now I think about it, doesn't work and only serves to make him irritated.'

'You know the Asperger's aspect of him cannot be changed. There's no cure so, just like his parents found, if you want to help and understand him, it's you who has to adapt. He does talk about you quite a lot when we're working together. It's mainly about how much you know about genetics and how you've both discovered there are many similarities between genetics and robotics. He also talks about how you've helped both Simon and Jake and how he really enjoys the Mad Hatter's tea parties with you, although he does say you ask annoying questions which probably reinforces what you've just said yourself.'

William reached across the table and enveloped Alice's hand with his own, much larger hand. 'It can't be easy being in love with someone like Robert. I've never heard him use the word love, neither have his parents, so there's no guarantee you'll ever know whether he loves you back.'

Alice made no attempt to withdraw her hand and was fighting back the tears as she said shakily, 'I can't walk away now. I have to give it my best shot and believe that one day I'll know the answer.'

'Alright,' said William hesitantly, 'maybe one day.'

The mood was broken when the waitress approached with their bill. Alice pulled her hand away, took her purse out of her shoulder bag and started to count out some money. Just as William was about to do the same with his wallet, Alice looked at him firmly. 'Please let me pay for tonight. You've helped me a lot. I'm sure there'll be lots of ups and downs to come and, if we feel the need to do this again, it can be your turn.'

William put his wallet away. 'That's very kind of you, thank you. I'm very happy to do this any time you wish. It's helped me as well. Without your company, I would only have been sitting at the bar on my own. Old habits die hard.'

'It's a shame all this has happened so quickly and while I was in Dublin,' stated Alice. 'I did speak to Robert briefly over the phone but if I'd had a chance to talk to him in person, he might have been persuaded to let me drive him to the brewery. You know he won't even come in the car with me tomorrow. At the moment I feel he loves trains more than he does me. As it is, I suppose there's no option but to try to do it his way. At least my boss was in a good mood so I had no problem getting tomorrow off. Anyway, it's been a long day and what I really need is a good night's sleep. Don't forget the video conference tomorrow evening; fingers crossed it'll be good news.' With that she stood up, gave William a small kiss on his cheek, thanked him again and walked out of the pub to her car.

William watched her go then wandered to the bar for another pint of beer, which he drank slowly, before making his way home on foot as he'd done many times before.

Chapter Two

It had seemed such a good idea two days ago but, now it was time to catch his train, Robert Tait was having second thoughts. He didn't like to be underprepared but that was how he felt. This time it wasn't because he had left everything to the last minute, there just hadn't been enough time since receiving the phone call to find out all the facts, plus the text to confirm the meeting had only come through yesterday. At least he'd arranged for Alice to be there. He'd been staggered as to how easily she could get away from work at such short notice, as he'd been dismissed from his own job for that sort of thing. Also, there had been no difficulty in persuading Jake and Simon to be ready, although he was concerned they did not always work well together. However, he was most worried about himself. All of his life, he'd struggled to understand people, particularly strangers, and here he was, going on his own into the unknown to meet a total stranger. It was bound to stretch his internal elastic band but he was determined to stay in control. The best way of doing that was to have a logical plan and to stick to it. He was pleased to be travelling by train. He liked trains, even though on this occasion it meant going via Clapham Junction to get from Redhill to Southampton. As usual, he had reserved a forward-facing, first-class window seat with a table and a computer charging socket. He could work on the train rather than having to talk to Alice, who would no doubt have asked annoying questions. He did have the outline of a plan and he boarded the train determined to decide on his strategy well before he arrived in Southampton.

It was early September and the temperature had started to drop as the 16.23 from London Waterloo was pulling into Southampton Central station. It was due to arrive at 17.57 but, as he packed away his laptop into his rucksack, Robert noted the time was now 18.09. He didn't look like a typical first-class passenger. His chinos were faded, his trainers well worn, and his long-sleeved plain blue shirt was creased and fraying at the cuffs. With his shock of curly brown hair and badly trimmed beard, he attracted a number of glances from fellow travellers as he stood up from his seat, excused himself somewhat clumsily past the lady in the aisle seat and moved towards the door of the carriage, leaving the remains of his complimentary tea behind him. Late as usual, he thought to himself as he was waiting to disembark and, in spite of starting to feel quite nervous, no chance of compensation this time.

Determined to focus on the job he was there to do, he alighted onto the platform but, instead of heading for the exit, he turned in the opposite direction and walked rapidly towards the end of the platform, approaching a bench on which a man was sitting alone. The man was thick set, middle aged, with a full head of slightly greying fair hair and wearing a dark pin-striped suit. Robert paused for a moment, making sure it was the same person whose photograph he'd been studying on the train, but, before he had chance to speak, the man turned and, with a somewhat superior air, said, 'Mr Tait, I presume? I do hope this isn't going to be a waste of time. My secretary was very sure I should come and pestered me until I agreed, but I must say meeting you like this does seem an unnecessarily clandestine and complicated arrangement over just one email.'

Robert was a little taken aback but resolved to stay positive and replied, 'I do not agree, Mr Watson. Neither of us knows the true facts of the situation and, until we do, it is better to be cautious. I do not believe it is just about one email. You are the Chairman of a family-owned brewery with a lengthy history which had been steadily increasing its profits over recent years until last year, when there was an inexplicable decrease in profit. You now think your brother might be conspiring against you. It is not surprising you are concerned and unsure of the next steps to take.'

'That's a lot to read into a chance conversation between my wife and your mother, Mr Tait. My wife has the impression you are some sort of computer wizard who would be able to tell if my brother did in fact write the email. Is that correct?'

'I have not spoken to my mother about this and I do not propose to do so. The only information I have gained is from speaking to your secretary, Miss Pauline Sharples, and from looking up your company on the internet.'

The train started to move and rumbled slowly out of the station towards its next stop at Brockenhurst and then on to its final destination in deepest Dorset. When it was almost out of sight, Robert continued. 'I usually tend to be thought of as more of a geek than a wizard but, as you say, your wife has obtained her information from my mother and my mother has a very limited understanding of what I actually do. Tracing the source of the email should be relatively straightforward but I suspect that knowing the answer will not solve your problems. However, now the train has moved on, we are rather exposed here at the end of the platform so, if you wish to continue this conversation, I suggest we find a quiet corner in the pub across the road.'

Without waiting for an answer, Robert turned and walked briskly towards the exit, swerving around but carefully avoiding anyone on the platform who was in his way. Derek Watson, who was not particularly fit after many years of good living, looked somewhat bemused, stood up and followed, struggling to keep up.

The King's Head was full of people enjoying a drink after work before catching their train home but the two unlikely companions took their drinks and managed to find a free table where they would not be easily overheard. As a brewer and owner of many public houses, although the King's Head in Southampton was not one of them, Derek had naturally made his way to the bar to buy the drinks. Usually he would have been interested in assessing the competition by closely checking the quality of the beer and the level of service but, today, he felt strangely out of control. He wasn't used to being kept waiting, particularly on a cold railway platform. Also, he didn't need Robert Tait to tell him his company was in trouble, he knew that all too well. He found he had drunk more than half his pint of beer by the time they reached their table. He felt he was clutching at straws by pinning his hopes on this strange young man with his quirky ways and odd mannerisms, who had requested an apple juice whilst explaining why he didn't like any form of alcohol.

Almost as soon as they were seated, Robert abruptly asked if Derek had brought a copy of the offending email as he had been instructed to do. Derek extracted a single sheet of paper from his inside pocket and, after a moment's hesitation, passed it to Robert who photographed it using the camera on his smartphone and, after tapping away for a minute or so, passed the paper back to Derek.

'Are you telling me just by doing that you can find out who sent it?' asked Derek, who was something of a technophobe.

'No,' replied Robert. 'I can only trace the computer it was sent from. If you really want my help, I need you to tell me the background behind the email and why your company is performing so badly, but before you start, I should warn you that I am only interested in the truth and in clear facts. My approach is based on logic and analysis of the facts, so any untruths or supposition will just slow me down.'

Derek hesitated and took another large mouthful of his beer. After careful consideration he said, 'Before I give you any detail of that sort, I must be certain everything is going to be treated extremely confidentially. I'm not even sure I should have let you take a photograph of the email. In the wrong hands it could do a lot of damage. Also, I expect you will want to be paid for your services, so hadn't we better agree your fee and the terms of reference first?'

Derek quickly drained the remainder of his beer. Realising he still had most of his apple juice left, Robert caught up by gulping down the rest of his drink. Almost before he finished, a young lady wearing a King's Arms tabard and hygienic blue gloves courteously asked if they'd finished and could she clear the glasses, which she quickly whisked away. Derek doubted whether his own pubs would have provided such efficient service.

Robert looked up and made a pronounced effort to look Derek in the eye.

'Mr Watson,' he said, 'from the limited facts I have gleaned so far, the most logical explanation is that someone is mounting a cyber-attack on your business. I am confident I can help you overcome this and get your business back on track but I am only willing to do so if our relationship is built on total trust. I promise I will not divulge any information you give me to anyone other than my close associates, who will need some of it to work with. I do admit I would be likely to give everything up under duress, as my pain threshold is very low, but

I do not expect it to come to that as I intend to keep my involvement undetectable.

'As for a fee, I think that should be based on the potential benefits of success. I also have much to lose if confidentiality is not maintained. I should inform you I have already taken out insurance, in case you choose to expose my involvement and my methods. I did try to explain this to your secretary but I don't think she quite understood. Her solution is to call me Roger Thompson rather than Robert Tait but that is unlikely to fool anyone who is capable of sending that email.'

'What do you mean by insurance? That doesn't sound like a relationship built on trust.'

'The young lady who cleared our glasses is, in fact, one of my associates. She will use your beer glass to obtain a sample of your DNA and your fingerprints. These could be used against you but that will only happen if you fail to keep your side of our agreement. As an example, I have been informed your relationship with Pauline Sharples may be more than just boss and secretary. Whether it is or not, it would be fairly simple for her home to be broken into and for your DNA and fingerprints to be found during the subsequent police investigation.'

Derek Watson's face started to turn red and he looked about to explode, although he kept his voice low as he said, in a way that seemed to Robert like he was shouting, 'I thought you said you only dealt in the truth and in facts. That is akin to blackmail. It would certainly be falsifying evidence, which is highly illegal. I don't think I like your methods, Mr Tait. This conversation is over and I now wish I hadn't wasted my time by coming here. It would be better if you don't try to help me after all. Meeting you like this has been a mistake and I am going to leave before I really lose my temper.'

Robert could tell the meeting was not going as he'd planned but didn't really understand why. He could feel the familiar rumbling in his brain starting to build up to the level that could trigger a meltdown, but he resolved to stay calm and in control of the situation. As Derek was starting to get up from his chair, Robert spoke in as confident a manner as he could.

'Fight or flight, Mr Watson, it is entirely your choice, but, if you do walk away now, logic tells me that within twelve months you will no longer be in charge of your brewery. I may well be your only hope of survival so you may wish to reconsider your decision.'

Derek paused, thought for a moment and then slowly sat back down.

Robert continued, 'I apologise if I am not explaining my approach very clearly. Let me try again. Your actual relationship with Pauline Sharples is currently what I term an "unproven fact" as I do not yet have enough evidence to be certain of its nature. In my example, the actual nature of your relationship would not matter as it would become a fact that your DNA was found in Pauline's home. What the authorities would make of this may or may not be the truth. However, I accept that people skills are not my strongest quality. I am much more comfortable with machines but the principle of unproven facts applies everywhere. For example, it is currently an unproven fact your brother sent that email. It is also an unproven fact there is a link to the bigger issue of your failing business. Determining the actual facts is the only way to resolve these questions. I have the ability and resources to do just that and, yes, I do expect to be paid appropriately.'

Robert paused long enough to draw breath. 'Although Watson & Charles is a private company, I still managed to find out enough about yourself, your brother and the value of your business by searching the internet. By my calculations, if your business continues to be undermined and sold, you, personally, will be at least 10 million pounds worse off. I think a fee of 5 per cent of that would be reasonable. Therefore, I ask you to transfer the sum of five hundred thousand pounds into your personal bank account and keep it there until the issue is resolved. Of course, it remains your choice if you want to walk away now.'

Still looking angry, Derek retorted. 'I don't understand what you possibly think you could do for me that would be worth anywhere near half a million pounds of my own money. We've already looked very closely at the reasons for the dip in performance and I'm certain we would know if we were the victims of any criminal activity. I came here thinking a few hundred pounds would be a fair reward for confirming the source of the email. It's only because of the sensitivity regarding my brother that I came here at all.'

Robert's foot was tapping on the floor as he said, 'As I have stated before, the email is likely to be just the tip of the iceberg. I am sure my associates and I are not the normal type of consultants you are used to dealing with but I can assure you we are the best in our fields and also your best chance of resolving your very serious problem. I am, however, not the best salesperson in the world and it is clear I am not yet succeeding in making you understand what we are offering. Although you and I look and behave very differently, there are many similarities between us. I am sure you choose the people you employ because of their ability to provide the wide range of skills you need in order to make your business successful and you reward them well, to buy their loyalty and hard work. I, too, work with extremely talented people but these people are not my employees, they are my associates and are motivated by far more than just money. They have an extremely strong desire to prove they are the best at what they do.'

As he was talking, Robert's phone vibrated slightly. He glanced at it for a few moments and then continued.

'Perhaps one way to help you understand is to demonstrate by means of what I think you would regard in business terms as a loss leader. I will give you a big part of the answer to your email question for nothing. That message was from my associate to tell me it is highly unlikely the email was sent by your brother. No disrespect to your brother but it was planted by someone who has far more knowledge of your IT systems than your brother is likely to have and, even if your brother had paid someone to plant the email, it is not logical he would have done so in a way to point the blame at himself. I seriously suggest you start to accept your business is under attack and that you need to take appropriate action to defend it. You told me earlier the only other person to know your brother is under suspicion is your IT manager. Are you absolutely sure no-one else knows?'

'Well, I suppose I may have mentioned it to my secretary,' replied Derek, looking confused. 'Wait, are you saying the waitress who walked off with my beer glass has already had time to get that far with the email?'

'No, it was from a different associate who specialises in computer technology. Now, please answer my question properly; did you tell your secretary?'

'Yes.'

'Did you tell your wife?'

'No. I only told Mary that Ian Walters, our IT manager, was sure it hadn't actually been sent, as it first appeared, from Butcher's Brewery, as he had found it was really sent from someone inside our own brewery.'

'I find it interesting you told your secretary and not your wife. That adds weight to my theory that there is something more to your relationship with your secretary. We can either leave that as an unproven fact, or are you now convinced I can be trusted with the truth?'

'Whatever my relationship with my secretary is, it is totally irrelevant to the issue at hand.'

'Mr Watson, at this stage neither of us is in a position to decide what is relevant and what is not. As I have tried to explain, the more information you hide from me, the more difficult it will be for me to help you. I am, however, becoming increasingly certain you are having an affair with your secretary.'

Derek responded instantly. 'I categorically deny any affair. I admit I find Pauline a very attractive lady. She has recently split from her long-term partner and I do accept I may have influenced that decision. We've been out for a meal occasionally together and we've kissed a few times, possibly a little more passionately than we should have, but that is definitely as far as it has gone. The fact is, Mr Tait, I love my wife, whom I trust entirely and who I believe would be devastated if she suspected I was being unfaithful. I did not expect to be grilled about my personal life but I've told you this in an attempt to prove I am taking the whole issue seriously and am prepared to do whatever is necessary to resolve the situation.'

'Thank you, Mr Watson. I will take what you have just said as the truth.' After consulting his phone, Robert continued, 'I have to leave shortly. It is nearly 7 p.m. and I have a bus to catch.'

'Ah yes, Pauline told me you were coming down anyway today, to see your uncle on his birthday, I believe.'

'I am pleased you mentioned that. You may be interested to know my uncle died two years ago.' Robert continued to tap his foot as he spoke and to look anywhere but at Derek.

'So why did you lie to Pauline when you claim you only deal in the truth?'

'I did not lie. I do not lie. I chose my words very carefully when speaking to Pauline in order to give you an example of how facts can become misunderstood and distorted. I actually said it was sixty-nine years today since my uncle was born near here, that he is still in the area, and I would have to leave by 7 p.m. to attend a family meal. The facts are correct. However, my uncle is buried in the graveyard of a local church and it is his widow, my Aunt Janet, whom I am visiting. If Pauline had been aware of these two additional facts then she would have communicated more accurately with you. Avoiding distortion of the facts, Mr Watson, is another skill I possess!

'In a similar vein, I told my aunt I was hoping to be catching a bus at 7 p.m. so she would be expecting me to arrive on the train due in at 18.55. I see from my phone this train is running 6 minutes late so I do have a few extra minutes to spare. Trains are something else I know a lot about because I like them a lot but not when they are late. I am a strong believer if train companies offer compensation then any passenger who has a valid claim, no matter how small, should pursue that claim, otherwise how will the train companies get the message that they need to improve their performance?'

Derek was wondering what this mini rant had to do with anything when Robert suddenly reverted back to the previous theme of the conversation.

'In terms of deciding whether to go ahead with our contract, Mr Watson, when you get to work tomorrow, I strongly recommend the first thing you do is ask your IT manager to double check on the sender of that email. You can tell him you need to be absolutely certain before accusing your brother. When he reports back to confirm you brother's innocence, I suggest you ensure your secretary is also made aware of this fact and, at the same time, you can instruct her to text me either "Yes" or "No" to indicate if you want to go ahead.

'Oh,' Robert continued as he was standing up, 'assuming it is a "Yes", which I fully expect it to be, there is one other non-negotiable condition. There must be no further communication whatsoever between your wife and my mother on this issue. Good evening, Mr Watson.'

Derek grabbed Robert's arm and whispered. 'Wait a minute. What contract? We haven't arranged to sign anything.'

'No,' replied Robert, also in a whisper whilst releasing his arm. 'This is a verbal contract only, as the fewer people who know about it the better. The contract states I will resolve your issues and restore your business to its previous level of performance, to your entire satisfaction, for a fee of five hundred thousand pounds. I am comfortable my position is fully protected and you should be equally comfortable as you now know, as a fact, I can be trusted. I believe it is traditional to cement such an arrangement with a handshake.'

Now standing, Robert held out his hand. Almost before Derek realised what was happening, he automatically responded by also standing and holding out his hand to receive a very firm handshake indeed.

'Thank you for my drink, Mr Watson. Goodbye.'

Derek sat back and watched him go. What a very strange chap, he thought to himself, and a bloody train-spotter as well. Nevertheless, he resolved to see his IT manager first thing in the morning. Then he walked up to the bar to order another beer. The waitress who had taken his previous glass was nowhere to be seen.

*　*　*

Almost three hours later, Robert was saying good night to his aunt after an enjoyable meal. He told her he was tired, which was true, but he really wanted to get up to his bedroom so he could be in time for the 10 p.m. video conference.

Robert quite liked visiting his aunt. She was a good cook and knew what sort of food he liked and, more importantly, what he didn't like. He wouldn't have thought about coming today had it not been for a prompt from his mother telling him it would be a nice thing to do, given it was the anniversary of his uncle's death and his aunt would otherwise have been on her own. Robert didn't understand why being on her own would be a problem as he quite liked being on his own. In fact, after the meeting with Derek Watson, he wished he could have been on his own to recover from the effort of it. As he'd expected, his elastic band had been stretched almost to breaking point. Even though he knew his Aunt Janet well, he'd only relaxed a little during their meal together as he still had to worry about the conventions of eating in company, making small talk and remembering to use his cutlery properly.

Fortunately for Robert, the bus had been on time and there had been no reason for his aunt to suspect he hadn't caught the later train. She just asked if it had been a good journey, so he was able to answer truthfully that all went smoothly apart from his train being slightly late but not late enough to trigger a claim for compensation. They'd talked about trains for the majority of the meal. Robert discovered Janet had recently had two train journeys where the trains were late enough for compensation to be due. After the meal was over he insisted on helping her fill in the relevant claim forms. Being the sister of Robert's mother, Janet knew Robert well, having been very aware of all the issues during his childhood. When he was younger, she had often looked after Robert for short periods to give his parents a much-needed break. Janet knew which subjects to avoid in order to prevent Robert getting annoyed and she was happy just to listen to Robert talk about the things he was interested in. Of course, Robert made no mention of his meeting with Derek Watson or of what he was planning to do next.

Chapter Three

Once upstairs in Janet's spare bedroom, it didn't take long for Robert to set up his laptop. Janet had cleared all the usual items off the dressing table as she knew Robert would want to use it as a desk. While waiting for his laptop to boot up, he closed the heavy blue curtains so he would feel secure and hidden from any prying eyes. He was aware of the matching bed cover and decided to fold it up carefully so it didn't get damaged. He never really saw the need for fancy furnishings; all he required from the things around him was functionality.

Robert sat down and logged in. As soon as the computer came to life, he smiled inwardly as yet again he was correct. They were all there, ready to hear his news. He was looking at the split screen in front of him with four very different faces, one in each quadrant, looking back at him. Before he had a chance to speak, Alice's voice came through the internal speakers, saying, in quite an impatient tone, 'Well, tell us what happened then. I've already told the others I couldn't gather anything from the little I overheard in the pub but the visual signs didn't look great.' Alice was often described unkindly as a mouse because of the colour of her shoulder-length wavy hair, her thin oval face, longish nose and green eyes. This evening she was not her usual smiling self. She looked quite stern and concerned, a combination of being upset at Robert for not accepting her offer of a lift earlier in the day and worried the meeting had not gone as smoothly as they had all wanted.

Robert felt he should be addressing the group as a whole but Alice was the dominant personality and he replied as if talking just to her.

'I think it went alright. As you know, I cannot tell you how Derek Watson was feeling when I left him. However, I tried to stay positive and to sound confident, just as you had suggested, despite my elastic band being stretched. It did come close to snapping at one stage but I managed to stay under control. All of the pre-planned arrangements worked well. He was sitting on the correct bench when my train arrived, twelve minutes late. I managed to persuade him to go to the King's Arms without any difficulty, so you could take his beer glass to capture his fingerprints and to do your DNA thing with it, although I hardly recognised you with your hair tied up like that.'

Alice interrupted. 'I'm surprised you even noticed. You don't normally notice what I look like. I didn't like pretending to be a waitress, which is my way of saying my elastic band was stretched too. However, the glass is safe and I'll process it tomorrow at work. I scarpered as soon as I'd taken the glasses. The landlord of the pub seemed surprised when I turned up earlier in the afternoon in place of his regular waitress and I'm sure there will be plenty of confusion tomorrow when she returns, thinking, thanks to Jake, that the pub had cancelled her shift today, whilst the pub manager was under the impression she was sick. However, as instructed, I chose my words carefully so I didn't lie but I don't intend to go anywhere near that pub for a very long time. As I was leaving, Mr Watson seemed to be getting quite angry with you, so are you sure you didn't upset him?'

'I do not think so,' replied Robert. 'I raised the issue of his relationship with his secretary, again as you suggested, which he didn't want to tell me about, but Jake's text came through at just the right moment. Thank you, Jake.'

Without really thinking, Robert looked to the top right-hand quadrant of his screen to see Jake's face beaming back at him. Jake Anderson had even longer and fairer hair than Alice. Even from a small image on the laptop screen, it was obvious his hair was greasy, as it hung like heavy curtains down the sides of his face, but it was still possible to see much of the pronounced acne that Jake had suffered from for most of his life.

'Yeah,' said Jake in his fairly strong Lancastrian accent. 'As soon as I had the domain name, it was dead easy to tell it wasn't from his brother. I knew it would be easy and I didn't need Simon's help to do it. I don't know why you didn't want me to dig any deeper but you said not to so I haven't.'

Robert answered. 'The reason for not going any further at this stage is I want us all to have a chance to contribute to the next steps of the plan. Also, Simon is our security expert so he needs to be happy with all of our planned interventions.'

'I'm happy Jake knows what he's doing with relatively simple stuff such as emails. It's with more complicated systems the risk increases but, as I keep saying, you can never be 100 per cent secure with anything.' This was the voice of Simon Skidmore, from the bottom left-hand quadrant. Everything about Simon was small, apart from his ears and his dark-framed spectacles with pebble lenses, which dominated his face. His hair had been recently shaved with only short dark stubble remaining, making his head appear even smaller.

'You still haven't told us how it was left, whether you did a deal and what he's going to pay us, if anything,' said Alice.

Before Robert could answer, William, who had so far kept quiet, said, 'I know this all happened very quickly and you did tell me a little about it but, if you want me to contribute to this discussion, I feel I need to know more detail.'

'Hello, Bill,' said Robert. 'Yes, you probably do know less than the others. It did happen quickly. I needed to get Alice and Jake lined up and there wasn't time to tell you everything.'

'Hello, Bob,' said William sarcastically, followed, after a slight pause, by 'flobbadob'. This Bill–Bob interchange between Robert and William was not new but none of the others understood what it meant, so, although it sounded strange and quite funny, nobody laughed.

'Robert,' said Alice, 'not just for William, but to make sure we all have the same information, why don't you go back to the start and give us all a recap? It would be good to be reminded of the order in which everything happened.'

'I was just about to do that,' said Robert tetchily. 'Derek Watson did give me quite a few facts from his side which helped to fill in some of the gaps. I will include these in the timescale to create a logical picture of events. Right, as you all know and as suggested by Alice, we have been looking for opportunities to earn money by using our various talents in a more worthwhile way. Last Friday afternoon, Mary Watson, the wife of Derek Watson, who is Chairman and Managing

Director of Watson & Charles Brewery located just outside Totton near Southampton, received an email that purported to be from Christopher Butcher, who is Derek Watson's equivalent at Butcher's Brewery, based in Havant near Portsmouth. Derek Watson showed me the email this afternoon. Jake, perhaps you could bring up the email onto the screen so everyone can read it.' Within a few seconds, the four faces were replaced with the email.

Subject: Future of Watson & Charles
From: Christopher Butcher c.butcher@butchersbrewery.co.uk
Date: 08/09/2017 17 12
To: Mary Watson <marywatson@watsoncharles.co.uk>

Dear Mary
I am sure you are well aware of the current difficulties facing Watson & Charles. After a disappointing financial performance during the last (2016/17) financial year, I am informed the results for the first half of the current financial year have shown a continuing decline. It is difficult to see how the full year's results for 2017/18 are going to show anything other than a significant loss, with the likely impact being a serious fall in the value of Watson & Charles shares.

As you know, I have been both a business acquaintance and friend of Derek for a number of years. I know how stubborn he can be, so I am writing to you in the hope you can use your influence as his wife to make him realise the magnitude of the situation.

Given the consolidation of the brewing industry worldwide, driven from the top by major international companies amalgamating and taking over smaller breweries, there is a lot of pressure on all members of the Independent Family Brewers of Britain. We, at Butcher's Brewery, are no exception but it does seem we are adjusting to the changing environment much better than Watson & Charles.

It is unlikely there will be room for both Butcher's Brewery and Watson & Charles to exist alongside each other for very much longer. I suggest, therefore, to you and all other members of the Watson family who hold shares, it would make sense to sell the Company now. Providing the decision to sell is made before the performance of Watson & Charles collapses to beyond the point of recovery, I assure you Butcher's Brewery will offer a fair price. The alternative, if the current position is allowed to drag on and deteriorate further, is Watson & Charles will end up being sold to a large, predatory company, with the value of the shares, once all costs and commitments have been covered, likely to be close to worthless.

I urge you, therefore, to try to persuade Derek it would be in the best interests of all Watson & Charles shareholders to consider this offer very seriously indeed.

Yours sincerely,

Christopher Butcher

Managing Director, Butcher's Brewery

After a couple of minutes, the email disappeared, the four faces returned and Robert continued.

'Mary Watson showed the email to her husband when he returned from work and, according to Derek, they spent a lot of time over the weekend discussing it and arguing about it. Apparently, Mary likes spending money and is worried their lifestyle might suffer. They have two children who are both at exclusive private schools. The Watsons live in an old country house with large grounds near the edge of the New Forest which is expensive to look after and maintain. Derek tried to reassure Mary that Watson & Charles was not at risk but failed to do so. Derek does know Christopher Butcher well because of the connection between the two breweries and also because they play quite a lot of golf together. Derek promised Mary he would speak to Christopher Butcher on Monday morning and he did. Christopher Butcher denied all knowledge of the email and, because they were friends, Derek wanted to believe him despite having seen the evidence for himself. Derek then explained the situation to his IT manager, Ian Walters, and asked if there was any means of confirming whether Christopher Butcher had actually sent the email.'

The Cubic Pea

'Of course there is,' interjected Jake. 'Even Microsoft technical support could do that!' Everyone laughed, even Alice.

Again Robert continued.

'Later that same day, Ian Walters, reported back to Derek that he had looked into the matter and found the email had not been sent by Christopher Butcher but appeared to be an internal email sent by Stephen Watson. This put Ian Walters in a very difficult situation as Stephen Watson is the Production Director, the brother of Derek and the boss of Ian Walters. Derek was very taken aback by this news. He told Ian Walters to say nothing about it to anyone else until he had time think what to do next. Derek did, however, telephone his wife straightaway to tell her the email definitely did not come from Christopher Butcher and was not, therefore, an attempted takeover of Watson & Charles by Butcher's Brewery. He also told her he didn't know where the email had originated from but he had asked his IT manager to investigate further. Derek admitted to me he really didn't know what to do about it and had stayed at the brewery quite late that evening to think about how to raise the issue with his brother. On the second Monday of each month, which this was, Mary Watson attends an evening art class which happens to be run by my mother. Apparently, Mary Watson and my mother talk about me quite a lot.'

'What a surprise!' muttered Alice under her breath.

Not having heard her Robert carried on.

'Mary knew I was now an independent consultant on computing issues and told my mother about the email. Derek said that had he got home before Mary left for her art class, he would have stopped her from mentioning it but he did confess he had previously told her he didn't have a lot of confidence in the ability of his IT manager. Anyway, my mother told Mary she thought I might be able to help and gave Mary the number of my mobile. Mary passed this on to Derek when she got home and insisted he call me in the morning. Derek was far from convinced this was a good idea so they ended up having another argument.

'On Tuesday morning, Derek still had not worked out exactly what to do. He wanted to talk it through with someone and the only person he felt he could trust was his secretary, Pauline Sharples. He called her into his office and explained the whole situation to her, including the

31

part about his brother, his concern over Ian Walters, and his wife's wish that he should call me. Pauline took the view this was such a potentially serious situation that Derek needed to be very sure about the facts of the matter before he spoke to his brother. She also said it could not do any harm to talk to me to try to gain more understanding of the technical side of how emails worked. Pauline volunteered to make the call herself so it would not come across as such a big issue.

'I picked up a message from her on Tuesday afternoon asking me to call back, which I did. She explained the situation to me but was reluctant to tell me about Stephen Watson until I told her I could easily explain how emails could be tampered with but would only help if I had all the facts. I also told her I was going to Southampton on Thursday afternoon and was prepared to adjust my plans if it would help. She said she would talk to Derek and try to persuade him to meet me at Southampton station. She stressed the meeting would have to be highly confidential and I told her about the bench at the end of the platform. On Wednesday morning, I received a text confirming he would be there to meet my train. All of you knew about this last part because, after the meeting was confirmed, I spoke to you all individually about it. Even though I only had a short conversation with Alice because she was in Dublin, she made me go through the conversation I had with Pauline word for word, from which Alice deduced that Pauline cared more for Derek than she did for the business and suggested I use this as ammunition during the meeting.'

'I like the sound of Pauline,' blurted out Jake. 'I bet she's got big tits.'

'Jake,' reprimanded Alice. 'That's a horrible thing to say about any woman.'

'Sorry,' said Jake, 'but I bet she has and I will picture her that way if I want to.'

'You picture all women that way,' said Simon. 'All of the dreams you tell me about feature women like that.'

'Can we please move on?' said Alice in a firm voice. 'It does seem I might have been right about Pauline and Derek.'

Robert carried on. 'The other thing Alice and I decided on was it seemed a good opportunity to try out the DNA plan we've been talking about for some time. I asked Jake to send an email to one of the agency waitresses at the King's Arms pub to let her know that her shift on Thursday had been cancelled. I thought it would give him a bit of practice in finding the information from the King's Arms system and making it look like the email came from the pub. It struck me as being very similar to what had happened at Watson & Charles. I gave Alice the details of the pub and she agreed to do the shift instead so she could collect Derek Watson's beer glass.'

'Reluctantly agreed,' stressed Alice, 'and I still don't understand why you didn't come down with me in the car. You could've explained in more detail what you had in mind and I could've helped you approach it in a better way.'

'I had already bought my train ticket,' said Robert, pointedly. 'You know I prefer trains to cars. Also, I used the time on the train to do more research into Watson & Charles which helped me to formulate a clear plan.'

'That's exactly what worries me,' said Alice in a rather exasperated voice, 'but you still haven't told us the outcome.'

'I do not yet know the outcome,' said Robert. 'I knew a little about Watson & Charles because my parents often visit their pubs and my father likes their beer. I looked up more about them yesterday. However, when I got on the train, I was still puzzled as to why anyone should send an email like that and in such a way. I thought about it logically and came to the conclusion it must be with the aim of dividing the family. Derek and Stephen are the two main shareholders. Only members of the Watson family are allowed to hold shares. It's clear from what Pauline Sharples told me that Derek Watson would never vote to sell the brewery, so it leaves his brother Stephen as the obvious person to be got at. If Derek and Stephen fall out over the email, a rift could start between them which would be to the advantage of anyone wanting to buy the Company.'

'That's very perceptive,' said Alice sarcastically, 'for someone who's not supposed to understand the way people think.'

'It is not a people thing. It's just logic,' Robert replied. 'Also, it is logical whoever is behind the email is also doing other things to undermine the performance of the business which could well lead to the Board of Directors losing confidence in Derek as the Managing Director. My conclusion, therefore, was the sending of the email and the recent poor performance of the business were linked. From the information I could find, I calculated the likely impact on Derek Watson of Watson & Charles shares becoming worthless, as the email had suggested. I then used that figure as the basis for working out how much he would be prepared to pay us if we stopped it happening.'

'But,' said Jake, 'what about the £500 for looking into the email we agreed you would ask for? Surely he was happy to pay that, especially as it was good news for him as I found it wasn't his brother?'

'I decided to give him that information for nothing.'

Before he could explain further, Alice butted in. 'I knew it was a mistake to let you do this on your own. What figure did you come up with?'

'Half a million pounds,' said Robert.

'So how much of that would we get?' asked Simon.

'I have just told you, half a million pounds. Sometimes I think you just do not listen to what I say,' said Robert, getting annoyed. 'I admit my calculations were based on quite a few unproven facts but I calculated Derek Watson would personally be 10 million pounds worse off, so paying us 5 per cent of that was not unreasonable.'

Simultaneously, he was greeted with loud responses of 'What?', 'How much?', 'No, never,' and, from Alice, 'You bloody idiot. No wonder he looked so angry. I suppose he said no in no uncertain terms?'

Robert was now getting even more annoyed. He couldn't understand why they were all shouting at once. He said, in a loud voice, 'Look, I did my best. He did not say no but he did not say yes either. We shook hands and parted amicably enough.'

'So what happens now?' asked William, trying to impart a calming influence.

Robert took a deep breath, as he had been taught to do when he felt himself fighting to stay under control. 'He is going to decide tomorrow after speaking to his IT manager again. I think there is a very good chance he will say yes but, with Jake's help, I have a plan to give him a bit of push in the right direction.'

'What do you want me to do?' asked Jake.

'Before you go to bed tonight, I would like you to go back into Watson & Charles's email system and make sure Ian Walters can find out for himself the email didn't come from Stephen Watson. Remember, Ian Walters has already looked once. It needs to be done in a way he thinks he missed something. Also, can you send him round in a loop as I do not want him to get as far as finding the real source. Is that possible?'

'No problem,' said Jake. 'It will be a doddle. I don't normally go to bed for hours yet, although I am looking forward to dreaming about Pauline.'

'Ugh,' groaned Alice.

'I'm happy to help if you would like,' said Simon.

'I can do it on my own.' said Jake defiantly.

There was a gentle knocking on the door of Robert's bedroom. Robert turned his head away from the screen to hear Janet's voice say, 'Robert, are you alright? I was just about to go to sleep when I thought I heard you shouting.'

Robert replied through the door. 'Sorry, Aunt Janet. I was just talking to my friends on the internet. We've just about finished. I'll be quiet now. Good night.'

Back talking to the screen, Robert said, 'That was my aunt. I probably should have brought my headphones so you all didn't sound so noisy. I do not think there is anything else to say tonight. Whatever the answer from Derek Watson, I think it would be a good idea if we all meet at the weekend. I hope Alice and Bill are free. I have some management-course training exercises that would be good for us to do, starting with SWOT analysis. I had better go now so I don't disturb my aunt again. I will be back at home tomorrow afternoon. Good night.' Robert turned off his laptop, visited the bathroom, changed into his pyjamas and got into bed, knowing it would still be a long time before he was ready to go to sleep.

* * *

When there was no sign of Robert by 10 o'clock the following morning, Janet went upstairs and knocked firmly on Robert's door. 'Good Morning, Robert,' she said loudly without opening the door, 'there's bacon sandwiches for breakfast if you get up soon.'

A sleepy voice replied. 'Thank you, be there shortly.' Robert checked the time and, within ten minutes, he was downstairs in the kitchen, dressed in the same clothes he had worn the previous day. He didn't like to have a bath or shower away from home and he only changed his clothes after having had one. However, he did like bacon sandwiches and he also had a train to catch.

*   *   *

Whilst Robert was eating his breakfast, Ian Walters was busy in his office, revisiting the strange email that had caused him so much heartache earlier in the week. Although his role as manager of the IT department was mainly concerned with helping people to use commercial software, he did know how to trace IP addresses. Almost as soon as he'd arrived at work, he'd been summoned into Derek Watson's office and asked if he was certain the email had been sent by Stephen Watson. He'd tried to explain he could not be sure Stephen himself had sent it but it did come from the IP address of Stephen's work computer. Derek had asked him to look again, on the basis that he wasn't prepared to accuse Stephen unless absolutely sure. Ian felt he had a loyalty to Stephen as his boss and had very nearly disobeyed Derek and told Stephen himself. However, he was now very pleased he'd said nothing. It did seem as if he hadn't looked deep enough the first time around, no doubt because he was only asked whether Christopher Butcher had sent the email. This could be the only explanation, although he was still surprised he'd missed what now appeared to be obvious. This time he could see the email had originated from an IP address that was nothing to do with Watson & Charles and then had intentionally been directed through Stephen's computer. 'What the fuck is going on?' he thought to himself. 'I'd better make damn sure I really get to the bottom of this before I go back to Derek!'

Ian continued to work through his lunchtime, ensuring he was not disturbed but getting more and more concerned. At just after 3 o'clock, his phone rang. It was Pauline to say Derek was getting impatient and wanted to see him immediately for an update. Knowing he had no choice, he went with trepidation to report to Derek and tell him he'd made a mistake and it wasn't Stephen after all, but some external source that had interfered with the Watson & Charles system. He apologised and said he'd not been able to trace the real source. He admitted he'd followed a trail of five different IP addresses but they had only led him back to the original one. He confessed he didn't know how to progress any further, expecting Derek to be angry because of his failure. Instead, Derek had smiled and thanked Ian for his efforts, saying he was pleased it wasn't Stephen, that he would take it from here and there was no need for Ian to say any more about this issue to anyone. After assuring Derek he would comply with his request, Ian left, feeling confused but immensely relieved.

After Ian had gone, Derek leant back in his executive leather chair, stared at his own computer sitting on his large antique desk and contemplated what to do next. He thought to himself, Robert Tait does seem to have been right so far. If he is also correct about there being a conspiracy against the Company, that would put a totally different complexion on things. I may as well find out what else he can come up with. After all, it's unlikely to cost anywhere near half a million pounds as we have no legal agreement and he had no real idea about how to negotiate any sort of contract. It was pretty naive of him to ask me to set aside the money and only pay him if I was satisfied. I only have to say I'm not satisfied and I don't have to pay him anything. The bigger question is what, if anything, to tell Stephen – probably best to say nothing for the time being.

Having made his decisions, he asked Pauline to come in. After she had closed the office door and sat down in one of the two armchairs at the opposite side of the desk to Derek, he said, 'I have some better news for a change. Robert Tait, or Roger Thompson as you decided to call him, has come good. He's found out it definitely wasn't Stephen who sent the email. I've decided to go ahead with the proposal he and I talked about yesterday. Please will you text him to say "Yes". It's incredibly important this is kept quiet and highly confidential with only you and me knowing about it. The future of the Company may depend on it. I trust you completely and want you to be the only point of contact with Tait. Given the findings in relation to this email, we should work on the basis that, at the moment, any means of electronic communication may not be secure, so please be very careful.'

*　*　*

Robert's transport arrangements had worked smoothly but he'd still only been at home for about half an hour when his phone vibrated to alert him to a new message. He was in his kitchen putting together a plateful of mature cheddar cheese & biscuits, the benefits of Janet's bacon sandwiches having worn off. Tentatively, he pulled his phone out of his pocket and, once he had seen the sender was Pauline Sharples, his hand was shaking as he opened the message. However, his apprehension evaporated very quickly as he read, 'Dr Mr Thompson, DW has asked me to tell you he says YES. Please direct any future communication through myself. Rgds, PS.' Feeling incredibly overjoyed and elated, Robert raced upstairs and banged loudly on the doors of both Simon's and Jake's bedrooms. They both quickly appeared on the landing to be met by Robert's grinning face, and him waving his phone and shouting, 'He said yes. He said yes. I knew he would.'

'That's fantastic news,' responded Simon.

'It's brilliant,' said Jake, 'so can I start now?'

Robert suddenly looked a lot more serious. 'No, we need to stick to the plan and work together on this. It is extremely important we get it right. I have to text Alice and Bill to let them know and then think about what to do tomorrow.'

Chapter Four

Sitting in his study at home, Derek Watson was starting to become seriously worried. He'd overcome many business problems in the past but, even though the current issues could now be classed as a crisis, the situation at home was causing him the most concern. It was only a week ago that the email had been sent to Mary. Since then they had argued a lot more than usual. Mary was continually questioning him about the future of the Company and whether the value of the shares really was likely to go down significantly. He didn't like having to defend his position at home as well as at work. He was thankful that Mary was out with her friend Jenny for their usual Saturday morning horse ride. He'd received the paperwork for the forthcoming board meeting just before he left work the previous day but had intentionally waited until Mary was not around before looking at it in detail. He knew it would be more bad news and he was correct. The papers included the half-year accounts which showed the downward trend was continuing. There was still no obvious explanation for this despite him asking for a detailed analysis to be carried out.

The main problem was that the managed houses were just not performing as expected. He had discussed the situation with the Managed House Director, John Hargreaves, on many occasions but could not find any fault with the way the division was being run or the actions being taken to try to rectify the situation. Should he consider firing John Hargreaves? Could anyone else do any better? Was Robert Tait right? Was the Company being attacked in some way as to cause this drastic dip in performance? If so, then firing people was not the answer as he needed to understand the root cause of the problem before making any major decisions. However, if the current level of performance continued for a further six months then the full-year results would show a loss. There would be a lot of questions asked and the shareholders, all members of his family, would lose confidence in his ability to run the business successfully. He knew Mary had every right to be concerned but decided not to share the latest piece of bad news with her just yet as he was certain she would overreact. He really needed her support but had the feeling she was more concerned about the financial impact upon herself and her own standard of living than she was about him. Derek wondered whether that was the sort of thing Robert Tait would consider to be an unproven fact and he resolved to find out the true facts about Mary's priorities.

*   *   *

Meanwhile, at Robert Tait's house in Redhill, things were not going according to plan. Everyone had turned up full of enthusiasm and in plenty of time for the 11 o'clock meeting which was taking the place of the usual Saturday morning Mad Hatter's tea party. Robert had set up the lounge so that everyone could easily see the large 52-inch TV screen linked to the computer on the desk nearby. Jake, who had made a special effort to get up early, have a shower and put on clean clothes, controlled the keyboard. Simon had scanned the room to make sure they could not be overheard, and also checked the footage from the infrared security cameras that protected the outside of the house to ensure no-one had been nearby overnight. This was part of his daily routine but he had become even more vigilant than usual since the Watson & Charles project had become a possibility.

Alice, who was still tired after a restless night, had arrived complete with sandwiches, purchased from Sainsbury's and pre-ordered by everyone by text message. She had decided that food would be a good way to exert more of an influence on the group and, hopefully, to create opportunities for private conversations with Robert on non-technical matters. Although Nancy had been at William's shop in plenty of time, William was the last to arrive. He had parked his van on the drive behind Alice's red Ford Fiesta. Robert had answered the door to him and Alice had overheard their usual greeting. 'Good Morning,

Bill,' Robert had said. William had replied, 'Good morning, Bob, flobbadob.' Neither of them had laughed and William had entered the lounge looking quite sad.

Robert had made tea in the kitchen and brought through five mugs which he carefully handed out. He liked being in control. He was pleased they were meeting in his house and were going to be following his ideas. At precisely 11 o'clock, he formally opened the meeting and explained how important it was that, before getting into the detail of the Watson & Charles project, everyone understood how they were all going to operate as a team and had an opportunity to contribute to the plan. He reiterated that he had chosen SWOT analysis as the first exercise for them to do as this had worked well for similar projects he had been involved in at Crawtech. He was disappointed to learn no-one had taken the trouble to find out what SWOT analysis was, so he had to explain it was a tool for helping to develop the most appropriate strategy for tackling projects. It required the Strengths and Weaknesses of the organisation to be identified along with the Opportunities the project presented and any external Threats to success. He asked Jake to fill in the respective boxes on the screen with what was said and stressed that all comments should be positive and constructive. No negativity would be allowed.

It all started well, with their individual strengths being called out one by one and the list on the screen growing steadily, although Jake was capturing the minimum he could get away with. From the odd comments Jake made in between his typing, it soon became clear he would much rather be getting on with tracing the real source of the original email, which he saw as the obvious next step. Robert was having difficulty keeping control and was getting louder and louder, trying to reinforce his view that it was important to carry out these exercises first. The situation was not helped when Robert suggested that Asperger's should be listed as a Strength. Alice queried this by stating it caused as many weaknesses as strengths and, after quite a debate, Robert reminded her not to be negative. Having noticed the time, Alice responded by pointing out they had already spent a whole hour just on Strengths and, at this rate, it would take all day to complete the SWOT analysis exercise. Somewhat to Alice's surprise, Robert agreed they were moving too slowly and suggested they could speed up by doing Weaknesses, Opportunities and Threats in parallel. Alice realised she had inadvertently given Robert a way out of a difficult situation but noted how he managed to make the solution sound like it was his idea. Interesting, she thought to herself. I'd better keep trying to help Robert make this work or we really will be off to a bad start.

However, before Alice had a chance to say anything more, Simon leapt in. 'I've been waiting for Opportunities,' he said excitedly. 'For me the biggest opportunity is to do some good. We spend so much time developing and testing all the skills we've listed under Strengths but we never use them in a way that achieves anything.'

'I agree,' said Jake forcefully, 'I know how to hack into pretty much any system in the world. I think we've an opportunity to change the world, in a good way of course.'

Alice was starting to get worried again but it was William who spoke next. 'Without wanting to sound negative, I think we need to be careful not to get too far ahead of ourselves. There's no doubt, if we pool our resources and work together, we should be able to reach a point where we can be proud of our achievements. For me though, the biggest opportunity is to build on the friendships we've made and develop them to the point where we can really trust each other in times of difficulty. One of the things that has brought us together is we've all had difficult periods in our lives. Until we reach the point where we can be totally open about these, I believe we'll be unable to work effectively as a team, so I think it remains a weakness.'

Alice couldn't resist any longer. 'As I tried to say before, I think Asperger's should be listed as a weakness. As well as the direct effects of not understanding emotions or being able to read people, it provides too easy an excuse for not even trying to do those things.'

Robert started to speak, 'But being Aspie cannot be changed and—'

Before he could get any further, Alice interrupted, in a jokey voice, saying 'Now, Robert, remember no negativity!' Everyone laughed, including Robert.

Although Robert felt as if he was no longer in control, the discussion continued with various other Weaknesses, Opportunities and Threats being called out and justified. Just as the suggestions were starting to dry up, Alice broke the silence.

'I can think of a very serious threat. We've already said, in a variety of ways, how each one of us has particular strengths and skills to contribute to the group as a whole and how we need to perform as a team by supporting each other. We can only do that if we stay healthy and, before any of you think of arguing, this is nothing I haven't said before. None of you live healthy lifestyles. Despite his effort today, which hasn't gone unnoticed, Jake's level of personal hygiene is appalling and his limp, whatever that is due to, is getting worse. Simon hardly eats anything, doesn't get enough exercise and his skin is showing the effects of not getting enough daylight. William is overweight due to eating mainly junk food and drinking lots of beer. Robert is the fittest of the four of you because of his walking and cycling but his teeth always look as if they need cleaning and he gets so engrossed in what he's doing he forgets to eat and then binges to catch up, eating too many biscuits and snacks rather than proper food. Whilst you all may have got away with living like this until now, any one of you could succumb to serious health issues and then be of no use to the team. If I'm going to continue to be part of this group, I would like a firm commitment from each of you that you'll do your best to minimise this risk. I'm willing to help but only if you are honest with me and listen to my advice without getting upset.'

Robert sighed. 'I do not think there is much of an issue. As we have all got to this point without any major health issues, logically, I don't see why anything is likely to change suddenly. Also, I do not understand exactly what Alice is asking us to do.'

'Why don't you look at it in terms of probability,' said Simon. 'The more we do to look after ourselves, the higher the probability we will stay healthy. I think we can all agree Alice knows more about healthy living than the rest of us. If we're serious about trusting each other, surely we need to trust Alice on this.'

'It is not that I do not trust Alice,' said Robert firmly, 'I just do not think we are doing anything wrong.'

Alice thought for a moment. 'OK, let me see if I can find a way to show you the sort of thing I mean. We're all coming back here tomorrow to continue our planning. Instead of bringing more sandwiches, I'll offer to cook you a meal, a proper Sunday roast. It may not be the healthiest option but if you don't all think it an improvement on what you would otherwise have had, I'll take back all I've said. Robert, may I have the use of your lovely kitchen?'

'Of course,' said Robert, looking a lot happier, 'I always used to like Sunday roast dinners. Can we have roast pork with crackling, and is there any chance of Yorkshire pudding to go with it?'

'Unless anybody objects. It ought to be a collective decision and we need to get used to deciding things together,' said Alice. As nobody did object, Alice fabricated a yawn. 'All this talk of food is starting to make me feel hungry.'

'Does anyone have anything further to add?' asked Robert, feeling the need to get back in control. 'If not, I suggest we break for lunch and reconvene in one hour's time for the next exercise, which will be to establish the principles of how we will operate.'

'When can I get stuck into tracing the real source of that email?' asked Jake, irritated. 'Surely that's a major priority.'

'Jake, just be patient for a little longer,' replied Robert. 'You may well be right but I am determined to have a disciplined and structured approach to this project. The main aim of tomorrow will be to put together a detailed action plan for progressing the Watson & Charles project. We will talk more about the email then.'

Without saying anything more, Jake stood up, opened the double doors into the dining room, took the egg and cress sandwich he'd asked for off the dining-room table, helped himself to a glass of water from the kitchen and disappeared upstairs. The others ate their lunch downstairs. Alice was disappointed to find Robert and William had quickly fallen into a technical conversation about the latest server William was building, so she returned to the lounge, sandwich in hand, and studied the morning's work which Jake had left up on the screen.

Strengths	**Strengths**
Engineering skills – W	Analytical problem solving – R
Statistical expertise – S	People skills – A,W
Computer security expertise – S	DNA skills – A
Computer hacking expertise – J	Asperger's – R,J,S
Computer software knowledge – J,S,R	Knowledge of beer – W
Internet skills – J,S,R	Business acumen – W
Computer hardware expertise – W,R	Domestic skills – A
Logical thinking – R	

Weaknesses

Lack of emotional understanding
Asperger's
Not wordly wise
Lack of business understanding

Weaknesses

Limited equipment resources
Shortage of time
Scarred by past issues
Limited knowledge of the brewing industry

Opportunities

To do something good
To change the world
To build friendships
To make money
To buy more equipment
To make a difference
To use our skills for good causes
To help people with Asperger's-
    related issues
More time with Alice

Threats

Being caught
Arguing with each other
Working as individuals, not as a team
Poor communication
HEALTH
Complacency
Carelessness
Making false assumptions
Relying on unproven facts
Not thinking logically

In spite of her initial scepticism and the difficult start, Alice had to admit they'd ended up with a reasonable summary of the group's capabilities and limitations. How to apply this to the Watson & Charles project was still difficult for her to picture. There seemed to be a lack of knowledge about the problems Watson & Charles faced. She was, however, impressed with the way they'd changed from thinking about themselves as individuals to acting more as a team when discussing the last three categories. It also made her realise that everybody, including herself, had something worthwhile to contribute and the only possible chance of success was if they really did help and support each other. She did not recall anyone suggesting 'More time with Alice' as an opportunity and realised it must have been Jake who sneaked it in at the end. She wished it had been Robert instead. Alice was starting to feel that there was enough intelligence, skill and ability within the group but also an awful lot of emotional baggage that could get in the way. Just as she was wondering what Robert had in mind for the afternoon session, Simon appeared by her side.

'What were you thinking?' he asked. 'You looked miles away.'

'Oh,' said Alice, 'I was just considering how we move forward from here to tackle the practical aspects of the Watson & Charles project. I could tell Jake was getting frustrated doing this general stuff and I'm a bit concerned Robert is so intent on applying his management-training exercises he'll alienate and lose everybody before we really get started.'

Simon quickly responded. 'I think Robert is right to hold Jake back. Jake can be something of a loose cannon. He has lots of knowledge and ability but he does have a tendency to leap into things without considering the risks. I've been trying for some time to make sure he doesn't go too far but it's difficult to monitor his every move. I've just carried out a security check and he's already started to trace that email despite being asked not to. If he gets caught for hacking into some system that he shouldn't, we'll all end up in trouble and any thoughts of getting this project off the ground will be finished.'

Simon's comments made Alice think of her conversation with William earlier in the week. 'Simon,' she said cautiously, 'do you think you could explain to me what the risks are? I don't fully understand the technical implications of what you, Robert and particularly Jake do. I was speaking to William and he said you had an analogy about robbing banks because what you do is illegal. That worries me. I don't like to think I've encouraged you all to get involved in something like Watson & Charles if it means you have to break the law and there's a serious risk of you getting caught.'

'Let's go into the snug and I'll try to explain how I see it,' replied Simon, leading the way across the hall and through the door opposite. As Alice followed him, there was a loud beeping noise. They both stopped. 'Do you have your phone with you?' Simon asked. 'I've set this room up as a safe zone so no communication technology is allowed.'

Alice took out her phone, placed it on the table in the hall and re-entered the snug. The beeping had stopped. She looked around and saw nothing but purple. The walls, carpet, ceiling and even the covers on the sofa, two armchairs and pouffe were all shades of purple. There was no other furniture. 'I've never been in here before,' exclaimed Alice. 'What a strange room to have in a house where there's so much technology everywhere else.'

'As I said,' explained Simon, 'this is a safe room. It's safe from two points of view. The first means it is secure from any attempt to overhear what is said, as any electronic bugging device or similar equipment would be detected by my security screening system. The second relates back to Robert's time at school when he, and other students who had been diagnosed with Asperger's syndrome, were allowed to escape to a special room in order to calm down when they became too upset. The school room had padded walls as well as only having soft furniture but it was purple. Robert will also tell you his parents have a snug at their home, where he remembers having nice conversations and feeling relaxed. We all use this room occasionally when we get upset or, in my case, feel threatened.'

'How do you mean, feel threatened?' asked Alice.

'I get very worried if strangers come to the door or if I feel our computer security is at risk of being breached. It all stems back to my childhood.'

'Do you mind telling me about it?'

'No,' said Simon, 'I feel very comfortable with you. Everyone else knows and almost the more I talk about it, the better I feel. William was very understanding when I told him. It really started when I first had my spectacles. I was only five and so pleased I could see more clearly but the other children teased me about them and would pull them off my face to have a look through them. At primary school, I did have quite a lot of protection from teachers and my mother walked me to and from school, but at secondary school it became a lot worse. Some of my so-called friends from primary school caught the same bus as me and "hiding Simon's specs" became a regular game for them. At school, I tried to keep away from them but they always seemed to find me. I hated not being able to see but they found it very funny watching me stumble around looking for my specs.'

'Couldn't you tell anyone who would make them stop?'

'I did tell one of the teachers but it only made things worse. The bullies had been told to leave me alone but they continued in a more physical way, not only hiding my specs but lifting me up, turning me upside down and even trying to lift me by my ears. I also told my mother but all she said was she would pray for me and that God would protect me. Well, HE didn't.' Simon pointed aggressively at the ceiling. It was the first time Alice had ever seen him appear to be angry.

'What about your father?' asked Alice.

Simon quickly calmed down and answered. 'He worked away a lot, on the oil rigs, so was hardly ever there. When he did come home, he was either sleeping or catching up on domestic jobs so everything to do with my education was left to Mum. I'm sure she tried her best but, when things got difficult, she turned to prayer which never seemed to make any difference. I still don't understand religion but I suppose it's her way of avoiding things she doesn't understand or want to face up to. Fortunately, I was very good at maths. I was top of the class and, unlike most people, I really liked statistics and working out probabilities. At school, I was allowed to stay indoors at break times and use the school's computers. At home, I had my own computer and I used to get engrossed in statistical problems in order to avoid having to go outside.

'Even as a small child, I would constantly toss a coin to check that there was a 50:50 chance of heads or tails. All my presents became computer orientated and I became fascinated with the difficulty of producing a truly random number from a computer. I even persuaded Mum to take me to the Science Museum to see ERNIE, the first computer used for selecting premium bond winners.

'I was just starting to feel a little happier and more secure when, one day when I was about thirteen, Mum said I must stop doing things on my computer because it was not safe. That concerned me a lot because I had always thought of computing as a really safe thing to do. It soon became clear Mum didn't understand what I was doing and that her concerns arose from speaking to her friends who had children using social media sites. A local man had been found guilty of grooming by pretending to be their friend. Anyway, I persuaded Mum I wasn't using social media. She allowed me to continue computing on the understanding I would ensure I always uploaded the latest versions of security software to protect me. I then became obsessed with understanding how these security programs worked. I would spend hours identifying the biggest weakness, predicting how the next upgrade would tackle it and working out the probability of whether I was right. More often than not, I was.

'Years later, when I met Jake through the Asperger's group, I discovered he'd a similar obsession but his was to break through any security protection to get at the data beneath it. That's where the bank analogy came from. He's like a bank robber and I'm like a locksmith. The part Jake doesn't like is, because I've focussed so much on the security side, I understand the risks of trying to break in more than he does and am better at avoiding them. I could, therefore, be thought of as the better hacker and, as you well know, Jake likes to think he is the best hacker in the world.'

'Well,' said Alice, 'that helps me to understand better how it all fits together. Thanks for telling me. I know all too well how hard it can be to talk about past problems. I was aware of some aspects of your upbringing from our discussions on previous Saturdays, such as how your mother helped you with your Open University degree by going with you to summer school. I think I do understand some of the differences between you and Jake but nothing you've said stops me from worrying about what you do. However, I do admit that I get lost when you all talk about spyware, malware, firewalls, worms, Trojan horses, earwigs, viruses and, particularly, worms that eat their own tails.'

Simon smiled. 'OK, firstly, you may have heard us talk of earwigging but there's no such thing as a computer earwig. Let's expand the bank robber analogy a little further. It's probably important you do accept what we do is the equivalent of robbing banks. We do break the law pretty much every day and the penalties for getting caught are extremely high. The secret, therefore, is not to get caught. If you think of a team of bank robbers preparing to rob a bank, the first thing they would do is to "case the joint" which means understanding the security systems, the locks and alarms that are in place to stop someone from getting in and to flag up if any breach of security has occurred. We aim to do all our initial "casing" by using the internet and we have various means to hide what we've been looking at.

'The next step is to plan how to get in by opening locks and by-passing alarms. If, say, a bank robber chooses to use explosives to blow open the doors of a bank's safe, then it's very obvious the bank has been robbed and the only option is to get in and out quickly, before the police arrive. Also, the robber would need to be extremely careful not to leave any traceable evidence behind. The alternative is to get in and out again without being discovered, so the police aren't called in the first place. We aim for this more subtle type of approach. Once inside, it's helpful to know exactly what you're looking for, where it is and to have a plan how to get both you and it out, whilst making as little noise as possible. Ideally, when we hack into a system, we want to be able to do so without anyone knowing we've ever been in. That way, no-one is likely to come searching for us. So far, we've limited ourselves to going in, looking at the data and then coming out without changing anything.

The risk increases significantly if you change something because the change is likely to be noticed and queried.

'One thing that helps is someone always has the key. In our bank analogy, it's likely to be the bank manager. Many bank robberies have been carried out by robbers forcing the bank manager to give them the physical key or the combination to the safe. For computer systems, it's the system administrator, known as the sys admin, who tends to have the key. If we can convince the computer we are the sys admin then the task becomes a lot easier. Sometimes accessing a system as an approved user is sufficient. Often this requires doing the same sorts of things as criminals who commit identity fraud in order to steal money. What you have to remember is a computer is programmed to decide whether to let a user through each level of security. No matter how complicated, the principle is the same. Data supplied by the user is compared with data held within the computer. So, if you know how, you can interrogate a system to find out the security data and then plug it back in as a user. This principle works for simple passwords as well as for things like fingerprint scans and retina scans because they are all just pieces of data waiting to be compared. If a match is found, the door is opened.'

'You make it all sound so simple,' said Alice, 'but I still don't like the idea of breaking the law and the fact that I encouraged you to do so.'

'I don't see it that way at all,' replied Simon. 'We, especially Jake, were breaking the law regularly before we knew you. I have tried to help Jake avoid getting careless and making mistakes but he doesn't always listen. In my view, it was only a matter of time before he got caught and ended up as another "hacker with Asperger's syndrome" making the news headlines. What you've done is convince us we can do some good by using our skills in a positive and constructive way. It may not have been exactly what you had in mind when you asked us why we didn't work together as a team of independent computer consultants but it has given us a sense of purpose and, perhaps more importantly, a greater chance of controlling what Jake does do and keeping him out of trouble. I'm not 100 per cent certain of many things but I am 100 per cent certain we're better off with you helping us than we would be on our own.'

'I'm not sure Robert sees it that way.'

'Maybe not. It's often difficult to know how Robert sees things. Robert is the most intelligent person I've ever met but he's only happy if he feels he's using his intelligence to come up with good ideas. After he lost his job, he really struggled. He wouldn't admit he'd done anything wrong but he didn't want to put himself in a similar position again so he didn't even try to find another job. He was doing nothing, going nowhere and getting extremely frustrated as a result. The change in him over the last six months has been immense. Now this Watson & Charles project has come along, he's as excited and enthused as I've ever seen him. Without you, that wouldn't have happened. Given Robert's logical way of thinking, he must know it's true but getting him to say so is a very different matter.'

As if on cue, there was a knock on the door. Simon rose and opened the door to find Robert standing outside complaining they were late for the afternoon session. Simon apologised and hurried though into the lounge. Alice, however, intentionally took her time. As she passed Robert she said pointedly, 'I've just been having a very interesting conversation with Simon. He's been helping me to understand more about how you all do things. I hope your afternoon exercise is going to be just as interesting.' Robert pulled the door closed with a bang and followed Alice into the lounge.

Chapter Five

Everybody was sitting in exactly the same places as for the morning session. Robert stood up to address the other four, sounding just like a corporate training manager, 'I trust you all found this morning's activities useful. I have reviewed the output and I believe the overall situation can be summarised as follows. We all have individual strengths and skills to allow every one of us to contribute to this venture and complete it successfully. There are some weaknesses, mainly linked to people issues. Also, for this specific project, we need to build up more knowledge of business operations in general and the brewing industry in particular. If we are not sure of what to do or how to do it, we need to ask for help, not just plough on regardless. The potential rewards are enormous as this really is an excellent opportunity to do some good, achieve financial security and build a basis for doing other projects in the future. However, there are clear risks and we will only be successful if we work well as a team, stay healthy and support each other in times of difficulty.'

Alice was wondering whether Robert actually knew what working as a team meant in practice but she decided to keep quiet and see what came next.

'As I said earlier,' continued Robert, 'I want to leave the detailed approach to the Watson & Charles project until tomorrow. This afternoon, I want us to focus on how we set ourselves up as an organisation. We need to start viewing ourselves as a business, which means agreeing and understanding how we will work together. In particular, we need to establish our underlying principles and values so all decisions we make are made with those in mind. The first thing we need to decide upon is a company name. I propose we call ourselves Roger Thompson Associates.'

'Who the hell is Roger Thompson? I've never heard of him,' asked Jake vehemently.

'Roger Thompson is a fictitious character,' replied Robert. 'The idea is we build up a picture of Roger Thompson as a person we admire, with all the collective qualities and attributes we want our business to reflect. We can then ask ourselves questions like "what would Roger do?" or "what would Roger think?". Major retailers adopt the same principle by defining a typical customer to help them decide how to market and sell their products.'

'Just hang on a minute,' said Alice forcefully. 'Why do we have to have a male name? Why can't we have a female name? Female qualities may be more suited to our business. We could be called Rachel Thompson Associates instead.'

'I like the sound of that,' said Jake excitedly. 'I can already picture Rachel. She has long legs and big—'

Before he could finish, Alice shouted over him. 'OK, OK, maybe not female but surely we can think of a gender-neutral name. I can only think of names like Frances or Lesley or, if you want an R, Robyn. The problem is that these sound the same in male and female forms but are written differently. Can anyone think of a name that's spelt the same for both males and females?'

Simon was the first to answer. 'Not immediately, but I quite like Robin. It makes me think of Robin Hood. It's likely to fit our values quite nicely if we considered ourselves a modern-day Robin Hood. We could identify people and organisations who have obtained riches through illegal means, hack into their systems and accounts and redistribute the money to good causes. That way, they would be unlikely to admit to the authorities they'd been hacked and lost anything, so it would be relatively safe.'

'I agree with the principle,' said William, 'but it might put limits on what we want to do. For instance, if we had sought out projects on that basis, would we have selected Watson & Charles? Also, I'm not sure we want to be called Robin Hood Associates.'

'That's a pity,' said Jake with a sigh. 'Robin Hood is already one of my heroes. Whatever we're called, I'm going to think of myself as

Robin Hood, stealing from the rich to give to the poor. What's more, there could be a really sexy Maid Marian. I was just starting to think about her.'

To stop him going any further, Alice said loudly, 'Oh I give up. You win. I've changed my mind. I vote for Roger.' Everybody laughed, even Jake.

There were no more objections so Robert continued to facilitate the discussion. It became a wider debate, not just about Roger Thompson but how they would operate as a group. Alice was starting to get bored as a lot of the points being made were the same as in the morning or had been talked about at previous Mad Hatter's tea parties. She thought they were starting to go round in circles so asked what gaps were left to fill. Robert took this as an opportunity to summarise where they had got to.

'I think we have pretty much captured the qualities of Roger,' he stated. 'To summarise, these are truthfulness, honesty, fairness, openness, loyalty, respect and incorruptibility. From now on, we should apply these qualities to the way in which we work together. Everything we do, whether it is as a group or as individuals within the group, should reflect these core values. Moving on to more practical aspects of how we work, we have agreed we will do as much as possible from within these four walls. This house will be our base. With Bill's help we have built up a lot of computing power. We have the capabilities for writing code with both offline and online testing, a bank of pre-written code which we have already tested and proven and, of course, thanks to Simon, a brilliant security system. We will always be looking to expand our range of equipment which will be dependent upon what we can afford but, with Bill's assistance, we are fortunate we can keep costs to a minimum. We will decide on our plan of action together as a team and we will help each other to implement that plan as much as we can. We will aim to keep what we do as secret as possible and avoid taking unnecessary risks. We will deal only in facts, which means we will question and challenge any unproven facts until we are sure they are correct.'

'You can never be 100 per cent sure of anything,' said Simon.

Robert laughed. 'Yes, Simon, I think we all know that by now.'

'One thing we haven't talked much about,' said William seriously, 'is the financial side. Are we going to set up as a proper business? If so, there are lots of potential implications and issues. Say we do succeed with Watson & Charles and they pay us half a million pounds, what would we do with the money? How do we apply the spirit of fairness to avoid falling out over money? What about the tax implications? At the moment, Robert and I are registered as self-employed. Jake and Simon are on benefits and Alice has her job. There would be financial implications for all of us '

'Why can't we just hide the money from the taxman?' asked Jake. 'I'm sure we could use our skills to avoid him finding out.'

'No,' answered Robert firmly. 'That would be contrary to the values we have just set. Bill is right. We do need to sort out the finances, be prepared to pay tax and keep everything legal and above board.'

'That sounds a bit odd,' said Alice, 'when so much of what you all do computer-wise is illegal. Also, I love my job and I intend to keep it, so I need to understand what my time commitment is likely to be.'

'I thought we identified William as our business expert,' said Simon. 'Can't you look after the finances for us, William?'

William replied, 'I tried to explain this morning. Although I have my own business, it's very simple and my turnover is nothing like half a million pounds. Also, I only do the book-keeping. I use an accountant to produce my official accounts and tax returns. For the five of us, whilst the principles would be the same, it'll be a lot more complex. I suspect the easiest way is for all five of us to become directors. Whatever we decide, I do think we should start keeping books straightaway as it's possible to claim expenses back against any income. We already have the cost of Robert's train to Southampton and Alice's fuel. I'm not sure if the food for tomorrow's meal would qualify but it's unfair to expect Alice to pay as well as cook.'

'We already have a house fund for food, so Alice can be reimbursed out of that,' said Robert. 'Bill, could you ask your accountant for advice on what we should do?'

'Yes, I could, Bob,' replied William pointedly, followed by, 'flobbadob.'

'Good,' said Robert, seemingly unaware of any frostiness. 'As far as time is concerned, I envisage Jake, Simon and myself doing most of the work during the week and then all five of us reviewing progress and agreeing subsequent actions at the weekends. That would allow both Alice and Bill to do their work as normal during the week. Are there any other gaps anyone has identified? If not, I suggest we finish for today and come back tomorrow at 11 a.m. to talk specifically about the Watson & Charles project.'

Everyone had clearly had enough as they all leapt up almost before Robert had finished talking. Jake and Simon quickly disappeared upstairs and William made his excuses, saying he needed to get back to check on the shop. Alice suddenly found herself alone with Robert. 'Come and sit down for a moment. That all seemed to go really well. Are you pleased with the outcome?'

Robert did sit but chose his favourite armchair in spite of there being room next to Alice on the sofa. 'Yes, I think so,' he replied. 'There didn't appear to be any major problems, apart from at the end when Bill brought up the financial issues. I don't like the idea of money becoming a reason for us to argue and disagree.'

Alice did her best to reassure him. 'I'm sure if we continue to talk about it, with William's help, we can find a way forward. I don't believe money is the main motivation for any of us but we do need to manage it sensibly if we're going to make this whole thing work. Are you not struggling a little for money now, given that it's a whole year since you left Crawtech?'

'There is still some remaining,' stated Robert defensively. 'My parents were very generous when they helped me buy this house so the mortgage is relatively small. Jake and Simon contribute to the mortgage payments through the rent they pay. I did calculate a few months ago, if nothing changed, I would only be able to afford to live here for another year before the money ran out. At least this year I won't have to pay off any more of my student loan.'

'Both Jake and Simon would be devastated if you had to sell and they had to find somewhere else to live. I really hope it doesn't come to that. I know what you mean about the student loan. Like me, you had many years of building up debt. I started to pay mine back a couple of years ago and it feels like it'll take forever before it's all gone,' said Alice. 'Talking like this makes it seem like there's a hell of a lot riding on this Watson & Charles project. Are you confident we can succeed?'

Robert paused before replying. 'It would require Simon to work out the likely probability of success. However, as we agreed this afternoon to be honest, my honest answer is no. I am not confident because we do not have enough facts to work with. In spite of what you all said on Thursday night, I firmly believe it is worth half a million pounds if we do succeed but I would rather we had started on a smaller project first. Tomorrow should give us a clearer idea because, if we can put together a detailed action plan, we can then find out more facts and come to some logical conclusions.'

Feeling that Robert was in a good mood and receptive to ideas, Alice decided to take quite a big risk. 'Thinking about tomorrow,' she said, 'I need to buy the food. Please will you come with me? I would really like your help. You know what Simon and Jake will and won't eat. It's only a few minutes in the car and if we bring it back here you can store it in your fridge. I don't think I have enough room in mine.'

'Well,' Robert said hesitantly, 'I was going to plan for tomorrow but I suppose I will still have enough time. Where are you going to go? Not Sainsbury's I hope.'

'Actually,' said Alice as casually as she could, 'I was aiming to go to Sainsbury's. I prefer their meat and they will have a wider choice of vegetables. Is Sainsbury's a problem?'

Robert stood up and started walking towards the door. 'I have not been there since ... you know, when I bumped into you. Given what happened then, I am not sure I want to go back. Maybe you had better go alone.' Alice quickly got up, intercepted him and gently held his arm. She felt him flinch slightly but he didn't move away.

'Robert,' she said softly, 'one of the other things we agreed today was we would trust each other I'll be with you and you can trust me that everything will be alright. Surely you would like to be able to shop at Sainsbury's again?'

'Well, yes, I suppose so,' replied Robert tentatively.

'Come on then,' said Alice in a sprightly voice, 'you won't get a better opportunity than this.' Before Robert had a chance to object, Alice headed towards the front door. Inspired by a sudden thought, she stopped and reached in her pocket for her phone. 'I'll see you in the car. Hadn't you better get some shopping bags and tell Simon you're going?'

Alice was just putting her phone away and had a smug look on her face as Robert got into the car beside her. Right, she thought to herself, I need to keep him calm and relaxed so I must make sure I don't ask any annoying questions. She skilfully manoeuvred the conversation to the safe ground of comparing DNA to computer code, something they had talked about many times before and she knew Robert found interesting.

They had to park some distance from the entrance to Sainsbury's, making Alice realise it would be quite busy on a Saturday afternoon. She asked Robert to push the trolley and they selected fresh vegetables under Robert's guidance, choosing carrots, cauliflower and sweetheart cabbage, as he explained Jake would eat these raw but not cooked. The only cooked vegetables Jake liked were peas, beans and sweetcorn. All was going well until Robert stopped suddenly and seemed to freeze. Alice was just about to ask what the problem was when she realised Robert was looking straight at Jane, who was walking towards them.

'Hello, Alice,' said Jane cheerily, 'how's your wrist?'

'It's fine,' replied Alice through gritted teeth and glaring at Jane, then changed her tone. 'Jane, this is Robert Tait. I think I mentioned to you that I met him again after we had our little accident here a few months ago.'

'Oh, yes, sorry,' mumbled Jane, struggling not to smile. Then she looked directly at Robert and spoke to him quite formally. 'Good afternoon, Mr Tait. On behalf of Sainsbury's supermarket, I would like to say how pleased I am to see you here again. We have missed your custom and we hope you do not hold Sainsbury's responsible for your unfortunate experience.'

Robert looked away and seemed slightly stunned but replied just as formally. 'Thank you. Alice and I have talked about the accident and decided it was just a combination of circumstances where no-one was really at fault. I have been uneasy about shopping here since the accident but now I am in a position to do so again.'

'That is good news,' said Jane. 'I look forward to seeing you in the future.'

She thrust her hand out towards Robert and received a very firm handshake in return. Robert and Alice moved away but, after a few steps, Alice turned back to look at Jane, raised both thumbs and mouthed, 'Thanks.' Jane, who by this stage was almost in hysterics, made a one armed gesture back. Alice was pleased to see that Robert was still looking forwards, as even he might have recognised Jane's meaning. Blushing slightly, she caught up with Robert and they finished their shopping without further interruption.

During the short drive back, it became obvious to Alice that Robert had relaxed and was extremely happy about being able to shop at Sainsbury's again. She was feeling very satisfied with the result and decided to push her luck a little further so, as she was pulling into Robert's driveway, she said, 'I could do with some help tomorrow with preparation of the food, particularly if you do want Yorkshire pudding. If I arrive early, around ten-ish, will you help me in the kitchen?'

'I suppose that would be alright as long as we can still make a prompt start to the meeting at 11 o'clock.' Without any further words, Robert got out of the car collected the shopping from the boot and walked towards the front door, which opened as if by magic to let him in and then quickly closed behind him.

Alice sat in the car for a few moments, her elation rapidly evaporating. Not even a word of thanks or a goodbye. Am I ever going to get used to this? she asked herself. She tried to console herself with the fact that Robert did not know that the meeting with Jane had been a set-up. She made a mental note to thank Jane properly, particularly as Jane, who happened to live just round the corner from Sainsbury's, had rushed in specially after receiving Alice's call. Alice had originally rung hoping Jane would already be on shift. She reversed out of the drive and headed home to spend Saturday night on her own. She had been invited to a party but, as usual, she had made an excuse not to go. She did not like parties. One day, she might pluck up enough courage to tell someone why. She thought again of what William had said. Maybe one day …

* * *

Mary and Derek Watson did have a dinner party to go to that Saturday night and Derek was extremely pleased they did, especially as the other three couples who would be there were all friends from the golf club and had nothing to do with brewing. It had been raining so Mary had got home from her horse ride earlier than usual and found Derek sitting at his desk in his study, still going through his board papers. As was becoming the norm these days, Mary had started questioning him and became quite aggressive when he stalled and tried to avoid telling her the bad news. Eventually, he felt he had no choice but to admit things were looking pretty bleak. She demanded to know what else he was doing to try to improve the situation and hoped he was not relying solely upon Robert Tait, whom she had only suggested because of the incompetence of Ian Walters. Derek sought to deflect the question by trying very hard to explain that her attitude was not helping and, if anything, was causing tension between the two of them, which was quite probably the aim of whoever sent the email in the first place. He stressed how important it was for the close family to stick together in times of difficulty and to support each other and that, personally, he felt he needed to be able to relax and have some downtime when at home so he was at his best when he was at work. Mary said that was all very well but she couldn't just stand by and watch the family worth be eroded, for the children's sake as much as her own. Derek responded by saying the children's trust funds would be unaffected but he did accept, if the brewery was sold, there would be no route for one or both of the children to follow in his footsteps. The argument reached its peak when Derek suggested, if the worst came to the worst, they could always sell the house and move to somewhere smaller, particularly as the children were older now and it would just be the two of them rattling around in such a large house. When Mary shouted her objections, Derek made the situation even worse by pointedly reminding Mary the house was in his sole name and, therefore, it had nothing to do with her. At that, Mary had stormed out, slamming Derek's study door behind her.

Realising that he'd probably gone too far, Derek thought he had better offer some sort of olive branch to Mary. Having given her a good half an hour to calm down, he went downstairs to find her sitting in the conservatory having a gin and tonic. 'Look,' he said gently, 'I'm sorry I upset you. I don't want us to fall out over money and I do understand your concerns. I am aware this is a very serious situation and there is no doubt the brewery is at risk, but I do believe we can find a way out of this mess. The board meeting on Wednesday is bound to be difficult. There will be a lot of awkward questions asked and I will not have the answers to most of them. Whatever comes out of it, there will be some tough decisions to be made. As a way forward, how about I invite my parents as well as Stephen and Anthea for dinner next Saturday? That way we will have more than 50 per cent of the brewery shares represented around the dinner table. We should then be able to tell whether there is a real risk of us becoming divided as a family or whether we're all committed to keeping the brewery, whatever the future holds.'

'I don't really want to fight over it either,' said Mary firmly, 'but I sometimes think you don't listen to what I have to say or take my feelings into account. I've got used to living as we do and I don't like the thought of that being taken away from me. I accept I don't fully understand the predicament the brewery is in so, yes, I would like to hear what your father and brother have to say on the matter.'

'Good,' said Derek,' so can we agree not to talk about it further until after the board meeting at least. It will be good for us both to take our minds of our problems and enjoy an evening out.'

'I suppose so.' said Mary, turning her back and sighing as she went upstairs for a shower.

Chapter Six

For once, William was early. As it was Sunday, he didn't need to worry about the shop. He drove his van onto Robert's drive and parked, as he'd done the previous day, behind Alice's Fiesta. He walked towards the front door but, just as he was about to press the doorbell, the door swung open. After entering the hall, he pressed the No 2 button on the intercom. 'Thanks, Simon,' he said into the microphone.

There was a click and then a rather tinny reply. 'No problem, William, I was looking out for you. Alice has been here a while. I'll be down soon, when I've made sure Jake is awake.'

William walked through to the kitchen to be greeted by a typically domestic scene. Alice was inspecting a large piece of pork, wearing a colourful but not particularly clean red and white striped apron over her blouse and jeans. Robert was sitting on a stool next to the granite island worktop, peeling potatoes. 'Good morning,' said William cheerily, 'this all looks very appetising.'

'Hello, William,' said Alice brightly. 'Yes, we're pretty much under control. I'm doing the meat and Yorkshires and Robert's in charge of the veg.'

'Hello, Bill,' said Robert. 'Would you like a cup of tea?'

'Yes please, Bob, but I'm happy to make it myself as I can see you're busy.' Then, whilst filling the kettle William said, almost under his breath. 'Flobbadob.'

Both Simon and Jake came downstairs with five minutes to spare before the meeting was due to start, just long enough to make a cup of tea and, in Jake's case, to grab a couple of cereal bars as a late breakfast. As usual, Robert opened the meeting right on time. He reminded everyone of the conclusions they had reached on Saturday and stated that the main aim of today was to agree a way forward with the Watson & Charles project. Before he could get too far, Jake leapt in. 'Does that mean I can get started on that email?'

Simon could not resist responding. 'What do you mean get started? You already have started despite being asked not to.'

Jake looked very sheepish. 'I only wanted to get ahead of the game. I've been very careful and, anyway, you said you trusted me with emails.'

'That is not the point, Jake,' said Robert forcefully. 'We agreed yesterday that we would operate as a team and that we increase the risk of failure if we don't. You should have waited until after this meeting. Please do not go against the wishes of the group again.'

'OK,' said Jake quietly and then in a louder voice, 'but it's an obvious next step.'

Alice sensed that yet again the meeting was starting badly and wanted to defuse the tension. 'Just as a matter of interest, Jake, how far did you get?'

'Not very far yet,' admitted Jake. 'I've traced it through six different IP addresses but it feels as if I'm following the sort of email chain I set up myself. Whoever's done it must be an expert in ghosting.'

'Precisely,' said Robert. 'The reason I wanted you to wait is that it is too obvious a next step. Whoever is behind sending the email may well be monitoring one or more of those IP addresses, so it is likely that you have just done what they wanted us to do.'

'I hadn't thought of that,' confessed Jake. 'Sorry, next time I'll try to do only what's been agreed.'

'It is also why I want Simon to be involved,' Robert continued. 'We need to know if anyone is tracking our movements as that may give us an opportunity to trace them.'

'I haven't noticed anything yet,' said Simon, 'but I'm trying to be extra vigilant and I'm putting in an additional layer of security around everything we do. That was how I found out what Jake was doing.'

'You're not supposed to spy on me,' said Jake angrily. 'I didn't realise you were watching my every move.'

'Look,' said Alice, trying to be the peacemaker again, 'I admit I don't understand the technical side of what you're doing but if you two start falling out before we've really got going, we're not likely to achieve anything. We're back to trusting each other. Surely it's a good thing if

Simon's security systems are not that obvious. We have to trust Simon to do whatever he can to give us maximum protection. It should give us all confidence that Simon's systems worked out what Jake was doing, so I see it as a good thing. Simon, you also have to trust us, particularly Jake, and make sure he knows what you're up to as much as Jake needs to tell you what he's doing. It's about communicating effectively.'

'Alice is right,' stated Robert. 'That's why we did yesterday's exercises. We all agreed how we would work together and now we need to put it into practice. We should get back to where we are supposed to be and talk about building an action plan for the Watson & Charles project.'

Having felt she had calmed the waters, Alice couldn't resist asking the question which had been on her mind for some time. 'Again, I know I don't understand all aspects of IP addresses but isn't the whole point of having IP addresses in the first place so you can trace the owners of them? As long as we act carefully, why can't we do as Jake wants and track down the sender of the email from their IP address?'

Surprisingly it was Jake who answered, beating the other three to it as it was obvious all of them had an answer to her question. 'IP addresses are not straightforward. You can use the same computer with two different internet service providers to create two different IP addresses. You can easily hide your IP address using means such as virtual private networks. For hackers like me, playing with IP addresses is all part of the fun. Making things appear to come from somewhere else is a pretty fundamental requirement of being a hacker, otherwise you could be easily traced. Simon would no doubt describe it as a security issue but, for me, it's about trying to appear invisible. That's why it's known as ghosting. You can buy software to do it but I prefer to write my own.'

Although slightly stunned from listening to the longest statement she had ever heard Jake make, Alice rationalised this was because it was a subject Jake liked. Therefore, she decided to plough on further and addressed Jake directly. 'So, are we saying there's nothing to be gained from trying to trace the source of the email, that it has been set up by someone like you and in such a way as to make them invisible? Can't you use your knowledge and skills to reveal anything about them?'

This time it was Simon who replied, trying to use layman's language to help Alice understand. 'I think what we're saying is we've found out enough to know that by trying to trace the sender, we would just be playing into their hands as they could just as easily trace us. It's clear they know how to muddy the waters and are likely to have set it up to send us all, including Jake, on a wild goose chase. We could waste lots of time following the chain Jake has started going down but identifying any really useful pieces of information would be like searching for a needle in a haystack. We need to come at the problem from a different angle, find another key if you like, so that we can unlock a door they're not expecting.'

Alice was not really any clearer on the matter, but recognised the effort both Jake and Simon had put in to try to explain things to her. 'Thank you, both of you, I think that's helped a lot.' William, sitting quietly but observing closely, struggled not to laugh out loud.

'However,' said Simon, this time with a more severe tone and looking pointedly at Jake, 'it is the way in which a lot of hackers are caught, by packets being traced back because they were not careful enough. We should not forget that.'

Robert was starting to get irritated. He'd lost control of the discussion for a second time and was no closer to establishing an action plan. He knew precisely what actions they should take and just wanted to tell them what to do. However, telling people what to do was one of the reasons he had lost his job with Crawtech and he didn't want to lose his friends in the same way. Sensing Robert's discomfort, it was William who came to the rescue. 'I feel we need to speed this up a bit otherwise we won't have finished by the time lunch is ready and I, for one, am really looking forward to our Sunday roast. Can I suggest we let Robert explain his thinking and ideas for what to do next? We can then either accept what he says or debate the points we're unsure about.'

'Thank you, Bill' said Robert, grasping the opportunity and failing to hear William replying under his breath, 'you're welcome, Bob … flobbadob.'

'I am confident,' continued Robert, 'that the main question we need to answer is why the email was sent in the first place. There must be a reason for someone to have gone to so much trouble. It takes a lot of time and effort to set up something like this and I don't think even Jake would do it just for fun. This was my logic before I even knew for certain the email didn't come from either Christopher Butcher or Stephen Watson, Derek's brother. It was this logic that made me dig into the business side of Watson & Charles before I met with Derek Watson. Even though I had limited time, and the fact that Watson & Charles is a private company meant information was not readily available, I found out enough to suggest they are in serious financial difficulties for which there is no obvious explanation. I treated this as an unproven fact when I went to meet Derek Watson. When I suggested to him the two things were connected, he did not agree but he did not contradict me either, which added weight to my theory, and it was this that led me to ask for a fee of five hundred thousand pounds. It remains an unproven fact that the two things are linked but, if we asked Simon to work out the probabilities, I am sure he would find it more likely the business was being made to fail so the email could be sent rather than the email was sent just because the business was failing. Logic dictates, therefore, that our efforts and actions should be focussed on three questions. One, why is the business failing? Two, who has the motivation to cause such a failure? And, three, what we can do to reverse the trend in order to make it a successful business instead?'

Everyone was stunned into silence. Alice found herself mesmerised, not for the first time, by Robert's ability to analyse situations based purely upon fact. Was this why she felt as she did about him? Could it be admiration rather than love? Maybe the fact was he could only do what he did because his thought processes were not cluttered by emotions and feelings. He did not take account of people issues. That's the problem, thought Alice to herself, I'm a people issue. He doesn't do those. As she felt tears starting to form, she stood up, forced a smile on her face and walked out of the room saying, 'Carry on without me, I just need to check on the meat.'

She had intentionally left the doors open so she could hear the continuing discussion and in case she felt the need to go back and smooth over any arguments. She busied herself in the kitchen to take her mind off her feelings for Robert and also thought more about the Watson & Charles project. She was sure Robert was right about the business issues, but very unsure about what they could all do about it. From the sound of the raised voices coming from the lounge, she wasn't the only one. Surprisingly, William's voice was one of the loudest, shouting more than once that he was not a business consultant.

After she had confirmed the meat was progressing nicely and worked out a timescale for cooking the rest of the food, Alice moved into the dining room under the pretence of laying the table but really to hear the discussion more clearly. The noise level from the lounge had reduced and she realised Robert was progressing well with his action plan, using many of the points that had come out of the previous day's exercises to counter any objections. It was as if the exercises had given him a bank of ammunition which he could use to support his logical approach. She also noted that without her, the discussion had become a lot more technical, particularly when it reached the point of hacking into the Watson & Charles information systems. She wondered if her lack of understanding was holding them back but then convinced herself that, by being able to ask 'stupid questions', she played a valuable role. She had found from the early days of knowing them that they had a tendency to overcomplicate situations and could easily miss a relatively simple explanation.

Recognising she had little to contribute to the current theme of the discussion, Alice decided to focus on the house, as this was her first real opportunity to explore on her own. It still seemed a strange set-up to her, three young men living in a large detached four-bedroom house, even though it had been explained to her it was bought by Robert with his parents' help when he had obtained the job at Crawtech. She had never been upstairs but knew that part of the arrangement was that the main bedroom, complete with en suite, was reserved for the visits of Robert's parents so Robert, Simon & Jake had the other three bedrooms and shared the main bathroom. She thought about going upstairs now but couldn't think of a valid reason apart from pure nosiness. She had already explored all of the cupboards and drawers in the kitchen and dining room and had no trouble finding everything she needed to prepare, cook and present the meal.

Having so much space made it far more enjoyable than cooking in the cramped conditions of the small kitchen in her flat. Recognising that there was still a lot to do in cooking the vegetables and the Yorkshire pudding, she decided to stay out of the meeting. She couldn't really see how she could contribute anyway and certainly didn't want to be given any actions just because she was there. Instead, she opened the door from the dining room into the conservatory and then from the conservatory into the garden. It was a nice sunny September day and the sun was just coming round onto the conservatory windows. They often had their Saturday morning tea in the conservatory during the summer but only once in the garden, at Alice's suggestion but not really welcomed by the three boys. Lost in her thoughts, she jumped when Simon appeared by her side saying, 'I thought it must be you but I just wanted to check. I'd left the alarms on at the back as I didn't think anyone would be going outside today.'

'Oh, I'm sorry,' said Alice. 'It's such a nice day I thought I'd let some fresh air in and take a stroll in the garden whilst waiting for the veg to cook. I didn't want to keep disturbing you all by coming in and out of the meeting. I didn't hear any alarm.'

'No, the alarms are set to silent. They just alert in my bedroom and on Robert's and my mobiles. I'll cancel them now so you don't have to worry any more.'

Regaining her composure, Alice said, 'Can you tell everyone lunch will be ready in half an hour? Yorkshires won't keep.'

Having rechecked everything in the kitchen, Alice ventured, via the patio area adjoining the conservatory, into the sizeable but very low-maintenance garden. It was rectangular in shape, bordered by 6-foot-high fencing with a central lawn area paved on all sides. A few shrubs were in the small areas of border which remained. Two large sheds were a feature of the left hand side. Afraid to try the doors in case they too were alarmed, Alice peered in through the windows but all she could see were heaps of what appeared to be old computers and other mechanical items. As she walked round the path she thought the grass could do with a cut and remembered Robert had talked about replacing it with artificial grass. She wondered whose turn it was to cut the grass as she knew Robert, Simon and Jake had rotas for all of their domestic chores. She continued around the garden and came to the rear of the large double garage. Again, peering in through the window, she could see nothing but computers. However, unlike the sheds, these all appeared to be neatly ordered and working, as indicated by the myriad of small flashing lights. The only piece of non-computer equipment that she could make out was a solitary bicycle standing close to one of the up-and-over doors. In theory, she could get back into the house by entering the garage and passing through the utility room but, being certain the doors would be locked, she returned to the kitchen via the conservatory. As there was both a double oven and a heated drawer, she had plenty of options for resting the meat and keeping the vegetables warm. She had also remembered to save some of the carrots and cauliflower for Jake to eat raw.

As soon as it was ready, Alice had dished up the Yorkshire pudding into five equal portions, put the plates on the table and sat down before she called the others through. As they came in to the dining room, Alice told them if they wanted anything else to drink other than water to get it themselves. Nobody did. William observed there was a slight jostle for position to sit next to Alice and he was sure he saw a disappointed look on Robert's face when Simon ended up on one side of Alice and Jake on the other, which made him think there might be hope for Alice after all.

'Where's the meat?' asked Jake quite brusquely.

'When a Yorkshire lass cooks Yorkshire pudding for you, you eat it the Yorkshire way, like this as a starter. It's delicious with gravy from the meat,' replied Alice as she poured gravy onto her own plate.

'I don't really like gravy,' said Jake as he picked up his piece of Yorkshire pudding with his fingers and took a bite. Alice wondered if she should have reminded them all to wash their hands. Everyone else had gravy and told Jake how good it was but still he avoided it.

William offered to carve the pork while Alice put the rest of the food on the table It was an oval table and she had opened out the extension to give them plenty of room. Everyone piled their plates quite high, including Alice. The conversation was mainly about how good the food was. Alice again noted Jake hadn't had any gravy and that he and Robert both ate one element at a time, starting with the meat and ending with the peas. Towards the end of the meal, Alice asked whether the meeting needed to be reconvened and how much she had missed. Robert replied that he was happy they had a created a suitable action plan but it would be a good idea to summarise it for everyone's benefit, not just Alice's. After they had all finished second helpings, William suggested he make a pot of tea and they do the summary in the conservatory rather than go back into the lounge.

William took the tea tray into the conservatory and placed it on the rectangular glass-topped table around which they were all sitting. Robert and Alice were in the single wicker chairs at opposite ends of the table and Simon and Jake each sat on one of the matching wicker sofas, both favouring the ends nearer Alice. Although there was more space on the sofa next to Simon, William chose to sit next to Jake, a decision he quickly regretted as the effects of Jake's shower were already starting to wear off.

As soon as the tea was poured, Robert launched into a summary of the action plan. 'As identified yesterday, we have significant gaps in our collective knowledge about how businesses operate and about the brewing industry in particular. Of all of us, Bill is the only one who knows anything about beer or running a business. Bill made it clear his knowledge is limited but at least he knows some of the questions to ask and has agreed to do whatever he can over the next week to boost his understanding. Is that a fair summary of what we agreed, Bill?'

'I suppose so, Bob … flobbadob,' replied William, 'but don't expect too much progress as I will have very limited opportunities to ask worthwhile questions.'

'Understood,' said Robert. 'I will also aim to help by carrying out research using the internet. The other main priority is to tap into the Watson & Charles information systems, including emails, so we can see everything Derek Watson sees. Jake and Simon are going to set this up and Jake has promised to check with Simon before entering any new system, as we want to ensure that we do this side of things in as undetectable a way as possible. I have also asked them to look into Derek Watson's personal finances to make sure he is in a position to pay us the money. For the time being we are not going to do any more about trying to trace the real source of the email for fear of giving ourselves away. That's about it and there should be enough to keep us busy for the next week.'

'What about me?' asked Alice. 'Have I got any actions?'

'Not specifically,' answered Robert, 'but you might like to give some thought as to why the original email was sent to Mary Watson. I can see no logical reason so I suspect there might be a people element that I am missing.'

'What about Derek Watson's fingerprints and DNA? I knew that would prove to be a waste of time,' said Alice irritably.

Robert quickly responded. 'That remains for insurance purposes only. Hopefully, it will not be needed. When we have time, however, it would be good to treat it as a test case and see if we can add them to the national databases. Jake, Simon and I have already had a look at the DNA database and are confident we can get in and add data. Even if we find we don't require it for the Watson & Charles project, it may well prove useful in the future. As we move forward and get ourselves established as a business, I think it would be a good goal for us to have access to all the same resources as the police. Another database we have already been able to access is the vehicle licensing one so we can trace owners from licence plates. It is important to prioritise as each one will take a lot of time and effort. It is critical that whatever system or database we want to access, we aim to do it carefully and with minimum risk. At the moment we have other priorities.'

'OK, but don't start thinking of my works lab as your own forensic facility. It's there for cancer research purposes and I've already abused my position by using the facilities to process Derek Watson's samples. Even though I've done it in my own time, I don't feel very comfortable about it.'

Sensing the conversation was getting awkward and in danger of spoiling the good mood generated by their lunch, William decided to intervene. 'As the summary is over and Alice did the cooking with Robert's help to prepare the vegetables, it's only fair Simon, Jake and I do the clearing up. Come on, you two, let's make a start.'

'Oh, do we have to?' asked Jake petulantly.

'That probably depends on whether you want Alice to cook for us again,' stressed William. 'Personally, I thought it was an excellent meal and I hope we have a repeat some time soon.'

'Come on, Jake,' said Simon, standing up. 'We haven't done anything else towards it. William is right. We need to do our bit now.'

Reluctantly, Jake stood up and the three of them went through to the dining room and started to clear the table.

Recognising she had some precious time alone with Robert, Alice softened her tone. 'I'm pleased the weekend went well and you're happy with the outcome. Are you sure there's nothing else you would like me to do?'

'No, you've already done a lot. Even if we don't use Derek Watson's DNA, obtaining it showed we are serious and helped with the negotiation. I suspect, however, we will find that Derek Watson has done nothing towards putting any money to one side but, if that is the case, I have a plan in mind to show him more of what we are capable of.'

Alice realised she was sitting opposite Robert so, on the pretext of looking to see if there was more tea in the pot, she moved onto one of the sofas and closer to Robert. 'I still can't believe we'll be paid half a million pounds but I'm starting to understand why you asked for that much. If there really is a conspiracy to undermine the Watson & Charles business which is costing them millions of pounds, then half a million for solving it is not ridiculous and I'm sorry for being cross with you. My difficulty now is, whereas I could understand how you, Jake and Simon could answer the email question, I'm not so sure about resolving a major business problem. I heard William shouting about not being a business consultant so I presume he has similar concerns as well.'

'Bill was pointing out that just because he ran his own shop, drank beer and was a member of CAMRA didn't make him an expert on the brewing industry. I responded that he was in a position to find out general information which could be helpful to us and, as you heard, that's what he agreed to do.'

'What's CAMRA?' asked Alice.

'It stands for the Campaign for Real Ale. Bill has told me a little bit about it in the past. It is an organisation for beer drinkers that was formed in the 1970s to fight for traditional methods of producing and dispensing beer. It was mainly in response to large breweries making mass-produced beer such as Watney's Red Barrel and selling it in kegs not casks. Cask beer is viewed as real ale because of the traditional way it is produced. It is not filtered whereas beer in kegs is chilled, filtered and then has extra carbon dioxide added. I am not certain if knowing more about the likes of CAMRA and the different types of beer will be of much use but, at this stage, it is important to build up a clear picture of the Watson & Charles business and the environment in which it operates. We definitely need as much information as possible in order to analyse the situation logically. I accept, at the moment, we have very little knowledge but I am confident we can gain a much greater level of understanding. The element that may not be on our side is time. That is why it is important to prioritise what we do and to review our progress regularly.'

'I suppose the same applies to the Mary Watson question,' mused Alice. 'She may or may not be relevant. At the moment, we don't know much about her. Would it be worthwhile asking your mum? You said that was where the first contact came from.'

Almost before she finished speaking, Robert said forcibly, 'No, I do not want my mother involved. I made that extremely clear to Derek Watson and I meant it.'

'OK, OK,' said Alice, holding her hands up. 'I'll do it your way.'

'You could try looking her up on the internet', suggested Robert. 'There may be something useful in the public domain. In theory, Jake could help with databases such as census information but, as I said, I don't want him distracted at the moment. He has plenty to do. He makes it all sound so simple but it isn't. It takes a lot of time for him to write and modify his worms and viruses, even though he spends most of his waking life doing it.'

'Ah yes,' said Alice with a smile on her face, 'worms that eat their own tails.'

'That is all due to Simon,' explained Robert seriously. 'It's a brilliant concept and one that greatly reduces the risk of detection although, as Simon would say, nothing is 100 per cent secure.' They both laughed. Robert continued, 'I am, however, concerned about Jake's ability to work with and listen to Simon. When Simon was trying to explain his methods to Jake a few months ago, they were continually arguing. Jake had a number of meltdowns and spent many hours in the snug recovering. They have been a lot better recently. In fact, there is a strong correlation between the improvement in their relationship and Jake starting to join us for our Mad Hatter's tea parties. Even this weekend, there were two occasions when I thought they were going to have a serious argument but, both times, you said something which stopped them.'

'I don't think it can be all down to me,' said Alice. 'I'm not trying to do anything special but I admit I don't like it when anyone is heading for an argument, so I suppose I naturally try to do something to head it off.'

'It will be interesting to see how they cope with the Watson & Charles project as it is likely they will be under quite a lot of pressure, particularly Jake.'

'That sounds to me like a people issue. I thought you didn't do those.'

'It's a logical conclusion from the evidence I have witnessed in the past.'

'So you can cope with people if they are logical. It's when they act illogically that gives you difficulty, is it?'

'You are starting to ask annoying questions again. I do not think I want to listen to any of those now,' said Robert, starting to get to his feet.

Quickly, Alice changed the topic. 'Sorry. Tell me instead what you thought of the lunch.'

Robert sat back down and said enthusiastically, 'It was excellent. It reminded me of the Sunday roasts we used to have at home. You are obviously a very good cook.'

'I had plenty of practice cooking Sunday roasts when I was doing my PhD. My flatmates would often go out partying on a Saturday night and then not get up until late on a Sunday morning. I preferred quiet Saturday nights so on Sunday mornings I had the kitchen to myself and spent the time cooking lunch for the whole flat. I used to enjoy doing it but not as much as I enjoyed cooking in your kitchen today. It was great having your help this morning and also having so much space to work in and flexibility with the two ovens as well as a microwave. This is a lovely house. Sorry for setting the alarm off by the way.'

'Don't worry. It happens a lot. Simon gets a bit carried away with the security side of things.'

'Yes, but it obviously matters a lot to him. If he applies the same approach to Jake's hacking activities, it can't be a bad thing.'

'I suppose not,' admitted Robert.

'When I was wandering around the garden, I had a peek in through the garage window. There seemed to be an awful lot of computers inside. I hadn't really thought about it before but I suppose you do need a lot of computing power to do everything you all talk about.'

'Yes, we need a lot of servers but we're very fortunate. Most of the equipment was built by Bill. There's not much he can't do when it comes to building computers. He's brilliant at controlling power levels. We also have air conditioning in the garage to keep the temperature under control. I enjoy working with Bill to define all the specifications and then sourcing and ordering the parts. Unfortunately, we've had to slow down recently as I have very little money left but when we get paid by Derek Watson we will be able to expand further.'

Alice wished she shared Robert's confidence. Although she was worried about the effect on him should the Watson & Charles project fail, she was enjoying her time with him and continued the conversation. 'I also looked in the sheds. I couldn't make out exactly what was in them but they didn't seem as well organised as the garage.'

'They contain mainly old parts from some of my past robotic projects,' Robert replied somewhat sheepishly. 'Most things in them are either unfinished or don't work any more. Bill has offered to help me go through everything to identify what is worth keeping but we have not got round to doing it yet. I do not like throwing things away.'

Just as Alice was thinking she was in danger of becoming annoying again, in walked William. 'Right, that's all done,' he said. 'The table is clear and the kitchen is nice and tidy. The dishwasher is running so will need emptying later. Jake has gone upstairs. I think he's had more than enough socialising for one day or, as you would put it, his elastic band was reaching breaking point. Simon has also gone, no doubt to make sure that Jake keeps his promise. I do, however, have a question from Simon which is – can we do this again next Sunday?'

Robert looked at Alice and said, 'I do think we will need to review our progress some time next weekend. Whether we do it on Sunday with another lunch is really up to Alice.'

Alice responded quickly, 'I would love to do it again, particularly if Robert will help as he did today.'

William was also enthusiastic. 'That would work well for me. Sunday is preferable as I don't really want to ask Nancy to look after the shop for another Saturday and I thoroughly enjoyed today's meal.'

'Alright,' said Robert, 'that is settled. We will review at the same time next Sunday followed by another Sunday roast.'

'Excellent,' said William, 'I'll let Simon know on my way out. I'm sure he'll be delighted. Thank you for a lovely meal today, Alice. Goodbye.'

Suddenly inspired, Alice leapt up and gave William an enormous hug and a kiss on his cheek, whispering into his ear, 'Thank you'.

As soon as William was out of earshot and before Robert had time to move, Alice sat down again, put her hand on his arm. 'Robert, there's something I've been meaning to ask you about William. Can you explain what all this flobbadob business is about? It means nothing to me.'

'Oh that,' replied Robert, 'it's just a bit of banter between the two of us. It comes from a children's television programme of the 1950s called *The Flowerpot Men*. I'm surprised Bill is familiar with it as even he could only have been a baby when it was first broadcast but I think it was repeated a lot and, of course, Bill always had a television because of his father's repair shop. The two main characters were puppets called Bill and Ben who lived in flowerpots, with a third character called Little Weed, who spoke in a high-pitched, squeaky voice, in between them. They had their own language called Oddle Poddle with words like flobbadob and flobbalobbalob and the audience had to work out what they meant. In fact, flobbadob was particularly associated with Ben as he said it at the end of every episode. If you want to join in, I suppose you could be our Little Weed.'

'No, I definitely don't want to join in. My concern is William seems to call you Bob in retaliation for being called Bill but he always seems unhappy when he does so. Are you sure William views it as banter?'

'I do not know,' replied Robert testily. 'You know that is the sort of thing I don't pick up on but Bill has never asked me not to do it. All I do know is *The Flowerpot Men* were Bill and Ben, not Bill and Bob.'

Sensing that Robert's elastic band was starting to get stretched again and conscious she had spent a significant amount of time with him already, Alice reluctantly decided it was time to leave. She stood up.

'I hadn't realised how late it's getting. I have things I need to do to be ready for work tomorrow. I have enjoyed this weekend, particularly today. Given we're planning to do the same again next Sunday, are you happy to buy the food?'

'I'm not very confident about buying meat but I'm sure I can manage to get the vegetables.'

'OK, I'll get a piece of beef and bring it with me,' said Alice, preparing to implement her plan. 'Will you open the front door for me? I don't want to set off any more alarms. By the way, does Simon have cameras and microphones set up inside the house?'

'No,' replied Robert, getting to his feet. 'He's only allowed to have cameras outside. He does have sound detectors as part of his alarm system but not microphones that can pick up speech.'

As they were walking through the dining room into the hall, Alice, leading the way, said, 'Thank you for a lovely weekend. I'm pleased it went so well and good luck with implementing the action plan.' Then, before Robert had time to react, she turned and gave him the same sort of hug she had given William, ending with a slightly longer kiss on his cheek. Somewhat stunned, Robert opened the door in silence and with a cheery 'Goodbye', Alice got into her car.

As she was driving home, Alice was feeling very pleased with herself. She was slowly learning how to manage situations with Robert to her advantage. Her only concern was Jake would find out it was now going to be the norm for her to say hello and goodbye to Robert with a hug and a kiss.

Chapter Seven

Pauline Sharples had made a special effort to be at work early so she could be fully prepared for the board meeting that Wednesday morning. She had chosen to wear a smart maroon suit with matching shoes and a pure white blouse. She had thought about tying back her dark shoulder-length hair but decided to leave it down and free flowing as that was the way Derek preferred it. It had been four years since she first took the minutes of a board meeting. She recalled being very nervous and intimidated by the imposing nature of the board room with its antique table and chairs and historic pictures on the walls of past chairmen from the Watson family. The atmosphere of the first few meetings had been relaxed and she had quickly settled into her role as secretary to the board and personal assistant to the Managing Director.

Although there had been the occasional controversial issue and heated debate, the meetings had always been followed by lengthy lunches at one of their flagship pubs. Recently, the atmosphere in board meetings had changed and grown to be much more tense and fraught. She was sure that today the knives would be well and truly out. The fact that she had not been asked to organise lunch was a bad sign. She worried about Derek and how he would cope. He cared a lot about the people who worked for the brewery but this could make him too easily swayed when it came to making tough business decisions. The board was relatively small and the change in policy to employ non-family members with the aim of bringing in outside expertise was in danger of backfiring on Derek. These tended to be hard-nosed businessmen, like Jeremy Turner the Finance Director, who had no emotional attachment to the past or to the people. It was all about numbers for him and, at the moment, the numbers were not good.

Pauline ensured that biscuits, coffee, tea and water were available and resolved to take the minutes in a quiet and efficient manner, hoping that she would learn enough to provide Derek with a sympathetic ear should he need it after the meeting.

Stephen Watson was the first board member to arrive. He greeted Pauline saying, 'I'm not looking forward to this one. The situation is only getting worse and becoming extremely serious.'

'I know,' replied Pauline, choosing her words carefully. 'Derek is working harder than ever. I wish there was more I could do to help him but I don't know if there's anything I can do.'

'There's not a lot anyone can do at the moment. It's going to come down to what we decide as a family. I expect him to try to put off any difficult decisions from today until after our family get-together on Sunday.'

Although Stephen was three years younger than his brother, he appeared older. He had a similar stocky build to Derek but with fairer hair and a more rugged look due to his outdoor and high-energy lifestyle. He always looked uncomfortable when dressed in a suit, as he was now. He was much more at home in an open-necked shirt, chinos and a lab coat. As with Derek, from a very early age, Stephen's career in the family business had been carefully mapped out for him. Being the younger brother he had been steered towards the technical side of brewing. This had suited him well and his first job after leaving school had been as a technician in the brewery laboratory. Two years later, after he'd got a feel for the brewing life, he went to Heriot-Watt University where he obtained a first-class degree in brewing science, returning to the brewery as Laboratory Manager. He continued his studies through the Institute of Brewing and Distilling and obtained a Master Brewer diploma. He was appointed Head Brewer at the age of 32. When his father retired and the business was restructured with Derek becoming Chairman, Stephen was made Production Director. His responsibilities included the sales and marketing of small-pack beer as well as all the elements of production, from buying raw materials through to warehousing and distribution. He quickly set up a new managerial structure within the Production Division and tried to achieve a balance between giving his managers the freedom to operate as they chose whilst keeping a close eye on the quality of the beers. He made an effort to walk regularly around the brewery site and was always willing to listen to people talk about their issues. He even made an effort to meet with buyers from major retailers whenever his Sales Manager suggested it, on the basis that the Watson name carried some weight. As a result, he was liked and respected by everyone who worked for him.

The rest of the board arrived within a few minutes of each other and took their usual positions at the table, with Derek sitting at the head. There had been relatively little small talk while people were obtaining their respective cups of tea or coffee, indicative of the amount of tension in the room. The early formalities proceeded smoothly with the previous minutes being signed and everyone agreeing that the actions identified had either been completed or would naturally arise during the course of the meeting.

The next item on the agenda was the Finance Director's report. Jeremy Turner, who was a short, squat, thick-set man with a shaved head and relatively large bulging eyes, took a deep breath and began his report.

'Gentlemen, you have all received the half-yearly accounts. As you know, this meeting is timed so we can review these accounts as soon as they are available and take any actions we deem necessary to improve performance during the second half of the year. The information contained in these accounts should not come as a surprise to you as they show a continuation of the trends we discussed at our previous meeting. To summarise, these results are nothing short of disastrous. We are now past the key summer months which are our peak trading periods. There are no excuses. The weather has been excellent and, unlike last year, there has been no major football tournament where we have lost projected beer sales because the England team were knocked out early. Our budget for this year was to achieve a profit of just over ten million pounds. Whilst we knew this would be a stretch we all did agree to this budget. By this stage of the year, we should be showing a profit of just under eight million. The actual profit to date is only £300,172, so we are more than seven and half million behind target. This underperformance has been going on now for more than a year and there is no indication that it is likely to change. Extrapolation of the current trends for a further six months will result in an overall loss rather than any profit at all. I am already having very difficult discussions with our bank over the various loans we have and I've no doubt that such a result would have a serious impact on our interest rates and our ability to raise more finance.' He paused and shuffled his papers for dramatic effect, before delivering his final sentence. 'It is, therefore, imperative we take major action now, albeit, in my view, it is already far too late to rescue this year's result.'

'Thank you, Jeremy,' said Derek through gritted teeth. 'What specific actions would you recommend?'

Jeremy made a point of having a drink of water before replying. 'As we all know, it is extremely clear the major problem lies within the Managed House Division. The strategy of investing in larger and larger managed houses has failed spectacularly. Suspending this strategy immediately is an obvious course of action. My personal view is that this should have been done a long time ago and that we are already past the point of no return.'

Before he could continue, Derek interrupted. 'I think before we get into detailed discussion about future actions, it's only right we hear the reports from the other divisions. Stephen is next.' Jeremy Turner slammed his papers down on the table in an expression of frustration.

Taken a little by surprise, Stephen separated his papers so he could gather his thoughts and commenced his report.

'Although the Production Division is slightly behind budget, I'm generally pleased with our performance so far. Our budget is to break even. The transfer pricing system for large-pack beer to our own pubs and the reciprocal agreement with S&N, which is part of the lager contract, means we have little control over potential profits from these streams. We can only be successful by maximising production volumes and controlling costs. As I've said many times before, we do have an ageing brewery which is labour intensive and energy inefficient. Without investment, this situation will not change.

'The take-home market is our main variable and we have managed to hold up our volumes quite well. Bottled beer sales are ahead of last year, which was helped by the hot summer, although they are not quite keeping up with the market as a whole, although I've heard it said the temperature did at times become too hot to drink beer and people turned to water instead. To maintain these bottled-beer volumes, we need to be almost constantly on promotion with one or more of the major multiples so profits are slightly down. We are getting more and more squeezed between the larger breweries who have scale on their side and the small local breweries who are benefiting from the lower rate of duty and a larger allocation of shelf space in the major supermarkets. In spite of the poor performance of the managed houses, the sales of large pack are holding up well. As we only have small volumes going to Free Trade these days, this means beer sales through our own pubs are on course. The small amount of contract packaging we do for others is also on budget. If nothing significant changes for the rest of the year, I forecast we will end the year approximately forty thousand pounds short of target.' He drew breath, looked up and circled the table with his eyes.

'Thank you, Stephen,' said Derek. 'Any questions for Stephen before we move on to John's report?'

There were no questions as everyone was waiting to hear what John Hargreaves had to say in defence of the managed-house position. However, just before John was about to speak, Howard Watson, Derek's father, intervened, speaking slowly in his distinctive Hampshire drawl.

'In my role as a non-executive director I am supposed to represent the views of the shareholders. Over 50 per cent of the shares are represented by the three family members around this table. In my 25 years as Chairman, the shareholders supported the business through many ups and downs, whether caused by external issues such as drink-driving legislation or smoking bans or anything else. The key has always been to adopt an open and honest approach and present a credible plan for recovery. There is little doubt that the current situation constitutes a major crisis and may well require radical action to overcome it. However, I want to make it very clear that selling the business is not an option. All our efforts need to be concentrated upon resolving this issue by other means.'

Although Derek was unhappy his father had behaved as if he was still in charge, Derek thanked him for his comments and then asked the Managed House Director, John Hargreaves, to give his report, along with his latest findings from investigating the cause of the poor performance of his division.

John Hargreaves was a tall man with a long, gaunt face and thinning black hair. In spite of his appearance, he had a naturally buoyant and enthusiastic personality but, today, he was subdued. He ran his fingers through his hair, removed his dark-rimmed spectacles and began.

'I know you are all hoping for some good news and a potential way out of this horrendous situation but I'm afraid I have nothing new to offer. I remain at a loss to explain why the performance of the managed houses has deteriorated so much. We have analysed the data from just about every angle we can think of. Jeremy's people have looked at the overall performance, comparing this year with last year and beyond. I have personally visited every single one of our sixty-nine pubs and spoken in detail with all of the managers. I have picked the brains of my area managers, most of whom are vastly experienced. I have gone through various strategies to improve the situation with Derek, aiming to make use of his knowledge from the time he spent in the Managed House Division.

'No single factor has emerged which is consistent across the estate. In fact, we have identified a number of inconsistencies. Some pubs have good periods followed by bad ones. Others show a more consistent rate of falling performance. None of the more recent acquisitions or major refurbishments are close to their budgets but all are showing steady improvements, just far more slowly than budgeted. We have implemented changes to some individual pubs to try to achieve improvements, such as modifying menus and reducing staffing levels. Although these steps have reduced costs, they have led to an increase in complaints about reduced choice and poor service.

'All pubs report being busy, particularly during the peak summer period, but this is not reflected in the takings. I can only put this down to the fact that a large pub taking, say, forty-five thousand a week appears busy even if it's budgeted to take fifty thousand. However, it is the additional five thousand per week which makes the difference. Averaged out across the whole estate, it equates to the overall 10 per cent that we are behind budget. I have revisited the arguments and calculations made in setting the budgets but there is very little I would have done differently given we all wanted to hit a total profit target for the group of ten million. We have looked at external factors but again can find nothing major. There is no suggestion our competitors are suffering in a similar way. I have spoken with Neil and, as I am sure we'll hear from him shortly, tenancies are holding up well with none of the same issues we seem to have. I feel my whole team have done and are doing as much as they can to understand what is going on. I freely admit we are running out of ideas and I would very much welcome any suggestions we haven't already thought of.'

In order to avoid a lengthy and unpleasant discussion at this stage, Derek moved swiftly on and asked Neil Martin, director of the Tenanted Division, to give his report. Everything about Neil Martin seemed to be average. He was of medium height and build with few distinguishing features. He had dark-brown hair, regularly shaved to a 6mm cut to hide his widow's peak. He spoke clearly and confidently.

'As our rents are set in advance, tenancies are not subject to market fluctuations as much as managed houses so this helps to keep us on track. Most other indicators are positive so our current performance is slightly ahead of budget and our forecast is to maintain that position through to year end. Overall, beer sales are encouraging and fit in with the picture that Stephen has described. Our main thrust has been to continue to move all of our 176 pubs onto the new tenancy agreement, which incorporates intelligent tills and open-book accounting using the Brewdat system. The vast majority of tenants are finding it works well. It definitely helps our area managers to provide better guidance and advice and, in most cases, when the tenants take this advice on board, they are able to reap the benefits. Rent reviews are still not easy but at least there's no arguing about the facts. The few tenants who haven't changed to the new agreement are likely to be hiding some of their profits in the hope this will keep their rent down. These tend to be long-standing tenants who are resistant to change but are performing well enough for us not to want to rock the boat. There are a few tenants who I would like to get rid of but we don't have a list of high-calibre candidates waiting to take their places.

'As John has stated, there's nothing obvious from our side which would help to explain why the managed houses are struggling. In fact, the managed house cast-offs that were transferred to tenancy during my two years with the Company are among the better-performing houses. If we were not facing the current situation, I would be recommending a couple of larger tenancies for transferring to John. The tenants are making very good money and there's no reason in my view why we couldn't make those pubs work well as managed houses instead. One of these, The Black Dog, is due for rent review next year so, if we do want to give notice to the tenants, we need to do so soon.'

The room stayed silent, awaiting a response from Derek, but again, he refrained from commenting or inviting questions and just moved on.

'That completes the reports from the three divisions. The next item is to identify a full-year forecast and then decide on the actions required to improve it. Thanks to Jeremy's simplification of the accounts last year, central overheads are now allocated across the divisions so are included in each division's profit target. It is, however, worth noting that the total for central overheads is very close to budget. As we have already heard from Stephen, the Production Division will be close to its budget of break even and Neil expects tenancies to hold their current position. This just leaves the managed house forecast. I've discussed this with John and agreed it's not possible to put a justifiable number forward until we understand the factors behind the poor performance during the first half of the year. These factors remain a mystery. It would appear we're left with a best-case scenario of achieving the managed-house budget in the second half of the year or, heaven forbid, a worst-case scenario of falling a further seven and a half million behind. In the former case, this would give a total group profit at the end of the year of around 2 million and, in the latter case, a group loss of almost 6 million, which would be absolutely disastrous. In past years, as you know, we've been able to manipulate the final result by planning the timing of property profits from selling pubs with a low book value compared with their current market value. We have, however, now exhausted this option, particularly as the pub market is flooded and property prices are static at best. We are desperate for an alternative route by which we can boost the forecast and give us the best chance of delivering the highest result possible. In my view, turning around the performance of the managed houses is our best, if not only, option and I believe we should all do our utmost to help John identify what has gone wrong so we can collectively devise a plan for putting it right.'

As he was speaking, Derek realised how weak he sounded but he was conscious of not revealing anything about the email. Rather reluctantly but knowing it needed to said, he added, 'I am, of course, willing to listen to other ideas or suggestions.'

Not surprisingly, it was Jeremy Turner who responded first.

'The problem is the numbers do not lie. Whatever the reason, the poor performance of the managed houses stands out like a sore thumb. The rest of the business is performing satisfactorily but, as three-quarters of the profits are supposed to come from the Managed House Division, we just cannot afford for this situation to carry on any longer. I do not feel comfortable having this conversation in John's presence but I do think John's position has become untenable and I do not understand why a change in leadership has not already been made.' Even Jeremy was now looking uncomfortable as he continued. 'Surely it's past time we let someone else try to turn things around?'

Trying to stay calm, Derek replied. 'As I've already explained, if we understood why this has happened then it would be possible to judge if John has made mistakes. We've thrown lots of resources at this issue and I have personally looked closely into it. I believe I would have reacted very similarly to John. I am, therefore, far from convinced anybody else would do any better.'

'There is also a strong argument that someone else could not do any worse,' retorted Jeremy in an accusatory manner.

After a slight pause, Derek replied somewhat defensively. 'I wasn't going to mention this but, before anyone else feels like attacking John, I think I had better tell you that he did give me his letter of resignation over two months ago. I decided not to accept it for the reasons I have just outlined. As Managing Director and, therefore, John's line manager, I have the right to make this decision. As Chairman, however, any one of you has the right to challenge me by raising a vote of no confidence. If carried, then it would be someone else's decision as to what to do.'

It was Derek's father who spoke next.

'Calm down everyone. I'm sure we don't want to get into the area of votes of no confidence. That isn't going to help and we don't have time to complicate the situation further. There are only a few months left to make a difference to this year's result. I strongly suggest all efforts are concentrated on delivering the best result we can for this year. Longer-term decisions can be made once this result is known. I do, however, have a constructive thought for the meeting's consideration. It is clear Neil has done a good job in tenancies since joining the business and he now has almost two years' experience of how we operate. He also has past experience of managed houses from his time as an area manager at Limberts Brewery. I suggest it would be worth Neil and John exchanging roles so Neil can have a close look at the managed-house situation with a fresh pair of eyes.'

Concerned the conversation was heading into areas that he really wanted to discuss as a family before any major decisions were made, Derek closed down the discussion by committing to review the situation with John outside of the meeting. Derek could tell from Stephen's body language that he was waiting to contribute and was disappointed not to be given the chance. Derek again questioned whether he had made the correct decision in keeping the email to himself and resolved to tell Stephen about it as soon as possible after the meeting. He then moved onto the next item on the agenda which was to discuss major projects. After further heated debate, there was unanimous agreement to suspend all ongoing projects with immediate effect and also to seek out other short-term cost savings which could be made.

The next item was about property disposals. Derek tried to move quickly through this on the grounds he had covered it previously but Jeremy leapt in to say, 'I agree with your earlier statement in that we have exhausted the selling of poor-performing pubs capable of generating sizeable property profits. If we were to sell other pubs on the basis of poor performance, they would be ones we have only recently bought. Conversely, if we sold on the basis of maximising property profits, we would be selling tenanted pubs that are performing well. Neither of these approaches would make good business sense. There is, however, one area of property which is on the books at significantly less than its market value and that is the brewery site. The brewery has been on this site for almost one hundred years. Although the site has been re-valued in the past, the last valuation was over twenty years ago. I strongly suggest we have it valued again. We can then decide if we should consider moving elsewhere or whether we can justify having a brewery at all, given, as Stephen has just admitted, we know we can buy beer for less than we can produce it.'

This time Stephen did not hold back. He stood up and pushed back on his chair, causing it to scrape on the wooden floor. Glaring at Jeremy, he was almost shouting as he spoke. 'We are brewers. The heritage of this company is in brewing. Our values are clearly defined around the quality of our beers as well as of our pubs. Everyone working for Watson

& Charles is made aware of these values and should support them. I will never back a move for us to become just a pub company. I would rather sell the whole business instead.'

Jeremy stayed calm and responded, 'All I'm saying is we do not have up-to-date information to make any decision. There have been other independent family brewers who've been in the same situation with an ageing brewery. Some have redeveloped on the same site. Some have sold the site and moved to a cheaper site elsewhere, building a modern but smaller brewery. Others, as you rightly say, have become pub companies or sold up completely. I've tried to raise this topic before but we've hardly discussed it as a board. I accept it's too late for any decision to have an impact on this year's results but we can at least take steps to start the debate. As well as providing us with firm numbers to work with, given our formula for calculating share price, increasing the book value of the site would increase our total asset value and, therefore, negate some of the effect of low or zero annual profits.'

It was Howard Watson who intervened. 'From a shareholder's perspective, it's hard to oppose the financial reasoning for having the site valued. Also, given we are heading for a disastrous result, it may prove a useful topic to help deflect the criticism if we can say we are actively considering the future of the brewery site.'

'I just want it noted,' said Stephen passionately, his anger only just contained, 'I will always vote in favour of us staying in brewing.'

Realising that Stephen's outbreak of emotion had quietened the non-family members of the board, Derek moved on to ask for any other business and was relieved there wasn't any. As soon as Derek closed the meeting, Stephen leapt up and stormed out. The others followed silently and more sedately, leaving Pauline on her own to clear up and reflect upon the potential implications of everything she had heard.

*   *   *

Derek had chosen to have a quiet and reflective sandwich lunch alone in his office. He was pleased the meeting was over but felt it hadn't delivered anything new and had just exposed the level of unrest and bad feeling he knew was there but was hoping to contain. The animosity between Stephen and Jeremy Turner was not healthy. Like Stephen, Derek felt that brewing was fundamental to his family history, but he also thought Jeremy was only doing his job by pointing out the best course of action from a purely financial point of view. However, he did wonder if Jeremy gave as much thought to solutions which kept brewing within the Company as to solutions which did not. Derek considered whether the meeting might have gone better had everyone been aware in advance of the email and the possibility of a cyber-attack but he'd made his decision to keep this within the family for the time being. Hoping Stephen had now had time to calm down, Derek buzzed through to Pauline and asked her to see if Stephen was free.

As with most younger brothers, there had been times throughout Stephen's life when he had resented the favouritism shown to Derek. One of these had been when he had first realised that Derek was destined to become Managing Director purely on the grounds of being the elder brother, in spite of Stephen consistently achieving better results than Derek throughout their school years. However, this resentment had faded as Stephen grew to love his own role and he was now quite happy to leave all the tricky business decisions and political manoeuvring to Derek. Sitting in Derek's office and pondering the morning's meeting, Stephen felt some of his resentment returning and couldn't help thinking that Derek could have been more supportive about staying in brewing. Just as he was about to say as much, Derek started to speak.

'I know this morning was uncomfortable for you and I apologise if you feel I could have handled things better. There is something I need to show you. It's been preying on my mind for a few days and is the main reason why I asked both you and our parents to dinner at the weekend. I understand, by the way, we are getting together on Sunday evening rather than Saturday to accommodate our parents' hectic social life.'

'Yes,' replied Stephen, suddenly intrigued. 'What is it?'

Derek handed over a single sheet of paper. 'Read this but please don't say anything until I've finished telling you everything I know about it.'

As soon as Stephen had finished reading, Derek continued. 'It purports to be an email sent from Christopher Butcher to Mary offering to buy us out. I say purports as Christopher denied sending it, so I had it checked by Ian Walters who was able to confirm it did not, in fact, originate from Christopher. Ian told me it actually came from you but I found that hard to believe. I asked him to check again and he eventually discovered it had been placed on our system via a complex route and in a way in which the actual origin is well hidden and still remains unknown.

'I've employed external IT consultants to explore further and they've suggested it might be part of an elaborate cyber-attack on the business. If they are correct, it might be linked to the abysmal results we're seeing from our managed houses, although I'm far from clear what the connection might be. I've been thinking about the reasons for anyone sending such an email and in this obtuse way. The only reason I can think of is to cause splits and divisions amongst the family. Between you and me, if that is the intention, then sending it to Mary was an inspired move as she has taken it very seriously indeed. I'm showing it to you before I show it to Father as I fear he will not listen but just go blustering to Christopher Butcher's father and make the situation worse. It will be the focal part of our discussions on Sunday. I'm asking for your help in making sure we handle it as sensitively as possible.'

Stephen did not know how to respond and squirmed in his seat. His immediate reaction was of anger but this was quickly followed by confusion, so his reply was a mixture of the two.

'So, you're telling me you've been sitting on this for nearly two weeks, that Ian Walters knows about it but I don't, and you actually suspected I could have sent it. How can it be linked to our results? Even I agree with Jeremy that the numbers don't lie. Who are these consultants? Why should they know more about our business than we do?'

'Look,' replied Derek, 'I know this has taken you by surprise. Why don't you sleep on it and we can have another chat about it before the weekend? All I ask is you keep it to yourself and Anthea. The only other people who know about it are Mary and Pauline and, of course, whoever did send it in the first place.'

'Alright,' said Stephen firmly, 'but only because I don't understand what's going on. I didn't like the tone of this morning's meeting and I do think, as a family, we need to reinforce the message that we are brewers, we are going to stay as brewers, and coming out of brewing is not negotiable. I need to know you feel the same way.'

'Stephen, you know I strongly value our brewing heritage and, no, I don't want us to stop being brewers. What I'm trying to tell you is I fear we are in for a serious battle to save the whole company. If we lose, it will mean no Watson & Charles Brewery, no Watson & Charles pubs and the end of the Watson & Charles family business. You and I do not have enough shares on our own. We need to persuade others, starting with Father on Sunday. In spite of what he said this morning about selling not being an option, if it becomes the only credible option from the shareholders' point of view, I can see him reluctantly supporting a sale. Also, given the amount of shares he holds personally, he will want to protect his own position.'

'I really hope it doesn't come to that,' said Stephen with an extremely concerned look on his face. 'I'll talk it through with Anthea and try to make sure she understands the magnitude of the situation. Like both Mary and Mother, she has her own shares so will need to make her own decision.'

As Stephen left, he made an effort to wave goodbye to Pauline in the adjacent office. Pauline had just finished typing up the minutes from the board meeting and was sending them through electronically for Derek to approve. She was aware of their sensitivity so had flagged them as highly confidential, but this made no difference to the fact that, as soon as she pressed send, the minutes would be visible on multiple screens in a large detached house in the suburbs of Redhill.

Chapter Eight

Alice was surprised by how little chat there had been on their forum during the week. She suspected Simon was censoring many of the messages as there had been some debate about the difference between various types of pubs, but then nothing. She was still none the wiser about managed houses and tenancies but decided it was the role of the boys, as she called them, to spend all day looking up things like that on the internet.

But what was her role? Before she met Robert, she knew there was something missing from her life. She filled her time with work and social activities, mainly sporting related, with friends and acquaintances from work, but the Saturday-morning Mad Hatter's tea parties had become something she really looked forward to, even though the discussion was usually driven by Robert onto subjects like robotics, neural networks and artificial intelligence. Now the tea parties were being replaced by Sunday meetings that were more like work, she was unsure whether this was a good thing. However, it was Sunday again and she was very much looking forward to a repeat performance, remembering how much she had enjoyed the previous Sunday, more for the time spent outside the meetings than the meetings themselves. If she wanted to be able to contribute to the Watson & Charles project, she resolved she needed to be able to ask her questions and make sure she understood what they were all talking about. She left early for Robert's house so she could do as much food preparation as possible before the meeting started, taking with her the large piece of beef rib she had bought the previous day from the up-market butchers in Horley. She had messaged Robert twice, once to ask if he had had a good week and again to ask if he had got the rest of the food. On both occasions she had received a one word reply of yes.

When she arrived at Robert's house the door opened automatically for her. As she had hoped, there was no sign of Simon or Jake. Robert was in the lounge setting up for the meeting. She put down her bag in the hall and bounced into the lounge with a cheery 'Good morning' and gave Robert a big hug and a kiss on his cheek. Ignoring the surprised look on his face, she continued, 'I hope you're ready to help with the lunch preparations. I don't want to miss as much of the meeting as I did last week so I really need your help to get everything ready, including laying the table.'

'I'll be there shortly,' replied Robert as Alice picked up her bag on her way to the kitchen.

By the time Robert joined her, Alice had made two cups of tea and got out all the various vegetables from the fridge. She really wanted to know how Robert's week had been but she found it hard to have a proper conversation about it. As she had found the previous week, when Robert started peeling the carrots, he would talk about carrots. When he moved onto potatoes, he would talk about potatoes, and it was not easy for her to deflect him. However, she was learning it was not a good idea to push him too hard so settled just for enjoying the time alone with him.

They had just about finished everything when William arrived. As soon as he entered the kitchen, Alice, making sure Robert was watching, gave William a quick hug and a kiss. Simon and Jake came downstairs almost immediately, as if triggered by William's arrival. There were general hellos, even from Jake, who clearly had not made the same effort as the previous week and was back to his usual greasy look. Alice was pleased neither Simon nor Jake had witnessed her hugging William. She thought she wouldn't mind hugging Simon but definitely not Jake. She also noted that, in all the commotion, Robert and William did not go through their usual flobbadob routine. As they were moving through to the lounge for the start of the meeting, Alice smiled and said to William, 'It's going to be a good test of your carving skills today. I've got a lovely piece of beef but it's got two bones in it for you to carve around.'

William smiled back, 'I'm sure I'll cope. If today's lunch is anywhere near as nice as last week's it will be well worth the effort. I'm definitely looking forward to the lunch more than the meeting. I fear what I have to say may well disappoint Robert this morning.'

'Don't worry,' replied Alice, 'I've been trying to find out if Robert had a productive week but with little success. However, he seems in a pretty good mood today. I've explained to him I'll be nipping in and out of the meeting to keep an eye on the food so if I miss anything of note, please tell me afterwards.'

Robert called the meeting to order and started by reminding everyone that they were in the information-gathering phase of the Watson & Charles project. He said he was pleased to report, with Simon and Jake's help, he could now access anything on Derek Watson's computer. This mainly involved emails and attachments, which tended to be mostly Microsoft Office files, but they were providing a useful insight into the Watson & Charles business. Robert was extremely confident this access had been set up so it was undetectable from the Watson & Charles end. Simon and Jake were now in the process of setting up the same approach for accessing the computers of the other board members. He explained this was already generating lots of information and sifting through it would take time.

Other software systems, seemingly common throughout the brewing industry, were used for the day-to-day running of the brewery and the pubs. No progress had yet been made in trying to break into these and Robert was not certain it was worth the effort to do so, as they were primarily large databases from which the key information was extracted into Excel spreadsheets for manipulation and presentation. Just as Alice was about to ask a question, Robert pre-empted her.

'The most interesting documents so far are the minutes of a board meeting held on Wednesday this week and the half-yearly accounts which were presented and discussed at the meeting. As a result of having sight of these, we now have firm evidence the business is in serious difficulty and that the main cause is poor performance from the estate of managed houses. It would appear no-one at Watson & Charles understands the reasons for this. One of our key questions is: can we find out the reasons when they cannot? Before we try to find an answer, I suggest we hear from Alice and Bill about progress on their actions from last Sunday. Alice first.'

Trying to keep the mood light hearted, Alice responded, 'My main action was to buy the beef for lunch, which I have completed successfully.' There was only a small titter from the others so she moved swiftly on. 'My other action was to find out about Mary Watson. I haven't got very far with this but I did look her up on Facebook and I also found a few local news articles about her. She's been married to Derek Watson for 24 years. They have two children, Joshua and Philippa. Mary is quite active in Hampshire country life, although she was born in Wiltshire, the daughter of a vicar. She is very into horses and supports charities such as Riding for the Disabled and is an AB whip. Also, as we already knew, she is an amateur artist who paints horses and country scenes although, from the few pictures I've come across, she's not that good. That's all really, nothing unusual so far. Do you want me to keep looking?'

'Probably not,' replied Robert, 'but we will review future actions at the end. Bill, how did you get on?'

'Not too well, Bob, ... flobbadob,' retorted William. 'I did call my accountant but struggled to explain exactly what we wanted to know. He said there were a number of possibilities for setting up a new business and we agreed to speak more about it when we next meet in person. On the beer front, I concentrated on understanding the different types of pub. You have no doubt found this out yourself by now, Robert, but I was told there are three types of pub; free houses, managed houses and tenancies. Typically, free houses are owned by the licensee and are, therefore, free to buy their beer from any brewery they choose. The other two types are owned by companies who stipulate which beer brands are sold. These may be pub companies who just own a lot of pubs but don't own a brewery or breweries who want to sell their brands of beer in their pubs.

'The big difference between managed houses and tenancies is who gets the profits. Where a pub is managed, the licensee and all of the staff who work there are employed by the company who owns the pub and, therefore, all profit from the pub goes to the company. With tenancies, the licensee is a tenant who owns the business but not the pub, employs the staff and gets the profits in return for paying a rent to the company who does own the pub. Frank at the Red Lion is a tenant and he tells me, as part of his rental agreement, he is forced to buy beer from the brewery at a higher price than he would have to pay if he was free to buy on the open market. It sounds like a sore point. Apart from the beer part, the tenancy arrangement is similar to my shop, where I rent the premises to run my own business. I pay the business rates and all utility bills so need to make enough to cover those before I can generate any profit. In the current climate it is not all that easy and, talking to Frank, it is not very easy for him either. Unless you think otherwise, next week I was going to concentrate on building up a picture of the brewing industry as a whole. Some of my friends in CAMRA know quite a lot about the various changes and takeovers that have happened in the past. Until now, I haven't paid too much attention to it all but I should be able to learn a lot from them fairly quickly, although some of their views are likely to be somewhat biased.'

Trying to be inclusive, Robert then asked if Simon and Jake had anything to add. Jake's response was to moan about being slowed down by having to run his every move past Simon, whereas Simon just kept reiterating about the importance of being careful as nothing was 100 per cent secure. They then moved into detailed technical debate which was lost on Alice. She was thankful her timer beeped to indicate the oven was up to temperature, giving her an excuse to go to the kitchen. Even though all she had to do was to put the beef in the oven, she stayed in the kitchen a while to think about her best approach. She was still concerned she was not going to be lot of help to the project but wanted to find a way to prevent Robert from upsetting the others. When she heard William's voice again, she decided to return, taking with her a tray containing mugs of tea for everyone. When Alice asked what she had missed, it was William who replied.

'We were debating how to speed up the process without increasing the risk. I was just asking whether we would know if anyone else had been doing the same sort of thing as we're doing. It strikes me that whoever sent the initial email would have the skills to access the Watson & Charles systems. They may have already done so to obtain the same information we're now looking for. One potential way forward would be to find evidence of such activity and then trace it back to its source.'

Simon responded, 'It is a very good thought, William. In theory it should be possible to do as you say. We haven't really looked for evidence of someone else being in there but the knowledge we're gaining from protecting ourselves would help us to put together a tracing system. Again, it would need to be undetectable, otherwise we may just as well plough on trying to trace the original email.'

'I still would like to do that,' exclaimed Jake.

'I have a question on that topic, Robert,' said Alice. 'If you were right last week when you stopped Jake from going any further because he was being watched, will it not surprise whoever was watching us that we have stopped? Surely they will be wondering what we're doing instead. Would it be a good idea to go back to trying to trace the source of the email but to do it intentionally badly? That way they might think we're not as good as we actually are, and also they would not expect us to come at them from a different angle.'

Before Robert could answer, Jake butted in, 'I like the idea of that. Lead them into a false sense of security and then, BANG, hit them when they're not looking.'

Concerned Jake was starting to behave like one of his superheroes, Robert replied, 'Alice makes a good point. As well as planning what we are going to do, we should also look at it from the opposition's point of view and make sure our actions are not predictable. We mustn't forget it's an unproven fact the opposition have similar skills to our own and maybe we should try to predict what they will do next and consider playing them at their own game.'

'If it were me,' said William, 'I would approach more shareholders with the aim of creating more and more unrest. In fact, how do we know this hasn't already happened?'

'We do not,' responded Robert, tapping his foot and fighting to stay calm. 'We cannot do everything at once. All these are good thoughts and suggestions but we simply do not have enough time or resources to pursue them all. We still need to prioritise. I have given you all the chance to report what you've done and to say what you think. I have not yet reported my findings. I will do so now. We should then be in a position to agree on the actions for next week. There is no doubt we know more today than we did this time last week and it is critical that this time next week we know even more.'

Even though she thought they were still a long way from being able to do anything to change the situation, Alice felt the need to support Robert. 'I agree,' she said, 'we need to stick to the approach we all agreed last week. Even though I will never understand the technical detail, it does feel like we have made good progress. Let's listen to what Robert has to say and then we can decide on where to go next.'

Robert then commenced what was clearly going to be a lengthy report. 'I have concentrated upon Watson & Charles as a business and their financial situation. As I reported last week, because they are an independent family-run company, there is very little information available from normal internet browsing so having access to internal Watson & Charles documents has made it a lot easier. I have found annual reports, financial accounts, board papers and management committee minutes going back at least 10 years.' He then proceeded to give a detailed account of the financial performance with the intention of explaining what had changed to cause the current financial crisis.

Alice soon realised that everyone was losing interest. William was struggling to keep his eyes open, and Jake seemed to be thinking of something else entirely but she didn't want to imagine what or who! Simon was manfully trying to keep up with Robert but even he seemed to be losing track of all the numbers. Thinking of a way to bail Robert out, Alice said, 'Sorry to interrupt but it will soon be time to do the final preparations for lunch. If we don't get to the action plan part soon, we will need to reconvene after we've eaten.'

Everyone seemed to perk up at the mention of lunch, and even Robert didn't want to extend the meeting so he took the hint. 'To speed things up, I will just give you a general summary of what I have discovered so far. If any of you want more detail, I will leave it to you to ask, or I can send you any specific documents you may wish to see. Watson & Charles was founded in 1793 in a time when most towns and villages had their own breweries. It was traditional for family businesses to be handed down the male line. As the first Mr Charles had no sons, he sold out to the Watsons but the name continued. Only members of the Watson family are allowed to hold shares. There are strict rules on buying and selling, with all transactions carried out through the company. This is why it is difficult for anyone to try to take over the company. There are currently sixty-three shareholders but almost 48 per cent of the shares are held by Derek Watson, his brother, Stephen, and their father, Howard. A further 5 per cent is held by their respective wives. There is a formula for calculating the value of shares which is based upon the capital assets of the company and the previous year's profits. Once calculated, the share price remains unchanged for a full year.

'Only family members used to be allowed on the board and the board seemingly manipulated the asset value and profits to keep the share price rising steadily and dividend payments healthy. This was done by growing the business, mainly through acquiring more and more pubs. However, ten years ago there was a major change in policy. The Finance Director, who had been there for nearly thirty years and was married to Howard Watson's cousin, retired. The rules on non-family members on the board were relaxed and a new Finance Director was employed. At the same time, Howard Watson moved from being Chairman to become a non-executive director, and Derek Watson took over as Chairman and Managing Director with Stephen Watson being appointed Production Director.'

'That sounds like it might have caused a few family ructions,' commented Alice.

Robert continued in a serious tone. 'The documents I have read do not suggest any disagreements. Since then, the family directors in charge of the managed and tenanted pubs have also retired and been replaced with non-family members. Seemingly related to these changes, there has been an overall reduction in the number of pubs, with a lot of the smaller tenancies being sold off. In parallel, there has been significant investment in new, very large pubs or in the enlarging of existing pubs. This has led to increases in bank loans and there is some suggestion that the bank is reluctant to lend much more.

'Anyway, the main reason for the current financial crisis is the sixty-nine large managed houses are a long way behind the budget set for them. As I said earlier, there is no obvious explanation for this underperformance. On the other hand, the tenancies and the brewery itself are performing as expected. In my opinion, we are left with a number of unproven facts and some key questions which, if we had the answers, would help to either prove or disprove them. The biggest unproven fact is someone, most likely another brewing or pub company, is seeking to take over Watson & Charles, either by taking advantage of their poor performance or by directly influencing it. As a priority, therefore, I suggest we focus on this and try to answer the following questions. Who would want to buy Watson & Charles? How could they adversely influence Watson & Charles's performance? Has this been done before with other family brewers?'

William recognised that he could at last contribute something to the discussion and jumped in before Robert could explain further. 'One possibility that springs to mind is Marston's. They bought

Ringwood brewery some years ago and the Watson & Charles estate of pubs would probably be a good fit for them. I suspect that if Watson & Charles were not protected by the family rules you have just described, they would have been swallowed up by some larger national or international brewer a long time ago. This is an area that CAMRA are interested in, trying to protect and support the smaller breweries. I vaguely remember that it was a Monopolies and Mergers Commission ruling, involving Courage I think, which restricted the number of pubs a brewing company could own. This effectively led to the formation of pub companies who do not brew their own beer and, since then, the pub situation throughout the country has changed significantly. Lots of smaller pubs have closed. Others have got larger. You only need to look at any major high street to find a large Wetherspoons pub. All pubs these days are expected to serve good-quality food and, for many customers, the food is more important than the beer. It sounds to me as if Watson & Charles are just following the national trend but I'm not really up to speed on this area and I hope to find out more next week.'

'You know a great deal more than I do,' said Simon encouragingly, adding, 'I've never even been in a pub.'

'My brothers made me go with them a couple of times,' blurted out Jake. 'I hated it. It was too noisy and I have not been since.'

'You two hardly go anywhere these days,' chipped in Alice. 'Perhaps we should all go to a pub together,' adding quickly, 'at a quiet time of day. At least then you would know a little more of what we are talking about.' Realising her suggestion was met with stony silence, Alice went on, 'I really need to check on the meat as it should be time to give it its rest and get the Yorkshire pud in the oven, but I do have one thought first. What if it's not a company? What if it's a person such as Pauline Sharples? She would fit a lot of the facts.'

Robert responded immediately, 'I don't see how. She is unlikely to have the necessary technical knowledge or motivation.'

'No,' replied Alice, rising to the challenge even though she knew she shouldn't. 'It's a people thing so I wouldn't expect you to understand. Pauline Sharples is a secretary so is unlikely to have a lot of money. She is working for a man who does have a lot of money and, by the sound of it, she has already got her talons into him. If she suspects there are cracks in his marriage, what better way to make the cracks bigger than to send an email to his wife suggesting his beloved brewery needs to be sold. She has access to all the internal Watson & Charles information and has set herself up as the intermediary between him and us so she can keep tabs on what we're doing. All she would need would be a link to someone like Jake to do the technical stuff for her.'

William laughed. 'Well, Robert,' he said jokingly, 'you can't argue with the logic. It must at least qualify as another unproven fact.'

Recognising that Robert was struggling to see the funny side, Alice tried to diffuse the situation. 'How about I give myself the action to find about more about Pauline in the same way I did about Mary Watson?' Before anyone had chance to respond, she leapt up saying, 'I'll leave you to sort out the other actions. It's twenty minutes to lunch. Please be ready on time and, Jake, make sure you wash your hands first.'

The conversation over lunch was both lively and positive. It was mainly about updating Alice on the actions agreed for the forthcoming week, punctuated by compliments about the food, especially the beef. It seemed to Alice that Robert was pleased about the progress so far and, when Robert was happy, everyone else tended to be happy as well. Even Jake and Simon seemed to be working a lot better together. Simon had explained to her they were still in the process of 'casing the joint' and deciding which 'tools' to use before going beyond just accessing emails, which was relatively safe and straightforward. Alice hoped Jake wouldn't reach the point of wanting to 'blow the safe open' before Simon was ready. Alice had also asked if they could set things up so she could see the emails of Pauline Sharples.

As they were coming towards the end of the meal and the conversation about Watson & Charles was dwindling, William said, 'I've been meaning to tell you all for a little while now that I am planning to give up the shop. I thought about it again today when we were talking about the poor performance of Watson & Charles's business. My business isn't doing very well either and I have lost a lot of interest in running the shop. Also, I need to change my van. It cost quite a lot to get it through its last MOT. I don't need such a big van for just moving computer equipment around. An estate car would do fine. I've found one that's suitable and am hoping to part exchange my van for it in the next few days. If all goes well, I'll then concentrate on running down the business so I can retire some time next year.'

'Oh, William,' exclaimed Alice, 'I knew you were thinking about retirement but not that you'd made a definite decision. I hope you're not relying on Roger Thompson Associates to support you. We might be unsuccessful and not get paid anything.'

No,' replied William, 'I've worked everything out and I can live reasonably comfortably given the savings I've built up over the years. My lifestyle is not very extravagant. It's better to stop now than to continue making a loss which would eat into my savings and make things more difficult in the future.'

'It won't be the same without your van,' said Simon. 'I'm used to looking out for it. An ordinary car won't be anywhere near as distinctive.'

Robert, sounding concerned, asked, 'You will still be able to build our computer equipment for us, won't you?'

'I hope so,' responded William. 'In fact, I expect to have more time to do just that. I do need to work out how and where to do it. Building computer stuff for you is what I really enjoy these days and that's what retirement should be about, doing what you enjoy.'

'I enjoy what I do,' said Jake vehemently, looking at Simon, 'when I'm allowed to do it. I don't really care about making lots of money. I fancy the idea of being like Robin Hood, taking money from the rich and giving to the poor.'

'We will need enough money to buy new kit and expand our abilities,' said Robert. 'There's always something new we could do with. Remember what we said about being a team and thinking like Roger Thompson, who does not have quite the same ideals as Robin Hood.'

Simon said excitedly, 'I don't really think of us as a team. Look at us now, having our Sunday lunch together. Isn't it great? I haven't enjoyed doing this sort of thing since I was a small child. I think of us more as a family with William as father and Alice as mother. I hope we can do this many more times together.'

All of a sudden, Alice burst into tears, stood up rapidly, knocking her chair over in the process, and ran through the kitchen, down the hall and into the snug, slamming the snug door behind her. A loud beeping noise emanated throughout the house. Above the beeping, the four amazed members of the team still sitting in the dining room heard the snug door open, a mobile phone being thrown onto the hall table and the snug door closing again. The beeping stopped.

Breaking the stunned silence, Jake cried out, 'What the hell was that about? We're the ones who are supposed to have meltdowns, not Alice. She's not Aspie.'

It was William who answered. 'It seemed to be a reaction to what Simon was saying about being like a family. Let's give her time to calm down and then we might find out more.'

'I didn't mean to upset her,' said Simon, sounding worried. 'I was only trying to say how much I was enjoying doing all this.'

Looking extremely confused, Robert exclaimed, 'I don't understand either. It's Alice who has been pushing us to be more like a family. It doesn't make sense for her to behave like that.' This was followed by a shake of his head and a large sigh. 'People.'

Trying to reassure them, William said, 'I don't think we could have predicted her reaction and I doubt very much she's upset with any of us. It's more likely to do with something she hasn't told us about. I've been wondering for a while if there's something troubling her. I'll try to get her to talk about whatever it is.'

'Good idea,' said Robert, 'you are more likely to be able to help her. The rest of us would not know how to help. We would say the wrong thing and make the situation worse.'

'Given we've finished eating,' said William, 'one thing we can all do to help is to clear up. At least then she won't have to come back to a lot of mess.'

To William's surprise, they all leapt into action. Any leftover food was put in the refrigerator, the table was cleared, the dishwasher loaded and the hand washing up done. As they were finishing, Jake couldn't resist putting his ear to the snug door. 'She's still sobbing,' he reported to the others. 'Should we take her a cup of tea?'

No,' replied William, 'she'll come out when she's ready. Think about how you feel when having a meltdown. You don't want to be disturbed, do you? We just need to be patient. I'm happy to wait for her.'

The others, who clearly didn't want to be around when Alice emerged, seemed to take this as permission to leave. Robert was about to follow Jake and Simon up the stairs, when William stopped him and said, 'I don't know whether Alice would want you to be here when she comes out or not but, if you are going to disappear, you'd better tell me how you feel today has gone regarding Watson & Charles. Alice is bound to ask.'

Thinking carefully about his response, Robert replied, 'Tell her today went well and I am pleased with progress. However, I am starting to consider whether the email could have been sent from someone just trying to take advantage of the poor performance of Watson & Charles, rather than causing it in the first place. The question we didn't really get round to is how they would go about adversely influencing Watson & Charles's performance. If we could answer that then we would know what to look for.'

'I did have a couple of thoughts on that,' said William. 'One was to do something to affect quality; even just spreading the word that Watson & Charles's pubs had gone downhill may be enough. The other was controlling the competition. If other pubs are offering attractive promotions and undercutting Watson & Charles, they would lose business that way.'

'Thanks,' replied Robert as he moved towards the stairs to make his escape, 'I will think about it.'

As there was still no sign of Alice emerging, William settled down in the lounge to read the Sunday newspaper he had brought with him, leaving the door open so he could keep an eye on the snug door opposite. Having read about the Parsons Green bombing and caught up on the sport, William was thinking he ought really to be considering the potential impact of Brexit on the brewing industry when he heard the click of the snug door. He looked up to see Alice peeking sheepishly through the crack in the door. Her eyes were dry but extremely bloodshot.

'Hello,' he said softly. 'That took us all by surprise. How are you feeling?'

Alice slowly looked around and whispered in return. 'Where is everyone?'

'They've all run away upstairs, so you're safe, it's only me down here.'

'Oh. I've made a right fool of myself, haven't I?'

'I wouldn't worry too much,' said William comfortingly. 'It won't do any harm for them to realise you're not infallible. It might help to prevent them from taking you too much for granted. However, if you were to do it too often, they might find it difficult to cope with. Would it help to talk about it? Should we arrange another evening in the pub?'

'No,' said Alice firmly, 'I don't want to talk about it. I just want to go home and forget it ever happened.'

'Alright, but consider what we did say in the pub. It does help to talk. If you just bottle it up, there's a good chance something similar will happen again. Also, at some stage, Robert will want his logical explanation.'

'It's got nothing to do with Robert. It's about something that happened over ten years ago. I haven't spoken to anyone about it since and I don't think I can talk about it now, certainly not in a pub.'

Sensing she could be persuaded, William continued, 'It doesn't have to be in a pub. You could come round to my place and we can talk in private. I hope you know I wouldn't tell anyone else anything you didn't want me to.'

'No, it's not that I don't trust you. You're probably the only person I could tell. I suppose you're right and I ought to try, otherwise I'll let myself down again in front of Robert. I would prefer if you'd come to me. I would feel more comfortable in my own flat.'

'Not a problem,' said William. 'Do you want to strike while the iron is hot? I could do tomorrow evening or any other evening this week apart from Wednesday.'

'Not tomorrow but I suppose I could do Tuesday,' said Alice cautiously.

Before she could change her mind, William said, 'Tuesday it is. I know vaguely where you live but I can text you for details so the others don't find out. Let's say 7 p.m. and I'll bring pizza. Are you OK to drive home?'

'Yes, I'm fine now. I just want to get out of here before Robert comes down,' said Alice, grabbing her things and making for the front door. William picked up his paper and followed her, buzzing up to Simon on the way. They both got into their respective vehicles and drove off without exchanging another word.

Chapter Nine

A few hours later, Derek Watson was serving drinks to his visitors, who were sitting in the plush drawing room of his large country house. All four visitors had arrived together as Anthea had volunteered to drive. There was an eclectic mixture of regency-style sofas and easy chairs to choose from, all with occasional tables within easy reach. Howard Watson had quickly accepted a very large gin and tonic and parked himself in the biggest chair close to the open fire roaring away in the mock Tudor fireplace. Mary had guided Anthea to one of the two-seater sofas so they could catch up on the latest news about their respective offspring. Stephen had chosen a large chair on the other side of the fireplace to his father, leaving Derek little choice but to sit next to his mother who, otherwise, would have been on a three-seater sofa on her own.

Mary was acting more like a visitor than a hostess. She had been calling it a family meeting all week, rather than a dinner party, and had insisted Derek find an off-duty chef to come in and cook for them. Derek was always reluctant do to this as he felt it was an abuse of his position but he had managed to persuade Roberto from the Rose & Crown, one of their best gastropubs, to do it, albeit for an exorbitant fee.

Aware that once the alcohol was flowing his father would get louder and dominate the conversation, Derek was keen to get the meeting part of the evening started. Also, he had chosen a rather nice bottle of Pommard to accompany the beef wellington Roberto was preparing, so he wanted to be in a position to enjoy the meal himself. As soon as there was a suitable pause in the various conversations, Derek cleared his throat loudly to attract attention.

'Normally, when we have these family get-togethers, we try hard not to let the conversation be dominated by business issues. However, I've arranged tonight specifically because there is a business issue we need to talk about as a family. Within this room, collectively we hold more than 50 per cent of the shares in Watson & Charles. In the past we've received various offers, mainly from larger breweries, to buy our business. These have all been rejected because we've been united as a family that we do not wish to sell. The only way, therefore, the business can be sold is if the six of us are divided. It would appear someone is in the process of trying to do exactly that, divide us up, by carrying out a cyber-attack on our business.'

Around the room there were a number of confused looks and open mouths. 'What the hell does that mean?' asked Howard Watson, loudly. 'I thought cyber-attacks were to do with different countries spying on each other.'

'Please, Father, bear with me,' responded Derek. 'I'm not sure myself exactly what it means in our case but I believe the principle is the same. It implies someone is breaking into our computer systems with the purpose of disrupting our business. The only hard evidence we have for this so far is an email. I have copies of this for those of you who haven't seen it yet but it's the implications associated with it that are the most worrying. Before I pass the email around, I want to tell you about it first. It was not sent in the usual manner but was placed on our system in a very clever way. As a private company, we have always treated detailed information about our business as confidential and believed this information is not available to either our competitors or any prospective purchasers. Whoever is responsible for the email is also likely to be clever enough to break into our other computer systems without our knowledge. We can assume, therefore, we no longer have any secrets and that includes the fact that we are going through a bad patch at the moment.'

This time it was Sharon Watson, Derek's mother, who interrupted.

'Darling, I'm afraid you've already lost me. I know I hold around 2 per cent of the shares in my own name, as do both Mary and Anthea, but I've never understood or wanted to be involved in the running of the business. I certainly don't understand about cyber-attacking or whatever it is. I'm more than happy to leave the business decisions to Howard, Stephen and yourself and I'm sure Mary and Anthea feel the same. On the few occasions where anything comes to a vote, I will always vote as Howard says I should.'

'Thank you, Mother,' replied Derek softly. 'I am not asking you to get more involved in the business. I'm just trying to explain, on this occasion, we could well be facing a new and bigger threat than we have ever faced before. Stephen, Father and I do not see eye to eye over every key business decision but we've always agreed we'll do whatever it takes to protect and to keep the family business as just that, a family business. I'm extremely concerned someone is trying to drive a wedge between us with the aim of making the business vulnerable to a takeover. Perhaps if I tell you more about the email it will help you understand my concerns.'

Derek handed them copies of the email and continued. 'This email looks as if it was sent to Mary from Christopher Butcher of Butcher's Brewery but it wasn't. Not only that, it was set up so when Ian Walters, our IT manager, locked into it, he came to the conclusion it originated from Stephen but that has also proven to be wrong. Stephen and I have already had a heated discussion about it and, from the conversations Mary and I have had recently, it has unnerved Mary as well.' Derek paused and intentionally looked directly at Mary. 'This, I believe, was its true purpose, to cause friction and discontent between us.'

Mary butted in. 'It did more than unnerve me. It opened my eyes to the very real possibility that, come April, my shares may well be worthless.'

Taken aback by Mary's selfish attitude, Stephen retorted. 'It wouldn't just be your shares, it would be all of our shares. Anyway, they wouldn't become totally worthless with all the property we own.'

Howard Watson interjected in his low, steady drawl, keeping his head still and looking at no-one in particular. 'The exact situation would need to be worked out using the traditional formula. However, it is true the way we are performing this year is going to lead to little if any profit. The asset value would then be the only positive and would be offset against all debts and other liabilities. From where we stand at the moment, it certainly looks as if the share price will be taking an enormous hit at the end of this financial year and there will be a lot of explaining to be done at the AGM.'

'And I will be the one doing most of the explaining,' said Derek, 'but don't be surprised if, at the same time, we receive an offer for the business. If I'm correct and someone is manipulating this situation, potentially they could put in a bid that would be very attractive against the new share price, so attractive even some of us might find it difficult to resist. That's why I wanted to talk about this tonight. I felt I needed to make you aware of this possibility. Also, we do not know what other steps might be being taken to undermine us. Anything computer related that appears strange may be part of the strategy to disrupt us and not what it at first seems to be.'

'So, I take it we don't actually know where this email did come from?' asked Howard.

'No,' admitted Derek. 'It proved to be beyond the capabilities of Ian Walters to track it down. I've employed some independent consultants to carry out a more detailed investigation. We'll have to wait and see if they can get to the bottom of it. My own view is it would fit with some predatory brewing company wanting to buy us out. They could well be trying to adversely affect performance, create panic in the business and get through to shareholders, in the hope they can snap us up at a low price.' Derek had a sudden thought and the pitch of his voice increased.

'This sort of thing may have been done before. If you think about the bigger picture, thirty years ago there were over sixty family brewers in Britain. Now, over half of those have gone, snapped up by the likes of Marston's, Greene King and Limberts who have grown significantly as a result. We know some of them sold out because of splits in the family but we wouldn't know if those splits were prompted from outside by devious means.'

'Are you suggesting,' asked Stephen, 'this may have something to do with the fall-off in performance of the managed houses?'

'I honestly don't know but, yes, it might have,' replied Derek, well aware it was only Robert Tait who had put that thought in his mind. He knew what he wanted to believe. In spite of the fact that the Managed House Division had been underperforming for almost a year, he had been putting off getting rid of John Hargreaves for some time, purely because the strategy they were following was the one Derek himself had instigated. Robert Tait had given him a reason, or was it an excuse, for delaying further. If some outside influence was responsible then neither he nor John Hargreaves was to blame. 'Time is running out. I can't help wondering if that email was timed to push us into a change. If John is mismanaging the managed houses, I can't see what he's doing wrong. On the other hand, if we don't change anything, we could well get even more disappointing results. I don't want to play into their hands, whoever they are, but also I don't want to leave it too late if there is something we can do to improve this year's result.'

'I still believe swapping John Hargreaves with Neil Martin is worth trying,' said Howard.

'You may well be right, Father. I did speak to Neil about it after you suggested it at the board meeting. He wasn't overly keen. I think he sees managed houses as a potentially poisoned chalice. However, he gave me the impression, if there was enough financial incentive for him, based upon arresting the fall rather than recovering what is already lost, he could be persuaded. I've decided to leave John where he is for now but I'll work very closely with him until Christmas. If there's no sign of any improvement, Neil will move across. I realise Neil wouldn't have a chance to influence this year's result but at least we would be showing positive intent to the shareholders.'

Whilst Derek was talking, Roberto had silently entered the room and whispered in Mary's ear. As soon as Derek paused, Mary stood up and announced, 'Roberto tells me dinner is served. Although the avocado and prawn starter would keep a little longer, the beef wellington will not. I think we've had enough business talk for the time being so please take your drinks with you into the dining room.'

Mary had reverted to being lady of the manor. She was extremely proud of the dining room. It had only recently been redecorated to her specification with brand-new carpets and curtains. A sparkling chandelier overhung an oval polished mahogany table, large enough to accommodate twice their number. Six chairs were located around the table to match the place settings, laid with Mary's precious Doulton china and Waterford crystal that sparkled in the candlelight. A further six chairs were positioned around the room. All of the chairs had new upholstery of crimson damask embroidered with a golden fox, the symbol of the main Watson & Charles beer brand. A mixture of her own sizeable paintings and early family portraits adorned the walls.

Mary guided everyone to their places, having given her in-laws pride of place at the ends of the table. She had placed herself between Howard and Stephen so that Derek was sitting between his mother and Anthea. Roberto was unsure of the correct hierarchy so served all of the ladies first. As soon as he had left the room, Mary took the opportunity to accept all the credit for the quality of the meal as if she had prepared it herself.

In between the clatter of the cutlery, the group conversation steered clear of business matters and became much more light hearted. However, when the cheese and biscuits had been served and all the men had a glass of port, smaller conversations broke out. Mary took the opportunity to ask Howard about the likely impact of the current year's result on the share price. Taken by surprise and also affected by the amount of Pommard he had consumed, Howard blustered about it being quite complicated as many of the rules were archaic and outdated and probably should have been changed years ago. He also wondered why Mary was asking him and not Derek. Pushed harder by Mary, Howard eventually admitted he expected the value of the shares to be reduced by at least half. By this stage, all of the other conversations had stopped and there were audible gasps from the other end of the table when Mary stated, if the share price was going to fall that much, she would seriously have to consider selling her shares now, before the price went down.

Derek glared across the table, furious with Mary. Trying very hard to stay calm, he said, 'It's far too early to estimate what would happen. There are still five months of this year to go. Anyway, we're not supposed to be discussing business at this stage of the evening. We've all had a lot to drink and are unlikely to be thinking clearly. That's why we did the business part before the meal. If everyone's finished their cheese, let's move to the drawing room for coffee.'

Although there was no further talk about business, the mood of the evening had changed. Everyone was quite relieved when Sharon Watson, as soon as was polite to do so, announced she was feeling tired and ready to go home. Anthea quickly reached for her handbag and car keys. Even Howard, who at this point in the evening usually argued the case for just one more single malt, leapt to his feet to say his farewells.

Almost as soon as he had closed the door behind them, Derek started to feel depressed. The evening hadn't gone as he had hoped. There had been no meaningful discussion about how they would all vote in the event of a takeover bid but maybe he hadn't been direct enough in asking them. The only one who had said anything clear cut was Mary, who seemed to have had her own agenda for the evening.

He was extremely angry with her for blurting out her intentions and not being more supportive. Even though he knew it was not the best time for starting an argument, he couldn't resist following her into the kitchen and shouting at her. 'What the hell was that all about? It wasn't helpful you talking about selling your shares and asking my father about their value.'

Mary turned around and yelled back at him. 'They're MY shares so I need to able to make my own decision. Trying to get firm information from you is like trying to get blood out of a stone, so I thought I'd ask your father instead. It worked because at least he gave me a proper answer.'

'You do realise you were effectively given those shares when you married me. It is a tradition that goes back to the start of the Company. The intention is, as a wife, you will have a reason to take an interest in the business and to support your husband when needed. What you did tonight was not supportive.'

'That sounds like one of the archaic rules your father was referring to. What about the tax benefits of having shares in my name and not yours? Isn't that a reason too? Whatever the old-fashioned expectations, they ARE in my name and I can do what I like with them. I am interested in the business but sometimes it feels like you're burying your head in the sand and don't want to accept how bad things are. The only reason I know the business is in crisis is because that email was sent to me. Let me remind you it was me that found Robert Tait to look into it for you. You haven't thanked me for that and you haven't told me anything about what he's doing.' Pausing slightly, Mary softened her tone. 'Look, do we have to talk about this now? It will only make things worse. All I want to do is get the food put away and go to bed. The rest of the clearing up can wait until tomorrow.'

Derek was tempted to prolong the argument but realised it was better to walk away, especially as he didn't want to admit he had heard nothing further from Robert Tait. He helped to bring a few things through from the dining room, poured himself a glass of water and walked around the house, checking windows, switching off lights and locking up. On his way upstairs he called goodnight to Mary. It was one of the few occasions he was pleased they had separate bedrooms. He recalled it was after a similar boozy evening almost two years ago that Mary had insisted they stop sleeping together because of his heavy snoring. He still didn't like sleeping on his own but had to confess he was highly likely to snore tonight.

Once in his bedroom, Derek read for a while to try to take his mind off the evening's events. However, more than an hour after he'd heard Mary come upstairs and turn off the light, Derek was still wide awake. His mind was racing. He'd been through the numbers in his head to check whether his father was correct about the share price, only to come to the conclusion that halving of the share price would be a good result given how things stood at the moment. He made a mental note to get Jeremy Turner to do some projections so he would have a good idea of the reality of the situation. Whilst he was very upset with Mary, he did recognise that other shareholders who were making their decisions purely on results would be likely to react in a similar manner. As things stood, he was relying on those other shareholders not finding out about a drop in value until the results were announced at the AGM in April. However, if he was correct and whoever had sent the email did have access to the latest half-year results and chose to send them out to shareholders, he could be facing a deluge of shareholders wanting to sell before April. On the other hand, shares sold back to the Company and just sitting there come April had no vote. Alternatively, he could buy them himself, knowing he would be paying twice the price they would soon be worth. It was all getting extremely messy and complicated.

Derek was also trying to work out how his father and brother would be likely to vote if an attractive offer for the Company was to come in at the same time the share price crashed. He came to the conclusion he could not be sure of either of them. His father had intimated he would be prepared to put the interests of the shareholders above his own personal feelings. Stephen had made it very clear it was having a brewery that mattered to him and he was extremely frustrated the board kept rejecting his proposals for investment.

Derek also knew that whilst Jeremy Turner was Finance Director, the financial analysis presented to the board would always show far better returns for investing in pubs rather than investing in the brewery. In fact, Jeremy had told Derek privately more than once that Watson & Charles would be far better off without a brewery and they should become just a pub company. In his heart, Derek also wanted to invest in the brewery but Jeremy's arguments had always swayed him against.

Derek now wished he had gone against Jeremy. After all, Stephen was asking for only the equivalent cost of one large managed house. Jeremy wasn't part of the family and would not have factored in the importance of keeping the family happy. Given the latest results from the managed houses, there seemed to be a strong argument for having an efficient brewery to provide another string to the bow. Was it too late? Where would the money come from if the banks wouldn't lend more? Would it be viewed as just buying Stephen's vote?

He thought about what was said earlier about the demise of other independent family brewers. He was very pleased his father had played such an active role in setting up the Independent Family Brewers of Britain in 1993. Being part of this organisation had allowed him to build relationships with chairmen of similar breweries. There was no doubt collectively they carried more weight in lobbying government and influencing the brewing world in general. Nevertheless, there had still been casualties in Derek's time and the number of current family brewers was now down to twenty-nine. Would Watson & Charles be the next to go? He had to fight to stop that happening, but how?

It wasn't just family brewers; there had been a lot of consolidation in the brewing industry worldwide. Even Bass had succumbed, despite all their history and famous No 1 red triangle, the oldest trademark in the country. They were now part of Molson Coors, one of the biggest brewing companies in the world. Derek thought back to 2010 when he had rejected a formal approach by Molson Coors, who then ended up acquiring Sharp's Brewery instead. Could Molson Coors be behind that email? Would they use such underhand tactics? Surely not. Not all of the current independent family brewers had survived by adopting the same strategy but they were all protected by their respective family ownership. They were only vulnerable if enough of the family wanted out.

Derek remembered his father telling him about Bateman's, who had a very public family split in the 1980s and only survived because one side of the family bought the other side out. Derek didn't want his family divided over this issue but could see there was a real possibility of that happening. Had he got his strategy so wrong? When he took over from his father, he had tried to keep things simple. He focussed on rationalising the estate of pubs, selling off some of the smaller tenancies which had no potential for development whilst investing in others that could be made large enough for management. Similarly, he had set a minimum size for managed houses and transferred some of the smaller managed houses to tenancy. He viewed the tenanted estate as a stable source of steady income and the managed estate as the area for growth. He had tried to buy additional pubs wisely, using proper market assessment and modern demographic tools, aiming for no more than two new flagship pubs a year so that resources were not overstretched. It all seemed to be working well until the middle of last year. Now it felt as if the wheels had well and truly fallen off. Maybe he had ignored the brewery in favour of the pubs.

Many of the other family brewers had invested in their ageing breweries and seemed to be doing well. Companies such as St Austell, Thwaites, Adnams and Wadworth had all spent money on improving and expanding their brewing facilities and were still brewing on sites that would no doubt be worth a lot of money if sold for development. Robinsons had invested in both brewing and packaging and had built up their business of bottling and canning beer under contract for other brewers. Everards were in the process of moving to a new brewery site, having previously moved out of central Leicester to a cheaper site over thirty years ago. Brains were following a similar route in Cardiff, although Derek knew there had been a lot of heartache about their decision to move to the Cardiff brewery in the first place. Have I missed a trick? Should we have built a new, smaller and more efficient brewery many years ago? Or should we have got out of brewing altogether and become a pub company like Eldridge Pope did? Some brewers had merged or bought out each other. There seemed to Derek to be more survivors who had invested in brewing than had not, particularly as Eldridge Pope had ended up being bought by Marston's. Marston's, Greene King and Limberts always appeared to be on the lookout for new acquisitions and all had shown an interest in Watson & Charles in the past. They had emerged from the pack and grown to be major players. Could one of them be behind that email? Was he really resting all his hopes on Robert Tait coming up with the answer? Even if he did, how could it help the business turn around in just a few months? He didn't even know if Robert Tait could be relied on, whether he was making any progress or actually doing anything at all.

Derek was left with the overriding thought he had had for some time. His company was heading for a crisis but he didn't understand why and he didn't know what to do about it. All he could do was try to dig deeper but at least now he could be more open about the email. He tossed and turned for a while longer before eventually falling asleep.

Chapter Ten

Alice was having second thoughts. She wished she hadn't agreed to William coming round. How could she possibly explain all of her past to him? Maybe she could just say it was a family falling-out. All that was really needed was an explanation to give to the boys; surely that wouldn't be too difficult to agree upon. She looked out of the window of her flat to see if she could spot William arriving. Was it too late to call him and cancel? She could have done earlier but then nothing would be resolved. She had been mulling the same thoughts over and over in her head all day and still had no clear idea of what to say and how to say it. She liked William and had felt comfortable talking to him about her feelings for Robert but this was totally different. This was something she hadn't talked to anyone about for more than ten years. Before she could go around her thought processes again, she saw William's van driving up the road. There wasn't a large enough parking space near to her front door so he had to turn around and park further down the road. As she watched, she could see him walking back in his lolloping style, carrying the pizzas as promised. She decided to tell him just enough to be able to explain her behaviour on Sunday but definitely not the whole story.

She thought she was like Simon as she watched William arrive but, as she could not see the front door clearly, she waited for the intercom to buzz before pressing the door-release button. It seemed to take William a long time to climb the stairs to her flat. When he did finally arrive, slightly out of breath, she gave him the now customary hug and kiss, trying hard not to show how nervous she felt. They decided to have the pizzas first. While they were standing in Alice's small kitchen waiting for the pizzas to cook, they settled into a conversation about the Watson & Charles project. Alice started to relax as William told her again how her suggestion of Pauline Sharples as a possible suspect had affected Robert's thinking.

'He now seems to have two unproven facts to consider,' said William. 'One is his original conclusion that an individual or an organisation triggered the fall in Watson & Charles's performance by some form of cyber-attack in order to pave the way for the email, which was then designed to create a rift in the Watson family. The second option is the email was sent by someone who is trying to take advantage of the fact that Watson & Charles are just performing badly.'

Alice responded, 'I woke up yesterday morning to find a text from Jake telling me he had set me up with access to Pauline Sharples' emails. He must have worked on it during the night. There's a lot to go through. I made a start last night after I got back from squash. I came across some of the documents Robert referred to, such as the minutes of their board meeting last week. Jake said I could open any attachments I wanted without there being any risk. The main thing I've noticed so far is she seems to be very efficient and to the point in her communication with everyone apart from Derek Watson. There are relatively few emails from her to Derek only. It might just be my imagination but she seems to adopt a more familiar style with these, possibly because she's got a soft spot for him or wants him to think she has, or maybe because they just have a very close working relationship. I'll look more deeply when I've more time but I suspect what I could really do with is access to her personal email account as well, not just her work one.'

'I'm sure Jake could provide you with that if you ask him,' replied William. 'All he would need would be a link from one to the other.'

'You may well be right. I worry about asking Jake to do things. He makes everything sound so easy but I'm sure it takes more time than he admits to, especially with Simon looking over his shoulder from a security point of view. I don't want to get in the way of them doing what Robert wants done.

'Fine, I can understand that but you could ask Robert to ask Jake. As long as you give Robert a logical reason for wanting it, he can then decide where it fits in Jake's priorities. One thing you can be sure about is Robert will make his decisions based on fact and logic. It makes no difference whether it's his idea, your idea or anyone else's idea.'

'No, he doesn't grind axes, does he?' replied Alice, almost breaking into a smile, 'although I do think he sometimes claims the credit when it's not totally due. I know it's only a couple of weeks since we all took this thing on but it doesn't feel like we're narrowing down the possible explanations at all. In fact, it feels the opposite. Surely, if we can gain access to Watson & Charles emails and the business information associated with them, then so can whoever sent that original email to Mary Watson. I only suggested Pauline Sharples because I could see she might have a personal motive but there must be many other people out there with motives that are business driven. I know Robert has a brilliant analytical mind and he can compartmentalise things and look at each of them logically. I really want him to succeed but it's not just his lack of people skills that worries me, it's his lack of business knowledge as well. Sometimes business decisions are not based on sound logic either.'

William thought for a moment. 'I do agree with you. There's no sign of a solution yet and there are so many unanswered questions. Why, for instance, was that email sent now and in the way it was? It doesn't make any sense to me. However, my main problem is we all agreed to help but I don't know how to. I was pretty sure on Sunday that everything I said, Robert had already found out for himself. I do intend this week to spend as much time as I can on the wider issues within the brewing industry as it sounds as though Robert is going to concentrate on the specific aspects of the Watson & Charles business. Hopefully, I can come up with something that paints a background picture of the brewing industry so Robert can put the Watson & Charles situation into context. Don't give up on him yet. Just think of it as being in the information collection phase of the project.'

'I do hope you're right,' said Alice as she opened the oven door to inspect the pizzas.

As soon as the pizzas were ready, they took them through to the main room of the flat and sat at the small dining table located by the bay window from which Alice had observed William's arrival. Alice could feel the butterflies returning and only picked at her food as she knew the discussion she was dreading was getting closer. Trying to avoid the subject being raised, she questioned William about his retirement plans and his new car. Although William could see through her delaying tactics, he happily explained he had arranged to part exchange his van for a 2-year-old Ford Mondeo estate car on Friday. He reassured her again that he could afford to retire, although he did admit money would be tight and he was hoping the Watson & Charles project might help to ease things. When they had finished eating, Alice offered coffee. William accepted but he moved to sit on the two-seater sofa located in the middle of the room facing the television screen. This was where Alice usually ate her TV dinners. When she returned with the coffees, she had little choice but to sit next to William.

'I know you aren't looking forward to this,' began William softly, 'but I do think it's time to do what we said we would and try to get you in a position where you can explain to Robert what happened on Sunday, without the risk of a repeat performance.'

Determined to stick to her plan, Alice replied in a firm but slightly shaky voice, 'I've given it some thought and I'm sure Robert will not be interested in a lot of detail so long as what I say makes sense to him. The reason I was upset was that when Simon said it felt like we were a family, I suddenly thought of my own parents and that they are no longer together. A bit like Simon was suggesting, I remembered fond times as a family when I was a child and it really hurt when it all came to an end.' She paused, hoping William would not push her to explain further.

'I didn't realise your parents aren't together. I'm sorry to hear that,' said William, choosing his words carefully. 'I suppose we've concentrated so much on the difficulties the boys had when they were young, I just assumed you had a normal upbringing without any major issues.'

'Don't forget yourself,' said Alice, trying to deflect the conversation away from herself. 'You had a tough time of it as well. Compared to all four of you, I did have it easy. I realised that when you told me about it in the pub. I wasn't bullied like all of you were.'

'It's not a competition to find out who had the worst experience. I was just suggesting it was an area of commonality. That you also have unpleasant memories may explain why you're happy to be part of our group. My concern is your memories are buried so deeply within you that, when they are triggered, like on Sunday, they explode out in an uncontrolled way. From my own experience, I believe it's better to find a way to release the emotion rather than keep it all bottled up. It doesn't mean the memories disappear but it does mean you can get on with life knowing you're in control of your emotions.'

Alice could feel her palms getting sweaty and knew she was on the verge of bursting into tears. She made a concentrated effort to draw a line under the subject. 'I'm sure you're right. Telling you about my parents has made me feel a lot better and I'm sure I will now be able to tell Robert without getting too emotional. Thanks for helping me.'

William was not so easily deterred and decided to push further. 'I'm pleased talking about it is making you feel better but I'm still somewhat confused. You're usually so composed and cheerful but, on Sunday, you spent over half an hour in the snug crying incessantly. I don't want to sound callous but there must be more to it than you've told me so far.'

All of a sudden Alice leapt up, stared William directly in the face and screamed at him, 'It was because of me. I did it. I made them split up. I am responsible for their divorce. Are you happy now? I get upset because it was all **MY** fault.'

This time she could not control the tears. She struggled to speak, sobbed uncontrollably, collapsed back onto the sofa and sat hunched forward with her head in her hands. William inched across to her and put his chubby arm around her slender shoulders. With his other hand, he just managed to reach a box of tissues from the side table and place a wadge of them in Alice's hand. Slowly her tears subsided and she spoke through her sobs in a very weak voice.

'I'm sorry. I shouldn't have shouted at you. You might think I'm intelligent but over ten years ago I did something incredibly stupid, so stupid it not only wrecked my parents' marriage but it also ruined my relationship with them both.'

Realising she now had no choice but to explain further, Alice pulled her legs onto the sofa, snuggled against William's jumper and continued. 'You're right. I did have a normal and very happy early childhood. We did lots of things together as a family, usually involving sport. Both my parents were keen tennis players and I would be ball girl for them. They taught me to play and encouraged me to enter junior tournaments. We had holidays at the seaside, often going with my aunt and uncle and my cousin Terry. I remember us all playing football on the beach. In fact, it was through football that my parents first met. I was told the story many times. Mum's family had long been supporters of Barnsley and she used to go and watch them regularly. On one occasion, she and my Dad were given tickets for the directors' box by a mutual friend who had connections to Plymouth Argyle. Mum always dressed in Barnsley colours when she went to a match. Dad was struck by the bright red trouser suit and black roll-neck jumper in Barnsley colours Mum wore. In fact, Mum kept this outfit in the wardrobe next to her wedding dress.' After a thoughtful pause, Alice continued, 'I bet it's not there now. Anyway, they found they had lots in common, including that they were both in the medical profession. Dad ended up becoming a surgeon at Pinderfields Hospital in Wakefield and Mum was a nurse. I was very lucky when it came to my education. My Aunt Penny was a teacher at the local primary school but she had given up work to look after Terry, who was a year older than me. She looked after me a lot as well to allow Mum to do some agency nursing. Penny went back to work as soon as Terry was of school age, having negotiated with the headmistress that I could sit at the back of the class. I ended up being part of the class so I was moved up with Terry at the end of the first year even though I was a year younger. That continued throughout my education, even when I passed the entrance examination to Wakefield Girls' High School. As a consequence, all my friends tended to be older than me.

'In high school, I had three very good friends, Shirley, Wendy and Michelle. We did everything together, sport, swimming, going to the cinema, having days at each other's houses. We dressed up, played music and talked about the pop stars and film stars we all liked. We made pretend microphones out of rolled up cardboard with a ping-pong ball glued to the top. As we got older, the conversation turned more towards boys. Our school put on plays in conjunction with the equivalent boys' school, QEGS. Shirley, who was the oldest and most attractive, and into drama, met a boy from QEGS called Tony, who was already in the sixth form. He had three very close friends, Paul, Roland and Brian. We started meeting with them regularly and doing things as a larger group. I didn't really like it and preferred being just with the girls. I particularly didn't like Paul who was a loud-mouthed bully. I was still only fourteen and it was the first time for a long time I felt younger than the others. Gradually, we all started to pair up; Shirley with Tony, Michelle with Paul, and Wendy with Roland. I was left with Brian who was quiet and shy but nice looking. He had very straight fair hair and a lovely smile. I also found I enjoyed talking to him, mainly about science as he was clever and keen on physics. When we were just girls together,

I would try to keep up by telling the others how much I liked Brian and I convinced myself I had a crush on him.'

Alice had felt relatively comfortable talking about the good times with her parents and her friends but now she was approaching the difficult part. 'William, I don't think I can continue. It's too embarrassing. It's about sex.'

Alice's head had by now slipped onto William's lap and she was curled up in a foetal position. William gently stroked her hair, which was bedraggled and damp from her crying. He replaced her damp tissues with fresh ones and reached across for a cushion to put under Alice's head, saying soothingly, 'Alice, you've done ever so well in telling me everything so far. I truly promise all you've said will remain just between the two of us. Having got this far, I'm convinced it would be best if you just let it all come out.'

In a strange way, from having been determined not to tell him, a big part of her now wanted to tell him. Her tears had returned but, between the sobs, her story spilled out.

'One day, shortly before the Easter holidays at the end of sports, I was just leaving the hockey pavilion when I heard a sort of groaning coming from behind the pavilion. I peered around from the side and saw Shirley having sex with Tony. I was mesmerised and couldn't help watching for a while until Tony saw me. All he did was smile and continue what he was doing. I turned and ran away. During the Easter holidays, I spent some time with Shirley and the other girls but I avoided the boys as I was embarrassed about seeing Tony. Shirley freely admitted she'd been having sex with Tony for a little while. He had obviously told her I'd seen them both. She didn't seem to mind. She admitted she had been a bit scared the first time but Tony had been gentle and, although it had hurt a little she'd enjoyed it. She then said she was on the pill; they had sex often, she loved it and couldn't get enough. I was fascinated and I started to include in my romantic fantasies about Brian what it would be like to make love with him.

'Anyway, after Easter, for me, sports changed to tennis. We shared the tennis courts with the boys' school. Having finished the first tennis session of the term, I was walking on my own down the back streets from the tennis courts to the bus station when Tony suddenly appeared by my side and started talking to me about Shirley. He wasn't at all worried I'd seen them together and Shirley had clearly told him I'd been asking questions. On one side of the road was a small park. Tony said it was in that park where they'd done it the first time and he would show me where if I was interested. I know it was stupid to agree to go with him but I did. He took me to a small clearing surrounded by sycamore trees and said they had done it right there. He then asked if I'd ever kissed a boy. When I admitted I hadn't, he asked me if I would like to and said he could teach me how. He even said it would help me to know what I was doing if I ever got round to kissing Brian. I had dreamt of kissing Brian but realised I didn't know how to do it so I agreed. He told me how to respond to his mouth and how to use my tongue. I quite enjoyed kissing Tony, although I kept wishing it was Brian instead. I did pull back when Tony started to put his hand up my skirt but then he asked me if I'd ever seen a man's penis. I replied I'd only seen pictures.

'Before I realised what was happening, he had taken down his trousers and underpants and was showing me his. He encouraged me to touch it and when I did he started to kiss me again whilst at the same time putting his hand inside my knickers. He asked me if I would like to find out what it felt like to have his penis inside me. I was feeling terrified but also quite excited. He went on to say he would be gentle and do the same as he had with Shirley on her first time. He said he would only go far enough to, as he put it, prepare me for Brian, as the first time did hurt a little and it was best to get it over with now. I tried to resist by suggesting Shirley wouldn't like him to be doing this with me but he just laughed and said Shirley wouldn't mind, she would just see it as him doing a favour for a friend. I then tried to say I might get pregnant but he just pulled out a condom from his pocket and rolled it onto his penis. He seemed to have an answer to everything. I still wasn't sure but enough of me wanted to do it that when he spread his coat on the ground and asked me to lie on it, I did. He was true to his word. He quickly removed my knickers and it was all over almost before I realised it had happened. It did hurt but I was left with half of me feeling relieved it was over and the other half of me wanting more. He stood up, discarded the condom, got dressed and then helped me to do the same. He even gave me his handkerchief to put inside my knickers so they didn't get blood on them. We then walked to the bus station together as if nothing unusual had happened.

'Exactly two weeks later, on a lovely spring afternoon, the same thing happened. Tony came up to me as I was walking back from tennis.

I was sure he'd been waiting specially for me. He asked me if I'd got anywhere with Brian yet. When I said no, he suggested we went to the park again to practise my kissing and to make sure I was ready to enjoy sex with Brian without it hurting. Again, stupidly, I agreed to go with him. As soon as we got to the same clearing, he kissed me and laid down his coat. This time he persuaded me to take off all my clothes before lying down. I felt quite ashamed of my skinny body and tiny breasts but Tony also undressed and lay down beside me. He told me how lovely I was and kissed me more and stroked my breasts and between my legs. I remember thinking how nice his body looked but I didn't feel relaxed enough to be able to touch him in the same sort of way he touched me. As he was about to move on top of me, I realised he hadn't put on a condom. He admitted he hadn't got one as he didn't need them any more now Shirley was on the pill. He promised he would pull out of me well before he came as he had done a few times in the early days with Shirley and she had been OK. He also said sex felt better without a condom.

'I didn't really want to continue but I thought I could trust him so did nothing to try to stop him. Just as we were getting going and I was starting to feel some enjoyment, I heard a rustling in the bushes and Tony suddenly stopped. I looked up and was horrified to see Paul standing over us with a great big grin on his face. "Well, well, well," he said, "I wondered what you two were getting up to when I saw you heading into the park. I'd heard you were a bit of a goer, Alice, but I didn't expect to find you like this. You must really love it."

'I wanted to explain but, before I could say anything Paul made it even worse by saying he had sent a text to Roland and Brian and they would be there any minute. All I could think of was Brian finding me stark naked with Tony lying on top of me. I tried to speak but Paul had knelt down next to me and started kissing me and pulling at my nipples. He called Tony 'lover boy' and told him to get on and finish the job. I expected Tony to stop and help me to explain but I was aghast when he started again until he eventually did come whilst still inside me. Paul seemed to take this as his cue to have a turn, boldly claiming that he was much better at it than Tony. He dropped his trousers and pushed Tony out of the way before he climbed on top of me and entered me. By this stage, I was numb and could hardly move or speak. Paul's penis was bigger than Tony's. He was a lot rougher and was hurting me. Inwardly

I was screaming but I knew I couldn't do anything to attract attention, so I just closed my eyes and waited for the nightmare to stop, all the time hoping I could run away before Brian got there.

'My hopes were dashed as, by the time Paul had finished, both Brian and Roland had arrived. Paul actually asked me if Roland could have a go too, as he didn't have much luck with girls and even Wendy wouldn't let him. He said they would save Brian for last, as they all knew it was Brian I really wanted. Roland didn't need much persuading and, although I kept my eyes closed, I could imagine his spotty face as he pounded up and down on top of me. All the time, I kept hoping Brian wouldn't do it as well but I could hear him being goaded by Paul who was telling him "little Alice loved to be fucked". It was as if none of them could stand up to Paul. I have no idea whether Brian really wanted to do it but he did. All my romantic dreams of him were destroyed in a flash. I hated him. I hated them all.

'At last it was over. Paul said he had a bus to catch and they should leave me to get dressed in peace. As they were leaving, Paul had the temerity to thank me and say we should all do it again some time. The only one to show any remorse was Tony, who mumbled sorry as he was retrieving his coat. After they had gone, I staggered to my feet and managed to get myself dressed. I was shaking all over and in a lot of pain. It was supposed not to have hurt but it did, it hurt a lot. Somehow I managed to get myself cleaned up enough to get the bus home. I sneaked into the house to avoid Mum and went straight into the shower but I couldn't wash away the pain and the shame. I called down to Mum that I had a bad migraine and was going straight to bed but I hardly slept all night. I just kept reliving the whole thing over and over again, berating myself for being so naive and stupid and resolving never ever to put myself in a situation where the same thing might happen again. The next morning I made a huge effort to behave as normal so my parents wouldn't suspect anything.'

By this stage, Alice had cried so much she was almost choking as she was trying to get the words out. Although she didn't seem to want to cease talking, William did encourage her to have a break and helped to raise her gently back up into a sitting position. William himself was shocked. He'd worked out there was something troubling Alice but had never imagined it was anything like this. He didn't quite know what to say next so he just wrapped both of his arms around her and they sat motionless and in silence. Eventually, Alice stirred, ran her hands through her hair and slowly looked around her as if she was coming out of a trance. She spoke as if she had only just remembered William was there.

'Oh, William,' she exclaimed, 'what's wrong with me? I've got myself into a right state again. Look at my hair, it's all matted and stuck to my face. I need to go to the bathroom and sort myself out.' She stood up and gingerly made her way across the room.

William also felt the need to move. He was very stiff from sitting in the same position for so long. He cleared the table and coffee cups and found everything he needed in the kitchen to make a pot of tea for them both, which he took back to the table. He was just starting to worry that Alice had been in the bathroom too long when she emerged, very sheepishly.

'I'm so sorry,' she said with a note of trepidation in her voice, 'I feel so embarrassed telling you all that. I didn't mean to go into that level of detail. What on earth can you think of me?'

William moved towards her and again put his arm around her shoulders, 'I think you've been extremely brave to tell me. There's absolutely no need for you to be embarrassed but, Alice,' William said as carefully as he could,' you do realise what you have just described was rape, don't you?'

'No,' she responded quickly and firmly as she pulled away from him. 'I've thought it over many, many times. Crying rape would just have been an excuse. I went willingly, expecting to have sex. I did have sex but it was just not as I hoped it would be. I had plenty of opportunities to object and to say no but I didn't. It was my choice just to lie there and take it. I'd obviously expressed too much interest when talking to Shirley and created the impression I wanted to have the same experience as her. I made some bad decisions and it all backfired on me.'

'Well, from how you've just described it,' replied William, 'I don't agree with you. With the exception of Tony, and even he went further than you'd asked him to, you did not consent to having sex with any of the others. As I understand it, that's the definition of rape.'

Realising Alice was feeling uncomfortable with the conversation, William said, 'I've made us some tea. Come and sit down and drink it and let's talk about something else, something a bit more pleasant.'

'Tea sounds nice,' said Alice as she moved towards the table, 'but I haven't told you the worst part yet, about my parents' divorce.'

Thinking there couldn't be anything worse than he'd just heard, but beginning to guess what was coming, William replied, 'Are you sure you want to do this now? I can come back another time if you'd rather.'

'No, I'd rather do it now if you don't mind. Then you'll know the full story.'

'OK, if you're sure. Do you want to go back to the sofa?'

'No, let's stay here at the table,' said Alice, sounding a little more like her usual self. 'I don't want to put you through any more of my blubbering. Anyway, I feel as if I'm all cried out for now.'

'Alright, but promise you'll stop if it gets too much for you.'

'I will, but this is the part that explains my reaction on Sunday. If I don't tell you about it then we can't work out what to say to Robert. I'll try to keep it brief.' She reached across the table to take hold of William's hand.

'As well as all the other thoughts going through my head, I was very aware that none of them had used condoms. My next period was due two weeks after I'd had sex with them and I prayed it would happen on time but it didn't. I knew I was pregnant. I went through a whole gamut of different emotions. Mainly I was scared and didn't know what to. As I said earlier, I had a very close relationship with my parents, especially my mother. They had both told me many times that if I had a problem, no matter what it was, they would always help me and support me. I decided, therefore, to tell my mum. It took a while to pluck up the courage but one day after school, just before tea time, I stopped her in the hall and told her I was pregnant. She looked stunned and then said she always thought something bad would happen as a result of me being associated with the likes of Shirley.

'I really wanted her to give me a cuddle and say everything would be alright but, just when I thought she was about to, the front door opened and in walked Dad. It was unusual for him to be home so early and he obviously expected us to be pleased to see him. However, he quickly realised something wasn't right and asked what the problem was. Mum said I had better tell him so I did. His expression changed to a look I had never seen on his face before. He exclaimed "What!" in a loud voice and then "Who was it? Who's the father?" I'd never seen him so angry so I blurted out that I didn't know and it could have been any one of them. This enraged him even more and, without warning, he slapped the side of my face so hard it almost knocked me over. At the same time he called me a dirty little slut. He was about to hit me again but Mum stopped him. I ran upstairs to my bedroom, slammed the door shut and lay on the bed crying my heart out. I couldn't believe Dad had turned against me in such a way.

'As I lay there, I could also hear an enormous argument taking place between Mum and Dad. I'd never heard them fight like that before but it was to become the first of many arguments between them. From then on the atmosphere in the whole house became extremely frosty. Dad would stay at work well into the evenings and I would avoid him by staying in my room. We hardly spoke, certainly not about my pregnancy, and he never apologised for hitting me. It was my GCSE year so I threw myself into studying for the exams. I gave up tennis and kept well away from Shirley and the other girls and especially the boys. Mum knew enough people through her work to arrange for me to have an abortion, which I had as soon as the exams were over.'

William could feel Alice's grip tightening but her eyes remained dry as she continued to speak. 'She even arranged for me to have counselling with a friend of hers to help me accept that abortion was the correct decision. It did help but I still wonder what would have happened if the baby had been born instead. One of the arguments was that I would be able to choose later in life to become a parent. My worry is this will never happen because I am now so scared to have sex with anyone ever again. That was another reason I was upset on Sunday when Simon said I was like the mother of the family. Anyway, I had a horrible summer holiday, hiding away from everyone and trying not to hear the ever-increasing arguments between my parents.

'The only good news was that my GCSE results were excellent. I chose science-related A levels, which also helped as my previous friends either chose other subjects or didn't stay to do A levels at all. It had become such a horrible environment I was determined to leave home as soon as possible. I even talked to Mum about it and she arranged for a family conversation about how we could all live together. Mum did all the talking. Dad hardly said a word but I was persuaded to stay at home until I finished school. I studied as hard as I could for the next two years and got exceptionally good results. I passed the Cambridge University entrance exam and, after some debate about my age, they offered me a place. By the time I went home for Christmas after my first term at Cambridge, Dad had moved out. I've never spoken to him since. Less than a year later my parents were divorced.' Alice paused and looked William straight in the eyes. 'Now will you believe that I'm responsible?'

William held her gaze. 'I understand why you believe you're responsible but I feel strongly that, if you were asking Simon, he would say you are definitely not 100 per cent responsible. Whether it was rape or not, those boys would have known what they did was wrong, so some of the responsibility must be theirs. Also, in my view, your father was very much in the wrong for hitting you. If he hadn't done, the situation may have turned out very differently.'

Alice considered for a moment before responding. 'I suppose you might be right but the fact remains if I hadn't gone willingly into that park, none of it would have happened so it was my stupid, stupid decision that caused everything.'

'Maybe,' replied William, 'but you were just a teenager who was starting to be curious about sex. Most teenagers are curious about sex and many do things they later regret or feel embarrassed about. You've been punished far, far too harshly for your error of judgement and you're continuing to punish yourself even now.'

Alice was starting to get cross and pulled her hands away. 'I didn't expect you to tell me I was wrong. I was the one who was there. I know what happened. Anyway, we were supposed to be doing this so we could decide how to explain my behaviour on Sunday to Robert. Have you got any bright ideas about that?'

Realising Alice had been through a lot and was mentally exhausted, William wanted to end the conversation but was well aware she wouldn't give in until she had an answer to her question. He also felt this was his best chance to convince her she was not all to blame. He tried to combine both aspects.

'Robert would probably accept the minimal explanation of you being upset because your parents were divorced and you could no longer have family meals with them as you used to do when you were a child. However, if you want to be really honest with him and build a relationship with him based upon trust, you need to tell him why you feel you are to blame. It depends whether you can do that without getting upset again. If you do tell him what you've just told me, don't be surprised if he doesn't accept it. Even though he struggles with emotions, he's unlikely to find it a logical explanation. I'm convinced he would argue there are too many unproven facts. For instance, did either of your parents understand the circumstances leading up to your pregnancy? You told me your father didn't but what about your mother? How much did you tell her? Also, how can you be sure there wasn't already an issue with your parents' marriage before you were raped?'

'I wish you wouldn't keep calling it rape. I was the guilty one, not the victim. I told you we had an idyllic family life until I became pregnant. I accept my mother doesn't know the circumstances, as you put it. She never asked me and I wouldn't have been able to tell her anyway, not in the same way I've just told you.'

'Look,' said William, 'It's getting late and you've put yourself through a lot this evening. Why don't you sleep on it? I know enough to fend off any questions from Robert and the others until you're ready to speak to them yourself. All I ask is you consider it from your parents' point of view. The way you explained it to me, they could easily have interpreted it as if you were sleeping around with every boy you vaguely fancied. You and I know that wasn't the case but did they?'

Alice hesitated before answering and then replied in a very considered manner, 'I really don't know what they thought. I must be tired as I can't seem to think straight any more. I promise that tomorrow I'll consider what you said if you promise to tell Robert enough to stop him worrying about me, that is, of course, if he ever does worry about me.'

'That's a deal,' said William, standing up and heading for the door. 'I'm sure Robert is worrying about you in his own way. Now try to get some sleep and I'll call you tomorrow to see how you are. Goodnight.'

Alice opened the door for him but was so engrossed in her thoughts that she forgot to give him a hug. She did, however, go straight to bed and slept peacefully until her alarm woke her in the morning.

Chapter Eleven

Although William hadn't spoken directly to Alice since the previous evening, he'd received a number of texts from her. As well as thanking him again for putting up with her outpouring of emotion, she had told him she had thought a lot about what he'd said about her mother. As a result, she had decided to take a week off work and spend it with her mother, particularly as it was her mother's birthday and, after last night, she felt she would be more able to talk about what had happened. She was going to drive up to Yorkshire on Saturday, so would have to miss the Sunday meeting. Could William let Robert know without, of course, saying too much?

William had decided it was best to break the news Alice would not be available on Sunday to Robert and the others in person. It was a fairly regular occurrence for William to call round on an evening to inspect their equipment and to plan how the latest addition could be fitted in, so Simon was not too surprised to receive William's message that he was coming. Both Robert and Simon met William when he arrived. Robert and William went through their familiar flobbadob routine. All three of them sat chatting in the kitchen with their customary cups of tea. As was usually the case, Jake remained in his room. After a short while spent discussing the computing equipment, William introduced the subject of Alice by saying in as casual a manner as he could, 'Oh, before I forget, Alice asked me to let you know she isn't going to be at this Sunday's meeting.'

'That's disappointing,' Simon responded without waiting to hear the reason. 'It's always much nicer when Alice is here. I hope it's nothing to do with what happened last Sunday and what I said that upset her.'

'No,' replied William, trying to placate Simon but choosing his words carefully. 'I've spoken to her about that and it was as we thought at the time. It was just the reference to being like a family made her think about her own parents. As they are divorced, she feels guilty she hasn't seen her mother since last Christmas. She has some holiday left, which she'll lose if she doesn't take it before the end of the year, and has decided to take a week of it now so she can be in Yorkshire on her mum's birthday next Tuesday.'

'So is that all there was to it?' asked Robert, looking bemused. 'When we have meltdowns it is usually because someone or something has made us extremely angry.'

'Yes,' said Simon, 'but Alice isn't Aspie so she wouldn't have the same sort of meltdown as us anyway.'

William tried to move the conversation away from Alice. 'As I understand it, not all of your meltdowns are the same. It seems to me Jake's are usually down to anger and frustration, Robert's to feeling out of control of a situation and yours, Simon, are more like anxiety attacks than meltdowns, when you feel particularly unsafe.'

'I suppose you're right,' said Simon. 'We are all different. The good news is I haven't felt the need to use the snug for a long time now and I haven't noticed Robert in there either. Even Jake seems to need it less than he used to.'

'I am happy to know it's there if I do need it,' said Robert. 'I am a lot better these days at walking away when the pressure is starting to build. Also, I try to plan ahead more. If I know I am going into a difficult situation, I will give myself time alone to prepare, like when I went to meet Derek Watson. I knew it was going to be stressful for me so I wanted to make sure my elastic band wasn't already partly stretched before I started. It is a little like making sure you have a full charge in your battery so you can last as long as possible without running out of power. That's one of the reasons why I didn't go in Alice's car. I enjoy her company most of the time but she does have a habit of asking annoying questions.'

William was very tempted to take this rare opportunity to find out more about Robert's feelings for Alice but resisted doing so in case it diverted the conversation back to Alice's outburst. He decided to settle for having his explanation accepted so changed the subject. 'That reminds me. Alice also asked me to report back on her action for the Watson & Charles project. Do you want to talk about that now or wait for Sunday?'

'Let us do it now,' replied Robert. 'She only had the one action so it should not take very long.'

'OK, it was just to say she has gone through Pauline Sharples' emails and found nothing untoward. Alice now thinks it highly unlikely that Pauline is a suspect but, to be absolutely sure, she would like to go through Pauline's personal emails as well as her work ones. Alice found the address from a work email that Pauline had forwarded to herself and thought Jake could use it do the same thing he has done with the work emails. However, she didn't want to ask Jake directly in case it took him away from more important tasks. She also suggested, if anyone else became a suspect, there was more likelihood of any incriminating evidence being found in their personal emails than in their work ones.' William smiled as he remembered Alice's exact words, 'because Robert would never think of that for himself'.

'It didn't make much sense to me to suspect Pauline Sharples in the first place,' said Robert, 'although I suppose it's a good thing to be able to rule her out.'

Simon butted in. 'With regard to Jake though, it wouldn't be a bad idea to get him to set us up with visibility of personal emails as well as work ones. It's a safe thing for him to do and we're struggling at the moment to give him enough things to do to keep him away from doing the things we don't want him to. If he knows it's for Alice, he's likely to be happy to do it as a priority.'

Robert considered for a moment. 'Jake is supposed to be helping to go through the work emails of the board members. There's a lot of useful information associated with them, mainly in the various attachments, and we're slowly building up an understanding of the Watson & Charles business. In order to try to speed things up, we've divided up the board members between us. I'm concentrating upon Derek Watson and John Hargreaves so I can focus on the managed-house problem. Simon is doing the family members, Stephen and Howard Watson. Jake is doing the other two, Jeremy Turner and Neil Martin. However, even I could tell he wasn't very pleased about it so to give him something he enjoys more would make sense. I have also come across personal email addresses. We should be able to find them for all six board members which, with Pauline Sharples as well, would give Jake seven to do. That should keep him busy for a while. I will talk to him about it.'

'Remember to tell him that it was Alice's idea,' said Simon pointedly.

'How are you getting on with your own actions, Bill?' asked Robert.

'Fine, thank you, Bob ... flobbadob ...' replied William. 'Most of what I'm finding is confirming and adding to what I already knew. There are many pubs up for sale and there's still an over capacity of beer production in the UK with consolidation continuing, but not as much as ten years ago. One of the few growth areas has been microbreweries and what is now known as craft brewing. However, I still have some work to do so would prefer to wait until Sunday to report fully.'

'I agree,' said Robert. 'Let's leave the rest until Sunday. I have a lot to do before then. It's taking a long time to do the background work. Maybe on Sunday we can find a way of speeding things up.'

'What are we going to do for food on Sunday?' queried Simon. 'I was hoping for another of Alice's scrummy roasts. It won't be the same without her.'

'Don't worry,' replied Robert. 'We can have pasta and a sauce. I'll make plenty so there will be enough for Bill as well.'

'We always have pasta and sauce,' moaned Simon.

Worried the conversation was heading back towards Alice's absence, William remembered the pretext for him being there. 'Anyway, I need to get into the garage to check on a few things. Am I OK alarm-wise, Simon?'

'I'll just nip upstairs and make sure they're all off,' replied Simon as he got up and left the kitchen.

Robert suggested going to the garage as well but William put him off by saying he didn't want to be responsible for Robert taking any more time away from the Watson & Charles project. Robert reluctantly agreed it was better to get back to all the emails but, from the body language Robert didn't even realise he possessed, William could tell he was not very happy. William spent only a little while in the garage, conscious that he too needed to get back home and make sure he did have something worthwhile to say on Sunday.

* * *

By the Friday morning following the disappointment of the previous Sunday's family meal, Derek Watson was feeling slightly better. At home he was still having arguments with Mary, but at work, he had decided to take action himself, starting with attending the weekly Monday morning meeting of the Managed House Division to review the previous week's takings. The numbers were surprisingly good, hitting the weekly budget for the first time for over a year. Although this was tempered by the fact they were now in a quiet part of the year, Derek had been encouraged, as he had by the unity shown by the group of managers present, who were all very supportive of John Hargreaves despite the dire situation they were in. They truly did seem to be all working together, desperately wanting to find a solution.

Derek had also held individual meetings with the three non-family directors to tell them about the email. Their reactions had all been very different. John Hargreaves was relieved there could possibly be an explanation other than his poor leadership for the deterioration in the results of his division. He was keen to have more detail and so was disappointed Derek couldn't provide any, but was a little happier when Derek did commit to exploring the implications with John at a later date. Jeremy Turner had initially been shocked and surprised but then said it fitted in with someone finding out about the poor performance of the business and attempting to undermine it further. Neil Martin had taken it very calmly, saying it was the sort of thing that could happen to any business these days. He questioned Derek upon the likely impact on the family and whether it could actually lead to a vote to sell by the shareholders. Derek had replied he believed the family were united but it would depend on how bad the end-of-year results actually were. Jeremy had already given Derek details of the effects of the likely scenarios on the share price. The potential impact of the worst-case scenario was greater than Derek had feared but his main concern was how much information to share with Mary.

Derek also had a follow-up meeting with Stephen in which he admitted it may have been a mistake not to invest in the brewery before now and, if they got through the current mess, they should seriously consider it, irrespective of Jeremy Turner's views. Stephen had been far from convinced, viewing it as just a sweetener to sway his vote, but he had agreed to go away and consider a variety of options.

That Friday lunchtime, Derek had arranged to go to lunch at the Hare and Hounds with John Hargreaves and look again at how anyone could interfere with the performance of one of their pubs. Shortly before he was due to leave, Pauline knocked and entered his office, vigorously waving a piece of paper.

'You need to see this,' she said nervously. 'It's from Roger Thompson.' Rather than pass it over to him, she started reading. 'Dear Ms Sharples, Please inform Mr Watson that it has come to our attention he has not yet complied with the financial arrangements of our contract. We have attributed this to an oversight on his part as a result of the strain of managing the current business situation. A few days ago, therefore, we took the liberty of instructing his bank on his behalf to sell enough shares in order for the agreed amount to be placed in his current account. It is now a proven fact that this transaction is complete. This oversight has not prevented us from commencing our investigations and these will continue providing the money remains in place. As proof of our progress, we now understand the relevance of the number 300172. Yours sincerely, Roger Thompson Associates.'

As she was reading, Derek was becoming more and more agitated. 'Let me see,' he demanded, reaching for the piece of paper and almost snatching it from her hand.

'Do you understand what it means?' asked Pauline, but Derek was too busy frantically tapping away at his keyboard to respond.

Pauline could see Derek's face reddening and he looked about to explode. 'I'll tell you what it means,' he shouted. 'The little bugger has sold half a million pounds worth of my personal shares. I've just logged into my online banking system and it's all there, just as if I'd done it myself.'

With a confused look on her face, Pauline asked, 'Was it not true that you agreed with him about transferring the money?'

'Well, yes,' admitted Derek reluctantly, 'but the whole point is he must have stolen my identity to do it. It means Tait is nothing more than a criminal. He's committed identity fraud.'

'But you still have the money,' pointed out Pauline, calmly. 'If he wanted to, he could have stolen the money as well but he hasn't, has he? If I understand correctly, all he has done is what you should have done yourself days ago. Not only that, he has demonstrated he is capable of doing those sorts of things without anyone knowing. What does the bit about proof of progress mean?'

Slumping back in his chair, Derek replied despondently. 'It means he's seen our half-yearly accounts. It's the measly amount of profit we've made to date. It also means if he's aware of our situation, others could be as well. I think we can now be damn sure our systems aren't secure and we have no secrets any more.'

In the hope of cheering him up, Pauline said, 'Look on the bright side. You were concerned you hadn't heard anything from him. Now you have. Alright, you're upset he knows your personal banking details but, if he's any good, wouldn't you expect him to be able to find out things like that? Surely, it's how he uses them that matters. It sounds to me as if he's doing his best to keep his side of the bargain. If you want there to be any chance of him helping you, you'd better keep your side as well.'

Derek suddenly remembered his discussion with Robert Tait about Pauline and DNA. 'Maybe you're correct. It could be worse.'

Pauline looked down at her watch. 'It's time for your lunch with John. Try to relax and enjoy it but remember your diet, don't eat too much. Have faith in Roger Thompson, I've a good feeling about him. Oh, and don't forget to take your coat, it's quite cool out there today.'

Although Derek was far from convinced, he did admit to himself as he was walking across the brewery yard to meet John, there was a small part of him that was impressed with what Robert Tait had done. Maybe he wasn't so naive after all.

*　*　*

The Hare and Hounds in Copythorne had been a Watson & Charles pub for many years. It was one of Derek's favourites. Two years previously he had pushed for it to be significantly extended and refurbished at a cost of over two million pounds so it could be transformed from a struggling tenancy into a flagship managed house. It was only a five-minute drive from the brewery and, whilst John was driving them there in his company-owned series 7 BMW, Derek was wondering whether it might have been better to sell it, as Jeremy Turner had wanted to do. It was a thought that had gone through Derek's mind a lot recently.

When they'd decided on the strategy almost twenty years ago to increase steadily the overall size of their pubs, either by buying new ones or developing existing ones, the decisions had been fairly straightforward, as had the decisions about which of the smaller pubs to sell off. However, over the years, those decisions had become more difficult as they had reached the point of having to deal with a number of borderline cases, of which the Hare and Hounds was one. To invest or divest had become a major part of board discussions. It was the only explanation Derek had come up with for the deterioration in performance. Had they been lured by the success of the initial investments and, as a consequence, drawn the line too low and invested where they shouldn't have?

Even though, as they both had hoped, the Hare and Hounds was nicely busy on a Friday lunchtime, Derek was treated as royalty. The manager, Ron Bentley, greeted them personally and showed them to a corner table in one of the larger rooms, from which they could see the bar but also with a pleasant view of the beer garden and countryside beyond. Ron took their order with Derek, trying to do as Pauline had requested and keep it to a relatively light lunch, asking for a steak and onion baguette and a pint of Frisky Fox. John followed suit, having a prawn baguette and, as he was driving, a pint of Gunners. As soon as their drinks had been served, Derek lowered his voice.

'One of the main reasons for wanting to come here is I've been giving a lot of thought to what actions we should take in response to the email. The impact on the shareholders and how we try to defend the sale of the business against any potential offers is one thing, but how we work out if we have been the victims of a cyber-attack that could somehow be causing our problems is another. I know you and I sat here only a few months ago and talked about theft as one of the possible explanations but discarded it on the basis that Keith Fairbrother convinced us there was no evidence of anything untoward. In the light of recent events, I think we should look again.'

'I've been thinking about that email too,' said John. 'I want to believe there are factors beyond my control that are the cause. However, Jeremy has been very good at releasing Keith's time to look into everything. After all, Keith is Jeremy's number two and a brilliant analyst. He has been through the numbers with a fine-toothcomb, looking at both the collective position across the whole estate and also just about every one of the sixty-nine individual pubs. Everything balances. That's one of the beauties of the Brewdat system. All the data is there.'

'Exactly,' said Derek, 'that's my point. What if someone has been interfering with the data? That's the sort of thing a cyber-attack means. Keith has no knowledge of the email or the suggestion of a cyber-attack, so wouldn't necessarily be looking in the right places. I think we should tell Keith our suspicions and ask him to look again.'

'I'd be very surprised if Keith has missed anything. He's explored everything to do with money extremely thoroughly, from the tills to the card readers to the bank. He's worked bloody hard, you know, cross checking the data in Brewdat with the bank statements and carrying out both vertical and horizontal audits across the whole system. I've a great deal of faith in him. He's extremely diligent and a wizard with spreadsheets. As you know from my management committee reports, every time he's found something that looks vaguely like a trend and worth digging into further, subsequent results have disproved it. That's why I'm at a loss to know what to do next. I truly believe we're doing the best we can to maximise the return from the estate and, although it may seem strange to say this, I'm fearful of changing our overall approach in case it makes things worse. If the results weren't so bad I would argue we've been too bullish with the budget, but to be so far behind both budget and last year does suggest we're missing something major. Yes, let's go back to Keith. I'm prepared to give anything a go at this stage. I'm no expert when it comes to data systems,' admitted John.

'No, I'm no expert either,' confessed Derek. 'I suggest we also involve Ian Walters. Ian already knows about the email. If there's anything to be found, then Ian and Keith working together are our best bet for finding it. The other thought I had is, let's focus all our efforts on this pub rather than spreading them across the whole estate. I know Keith has always said there are no obvious patterns or trends but it struck me on Monday, in spite of the overall position looking a little better against budget, this pub, along with the two other most recent refurbs, the Black Bear just outside Salisbury and the Jolly Sailor near Arundel, were the three worst performers last week. I really could do with knowing if investing in those three pubs was a good decision or not.'

Carefully considering his response, John replied, 'As every single managed house is well behind budget for the year to date, it does make sense to assume they're all affected and to concentrate on just one.

I can understand your reasons for choosing this one. However, isn't it possible the cyber-attack, if there is one, could be after the data from all of the pubs have been combined, so shouldn't we look at the collective position as well? Also, one thing we did notice a few weeks back was there was an increase in the number of poor reviews we were receiving on various websites. These didn't correlate with the feedback we were getting within the pubs themselves so we didn't worry too much about them. It may be worth digging into those in more detail as they might also qualify as some form of cyber-attack.'

Before Derek could respond, their food arrived. The conversation changed to the impact of the poor results on the morale and motivation of the staff, with Derek telling John how impressed he had been with amount of unity shown at the Monday meeting. When they had finished, Derek resisted the temptation to have another beer, settling for joining John in a coffee. Ron Bentley came over to check all was well and they all spoke for a while. Ron had no explanation for the disappointing results, insisting the pub was busy, staffing levels were under control and feedback on quality and service was good, with far more compliments than complaints. Derek was well aware most of the publicans, whether managers or tenants, tended to tell him what they thought he wanted to hear. On the other hand, he'd known Ron for a long time and had no reason to doubt what he said. When Ron had left them, Derek reverted back to the earlier conversation.

'As a way forward, John, I'll set up a working party led by myself and including you, Ian Walters and Keith Fairbrother with the primary aim of searching for any evidence of a cyber-attack in any of the new areas we've identified.'

'That sounds like a good plan,' said John, trying not to sound too negative, 'but I'm slightly concerned it might take too much of my time away from running the division. I would like to think the improvement we've seen in the last couple of weeks is due to the hard work everybody is putting in and, whilst I remain in charge, I would like to do all I can to deliver the best result possible.'

I understand that,' said Derek. 'It will only require a small amount of your time, initially to set Ian and Keith going and then for the occasional review of progress. There is, however, one last question I need to ask you. How do you feel about my father's suggestion of you and Neil Martin exchanging roles?'

'I wouldn't want to do that,' John responded without any hesitation. 'I have nothing against Neil. He seems to be doing a good job in tenancies and has tried to help me as well. In fact, if you find Brewdat is an issue, then Neil might be the right man. He was familiar with it during his time in managed houses at Limberts and has championed it within the tenancies here. There are now only a handful of tenancies who are still resisting putting it in. However, from my personal point of view, I would much rather you accept my letter of resignation than be moved to tenancies.'

'I thought you might say that. You'd better hope Ian and Keith do find something. If we're still in this same situation at Christmas, I'll be left with little choice,' replied Derek, as he stood up to go to the bar and pay.

Chapter Twelve

It was as William had feared. The Sunday meeting had gone badly. The best part about it had been going in his new car. He was home early and had just received a text from Alice asking him to call and tell her what had happened. He was beginning to tire of the role of intermediary he seemed to have inherited. Having had to choose his words carefully to tell Robert about Alice, he now had to do the same to tell Alice about Robert. In spite of agreeing with Simon's view that the meeting would have gone better if Alice had been there, William decided just to tell Alice the facts. She could draw her own conclusions. Before he picked up the phone to dial Alice's mobile, he opened a bottle of Fuller's London Pride and settled himself in his favourite armchair with its well-worn cushion. Alice answered almost immediately.

'Hello, William. How are you? How's Robert? What did you tell him? How did the meeting go?'

William responded in kind. 'I'm fine. Robert's fine. The meeting was short and not very productive. How's your mother? Did you have a good journey up?'

'Sorry,' replied Alice. 'It's just I feel a bit guilty for not being there. Yes, thank you, my journey was OK. The M25 was a bit slow as usual and there was a hold-up on the M1 around Sheffield but I got here safely. Mum is well. We went for a nice walk this morning in Bretton Country Park. So far, we've just been catching up. I haven't talked to her yet about what, you know, you and I spoke about. I'll wait until after her birthday to do that. I've offered to help her cook her birthday meal. It's going to be a bit of a party. She's invited a few of her friends round.

Aunt Penny and Uncle Bernard will be there as well as my cousin Terry and his fiancée Juliet. I've only met Juliet once before but they're planning on getting married in the spring. I've been invited. The invitations came in the post only last Friday so Mum held on to mine for me. It's for Alice Selby plus one. What chance to you think I have of persuading Robert to be my plus one; pretty much zero I suppose?' Eventually, she paused for breath.

'You'd definitely need to pick your moment to ask,' answered William, 'but I wouldn't rule it out completely. You never know with Robert. Assuming the wedding will be in Yorkshire, you would probably have to accept going by train.'

'That would be a small price to pay. I'd do anything to get him to say yes,' said Alice, a little more hopefully. 'Anyway, tell me more about today. It doesn't sound as if it went very smoothly.'

'Well,' said William with a sigh, 'it got off to a bad start and never really recovered. You know how Robert likes to be punctual. He was all ready to start at 11 o'clock precisely but there was no sign of Jake. Simon had to go up three times to call him. Even when Jake came down almost half an hour late, he was at his most sullen. I was in the middle of reporting what I had found out about the brewing industry but it was clear Jake didn't want to listen. All he did was moan and ask why he couldn't get stuck into something more interesting than just emails.'

'Oh dear,' exclaimed Alice, 'and I thought he was OK with that as I noticed when I got here he's set me up with access to Pauline Sharples' personal emails, just as he'd done with her work ones. He even sent me a nice message to say he'd done it.'

'It's not you he's unhappy with,' explained William. 'Robert's got him sorting out access to the personal emails of all six board members as well. He's also trawling through the work emails of Jeremy Turner and Neil Martin and now he's got to do their personal ones as well. That's not Jake's strong point and he got very vociferous about not understanding what he was looking for. All three of us tried to explain to him that we've only been working on this project for just over two weeks and we're all in the process of trying to understand what to look for.'

'I suspect all Jake wants to do is break into a bank. Aren't there information systems at Watson & Charles Jake could work on instead? It sounds as though Robert and Simon still don't trust Jake.'

'I think you're right. Simon admitted they're struggling to find enough things for Jake to do that are considered to be safe. I don't think Jake minds setting up the email accesses. It's going through them he objects to. My concern is he might miss something of importance. As far as Watson & Charles's systems are concerned, Robert did report on what he'd found but that only made the situation worse.'

'What do you mean,' asked Alice.

'Well, Robert managed to calm Jake down a little by explaining that one of the main aims was to try to find any links between my report on the brewing industry in general and the internal goings on at Watson & Charles. From what Robert himself has found, he believes a key unproven fact is that another company wants to buy Watson & Charles. Simon supported him by saying there was a high probability of this and added that if they could identify who this was then Jake would have a major role in investigating them. Jake did mutter about that just meaning more emails but quietened down enough to let me finish my report and Robert to start his. I wrapped mine up pretty quickly, limiting it to previous takeovers and explaining how companies such as Marston's, Greene King and Limberts had grown through acquiring other smaller companies, but recently there had been a slow-down in the number of acquisitions.

'Robert then took over. He acted as if he was Chairman of the Watson & Charles board, waving his hands all over the place and going through in great detail their current financial position. He explained it was only the Managed House Division that was failing. The reasons for this failure were not understood in spite of in-depth analysis by their accounts department. Apparently, all their information is held within a system called Brewdat which is pretty common throughout the whole brewing industry. Jake perked up at that stage but Robert said it was just a large database and, in his opinion, all they would achieve from digging into it would be to repeat the findings of Watson & Charles. It would seem that one of their people, an accountant called Keith Fairbrother, has spent loads of time on this and Robert wants to go through all his reports before deciding what to do next. Jake shouted he could do a better job than Keith Fairbrother as he could look underneath as well as on top. Simon didn't help matters, saying that would run the risk of Jake's activities being spotted and throwing back at Jake that he wouldn't know what to look for. Seemingly, Jake always says about any system he is going into that he needs to know what to look for. Jake leapt up, held his head in his hands and yelled that they were stopping him from doing what he was good at. He stormed across to the door, continuing to yell how he'd proved how good he was by selling Derek Watson's shares and putting the proceeds in his bank account. He slammed the lounge door behind him and then the snug door. He spent about twenty minutes in the snug and then we heard him come out and go upstairs. He wouldn't come back down, even for the food.'

'That sounds as if he was so frustrated he had quite a bad meltdown. Is he OK now?' asked Alice.

'I don't know but Robert and Simon didn't seem overly concerned. They treated it as the norm even though they admitted Jake hadn't had a meltdown for a while. They suggested he was best left alone to get over it,' said William, wondering if it would have happened at all if Alice had been there.

'So what happened then? Did you continue the meeting without Jake?'

'Not really because I got cross with Robert. I asked him what Jake had meant about selling Derek Watson's shares. According to Robert, Derek Watson hadn't done anything about moving money across to his personal bank account ready to pay us, so Robert had got Jake to do it for him by accessing his accounts and selling some of his shares. My problem is I knew nothing about this and I guess you didn't either.'

'No,' said Alice. 'It means nothing to me.'

'I told Robert in no uncertain terms there was no point in having discussions about how we were going to behave as a team if he then went off and did things without discussing them as a team first. I even threatened to have nothing more to do with the project if that was the way Robert was going to act. At one point, I thought Robert was going to follow Jake into the snug. He tried to defend his actions by saying he'd told us it was part of the contract and all he was doing was implementing the contract. Also, he'd needed to make a quick decision and Simon had stopped us all from using the forum for sensitive subjects. Fortunately, Simon intervened on my side and persuaded Robert he should have at least mentioned it before taking action and the lack of a forum was no excuse, using the argument that Roger Thompson would have found a way to tell us all. We talked generally about the values we had set for Roger Thompson which, probably because it wasn't personal, slowly settled things down. We even got on to how best to handle Jake using those values, although we didn't really come up with an answer. We then decided to abandon the meeting and have lunch instead. That's why I'm back so early.'

'I'm pleased the Roger Thompson stuff was useful. I was worried it might all have been a waste of time, something Robert had concocted so he could control the rest of us without following it himself,' Alice confessed. 'Well played, Simon, for using it against him.'

'You would probably have done the same had you been there.'

'Maybe. I would like to think I could've done something to help Jake. It seems as though we need to find a way for him to be more involved and not feel excluded.'

William was worried that Alice was going to ask him to carry out yet another tricky task in her absence.

'That's easy to say but not so easy to do, particularly when he won't come out of his room. He's much worse than Robert when it comes to finding opportunities to have discussions with him on difficult topics.'

'Yes, I know, but let's give it some thought anyway. One thing that struck me when you were talking earlier was that communication would be easier if we went back to using the forum. Jake could read things in his own time and be part of the debate without having to do it in person. Isn't Simon supposed to be working on making it more secure?'

'He is. We talked briefly about it over lunch. He's made improvements but is still reluctant to consider it secure enough. I suspect in his mind it falls into the category of never being 100 per cent secure. I'll try to push him on it.'

'So what did you have for lunch?' asked Alice. 'I bet it wasn't a roast.'

'No,' replied William. 'It was just penne pasta with a tomato sauce but, from my personal point of view, it was nice not to come home and have to prepare something myself. We also had a far more productive discussion over lunch than we had in the meeting itself.'

'That's good. What did you talk about?'

'We talked a lot about you,' replied William with a laugh, 'but nothing for you to worry about. It was just that we all agreed you're a much better cook than all of us put together. Simon wished he could eat your food every day. I joked that if he did then he would soon be as round as he is tall. Robert admitted your two roasts had shown him how boring and repetitive their meals usually are and said he will ask you for advice on new recipes that are within his capabilities, so be warned.'

'I'm not sure I know what his capabilities are,' replied Alice light-heartedly. Then, a little more seriously, 'If I did cook for them more often they would definitely have a healthier diet. What about the project? What happens next?'

'Well, on the positive side, Robert has lots more to do to catch up with and understand the investigations done by Watson & Charles. Simon and I are going to try to set up a version of Brewdat so Jake can have a play with it. Also, as long as Jake agrees to work with Simon, Jake will be asked to look at the banking side of Watson & Charles, not changing anything, just establishing how money moves through the business. We didn't come up with anything else for you to do at the moment.'

'Good,' said Alice. 'I'll just have a closer look at Pauline Sharples' emails when I get the chance. You said positive side; does that mean there's a negative side?'

'I'm afraid there is,' admitted William, 'quite a big one in my opinion. Over lunch, Robert confessed that the unproven fact with the highest probability or, as we would put it, the most likely explanation for the original email, is that it was generated by a larger company trying to exploit the poor performance of Watson & Charles and take them over. His initial thought that a cyber-attack had caused the poor performance is now less likely.'

'Why has he changed his mind?' asked Alice.

'He's come across evidence of potential business failures within Watson & Charles that could explain their bad results. Together with my report on the brewing industry as a whole, which suggests other brewing companies the size of Watson & Charles are also struggling, he no longer thinks millions of pounds need to have gone missing through fraudulent means to cause the problem.'

'What business failures? Surely even Robert can't believe he's become an expert on the brewing business so quickly, can he?'

'He mentioned pushing for an unrealistic budget, investing in pubs that would have been better sold and a potentially incompetent director who should have been fired. I suppose he did sound a bit like a brewing company chairman. Whether he feels he now knows as much as Derek Watson, I don't know.'

'What do you think, William?'.

Trying to avoid expressing his personal views, William stuck to the facts. 'I can understand Robert's logic. Recent history of the brewing industry does show any split in the owners of family breweries has led to them being snaffled up by a larger company, not for their breweries but for their pubs. There's no suggestion of anything underhand in those deals or, indeed, of any reason to attack Watson & Charles specifically. However, there is far greater capacity for beer production throughout the country than there is demand. Large breweries have excess capacity so brewing extra beer is relatively cheap for them. The property market is flooded with small pubs for sale because they're not viable as individual businesses. Microbreweries are on the increase because of favourable duty legislation. This increases the competition for space on supermarket shelves. Brewing companies the size of Watson & Charles are caught in the middle. They have to rely on family unity as well as finding the best strategy in order to keep going. Robert says there's quite a complicated formula for calculating the value of Watson & Charles shares and the share price is only changed once a year, after the end-of-year results are declared and shortly before the annual general meeting. He thinks it's very logical for a predatory company to take steps to undermine confidence and stir things up before putting in an offer that would appear very attractive against a falling share price. In the past, companies like Watson & Charles were able to keep their performance a secret but, these days, it's almost impossible to prevent information leaking out. Robert now believes it might be a cyber-attack to discover information rather than anything to do with stealing or fraud. If you think about it, it was relatively easy for Robert to find out so much just from accessing their emails, so anyone else could have done the same.'

'But we have to believe we're better than anyone else otherwise we have no chance of succeeding, and not just believe it but actually be better. If we can find out who is behind this then surely that will help Derek Watson fend off any offer, won't it?'

'It might help but it's likely to be too late by then. Time is already against us. Watson & Charles's financial year finishes at the end of February. That only gives them five months to turn things around and make a worthwhile profit, otherwise the share value will fall significantly. If that does happen, lots of companies will be interested in putting in offers and, if enough of the Watson family want to accept, the business will be sold and we will have failed.'

'Oh God,' exclaimed Alice. 'Robert would hate that. He doesn't cope well with failure and, given his Crawtech experience, that's the last thing he needs. Did he seem very worried?'

'He certainly wasn't all that happy but, in his inimitable style, he was trying not to show it. He wants Simon to work out some numbers and probabilities but, as Simon himself pointed out, that would require a lot of guesswork and assumptions, so the results would not be very accurate. Robert asked Simon to do it anyway.'

'Well, I can't see any other way forward than trusting in Robert and supporting him as much as possible. I assume there will be another meeting next Sunday. I should be back for that. I'm intending to travel on either Thursday or Saturday, depending on how my chat with Mum goes.'

'OK,' said William, wanting to draw the conversation to a close and get another beer. 'See you next Sunday and good luck with your mum. Bye.'

'Goodbye, but let me know of any other developments,' said Alice as she hung up.

As soon as he put the phone down, William realised he had forgotten to tell Alice about the forthcoming visit of Robert's parents that Robert had announced over lunch.

* * *

Two days later, Derek Watson was planning to tackle a critical discussion with his wife. The previous day he had received a little more encouragement from another week's reasonable results but then Jeremy Turner had spoilt his good mood by presenting a detailed assessment of the effects of various scenarios on the share price. Although Derek knew a significant fall in profits would have a negative impact, seeing firm numbers had really brought it home to him how difficult a situation he was in. Whilst Mary had been at her art class, Derek had debated with himself how much to tell her. He was fed up with Mary pushing him for information and arguing with him over money. After much deliberation, he'd decided to try to put an end to all the arguments by letting her see the facts for herself. He had emailed Jeremy's presentation to Mary to prove he wasn't hiding anything and to give her the time and opportunity to look at it herself and consider her reaction. They had agreed to talk in Derek's study after their evening meal but Mary couldn't wait and, whilst they were still in the dining room, she asked him about the formula for calculating the share price.

'I thought we were going to have this conversation after dinner,' Derek replied. 'It would be easier with the numbers in front of us.'

'Yes, I know,' said Mary, 'but it's the principle behind the formula I want to understand first.'

Not wanting to antagonise her, Derek started to explain. 'The share price is calculated by dividing the value of the Company by the total number of shares issued. As the number of shares is constant, totalling two million, and the current share price is just over ninety-eight pounds, this means that the Company is valued at around £196 million. The value of the Company changes every year, based on the formula set up when the Company was first formed. The various rules are based on protecting the position of all of the employees should the business ever be sold. Over the years there've been some changes but the principles have always been the same. The value is calculated as the positive elements minus the negative ones. The main positive one is the book value of all the assets held, which is mainly all of the pubs, as other assets are relatively minor. The other positive, or at least should-be positive, is the profit made in the latest financial year. This is where the main problem lies. It's based on just the last year and is multiplied by a factor of ten. Anyway, the positives are then offset by the negatives, which are the amounts owed to creditors. The main creditors are the bank, where we have substantial loans, and the pension fund where there is a shortfall in funding. A few years ago, the pension fund was given first call on some of the pubs to bridge the gap. Also, any other creditors shown in the accounts have to be covered along with half of the annual salary costs, to allow for generous redundancy payments and any legal costs. After each financial year end, the value of the Company is recalculated and divided by 2 million so that the new share price can be announced at the AGM. The accounts are supposed to be kept confidential before then and no active family director is allowed to buy or sell shares between three months before the year end and the AGM.'

'There's nothing to stop me selling my shares at any time though, is there?' asked Mary pointedly.

Feeling his temper rising, Derek took another mouthful of his now almost cold boeuf bourguignon, chewed and swallowed before responding in the calmest voice he could muster.

'We have had this conversation a number of times. In theory, you can sell your shares. When you were given those shares, the intention was you would never sell them. It was expected you would support me, support the family, support the brewery and, ultimately, pass the shares on to our children.' He closed his knife and fork together on his plate even though there was still some food left.

'If you've finished eating,' said Mary, 'let's go and look through the numbers as we agreed. I'm going to make myself a cup of coffee. Would you like one?'

'No thanks,' replied Derek as he stood up. 'I fancy a Scotch instead. I'll see you in there.' On his way to his study, Derek poured himself a rather large Laphroaig, certain he would need it.

'Look,' said Mary as she joined him. 'I really don't want to argue with you. I do try to support you, when you'll let me. All I ask is you try to see it from my side. I've looked through Jeremy's numbers and, given what you've just told me, I think I understand the situation well enough.' Pointing at the screen of Derek's computer where the key slide from Jeremy Turner's PowerPoint presentation was displayed, Mary continued.

'Correct me if I'm wrong. The current share price is £98. It fell from the previous value of £106 last year because of a decline in profits and increased borrowing. At the AGM last April, I remember this being explained away by a poor Christmas because of a dip in consumer confidence, concerns over Brexit and not enough time for the new pubs to reach optimum performance. You yourself said this was a blip, the first time in many years the share price had dropped from one year to the next, and you were confident this year it would recover to a new high. The majority of the profit is always made in the summer. Summer is now over and the half-year accounts show very little profit. In fact they are seven and a half million behind where they should be. Jeremy shows the effects of a worst-case scenario of another seven and a half million behind budget in the second half of the year against a best-case scenario of hitting budget to give a total-year profit of just two and a half million, along with various possibilities in between. Even in his best case, the share price falls to £72 and in his worst case to only £34. What's more, all I hear from you is you don't know what's caused such a fall and you don't know what to do about it. It seems to me the likely outcome is going to be much closer to the worst case than the best. What I really don't understand is why you would expect any shareholder who knows the facts to hold on to their shares until the next AGM when doing so is likely to cost them more than fifty pounds a share. Am I missing something?'

Derek had slumped down in his chair. He was taken aback by Mary's summary. She had sounded just like Jeremy Turner. He doubted if he could have expressed the despondency of his predicament any better. She clearly understood much more than he gave her credit for, far too much. He felt he had to try to defend his position.

'No, from a hard-nosed financial perspective you're not missing anything. What you don't see is all the hard work being put into trying to understand what's going on and to put it right. We're doing everything we can think of including, as you well know, investigating whether there might be some sort of outside influence that's pulling us down.'

'That's another thing,' said Mary sharply. 'I pointed you in the direction of Robert Tait to help you find out about that email I received. You tell me he got as far as finding it was from an external source but you haven't mentioned him since. Yet, last Sunday evening, it sounded as if you were pinning your hopes on all this being down to some sort of cyber-attack. Is that because you know more than you're saying or are you clutching at straws?'

Reluctant to tell Mary about Robert Tait accessing his personal finances, Derek replied, 'I have commissioned Robert Tait to look into it but have not heard anything back from him. I've also asked Ian Walters and Keith Fairbrother to review the numbers again, looking specifically for any sign of fraud. So far they have found nothing and, to be honest with you, the longer that continues to be the case the more I believe it's because there's nothing to find. The most likely explanation for that email is another company planted it with the aim of causing the sort of reaction from shareholders you've just outlined. It wouldn't surprise me if, whilst I'm in London over the next couple of days for meetings with other brewers, some of the big boys come probing for information and with hints of generous offers. That's why I'm asking you to put the family first and stop all this talk of selling your shares.'

'So, if you don't think it's fraud, what has led to such a change in fortunes? If you put the second half of last year together with the first half of this year, you get a whole period of twelve months with hardly any profit at all. It would be difficult to stomach if it's just down to poor business decisions.'

'Well, it could be explained by the fact we've hit a perfect storm,' admitted Derek. 'Trading conditions have been difficult because of external factors such as Brexit. The value of pubs has dropped because there are so many on the market. We've reached the point where we've invested in all the pubs obviously worth developing and expanding. We've sold the pubs that were obviously not worth keeping. We've bought some new pubs thinking we were getting a bargain. Over the last few years we've been left with about fifteen borderline cases. We decided to invest in most of them because the property market was so bad. With hindsight, maybe those weren't the best decisions. Also, with regard to the share price, we talked last year about changing the rules to make the profit element an average of the previous five years rather than just the last one but decided against as Father argued it conveyed a lack of confidence. I'm going to put that change forward at the next AGM but it may well be too late by then.'

'So do the results show those fifteen borderline pubs are having a significant impact on dragging down the overall result?'

Wondering why they hadn't had many conversations like this about the business before, Derek said, 'No, they don't … Well, they didn't because we'd looked closely for any clear trends but, strangely enough, over the last two weeks, the three worst performers against budget have been the three latest investments. The other thing that is strange is the majority of the tenancies have been holding up well, it's just the managed houses that have performed so badly. That's why John Hargreaves offered to resign.'

'Maybe you should have accepted his resignation and got someone else in. What about your father's idea of moving Neil Martin across from tenancies? It strikes me he couldn't do any worse than John.'

'You may well be right. I've been thinking about that myself. I'll talk to Stephen about it. The real problem is we need a drastic turnaround in fortunes to affect this year's result. Given the time of year and only a few months left, I can't see anyone being able to deliver that.'

Mary thought for a while, moved to the window to draw the curtains, took a deep breath and said, 'I'm sorry, Derek. Nothing you have said gives me any confidence the situation will be improved by the end of this financial year and it seems like there's every chance of it deteriorating further next year. That is, of course, if you manage to survive until then. I really do feel I have to look at it from my personal perspective. My 2 per cent of the shares are currently worth four million pounds. In April, they are likely to be worth no more than one and a half million. I simply cannot afford to lose two and half million pounds. It's more than half of my entire worth. I'm going to have to sell now.'

Feeling his temper rising once more, Derek looked her straight in the eyes and said, in a very steely voice, 'You do realise, don't you, if you decide to sell it will be the end of our marriage?'

Mary didn't respond in the manner Derek had expected. She shouted back at him. 'That's just typical of you, using emotional blackmail to try to get your own way. We don't have much of a marriage any more, do we? There's no physical side to it. We don't talk to each other. Since you've become Chairman, you're hardly ever at home and are certainly not interested in what goes on here, only on what goes on at your precious brewery. You don't involve me, unless you need me by your side at some brewery function or other. This is the first serious discussion about the business we've had for a long time and look how that has turned out. You expect me to sacrifice two and half million pounds just because you want me to. Well, I won't.'

Derek slammed his fist on the desk before swivelling around in his office chair. 'If it's the fucking money you want, then you would be better off divorcing me. Get yourself a good lawyer and you can take me for far more than two and half million pounds. Anyway, whose fault is it we don't make love any more? It was you who decided to have separate rooms.'

'Yes it bloody well was,' retorted Mary. 'The last time was not making love. It was you using me for sex. You came home pissed after one of your men-only brewing dinners. For some reason you were all stirred up and slobbered all over me in your drunken stupor. As soon as you had finished, which fortunately for me did not take long, and without any thought of pleasuring me, you staggered to the bathroom, threw up, crawled back to bed, crashed out and snored all night. Are you surprised I didn't want to continue to share my bed with you after that?' Mary did not wait for a reply. She walked towards the door and just before she left, she turned to him and said, 'I think you're right. A divorce could well be the best solution to this mess.'

Great, thought Derek to himself, now I've got a crisis at home as well as one at work. He decided it was a good thing he was going to be away for a couple of nights. It would give both of them time to think about what had just been said. He waited for a while before going to his bedroom to pack his overnight bag, determined to leave early enough in the morning to avoid having to see Mary.

*　*　*

'It wasn't just me,' screamed Alice down the phone as soon as William had answered her call. Before he had a chance to respond, she continued in the same excited manner. 'Oh William, I can't thank you enough. I just had to tell you. I can't stop long because Mum's just about to put tea on the table but it wasn't just me.'

This time she paused just long enough for William to say, 'That sounds great but can you slow down a little and tell me what's happened?'

'OK, I'll tell you the main bits. We had a lovely birthday meal for Mum on Tuesday. It was great to see Aunt Penny, Uncle Bernard, Terry and Juliet. I got on very well with Juliet. She's lovely. She did ask me about bringing a plus one to the wedding. I told her I had someone in mind but hadn't asked them yet. Fortunately, she didn't push it as Mum was listening and I didn't want to explain about Robert in front of all of them. Anyway, this morning Mum was in such a good mood that, over breakfast, I said I wanted to explain to her about the events leading up to my pregnancy. I used your words about being just sexually curious teenagers but things had got out of hand. I didn't go into any more detail. I told her I was worried she might think I really was a little slut who went around sleeping with anyone who caught my fancy and wanted to assure her that was not the case, and, in fact, becoming pregnant had put me off sex and allowed me to concentrate on my studies, which was why I'd done so well at university. She said she'd often wondered if I had boyfriends but didn't want to ask as it

was such a sensitive subject and, no, she had never ever thought of me
as a slut. She told me calling me a slut was something Dad had said
in the heat of the moment, that he didn't believe it either and he had
regretted saying it and hitting me ever since.

'I then said, because we hadn't spoken about it, I'd never apologised
to her and Dad about causing their divorce and how very, very sorry
I was. All Mum did was look astonished and then burst into tears. It
was as if she couldn't speak. I didn't know what to do. I felt terrible for
bringing it up but then slowly Mum did start to speak through her tears.
I could hardly take in what she said and had to ask her to repeat it.
I eventually understood what she was saying, which was that it was
not my fault and *she* was apologising to *me*. She hadn't realised I even
thought I was to blame for the divorce, otherwise she would never have
let me believe it for so long. We both ended up crying and hugging
each other and we've talked and cried on and off for most of the day.

'Apparently, Dad had an affair about a year before I got pregnant.
As Mum put it, some nymphomaniac nurse threw herself at him and
he was too weak to resist. When Mum found out she tried to forgive
him and they agreed to keep it from me. However, when Dad hit me
and they argued, it was because she'd realised she couldn't forgive him.
All the subsequent arguments were about what to do about it all,
ending in an agreement to get divorced, but not until I'd left home
for university. So, you see, it wasn't just because of me. It would have
happened anyway. I feel so relieved. It's as if a great big weight has
been lifted from on top of me and it's all because of you. If you hadn't
persuaded me to tell you the whole story, I never would have been able
to talk to Mum like I did today. I really, really can't thank you enough.'

'You don't need to thank me. It was you who were brave enough
to do it. I'm just delighted it's all worked out well for you. I'm pleased
you called to tell me. Have a good journey back and I hope to see you
on Sunday.'

'Ah, there's been a change of plan. You won't see me on Sunday
because I'm not driving back until then. Mum's arranged for me
to meet up with Dad but not until Saturday as he's busy with lots of
operations until then. Mum still keeps in touch with him although he's
now remarried. He rings her to ask about me. She told me he went
to both of my graduation ceremonies and just sat at the back where I
wouldn't notice him. Mum thinks it's the same with Dad as it was with

her. He thinks we don't speak to each other because I haven't forgiven him for hitting me and I think it's because I caused the divorce. Now I know about the divorce, I'm really excited to see him, although it will no doubt be another painful and emotional conversation. Please will you explain to Robert yet again about me not being there on Sunday. I should definitely be there the week after.'

Suddenly William remembered about Robert's parents. 'There might not be a meeting that week,' he said. 'I forgot to mention when we spoke on Sunday that Robert's parents are visiting next week. Robert is insistent there's to be no reference to the Watson & Charles project whilst they are there. When I left them, Robert and Simon were putting together a plan in preparation for his parents' visit which includes serious cleaning and tidying up, so there might not be very much to talk about this Sunday either. They were putting Jake's name against some of the chores. You can imagine how that's likely to go down.'

'Jake would no doubt rather be swamped with tons of emails,' said Alice with a laugh. 'Oh, Mum asked me about my plus one for the wedding and I told her about Robert. She knew a little about Asperger's syndrome but only in a negative way. I found it difficult to explain there are good bits as well but I think she's now rather intrigued as she keeps pushing for more details.

'Sorry, got to go, Mum's just called to say tea's ready. Take care, William. I'll always remember it was you who taught me it was better to let things out rather than bottle them up. I wish I'd known years ago. Goodbye.'

'Goodbye, Alice,' said William as he switched off his phone and, full of thought, trudged to the fridge to open a bottle of his strongest beer.

Chapter Thirteen

William was enjoying his Sunday lunch and feeling quite pleased with himself. He had told Robert that Alice would be missing another Sunday and implied it would be better just to talk over lunch rather than have a formal meeting, in a manner that Robert could claim the idea as his own. Robert had even found a way to use one of his favourite phrases. 'If we do the same as last week,' he had said, 'it is only logical we will end up with the same result.' Robert had then offered to cook spaghetti alla carbonara which, William had to admit, was excellent and very much within Robert's capabilities although given the cream and lack of vegetables, it would probably not be considered a healthy option by Alice. It was again just the three of them. Jake was still unhappy and had suffered further meltdowns during the week, caused, according to Simon, by a combination of having to go through emails and do chores in preparation for the visit of Robert's parents.

'It's typical Jake,' said Simon towards the end of the meal. 'He's quite looking forward to Susan and Thomas being here but doesn't want to do the cleaning and tidying in advance. He always leaves everything like that to the last possible minute. He's supposed to be going shopping with me tomorrow morning at 10 o'clock but I'm 99 per cent certain he won't be ready. He never is.'

'That is partly your fault for setting such an early time,' said Robert. 'You know he doesn't do mornings.'

'Yes I do know. It was his suggestion,' replied Simon. 'He said he wanted to adjust his body clock in time for Wednesday but I just know when it comes to it, he won't want to get up.'

'If he's not ready on time, you could always go without him to teach him a lesson,' suggested William.

'Simon won't go out alone,' explained Robert, as if Simon wasn't present. 'He needs someone with him. Jake will go out alone. He sometimes goes for a walk on his own to help him recover from a meltdown, but if it's for shopping, he feels under pressure, and tends to make the wrong decisions and comes back without half the things he went for. It is a good example of teamwork. Jake makes Simon feel safe and Simon helps Jake cope with the chaos of shopping.'

'So, what's the plan for when your parents are here?' asked William. 'I was wondering if there was any chance of Tom helping in the garage to replace some of the shelves with racks. We're running out of space for the new servers I'm working on.'

'I have already suggested that,' replied Robert. 'Tom always asks what he can do. He should have plenty of time to spare. They are arriving on Wednesday afternoon and going up to London on Thursday. They've got tickets to go to a special exhibition Mum wants to see at the V&A, something to do with opera but apparently there's lots of art in it as well. On Friday, Mum's going to cook her famous sausage, egg and bacon pie for all of us, including you, Bill, if you want to come.'

'That would be great, Bob, thank you,' answered William before adding under his breath, '... flobbadob.'

'On Saturday, Mum wants to go clothes shopping so I suspect she will drag Tom with her even though he would prefer to stay here,' added Robert. 'However, they are not going back until Monday, leaving in the morning to make sure Mum gets back in plenty of time to run her art class in the evening, so there will be time on Sunday as well.'

William suddenly had an inspired thought. 'I've had an idea. To make sure Tom has plenty of time to do the shelves and to get him out of going shopping, why not suggest Alice goes shopping with Susan? It would be good for them to get to know each other. They've never met before, have they? Alice would probably enjoy a shopping trip, certainly more than Tom would.'

Robert hesitated over his reply. 'I am not sure that's a good idea. What if they don't get on? No, I think Mum would prefer to go with Tom. Tom will still have enough time on Friday and Sunday to do the shelves.'

Realising too late he'd got it wrong by rushing in and making it his own idea, William was unsure how to recover from his mistake. Fortunately, Simon came to his rescue by asking excitedly, 'Is Alice invited on Friday as well as William? She's part of our group now. It wouldn't be right to exclude her. Robert, your mum gets on well with most people and there's nothing not to like about Alice, is there? If Alice comes to dinner on Friday, then Susan can decide who she wants to go shopping with on Saturday,' adding as an afterthought, 'assuming Alice does want to go.'

'Mum only mentioned inviting Bill but I agree. If Bill is coming on Friday, it is only fair to invite Alice as well,' concluded Robert. 'I had better warn Mum first though as it will mean that the pie will have to stretch seven ways.'

Not wanting to risk Robert changing his mind, William avoided his usual flobbadob response. 'Great, that's settled then. Just make sure Alice has plenty of notice.' Then, rapidly changing the subject, he said, 'We haven't spoken much about the Watson & Charles project today. Is that because there hasn't been any progress? I certainly don't have anything to report and it doesn't sound as though Jake's got anywhere either. What about you two?'

Simon was the first to answer. 'I've been concentrating on the emails of my two board members, Stephen and Howard Watson. I've been trying to build up my own picture of the Watson & Charles business from the various board papers all the directors receive. I think I now understand a lot more of what Robert said last week. There's very little about Watson & Charles in their personal emails and Howard Watson gets relatively few emails compared with Stephen, who gets masses. I haven't come across anything strange apart from Stephen emailing things backwards and forwards to himself, so he can do some work at home. I'm surprised he's allowed to do this from a security risk point of view.'

'Both Derek Watson and John Hargreaves do the same,' said Robert. 'I suspect they all do. There doesn't appear to be any form of remote access from their home computers into the Watson & Charles systems. It is not something we should focus on.'

'The other thing I've managed to do this week,' added Simon, 'is to transfer across a blank version of Brewdat. I got this straight from the supplier without their knowledge, so it has nothing to do with

Watson & Charles and should be safe for us all, mainly Jake, to play around with and get a good feel as to how it works. I made sure I got version 12, the same one used by Watson & Charles. It's a program that has grown out of an enterprise resource planning system, which has been modified, expanded and updated over the years to make it suitable for all aspects of a brewing company. It links to almost everything from beer production to pub tills. It's essentially a large, modular database. Modules include production planning, quality assurance, warehouse stocks, pub performance, payroll and accounts. Reports can be generated from it on almost any aspect of the business. However, my impression from the Watson & Charles emails is the reports are not very user friendly. It seems to be standard practice to have data from the reports downloaded into Excel for manipulation, analysis and presentation. When Jake is next in a receptive mood, I'll talk him through it. As I say, he can't do any harm.'

'Yes, I noticed that too,' said Robert. 'All the attachments sent from Keith Fairbrother are as Excel spreadsheets. He seems to be something of an expert in Excel. Although I haven't done as much this week as I would have liked, I have gone through Keith's analysis in some detail. I was quite impressed. From the data he has analysed, his conclusions are logical. The first reference I found about his investigation dates back over nine months, to just after last Christmas when the results took an unexpected dip. One of his main findings was that all money was accounted for, suggesting, even then, he was searching for evidence of possible fraud. He came to the same conclusion in June, after it became clear the expected summer peak was not happening. On both occasions he analysed the Managed House Division as a whole and also carried out analysis of a number of individual pubs. This included a very in-depth analysis of The Black Horse, which had been the best-performing pub in 2016 but had fallen back significantly this year. It is a fact that he has put in a lot of work on trying to find an explanation. He found nothing untoward and, in one report, he states he couldn't find any obvious trends because every time he thought there might be one, the next month's results would disprove it. This is the only aspect that strikes me as strange because it would be logical for trends to exist. The absence of any trend is, therefore, a trend in itself.

'However, whilst we still need to understand more about his work, we need to be careful not to waste time just repeating it. Recently,

Derek has asked Keith to work with Ian Walters to have yet another look for fraudulent activity. It is likely that this request was prompted by the original email and my suggestion of a cyber-attack. We should be able to keep track of their findings as long as they email their reports to Derek. Also in Derek's emails was an agenda for a management committee meeting to be held on Wednesday. This meeting is to review their period 7, which effectively is September. When all the various reports have been issued and the minutes circulated, we should have a good idea of the recent results and their latest thinking.' Pausing for a moment, he added, 'Realistically, I'm unlikely to be able to do much more until my parents have been and gone.'

'You might be otherwise occupied for a while,' said William, 'but I have some spare time. Can I help in any way?'

'You might be able to help Jake,' replied Simon. 'It's going through the emails he mainly objects to. We originally asked him to do it to keep him occupied and safe, as well as hoping it would give him an insight into Watson & Charles's business. He gets upset when we ask him about them because he's not really doing them and, if there was anything of interest to be found, he would no doubt miss it. If you could look through the emails instead, William, I'm sure Jake would be a lot happier.'

'That's not a bad idea, Simon. Listening to the two of you, I feel a little left behind as you both seem to have picked up a lot about Watson & Charles from the emails of the directors you've seen. Hopefully, I can do the same. It's the Finance Director, Jeremy Turner, and the Tenanted Trade Director, Neil Martin, that Jake has, isn't it?' asked William.

'Yes,' said Simon, 'those are the two directors allocated to Jake. I'll ask him to redirect all their emails to you. I'm sure Jake will be delighted not to have to do them any more.'

Robert chipped in. 'I found the best way is to get an overview from attachments like board meeting minutes and then dig down into more specific areas of interest.'

As they had all finished eating, Simon stood up and started clearing the plates. 'Would you both like some tea?'

'Yes, please,' replied William. 'Then I think I'd better spend a bit of time in the garage to make sure Tom has enough room to work in.'

Whilst Simon cleared up and made the tea, Robert and William agreed a specification for the garage shelves so that Robert could explain to his father exactly what was wanted. After a short while, Simon returned with the tea.

'Sorry it's taken so long,' he explained, 'but I thought I'd go and tell Jake the good news and also remind him there's some carbonara down here for him. He admitted he'd done very little about going through the emails so, William, I'm afraid you'll need to start from scratch. He did say to tell you he'd been doing the bank thing instead. He's found five accounts for Watson & Charles, all linked, which he can access as a user or hack into if necessary.'

'There is no need to do any more on the bank side at the moment,' said Robert forcefully.

'Well, to me that does at least sound like some progress,' said William. 'When Alice asks, I'll be able to give her better news this week than I could last Sunday.'

'Don't make it sound too good,' said Robert pointedly.

'Why not?' asked William. 'Is there something else I should know?'

Robert didn't answer. Simon looked at him and then said cautiously, 'You haven't told William about the probabilities I calculated, have you?'

'No, you can tell him,' said Robert loudly, becoming visibly agitated. 'I am taking my tea upstairs so I can do more preparation for my parents' visit. Don't forget, there is to be no mention of Watson & Charles while they are here.'

As soon as Robert was out of earshot, Simon said quietly and in a conspiratorial manner, 'I'm worried about Robert. He's starting to give up on the Watson & Charles project. I know I was holding things back from a security point of view but I told Robert a few days ago I'd put enough safeguards in place to allow Jake loose, providing he kept me informed of what he was doing. It's now Robert who's holding Jake back and I think it's because Robert believes there's nothing for him to find after all.'

'Is this because of your probability calculations?' asked William.

'To some extent,' replied Simon. 'It came out as an 88 per cent chance of everything just being down to someone trying to take advantage of a slump in Watson & Charles's performance, so only a

12 per cent chance of someone actually doing something intentionally to cause the slump. However, when I told Robert, he wasn't surprised. I think he'd worked it out for himself and now he's scared that his original theory is incorrect.'

'Having got this far,' said William, 'surely it makes sense to continue and at least find out for certain.' Thinking about his role as a go-between, he added, 'I suppose I'll have to tell Alice. She won't like it as she's already worried about how Robert would cope with failure. While I remember, Alice asked about the forum. She thinks it would help Jake to have it back and just aid with communication in general.'

'I'm nearly there with the added security. Tell her I hope it will be ready by the weekend.' Then, with a large sigh, Simon exclaimed, 'Oh, I do miss Alice. We all do, even Robert, although, as usual, he won't admit it or even talk about her. We need her calming influence. It's only two weeks since she was last here but already we're reverting back to disagreements and meltdowns. I do hope she's able to come on Friday evening.'

'I'm sure she'll be there,' said William reassuringly as he stood up to go the garage, 'providing of course that Robert invites her.'

* * *

Pauline Sharples was struggling to focus on the task of typing up the minutes of that morning's management committee meeting. She couldn't stop herself thinking about Derek. All week there had been something about him that struck her as different and the way he had chaired the meeting that morning had only reinforced her feelings. He had been far more open about the predicament they were in than in the recent board meeting, even though there were non-directors present. He had told the meeting about his various conversations with other brewery chairmen during his trip to London. He said he was certain they would receive formal enquiries about whether the business was for sale and said he would not be surprised if shareholders were contacted directly with potential offers. Even when Jeremy Turner became highly animated and critical of the managed-house performance and suggested selling the brewery site, Derek had remained in charge and in control. In a calm manner, he had explained about the in-depth study on the Hare and Hounds to search for any sign of fraudulent activity and reported personally that Ian Walters and Keith Fairbrother had not found anything untoward that would directly affect the financial position. However, they had found a number of adverse reviews on external websites that did not correlate with the direct feedback received by the pub. Derek had concluded that this fitted in with the theory that another company was trying to undermine their performance before putting in a bid. He reiterated that he would do everything in his power to fight this off and asked everyone to let him have constructive proposals as to how each division and department could improve their end-of-year result.

Since the meeting, Derek had been closeted in his office talking to Stephen over a sandwich lunch, which he'd asked her to arrange. Normally, they would have gone to a pub for lunch so Pauline was intrigued as to what they were discussing. It was one of the few occasions where she wished she could just press a button and listen in without Derek knowing. As that wasn't an option, she decided to take her own lunch break and tackle the minutes afterwards.

Stephen had brought a couple of bottles of the latest trial brew for them to taste over lunch. He, too, wondered what Derek wanted to talk about. They stood for a while discussing the beer and looking out of the office window towards the brewhouse building, before moving to the two comfortable chairs with the coffee table between them where the plate of sandwiches had been placed. Whilst they were eating, they spoke generally about the period 7 results being more encouraging than they had expected compared with the previous six months. As soon as they had finished their sandwiches, Derek launched in.

'There are two important areas I want to talk to you about. The first is, in spite of what we were just saying about period 7, there is no way we'll recover from the first half of the year in time to avoid a disastrous end-of-year result. I'm now convinced this is primarily because of poor business decisions. Ian and Keith have come up with no other explanation and neither have the external consultants I employed. Secondly, we can now be certain someone is out there trying to divide the family. Not only that, it appears they have access to our latest results so are sure to use that information against us. Putting these two things together, it's highly unlikely we'll be able to prevent the majority of the more distant shareholders from voting to sell. That leaves the close family, starting with you and me.' Stephen tried to interrupt but Derek carried on.

'I know how passionate you are about us being brewers and having our own beers. The reason for wanting to talk to you today is to tell you I agree with you. The last time we spoke, I admit I was just trying to keep you on side but I've since thought about it some more and I'm now convinced you are right. When I was with the other family brewers last week, I did some digging of my own. I spoke to the chairmen of companies like ours who have invested in their breweries, such as Robinsons, Hook Norton, Wadworths and Adnams. They all agreed that trading conditions are difficult at the moment but the one thing they have in common is that they are sticking to their chosen strategies and marketing themselves as family brewers producing traditional beers of high quality. We're not doing that and I think we should be. The first thing we need is a modern brewery so we can be cost effective for our current scale of brewing and confident of the quality of our beers. How far have you got with looking at possible options?'

'To be honest,' replied Stephen, 'I've only got as far as a few rough ideas. I haven't consulted any suppliers yet. I didn't think you were serious in wanting to invest and I didn't, and still don't, see how we would get it past Jeremy.'

'Leave Jeremy to me,' said Derek firmly. 'The person we really need to convince is Father. It's his vote we need to survive any takeover bid. To achieve that, we need to present him with a long-term plan that he can believe in. Also, I want to put forward a proposal at the AGM to change the rules regarding share price and make the profit element based on the average of the last five years. I wish we'd done that last year but, as you know, Father objected. I think I'll be able to persuade him this time around as it would pretty much guarantee the share price rising the following year.'

'Well I would certainly welcome that,' said Stephen, starting to feel a little more hopeful. 'Money will be an issue though, even if you do find a way past Jeremy. Without any profit this year, the banks aren't likely to want to lend us much more, certainly not at a favourable rate.'

'That's why the plan has to be long term, flexible and deliverable. Whatever Father says now and however much his heart may want to keep the business, he'll only vote to do so if he truly believes it's in the best interests of the shareholders. We'll need to convince him this year is just a blip, albeit an extremely large blip, and, in my view, the only chance we stand of doing that is if the two of us are truly united on the way forward. As far as money is concerned, if we need to sell a couple of the larger pubs to fund the brewery, then we'll do it.' Derek sat back and finished the last mouthful of his beer. 'There is, of course, the possibility that the results are so bad this year that one or both of us doesn't think it worth carrying on. All I'm asking at the moment is we give it our best shot and keep talking openly and honestly to each other.'

'I don't want to see us go under without a fight,' said Stephen, determinedly. 'I'll put some firmer ideas together on the brewery front along with some outline costs and then we can talk again.' He half stood up but then sat back again. 'You said there were two areas to talk about. Is there something else?'

'Yes,' replied Derek, 'I'm afraid there is and it won't help our cause. You recall the frosty end to our family meal the other Sunday, when Mary talked about selling her shares. Well, I've not been able to dissuade her. She has definitely decided to sell. Under the rules, the Company has no choice but to buy at the current price, so we'll face a further loss in asset value when the share price drops next year.'

'But,' muttered Stephen, looking uncomfortable and struggling for a response, 'that was never the intention of having shares in our wives' names. Also, when other shareholders get wind of it, what will they think? It could create a cascade of selling and the business hasn't the cash available to buy back many more. That, in itself, would be the end of the road before we even get a brewery plan in front of Father. Surely, you could explain the situation to Mary and get her to change her mind.'

'Believe me, I have tried,' replied Derek. 'We had a lengthy conversation, the result of which is that Mary and I are getting divorced.'

'Holy shit,' exclaimed Stephen. 'Are you serious? I didn't realise things were so bad between the two of you.'

'Yes, I'm serious. It did come a bit out of the blue,' explained Derek, 'but, having had a chance to think it through, I'm not overly unhappy about it. We have grown apart. We've had separate rooms for almost two years. We don't seem to enjoy each other's company as much as we used to. We rarely talk about anything meaningful any more and we've developed different interests. Having a few days apart last week helped us both to consider the situation. Over the weekend, apart from the occasional accusation of blame, we had a surprisingly calm conversation and we both agreed a divorce was the best way forward. We've asked Josh and Pippa to come home next weekend and we plan to tell them then. We're going to try to keep it as amicable as possible for their sake. I'm sure many other couples have said the same thing about putting their children first but we're determined to try to do just that. Money is likely to be an issue because Mary is clearly more financially driven than I'd realised and will no doubt want to take me for all she can get.'

'Well, I'm still shocked and very sorry to hear about it. I'm sure Anthea will be too. It's the last thing you need on top of everything that's happening here. If there's anything I can do to help take off a bit of pressure, just let me know.'

'Thank you for your offer. Just to know I have your support is helpful. There is some good to come of it,' added Derek. 'As well as agreeing to a no-fault divorce, which should make the whole process quicker and easier, Mary has agreed to say she's only selling her shares because we're getting divorced and she will no longer be a part of the family. That will help significantly to manage the message and avoid the knock-on effect you mentioned. Also, there is always the chance that some other family member, who doesn't know of the current predicament, may step in to buy some of the shares.'

'I'm not sure it would be morally correct of us to allow that to happen, given what we know.' Then, with a perceptible nod towards the wall adjoining Pauline's office, Stephen said, 'I have to ask. Are you sure there's nothing that will come out in the wash to jeopardise the no-fault approach?'

Realising his meaning, Derek leant back in his chair and laughed. 'You mean between me and Pauline. No, nothing at all. I rely on her a lot and I feel I can trust her with anything but we just have a very close working relationship. I appreciate she is a very attractive lady so I can understand why you may think there's more to it. The only time it's got anywhere near personal is when I tried to help her as a friend whilst she was struggling with her own break-up a couple of months ago.'

'OK, I'll say no more, apart from,' Stephen added, with a sly grin on his face that reminded Derek of when they were children, 'if you need a friend now, I'm sure Pauline would be happy to return the favour.'

After Stephen had left. Derek moved round to the other side of his desk only to find he was pushing papers around because he was still thinking about what Stephen had said. He had heard Pauline come back from her lunch so he walked out of his office and put his head round her door. 'Would you be free for a drink after work this evening?' he asked.

Pauline looked up, hesitated a moment before replying, 'I can be. Why, is there some good news at last? I've just passed Stephen and thought he seemed quite happy.'

'I suppose it could be considered good news,' replied Derek.

'Great, what will we be celebrating?'

'My divorce.'

Chapter Fourteen

Alice was extremely flustered as she approached Robert's house. Not only was she nervous but she was late. She decided a few more minutes wouldn't make much difference so she pulled in to the kerb to compose herself before she turned the corner into Robert's road. She tried to convince herself she had been here many times before, that it was like a second home and she had nothing to worry about. Robert's text to invite her had been both short and confusing. The main problem was she couldn't help imagining the worst. She knew Jake had been having meltdowns and was probably struggling to cope with other people in the house. Apart from William, she was very aware she hadn't seen the boys since her emotional outburst and had no idea how they would react, but was certain they would ask awkward questions. She knew the Watson & Charles project wasn't going well and thought everyone would be frustrated because they couldn't talk about it whilst Robert's parents were there. On top of all that, she would be meeting Roberts's parents for the first time and was sure she would be scrutinised as this strange woman who had inveigled her way into their son's life. She wished she had given herself more time to prepare but, having been away for a week, there had been a lot to catch up on at work, plus a trip to head office to give her monthly presentation.

Her head was still full of all the thoughts generated from visiting her own parents. At least she had got out her clothes in advance, but only because she had woken up in the middle of the night in a panic, and now she was questioning whether her choice of denim skirt and woollen tights was the right one. She told herself it was too late to do anything about changing now and also remembered the conversation with William in the pub as to how nice Robert's parents were and how she could learn a lot about Robert from them. Encouraged by these thoughts and determined to adopt a cautious and steady approach, with hugging definitely out of the question, she steeled herself to continue.

At first, she was surprised to see two cars already in Robert's drive but then remembered that William now had a car instead of his old van. She walked towards the front door, half expecting it to open as she approached it, but it didn't. Somewhat apprehensively, she rang the doorbell. A few moments later the door was opened by Simon who beamed at her, ushered her in and closed the door behind her. Then, before she had chance to take off her coat, he threw both his arms around her, saying, 'Oh, Alice, it's wonderful to see you again. I've missed you so much.'

Realising that it was going to be hugs after all, Alice reciprocated, feeling the bristles of his recently buzz-cut hair against her chin. 'I've missed you all too. It feels a lot longer than three weeks since I was last here.'

Eventually, Simon released her and said, 'Let me take your coat. We're all in the lounge having drinks.' He opened the door of the snug and threw her coat inside. Then he moved across the hall to open the door to the lounge before announcing in a loud and excited voice, 'Look, everyone, Alice is here.' Alice was suddenly aware the conversation had stopped and all eyes were on her. She was struggling to take in the blur of both familiar and unfamiliar faces when Simon continued. 'Alice, say hello to Robert's mum, Susan. Susan makes the most fantastic sausage, egg and bacon pie. It's become a tradition that she cooks it for all of us when she comes to stay. You'll love it.'

'No pressure then, Simon,' said Susan with a laugh as she stood up and moved towards Alice.

Quickly regaining her composure, Alice extended her arm. 'Good evening, Mrs Tait, I'm very pleased to meet you,' she said politely, whilst coming to terms with the fact that Robert's mother looked nothing like she had imagined. For some reason, Alice had imagined a tall, slender and elegant lady, whereas, in reality, Susan was quite short and plump with grey, wavy, slightly tousled hair, a lopsided mouth, spectacles and a crooked smile. She was wearing a bright orange flowery dress which was slightly too small for her and highlighted some unsightly bulges.

'It's lovely to meet you as well, Alice,' responded Susan as she took Alice's hand warmly into both of her own. 'There's no need to be so formal. I feel I know you already, I've heard so much about you. You must call me Susan and, over here, is my other half, Tom.' Whilst Alice was trying to work out what she would have heard and from whom, Susan guided Alice across the room to shake hands with Tom, a tall, bald man with a round smiling face and prominent dark eyelashes.

Tom had been sitting next to William, who had also stood up as Alice approached. After Tom and Alice had exchanged pleasantries, William, without saying anything, held out his arms and gave her an enormous hug. Alice suddenly started to feel very emotional and wanted to tell William all about the visit to her father. Instead, in an effort to keep her emotions in check, she said, 'I like your new car.'

As she pulled away from William, Alice noticed that Robert was standing next to her as if waiting for his turn. As she looked at him, he hesitantly moved his arms towards her and spoke softly. 'Hello, Alice.'

All of a sudden, Alice didn't care any more who was watching. She gave him a hug and a squeeze and kissed his cheek. 'Hello, Robert. It's good to be back. I've missed you. How are you?'

'Fine, thank you,' replied Robert in a factual tone as, hug over, he sat back down in his chair.

As Alice was looking around to find somewhere to sit, she realised Jake was sitting on the sofa next to Susan. He was not, however, easily recognisable. His hair had been washed and cut into an almost girlish bob. He was wearing a tailored dark-blue shirt and neatly pressed grey trousers, neither of which Alice even knew he possessed. Apart from his acne, his appearance was only spoilt by the scruffy old slippers he always wore. Having hugged all the others, Alice resigned herself to having to hug Jake as well. Thinking, at least he's clean, she took a couple of steps towards him but, before she could speak, he rose, extended his right hand in a very awkward fashion and, avoiding eye contact, said, 'Good evening, Alice.'

Happy to be saved from a hug, Alice shook his hand instead. 'Good evening, Jake. It's nice to see you looking so smart.'

Not sure what to do next, Alice was saved by Susan who said, 'Jake, Alice hasn't got a drink. Please will you do the honours?'

'What would you like?' asked Jake.

'Just an orange juice please, Jake,' replied Alice, still coming to terms with his apparent transformation.

'You can sit over here, next to me,' called Simon. Alice turned and recognised one of the sofas from the conservatory which had been brought through to give extra seating. Almost as soon as she had sat down, Jake returned with her orange juice. She noticed his limp was worse than she remembered.

Feeling a little more relaxed, Alice said, 'I'm sorry I'm late. It's been very hectic at work this week. Can I do anything to help? I hope nothing is spoiled.'

'Well, I did put 7 p.m. in my text and it is now 7.23,' answered Robert, pulling himself away from listening to the conversation between Tom and William.

'Given that you had very little notice, dear, we're just delighted that you could make it at all, aren't we, Robert?' said Susan pointedly. 'You don't need to worry. All is under control, isn't it, Jake? Although, saying that, it probably is time to go and put together the finishing touches. Please excuse us. Come along, Jake.'

As soon as they had left the room, Alice couldn't resist asking Simon quietly, 'What's happened to Jake? I've never seen him like this before. I thought I might not see him at all tonight as William implied that he had been very unhappy and was back to having lots of meltdowns.'

'He has had a few meltdowns,' whispered Simon in reply, 'but they've been more to do with the W & C project. Jake quite likes it when Tom and Susan are here. It's the preparation in advance he doesn't like. He gets on well with Susan most of the time. They tend to do lots of deals. For instance, it was Susan who cut Jake's hair on the condition that he showered both before and after doing it. He helps Susan before the meals so that, if it gets too much for him, he can leave at any time with no questions asked. By the way, you do know not to mention W & C tonight, don't you?'

'Oh, yes,' replied Alice. 'Robert made that very clear in his text, as well as it being the very first thing he put on the forum, now it's back up. Thanks for getting it up and running again, by the way. I'm sure it will help us all to communicate better.'

'I still don't consider it 100 per cent secure, so I don't recommend putting anything too sensitive on there.'

'Simon, as we've all told you many times before,' said Alice jokingly, 'we have got the message that, in your view, nothing is 100 per cent secure.' Simon laughed.

Raising her voice a little so the others could hear, Alice said, 'I'm pleased to see this room looking like a proper lounge. Sometimes when I come here, it looks more like some sort of computerised control room. Where has all the computer equipment gone? Is it in the garage?'

'I hope not,' exclaimed Tom in response. 'These two have told me everything that can be moved out of the garage has been. It was a bit cramped working in there today. We're just talking about how we might create a little more space for tomorrow. I could do with more room to work in as I'm worried about damaging some of the equipment.'

'The computing equipment from here is distributed throughout our three bedrooms,' said Robert, replying to Alice's original question. 'We will need to move it all back after my parents have left. We can all hardly move in our rooms. There is only just enough space to get to our beds. We are generally getting very tight for space. William and Tom are planning how to use the garage more efficiently.' It seemed to Alice there wasn't much planning going on but that William and Tom were just happily chatting over a beer.

'We're trying to make best use of Tom's DIY skills whilst he is here,' explained William. 'That's why it's good that you're able to go on the shopping trip with Susan tomorrow.'

'What shopping trip?' asked Alice, sounding surprised. 'I don't know anything about any shopping trip.'

'Yes, you do,' said Robert firmly. 'It was in my text and you replied yes to both tonight and shopping.'

'Oh, is that what "+ Sat shop" meant?' said Alice, with a sudden realisation. 'How on earth do you expect me to work anything out from that?'

'Well, if you did not understand, you should have asked,' said Robert defensively. 'You usually ask if you do not understand something. Anyway, you cannot change your mind now. We have got everything worked out and Tom says he will need the whole weekend to finish the job.'

Feeling her temper starting to rise, Alice responded in a loud voice. 'How can I change my mind when I didn't make a decision in the first place? I told you earlier I've been very busy. Your text wasn't clear enough. I thought it was just something to do with buying a bit of food. I bet you just assumed I'd be free because I'm usually free on a Saturday. If it had been the other way round, you'd have wanted to know all the details first, wouldn't you?'

Before Robert could respond, Tom, who had many years of acting as peacemaker between Robert and Susan, leapt in. 'Alice, it's not a problem if you're unable to go. We can change our plans and I can go instead. I can work on the garage afterwards.'

Alice was on the brink of saying she had better things to do, with the intention of trying to teach Robert a lesson, when she looked up and saw William staring at her, shrugging his shoulders and opening his palms towards her as if to say, 'Think about it'. Quickly realising that William may well have had a hand in setting this up so that Alice could spend time alone with Susan, Alice calmed down and changed her mind. 'No, it's fine. As it happens I am free tomorrow.' Unable to resist, she added, 'It would just have been nice to have been asked properly in the first place.'

The conversation was interrupted by the opening of the door into the dining room. They all looked up to see Jake standing in the doorway. In an uncharacteristic voice, he announced clearly, 'Lady and Gentlemen, dinner is served.'

They had been correct. Susan's sausage, egg and bacon pie had been delicious. The conversation had flowed well, no doubt helped by the presence of more alcohol than usual. Alice had offered William a lift home and to pick him up the following morning, so that he could have more beer and keep Tom company. Susan had a couple of glasses of red wine and even Simon had a small glass of wine with his pie. The rest of them settled for soft drinks. Everyone had seemed fully relaxed, even Jake, who had been seated between Susan and Alice. Alice had noted that contentious topics were avoided, apart from the occasional reference to the shopping trip. Alice was taken with the way Tom and Susan had handled this. Both of them had criticised Robert but also explained why he should have made it clearer for Alice to understand what he was asking. Instead of getting upset, Robert had just said 'stereo parents' with a smile and all three of them had laughed.

Having eaten far more than usual, Alice was feeling quite full as she was making her way back into the lounge, this time just with Susan for company. Jake had had enough and gone back upstairs. The men had been asked by Susan, in a way that sounded more like an instruction, to clear up. At the same time, she had excused Alice on the grounds that the two of them needed to plan their shopping trip. Susan closed the door and indicated they should sit together on the sofa so they could talk quietly without being overheard.

'I get the impression you have been coerced into going shopping with me tomorrow. Please don't feel you have to come. You must have much better things to do with your time than spend it trailing around clothes shops with an old fuddy-duddy like me.'

'No, it's not that at all. There was just some confusion over Robert's text. Now I understand what it meant, I'm quite happy to come.' Feeling much more at ease, Alice almost blurted out that she wanted to go to hear about Robert and Asperger's syndrome rather than the shopping itself but stopped herself just in time, instead asking, 'Are you intending to go into London?'

'I really don't mind, dear. If it had been Tom and me, we would no doubt have settled on Croydon. We've been a few times before. It's easy to get to by train but I suppose it doesn't have a lot more to offer from a shopping point of view than Bournemouth. I'm just as happy to go to London or anywhere else you suggest.'

'I don't mind either. London obviously has more choices for shopping but will be busy and expensive. I quite like Kingston. It's a bit further than Croydon but it's nice by the river and there's both the Bentall Centre and Eden Walk for shopping. If you haven't been before, it would be somewhere different for you.' Thinking about maximising the time available for talking, Alice added, 'I don't mind driving. That way we wouldn't have to carry everything back on the train. I've got to bring William here first anyway so it would all fit together nicely.'

'That sounds like a lovely idea, if you're really sure you're happy to drive. I've never been to Kingston before so it will all be new to me.'

'Good, that's sorted.' Then, feeling the need to be open and honest, Alice confessed, 'I have to warn you, I will no doubt want to pick your brains about Asperger's syndrome. I was extremely impressed with how you were with Jake this evening.'

'I half wondered whether you might have an ulterior motive,' laughed Susan. 'Just because I'm Robert's mum doesn't make me an expert in Asperger's syndrome but I suppose I have learnt quite a lot about it over the years. Like most parents, my son is one of my favourite subjects so I'll certainly be happy to tell you whatever you want to know. As far as Jake is concerned, I treat him just like I did Robert when Robert was in his early teens. It's a matter of doing whatever you can to help him through the chaos and confusion he feels in social situations. I try to explain in simple terms what's happening and to give him tasks to do so he feels involved. It doesn't work every time but it seems to work most of the time. Also, giving him choices as part of a task usually helps as it allows him to feel a degree of control. Like Robert, the more he does, the more he will learn for himself. Robert was very fortunate, being diagnosed so early. Jake was not so lucky and, therefore, has not had the same support and opportunity to practise in safe situations.'

'Still, it's quite an achievement to get him to be so presentable. What about his leg, though? He's always had a limp since I've known him and I thought tonight it was particularly bad. Do you know what causes it?'

'I wish I did but I don't,' replied Susan exasperatedly. 'I've tried asking him in different ways but it's clearly a sore point because he won't answer and he quickly gets annoyed and storms off if I try to pursue the issue. I've obviously not yet built up enough of his trust for him to feel comfortable to tell me. My best guess is it's from something that happened to him years ago when he was being bullied. One day he might feel able to talk about it.'

'Yes, hopefully one day ...' Alice replied, thinking about the conversation she had with William about Robert in the pub. Then, not wanting to give herself away, she changed the conversation slightly. 'I do have another question. I was intrigued earlier when you said you'd heard a lot about me. Who from and what?'

'Oh, nothing to worry about, dear. It was all good. Everybody seemed to want to tell me good things about you.' Pausing for a moment, Susan listened and then continued. 'Sorry, I thought I heard them coming in. I'll tell you briefly and then I suggest we leave the rest of this conversation until tomorrow. From Robert, as you might expect, it's all fact. He's told me that you are a brilliant scientist, that you and he talk a lot about the similarities between genetic codes in DNA and the coding of computers. I don't always understand the detail but it's clear that you challenge his thinking about robots in a way that interests him. Simon seems to look upon you as a mother figure, mainly because of your cooking, and Jake views you as the sister he never had.

'William is a real admirer. He says that the atmosphere within this house has been transformed since you became part of the circle. He says you've helped him to think a lot about his own situation, including his decision to retire. He particularly likes the way in which you stand up to Robert, not letting him have all his own way but, equally, not pushing him too far when he's vulnerable. I enjoyed hearing that as it's similar to my own approach. William also told me earlier today you haven't been around for a few weeks and that all three of them had suffered as a result. From the reaction I saw myself when you walked in the door tonight, I could tell he was right and they were all delighted to have you back.'

'Wow,' said Alice, feeling the colour rush to her cheeks. 'I wasn't expecting all that … Jake's sister … what a relief. Yes, let's move on and talk about something else now. This is all quite embarrassing.'

* * *

The following morning, Alice was pleased to see William was waiting for her outside his shop at 9 a.m. as planned. He had left it ready for Nancy to open up later. There was little sign of the after effects of the previous evening's alcohol consumption, despite Alice having to persuade William it was time to leave and not getting a sensible word out of him on the drive back to his flat. They had just enough time on the short journey to Robert's for them to catch up on Alice's visit to her father and the current status of the Watson & Charles project. Both of them were looking forward to their respective days; William working with Tom and Robert, Alice shopping and talking with Susan.

Whilst she was driving to Kingston, Alice was trying not to be too obvious about her desire to find out more about Robert. She also got the impression that Susan was keen to find out more about her. After Alice had thanked Susan for a lovely evening, they talked generally about their lives and interests so that, by the time they arrived, both knew much more about each other's backgrounds. Alice was growing to like Susan a lot. She found her easy to talk to and, although Susan hadn't asked any really prying questions, Alice had been surprised to find she was able to talk about her childhood and parents' divorce in a factual way without feeling overly emotional. Her feeling of guilt over the divorce seemed to have evaporated and she easily managed to avoid mentioning her abortion or the events leading up to it.

Having parked without too much difficulty, they headed for the Bentall Centre to begin their shopping. Susan had asked Alice if there was anything she particularly wanted to look for. The only thing Alice could think of was a new business suit, which she didn't really want but was conscious of the fact she always wore the same suit when going to her monthly meetings at head office. In response, Susan admitted her own requirements were more vague, saying she thought it was time to change her wardrobe to reflect her age. They had decided to start in Bentalls itself but, as they were going up one of the escalators, Susan spotted a sign for Costa Coffee and suggested they have a coffee first. Alice happily agreed as, for her, the shopping was secondary. All she was really interested in was finding out as much as possible about Robert. As soon as they had sat down, Susan with a cappuccino and Alice with a skinny latte, Susan spoke as if she had read Alice's mind.

'I know we're here to shop for clothes but we must make sure you have time to ask all your questions about Robert and Asperger's syndrome. Once we get back, there may not be another chance.'

Alice grasped the opportunity. 'Six months ago, I'd hardly heard of Asperger's but, having met Robert, Simon and Jake, I've tried to find out more. I've read some books and William has also helped me but I still seem to say or do the wrong things. Also, I know it's a spectrum but I don't understand the differences between the three of them so I was very interested yesterday with how you handled Jake as opposed to Robert. You said that Robert was diagnosed early. Is it as simple as that?'

'I don't think anything about Asperger's is simple. I do think, however, that you can take Simon out of the equation. In my view, the main problem with Simon is, as my grandmother would have put it, he's scared of his own shadow. When he feels safe and secure, as he seemed to be last night, he's fine. Look how he joined in the conversation and picked up on people's feelings, totally different from both Robert and Jake. In fact, that was the most relaxed I've ever seen him.'

'But he goes to the Asperger's group every fortnight with Jake,' pointed out Alice. 'How does that work if he isn't Aspie, and why doesn't Robert go too?'

'I see you've learnt the terminology,' laughed Susan. 'As I understand it, Simon's and Jake's mothers knew each other. Both were concerned their sons were becoming recluses and, for different reasons, felt it was past time for them to have left home. As Jake is pretty much a text-book Aspie, Jake's mother knew that was his problem but didn't know what to do about it or where to go for help. Simon's mother hadn't considered Asperger's but, when it was suggested to her, she was much more proactive in trying to do something about it. She found out about the Asperger's group and so Simon and Jake ended up going together. As they're both so heavily into computers, they got on pretty well and became friends, the only friend either of them had. You probably already know that's where they met Robert as well, although Robert doesn't talk about it much because of the Crawtech situation.'

'Not really. It's one of those subjects that, when I ask about it, Robert says I'm being annoying, won't answer and gets cross.'

'That's certainly typical of Robert. What happened was this. When Robert joined Crawtech, they obviously knew he was Aspie and there were also another couple of Aspies working there as technicians, who were in the same Asperger's group as Simon and Jake. They invited Robert to the group and, at one meeting, he gave a talk about how he'd been successful in getting to university and becoming a trainee manager at Crawtech. Simon and Jake got to know him and, when they found out he had such a big house, persuaded him to let them rent a room each. Shortly after they moved in, Robert lost his job and hasn't been back to the group since. It's because, having presented himself as a success, I don't think he wants to be reminded of his failure.' Susan paused for a moment to finish her coffee.

'One piece of advice I can give you is when Robert uses the word "annoying", it's usually best to change the subject fairly quickly. Then, look for an opportunity at a later date to tackle the same subject but from a different angle, making sure you explain clearly why you want to know. It doesn't always work but it's usually better than having a full-blown falling out. Also, you need to be able to work out if he's using it just to fob you off. One of the biggest problems Tom and I had when he was growing up was, because he's clever, he would use his Asperger's to play us off against each other and to get us to give in to him. We ended up coining the phrase "spoiled-brat syndrome" as we were convinced that was how he would end up if we put everything down to Asperger's and always took the easy option. The other thing was we tried to talk to each other and agree a strategy before broaching any tricky topic with Robert. Hence his reference to stereo parents last night.'

'Yes, I was fascinated by that,' said Alice. 'At one point, I thought it was going to spoil such a lovely evening so I was pleasantly surprised when it ended in laughter.'

'Humour can be a useful tool as well. Tom is much better at it than me. There were many occasions in the past where Robert was heading for a meltdown but Tom managed to get a hint of a smile from him which allowed us to recover the situation.' Alice was engrossed in the conversation so was disappointed when Susan went on to say, 'Come on, time for some shopping. Let's see if we can find you a nice power suit.'

Although Alice's heart wasn't set on shopping, she couldn't help getting caught up in Susan's enthusiasm, so much so that she wondered if she should mention also needing an outfit for Terry's wedding. Deciding against it, Alice committed to trying on a few suits and was quite surprised to find she really liked a light-brown one that Susan had suggested. As it was quite expensive, Alice wanted to think about it before buying so insisted they look for something for Susan. They browsed for a while but without any success, so decided to have a break for lunch. They both chose salads. Very quickly, the conversation returned to the subject of Robert.

'There's something I want to show you that might help you understand Robert better,' said Susan, 'but first let me tell you about Robert's diagnosis. The initial suggestion of Asperger's syndrome was made when he was at pre-school. We were very lucky as the head there had previous experience and said it would explain a lot of Robert's behaviour. He would seek out adult company in preference to other children and, when he did play with other children, it was not very long before he'd upset one or more of them. When he went to primary school, even though he was a high performer in many areas, he was labelled a troublemaker but, as we were able to suggest it was due to Asperger's, they put him forward for medical assessment. The whole process took almost a year, by which time Tom and I already knew the answer, although it was quite a relief to have it confirmed officially. Like you, we had to learn from scratch and we made many mistakes along the way. However, it also helped to explain a number of the issues we had when he was very little that we'd put down to us being poor parents. From a schooling point of view, having a statement of special needs allowed him to have a dedicated learning assistant to help him. Most of the time this prevented him from getting into too much trouble but there were still occasions when the phone would ring and I would have to go and collect him because the school couldn't cope.'

'That can't have been very nice for you,' remarked Alice.

'No, but it got a lot worse once Robert found out about robots.'

'What do you mean?' asked Alice. 'He's always told me that his interest in robotics is one of the main things that helped him through both school and university.'

'Maybe, but when he was younger, it was almost his downfall. All the way through his schooling and even early years at university, the main problem was an inability to match Robert's thirst for knowledge. He's always been like a sponge, soaking up facts and information on all sorts of subjects. He could read before he was two and was constantly asking questions. He kept Tom and me on our toes and we were always helping him to find out answers to his questions, as were his learning assistants at school. Consequently, in some subjects, he ended up knowing more than his teachers.'

'And robotics was one of those?' interrupted Alice.

'More than likely,' replied Susan, 'but that wasn't the issue. He got so engrossed and obsessed by anything to do with robots. He would go around the house shouting "I am a robot", "robots are based on logic and make sense", "human beings don't make sense". Tom and I could just about put up with it but you can imagine how it went down at school when he would shout out at the teacher "you are just a stupid and illogical human being".

'Yes, I can see why that would be a problem,' said Alice, smiling.

'We went to endless meetings and got to know a number of the teachers quite well. Tom and I talked a lot about how to deal with all the issues. One of the difficulties we had was we could see Robert's point of view. The teachers who really knew their subject would find a way to engage with Robert either within the classroom or outside it. He got on fantastically well with them and consequently got very high marks. It was the teachers who just tried to stay one step ahead of the class and didn't want to be questioned that Robert disliked and who called for Robert to be disciplined and excluded. It was having a statement of special needs that saved him. That's what I mean when I talk about someone like Jake not being so fortunate.'

'I suspect Robert was also very fortunate to have parents like you and Tom.'

'As parents, you do your best to help your child, whatever the issue. It just so happened for us the issue was Asperger's. Once we were able to understand a little bit more, we started to build up our own confidence that we were doing the right things. We were helped, when he was nine, by a major breakthrough that allowed us to get a feeling of how things looked from Robert's perspective. I'm sure you've noticed that when Robert eats his food, he eats one part at a time, usually meat followed by potatoes followed by veg. One tea time, I was bringing him his plate of breaded fish, chips and peas. As I put the plate down in front of him he had the screaming heebie-jeebies because one pea had rolled off the pile and ended up touching a chip. I wasn't prepared to put up with his behaviour so I told him how ridiculous it was to make such a fuss over just one pea. However, I had learnt by then that it was always a good idea to try to give him a logical explanation or reason. The previous evening, I had made Spanish omelette for tea and I had thrown in a few left-over peas. He'd eaten that without any fuss. I pointed out it wasn't logical for him to eat the peas all mixed in with the omelette and then object to one pea just touching a chip. That calmed him down enough for him to try to defend his reasoning by saying that in the omelette everything was meant to be mixed together whereas the fish, chips and peas were meant to be separate. He still refused to eat the offending pea and carefully moved it to his side plate.

'Trying to lighten the conversation, Tom suggested what Robert really needed was someone to invent a square pea that would stay put and not roll. Robert did start to smile but, being Robert, had to argue the case. He said peas were three-dimensional and, therefore, it would be a cubic pea, not a square one. He went on to say it reminded him of what had been said at school, that Aspies were like square pegs in round holes, but he had never understood the saying because pegs were three-dimensional like peas. We then had a debate about whether a round hole was two or three dimensional. Robert concluded he was happier thinking of himself as a cubic peg in a spherical hole, although when he said it he said pea instead of peg. We all burst out laughing. The whole situation had been diffused and the rest of the meal passed smoothly. Since that day, we've had many a conversation about cubic peas.'

'What a lovely story,' exclaimed Alice. 'I can just imagine Robert being like that. I must remember the part about giving him a logical explanation.'

'That wasn't the end of the story,' said Susan, as she rummaged in her handbag. 'Six years later, Robert came home from school one day and marched in the front door with an enormous grin on his face, saying he'd got a present for me. He gave me this.' Alice looked down and saw Susan was holding a green plastic ball. It was rather like an airflow plastic golf ball with holes in the outside and a solid green plastic cube in the middle. 'I knew immediately what it was,' said Susan, 'but Robert had to tell me how he designed it for printing on the 3D printer they'd recently acquired at school. He proudly said "It's a cubic pea in a spherical hole. It is a good analogy for how an Aspie like me views the world. I'm the cube and the struts of the sphere are like window frames. When I look out, I sometimes see clearly through the holes. Other times, usually when people are involved, the frames get in the way and I can't see clearly. That's when I get frustrated and annoyed." I was so excited, not just to have it but to hear him open up like that. You can only really judge his emotions through his actions and it was one of the rare occasions when I could tell he loved me. Then I blew it. Without thinking, I said it was very well made and reminded me of a ship in a bottle, in that you couldn't see how the cube had got inside and there was no obvious way out. Robert's face changed. The smile was gone and replaced with one of his thunderous looks. "That's the whole point, Mother," he said and raced up to his bedroom, slamming the door behind him.'

Alice was lost for words, caught between imagining the scene and wondering whether there were frames blurring Robert's vision of her. Susan continued.

'Initially, I was upset at spoiling such a lovely moment but, when I told Tom, his view was Robert's reaction was an important element of the story as it highlighted how easy it was for him to interpret something in a different way to how it was intended. Tom wanted a cubic pea for himself and, a few days later, asked Robert to make another one. Robert refused, saying there was only one of him and so there should be only one cubic pea. I know it's only a bit of cheap plastic but it's become one of my most cherished possessions.'

Somehow, the cubic pea story had cemented a bond between Alice and Susan. They completed their shopping trip in a relaxed fashion, both persuading the other to buy. On the journey home Susan invited Alice to stay for the evening meal, saying it was Robert's turn to cook, that he always did risotto and always made loads of it.

This time it was William who had to persuade Alice it was time to leave. He had decided not to drink so he could drive himself home and be refreshed for the final day on the garage project. Susan was intending to use the Sunday as a cleaning day to ensure the house was cleaner than when they arrived. Alice thought about offering to help but then remembered all her own chores that needed to be done. She didn't, however, need any persuasion to go back in the evening for another family tradition, Susan and Tom's farewell meal of slow-cooked pork chops.

As soon as Alice got back to her flat, she realised how tired she was. It had been a hectic two weeks but she had been well and truly invigorated and felt extremely happy. It was as if she had gone from having no real family to being part of two different families, her own and Robert's. She thought of all the nice things that had happened but, just before she closed her eyes, her overriding memory was of giving Robert his now customary goodbye hug and kiss, when she felt the gentle brush of his lips on her cheek in return.

Chapter Fifteen

'It's your father and he's not happy,' warned Pauline on the following Tuesday as she put the call through to Derek.

'Good morning, Father,' Derek said as soon as he heard the phone click.

'It's not a good bloody morning,' bellowed Howard Watson. 'What the hell is going on? Profits are non-existent. It was only last week you told us you were getting a divorce and now I've received official notification Mary is selling her shares.'

'You know Mary can't continue to be a shareholder if she's no longer going to be part of the family,' replied Derek calmly.

'Yes, but she didn't need to act now. She could have waited. It will take ages for the divorce to come through. How will it look when we tell the other shareholders that a large packet of shares is available? They're bound to find out they were Mary's. Given what we know about this year's performance and the impact on the share price, it's worse than insider trading. The wife of the Chairman, for Christ's sake. Morally, we can't let anyone buy them who doesn't know the current situation, so the Company will take the hit. That will be another two million down.'

'It's only a transfer of assets so won't affect this year's result,' said Derek defensively. 'I've explained all this to Mary but she's adamant she wants to sell immediately and there's nothing I can do to stop her. Neither she nor I have any problem with telling people it's because of the divorce. If anyone does enquire about buying them, I can have a quiet word and suggest they wait until after the year end.'

'Don't be so bloody naive. If you do, word will spread like wildfire and we'll have loads of others wanting to sell. It would bring the Company to its knees. It feels wrong not telling people how bad it is but, fortunately, we're not a public company otherwise we would have had to issue a major profits warning before now.'

'If we were a public company, we wouldn't have all these archaic rules about shares and share price,' retorted Derek. 'If you'd supported me last year in changing to an average of the last five years' profits, it wouldn't be half so bad. I assume you'll agree to changing the rules this time around?'

'Don't try and blame all this on me,' shouted Howard down the phone. 'I had twenty-seven years in charge and the share price didn't drop once.'

'Yes, but you had the option of taking property profits when you needed to,' argued Derek. 'You did have bad years operationally. Times have moved on and property values have stagnated so there's no back-up any more, so when we have a bad year like this one, there's nowhere to go to cover it up. That's why we need to change the rules so one bad year doesn't have such a drastic impact on the share price.'

'I thought I'd taught you better than that. Even though they are family, most shareholders don't care. They've been used to getting regular dividends and seeing a small but steady increase in the value of their shares each year. They were disappointed enough last year when the price went down, even though the dividend was maintained. You explained that away as a blip. How do you think they'll feel in April when you announce the share price is halved and the dividend is negligible? Another bloody big blip! And,' stressed Howard, 'don't think that's a guess on my part. I spoke to Jeremy yesterday and he sent me the same document he sent you over a week ago, which you obviously didn't have the balls to tell me about.'

Without realising, Derek was tightening his grip on the phone. 'That was just some theoretical forecasts. Results from the last few weeks have been better and we don't know what Christmas will bring.'

'It pains me to say it, Derek, but I can't support you any more. You're burying your head in the sand. We both know summer is when most of the profit is made and you haven't made any this year. You've lost control of the business and you've now lost control of your wife. You've sat on the fence over John Hargreaves and come up with this cock-and-bull idea of a cyber-attack, for which there seems to be no evidence whatsoever.'

Derek tried to explain. 'There is some evidence that fake adverse reviews are being placed on the internet with the aim of putting people off going to our pubs.'

'Derek,' said Howard, getting infuriated, 'that's hardly going to make millions of pounds' worth of difference, is it? The vultures have been circling for years and trying to do things to undermine us and get through to our shareholders. Just because these days they're using modern technology to do it makes no difference. Fending them off is all part and parcel of the job, a job which you are failing to do. Where's your fight? Where's your backbone? You're letting the whole thing fall apart around you.'

'Look Father, I know we haven't got any clear explanation for this year but, equally, we've confirmed there are lots of things we're doing well. All I need is time,' pleaded Derek. 'As long as you, Stephen and I stick together, we can get beyond this year and the AGM. I'm already working with Stephen on a plan for the future.'

'I don't think you're hearing me,' said Howard, resignedly. 'The reason for ringing is to tell you I've made my decision. I have to look at it from a shareholder's perspective. If a suitable offer comes in for the business, as I'm sure it will, then I will be voting to sell and encouraging other shareholders to do the same. There's no point in discussing this any further. My mind is made up. Goodbye, Derek.'

Derek slowly put down his phone. It was a very long time since his father had spoken to him like that. The reality started to dawn on him that, after over two hundred years of brewing, he was the one who would be responsible for the end of Watson & Charles.

* * *

Alice was beginning to wish the forum was not back up and running after all. All week it had mostly been negative comments. The main problem was the computer system had not been working properly since the weekend. Tom's part of the project had been completed successfully but William had been round every evening since trying to sort out the issues. Simon was getting quite apoplectic about the loss of security.

Robert was still able to access the Watson & Charles emails but seemed to be making little progress and continuing to lose interest. The one who was happiest was Jake because the Brewdat test system was unaffected. Alice got the impression he was treating it like a computer game as he was constantly posting about adding another pub and boasting how he could make money when Watson & Charles couldn't.

Alice had decided to keep out of the various discussions and focussed on catching up on her work and domestic chores. However, when Robert suggested a Sunday meeting, Alice felt she had to intervene. It was obvious William didn't think a meeting was a good idea and, from Simon's and Jake's responses, there didn't seem too much in the way of good news to report. Thinking about what she had learned from Susan, Alice suggested they just have a discussion over lunch, arguing that with the previous meetings, she had missed too much of the debate because of having to cook. She also added that she had been thinking of doing another Sunday roast, this time with chicken, but if they all wanted to have a meeting, she would be happy to bring sandwiches instead. Within just a few minutes of sending her message, she was not surprised to find she had received four replies, all opting for roast chicken and no meeting. Good for Susan!, she thought, and was just about to contact Robert about helping with the preparation when she was suddenly inspired. Instead, she sent a personal message to Jake, asking if he would help her on the same terms as he helped Susan the previous weekend. In other words, he would be excused from the clearing up if he was clean and presentable when she arrived and did what she asked of him in advance. Again, she received a very prompt acceptance. Feeling very pleased with herself, she promised herself that, on Sunday, she would go for three in a row and aim to find a logical reason for her and Robert to go to a pub together one evening, just the two of them, but making a mental note not to refer to it as a date.

* * *

By the time Sunday came, Alice had caught up with everything. Not only was she feeling happy about how she had handled things with Robert and Jake but she had also received phone calls from both her parents to say how much they had enjoyed seeing her.

Within five minutes of her arriving at Robert's house, Jake had appeared in the kitchen smartly dressed and with his hair still wet from his shower. She noticed his limp was as bad as ever. Both Simon and Robert had already greeted her with hugs and she got the impression, or maybe just imagined it because she wanted to, that Robert was disappointed he hadn't been asked to help instead of Jake. Knowing one of the things Jake was happy to do was be in charge of drinks, Alice suggested he make tea for them all. This done and after a brief conversation during which she discovered the computer problem had finally been identified and William was bringing a replacement part later that morning, Robert and Simon left Alice alone with Jake to prepare the food. 'You'll have to tell me what you usually do to help Susan. She told me generally how much she values your help but didn't give me many details.'

'I know where everything is and how everything works,' replied Jake proudly. 'I usually get out all the tools and equipment Susan needs. She prepares all the food. I operate the controls on things like the oven and the microwave when she tells me to. I also lay the table and do the drinks.' Then, to Alice's surprise, he added, 'And in between we just talk.'

Alice quickly got used to working with Jake as he was happy to do the most menial of tasks as long as she explained clearly what was required. Her biggest problem was finding enough to keep him occupied. When William arrived, she asked Jake to make him tea and also to go and tell Robert. She overheard the usual Bill, Bob, flobbadob exchange as they greeted each other before going out to the garage. It was not long before the chicken was in the oven, the potatoes peeled and the vegetables prepared. 'I think we can relax for few minutes, now, Jake,' said Alice. 'Thank you for your help so far. I can understand why Susan likes having you around. Tell me, what do you usually talk about with her?'

'Lots of things,' replied Jake. 'She always asks about Robert and the house. I like to tell her about my computing but Simon says I mustn't tell her too much. This time I wanted to tell her about Brewdat but I couldn't because it's part of Watson & Charles, so I didn't. I can tell you though, can't I?'

'Yes, Jake, of course you can. You can tell me anything you like. I've seen from the forum that you've been making good progress with Brewdat. Getting stuck into that seems to have cheered you up. I'd heard you'd not been very happy while I was away.'

'Brewdat's OK. I've set up a virtual brewery to make beer and sell it through some virtual pubs. There are lots of modules connected to a large database. All that happens is you put data in through one module and then pull it out again by running a report in another module. I don't understand how it helps with Watson & Charles. I'm still not happy about that.'

'Why not?' asked Alice carefully, not wanting to cause Jake to get upset.

'Because we aren't going to change the world after all, are we? When Robert made us do all those exercises, I thought Watson & Charles was going to be the most important thing we did together. I was looking forward to it but I haven't been allowed to do anything. They stopped me from tracking that email. I could have done that. Now I've got Will Scarlet ready to go into the real Brewdat but they won't let me send him in.'

Feeling lost but sensing Jake's frustration building, Alice said tentatively, 'I'm very sorry. Jake, but I don't know about Will Scarlet. Who is he?'

'He's one of Robin Hood's merry men. He's one of the goodies. I have designed him to spy on the baddies like the Sherriff of Nottingham. What I want to do is catch the baddies. I call all my worms after Robin Hood's outlaws,' explained Jake, brightening up a little.

'Oh, I see. He's a computer worm,' said Alice, trying to play along. 'So how would he help with the Watson & Charles project?'

'He can go underneath and see if everything is as it should be. I have practised with him on my version. I'm sys admin so I can set everything up as a user. Then I send Will in to look at how it all flows through at a lower level. He's great; even Simon thinks so but he still won't let me do it because he says the baddies will be watching for him.'

'Maybe I can help you to ask Robert what more needs to be done before you can send him in,' said Alice encouragingly.

'I've already tried that. Robert doesn't think there are any baddies any more.'

Having put two and two together, Alice drew the conversation to an end. 'William also told me Robert was changing his mind. It doesn't sound like him at all, unless one of his unproven facts is now proven in a way he wasn't expecting. Let's see what comes out of the discussion over lunch when we're all there together. In the meantime, how about you laying the table while I check on the chicken and mix the batter for the Yorkshires?'

When Jake returned to the kitchen having completed his task, he limped slowly towards Alice with a sheepish look on his face and said, in a very hesitant voice, 'Alice, can I talk to you about my big toe?'

* * *

Robert and William came to lunch in a buoyant mood, reporting the problem was fixed and everything was now running well. Simon was his usual cautious self, saying all the security aspects still had to be double checked but, before he had finished, there was a chorus of 'nothing is 100 per cent secure' and everyone burst out laughing, including Simon. While they were eating, there was a lot of discussion about the previous weekend, including a comparison of Alice's cooking with Susan's. Alice was getting quite embarrassed when Robert suggested Alice was the winner, so she was very relieved when William stated the diplomatic solution was to call it a draw. The mood changed for the worse when Robert made an announcement.

'That may have been the last time my parents come to stay. Tom asked me about my financial position and I had to admit it is not very good. One of his suggestions to help was to change the rules about keeping the master bedroom free for when they come to visit. He said just having it sit empty for most of the year didn't make much sense when it could be rented out and bring in some money. I don't think I like the idea but I can see the logic of it. Anyway, he said he would talk to Mum about it.'

'I don't want anybody else,' said Jake loudly. 'I've got used to it being just the three of us.'

'Neither do I,' added Simon worriedly. 'Who would you look for, another Aspie? They'd have to get used to the security systems. I would need to train them.'

'It is not decided yet,' stressed Robert. 'Tom said I should warn you so you can get used to the idea. I wish I hadn't raised it. Anyway, it's not just the three of us, it would have an impact on all five of us. One thought I had was it could be Bill. That way most things could stay the same. Bill, you keep saying you are retiring and will be looking to move soon, don't you?'

Somewhat taken by surprise, William floundered for words. 'Well … er … yes, I suppose I do but it wouldn't work for me. I've got used to having my own space and, although I am planning to give up the shop, I'll still need a workshop. I wouldn't mind moving closer to you all but I would want my own place with at least my own garage,' adding after a slight pause, 'thanks for the thought though, Bob … flobbadob.'

'I've just had a great idea,' exclaimed Simon excitedly. 'What about Alice? That would work. She already knows us and it would still be just the five of us.'

Before Alice had chance to respond, Jake leapt in. 'Yea, that would be great. I vote for Alice.'

Alice was stunned. She hadn't been expecting anything like this. She felt she should be like William and give them a categorical no for an answer but she couldn't bring herself to do so. She looked across the table to William for help but realised none would be forthcoming. She tried to assess Robert's reaction but, as usual, he was giving nothing away.

'I'm flattered,' she managed to say, 'I really am, but I've got my flat, which is really convenient for my work, and I like my independence.'

This time it was Robert who responded, full of logic as always. 'I remember you saying how you were often lonely in your flat and that it takes less than five minutes to drive here, so it wouldn't take very much longer to get to your work in Nutfield. Also, your flat is only rented. I would charge you less than you are currently paying, so it would be financially beneficial for you.'

Whilst Alice was trying to work out whether that was Robert's way of saying he wanted her to move in, Simon chipped in. 'It's a lovely room, Alice. It's ever so big with its own en suite bathroom. You've never seen it, have you? I'll show it to you when we've finished lunch.' Again Alice looked across at William but he continued to remain silent with a silly grin on his face. She could feel all eyes on her and was feeling pressured into making a decision but she really wanted to speak to Robert alone first. Fortunately for her, Simon continued. 'What's more, if you lived here, you could look after us all and cook more delicious meals for us.'

Alice took the opportunity to diffuse the situation with humour, 'If you lot think I'm going to move in here just to be your cook and housekeeper then you've got another think coming.' Then, trying to change the subject, she added, 'I thought we were going to talk about the Watson & Charles project. If we crack that, there'll be plenty of money and no need for anybody to rent the room.'

'Well, that's a big incentive then,' said William sarcastically but still smiling.

Ignoring him, Alice realised Robert wasn't going to follow her lead, so she continued, 'Come on, let's go round the table and see where we've all got to. Robert, what's your latest thinking?'

Reluctantly, Robert answered, 'I currently think there is a strong probability the financial problems of Watson & Charles are all of their own making. Simon agrees with me. I have found out that, ten years ago, when Derek Watson took over as Chairman, they ranked all their pubs in order. They put those most worth keeping and investing in at the top of the list and those to be sold rather than invested in at the bottom. They drew a line about one third of the way up and commenced an investment programme starting from the top and a selling plan starting for the bottom. Last year, they reached the line from both sides. I think they drew the line too low and I think Derek Watson believes that now as well.'

'Are you sure?' asked Alice. 'How can you know what Derek Watson believes?'

'The evidence is growing all the time,' replied Robert. 'The last pub above the line was the Hare and Hounds. Given the number of times he lunches there, this would appear to be one of Derek Watson's favourite pubs. If he made the decision to keep the Hare and Hounds for emotional reasons rather than sound business ones, he would have had to keep all the other pubs above it on the list as well. For the last few weeks, Derek Watson has been receiving weekly reports of each pub's performance. The Hare and Hounds has been doing badly, as have a number of the other pubs just above it on the list. This trend has emerged only recently. Also, he arranged for an in-depth analysis of the Hare and Hounds to be carried out and, as before, nothing untoward was found.'

'What do you know of emotional reasons?' asked Alice, searching for a way of proving him wrong. 'You don't make decisions for emotional reasons, do you?'

'No,' retorted Robert, 'but other people do. You have taught me that as much as anybody else. Anyway, it doesn't matter why he made the decision. It could be why they are struggling so we would just be wasting our time searching for something that isn't there.'

'You said "could". That means you're not certain. And don't give me that "nothing's 100 per cent certain" nonsense. This is serious. Are we really going to give up now? What about Will Scarlet?'

'Who on earth is Will Scarlet?' asked William, still smirking.

Alice was starting to get quite agitated. 'He's one of Jake's worms. I'm surprised you didn't know that. Jake told me earlier that he's all ready to go and all he needs is for Simon to be happy to send him in.'

'With all the security issues we've had, I'd need to do some double checking first,' said Simon.

Jake also started to backtrack. 'Maybe he's not as ready as I thought. I wouldn't want him to get caught.'

'What is wrong with you all? Before I went to visit my parents, you were all so positive and enthusiastic. Look at you now. Why are you being so negative?'

It was Jake who answered. 'You said if the Watson & Charles project is successful then you won't come and live here.'

'What!' exclaimed Alice. 'I didn't mean that. Is that what you all were thinking?'

She looked around the table to see three sullen faces and vague nods. 'That's what I meant about incentive,' explained William playfully.

'Oh, for Christ's sake,' said Alice loudly. 'Let me make it perfectly clear. If, and it is a big if, I was to come to live here it would not depend on the success or otherwise of the Watson & Charles project.' As she was speaking, she became aware of Jake standing up and preparing to leave. She addressed him personally. 'Jake, I know the arrangement is you can leave whenever you choose but, if you go now, you will miss an important discussion.'

Jake had almost reached the door but turned around and shouted, 'I don't care. We're never going to change the world. We talk too much. It always ends in arguments. We're just a load of geeks and misfits.'

Alice lowered her voice and spoke very gently to him. 'Jake, I want to change the world as well. We all do. Changing the world is not easy. It takes time and the only chance of it happening is if we all find a way to work together. That's why Robert was right not to rush into the

Watson & Charles project before we had at least tried to agree how to do things as a team. Jake, you are a major part of our team. If me coming to live here means so much to you all,' although she was really thinking just about Robert, 'I'll tell you what might make a difference to my decision.' Jake leaned against the door frame and continued to listen. 'What matters to me is the three of you make good use of the very special talents you all have. Ever since I met you, I've been hoping for a suitable opportunity to arise. Watson & Charles seemed to provide that opportunity but the key aspect for me was when we came up with the idea of Roger Thompson Associates. We've already talked about how many other potential projects are out there. It obviously would be great if Watson & Charles brings in lots of money but what's far more important is we complete it to find out the truth or, as Robert would say, to turn the unproven facts into proven ones. One of the qualities we didn't talk about for Roger was persistence in the face of adversity. We should have done, because very little goes smoothly all of the time. One thing we did agree, however, is to ask what Roger would do. At the moment, Roger has lost some confidence so the question is: what can Roger do to restore his confidence? Remember, Roger is made up of all five of us.'

Alice waited for a response but all she was met with was stunned silence and blank looks. Even William seemed unsure what to say or do, so Alice continued. 'No suggestions, eh? Well, in that case, I have one. I think Roger would want to understand how a different load of geeks and misfits had successfully changed the world in the past. Unless anybody has any objections, I propose that next Sunday, instead of a meeting or lunch, we all have a day out at Bletchley Park.'

Eventually, Robert broke the silence. 'Can we go by train.'

'No, I was hoping William can take us in his new car. It will be cheaper than five train fares and trains on Sunday are always unreliable.'

Once the idea had sunk in, there were lots of questions, particularly from Simon, who was nervous about going so far, but Alice reassured him that they would all look after him as that's what friends were for.

Eventually, Alice and William left. As they were alone in the drive, William said, 'That was a pretty impressive speech. Was the Bletchley idea a spur of the moment thing?'

'Not really,' Alice admitted. 'I'd had it in the back of my mind for a few weeks but, when Jake talked about geeks and misfits, it just seemed like a good time to suggest it.'

'So it had nothing to do with it finally sinking in how much they wanted you to take the room, then, or should I say how much Robert wanted you to?' questioned William light-heartedly. 'In spite of their reluctance to go anywhere, I think they would've all gone to the moon if you'd asked them.'

Alice just laughed, gave William a hug and a kiss and got into her car to drive home, so she could check her tenancy agreement and confirm she only needed to give one month's notice.

Chapter Sixteen

'That was a brilliant idea, Alice,' said William as he was driving them home from Bletchley.

'I thought you'd all enjoy it,' replied Alice, sitting behind Robert and next to Simon, who was squeezed in the middle of the back seat with Jake on his other side. 'When I went there as a little girl, there was much I didn't understand. The lottery funding has made a big difference. There are lots of new galleries and the story was much easier to follow. Anyway, it's Jake you really have to thank. It was when he was talking about a group of geeks and misfits not being able to change the world that made me think about Bletchley. As you now know, there's a strong argument that, without the people at Bletchley, the outcome of World War Two would have been very different. I know the scale of operation and the level of technology is very different to what we're trying to do from a house in Redhill with just the five of us, but a lot of the principles are the same.'

'You're right,' said Jake enthusiastically. 'I liked the bombes. How big they were. All that mechanical clanking just to compare codes. I wouldn't even need a Raspberry Pi to do that now.'

'The bombes reminded me of going to the Science Museum when I was little and seeing ERNIE, the first computer used for drawing out premium bond winners,' added Simon.

'Do you know,' chipped in Robert from the front, 'how difficult it is to generate a truly random number from a computer?'

'That's what first attracted me to computers,' answered Simon. 'I loved writing programs to try to produce random numbers and then checking how random they actually were. I always found a very slight bias.'

'So nothing was ever 100 per cent random then,' pronounced William. They all laughed, including Simon.

Simon tried to get his own back. 'If you were just a few years older, William, you could have been an engineer working on the bombes.'

'Ha, ha,' replied William. 'I'm not quite that old but I do have a family connection to Bletchley. Just before he died, my grandfather, who was an engineer in the RAF during the war, told me he worked on the British Typex machine. After he was demobbed, he started the family repair business which turned into the shop I now have.'

'It is all in the genes, Bill. Alice will tell you that.'

'I'm sure she would be correct. I would have thought even you, Bob, have noticed by now how Alice is usually right about most things … flobbadob.'

Not wanting the good mood to be lost, Alice asked, 'What about the people? I found some of their stories so inspirational. Bletchley gave them a purpose in life that otherwise they might not have had.'

'I liked the way they set out specially to find the right sort of people by getting them to do a crossword,' said Jake.

'I wish you could get qualifications and jobs these days by doing puzzles and crosswords rather than having to sit exams and write theses, just regurgitating stuff that is already known,' moaned Robert sourly.

Alice persevered. 'One thing I do think is, we should stop referring to ourselves as geeks and misfits. From what I could tell, everyone at Bletchley felt part of a team and were proud of what they were doing. Also, remember that no-one in those days knew anything about Asperger's syndrome, although I'm sure a high percentage would have been Aspies. Let's just think of the five of us coming together because of difficult experiences we've had in the past. We are who we are, friends who want to help each other to get pleasure and satisfaction from our lives.'

'We want to change the world,' pronounced Jake at the top of his voice.

'Yes, Jake, we do. To achieve that, we need to work as a team. Did you notice how people who preferred to work on their own were given the space to do so but still had a way of interacting with everyone else?

Also, you could sense there was a great deal of frustration at times. There were arguments and disagreements as well but they found a way past those. That's what I meant the other day about persistence in the face of adversity. They put in incredibly long hours and stuck at their tasks even when things weren't going well. We need to be able to do the same.' Worried that Robert wasn't being as positive as the others, Alice decided to ask him directly. 'Robert, you're not saying very much. Did you not enjoy today?'

'I was just thinking,' explained Robert. 'I did know quite a lot about Bletchley before today, mostly about the code-breaking side of things. Code breaking is all about logic so applying logic to breaking something like the Enigma code appeals to me. The part that surprised me today was the logic behind the strategy, particularly the misinformation sent out about the Normandy landings. As you know, I'm not good at understanding people but I came away today thinking that Churchill must have had a very logical mind. As he has a reputation of being a great leader, I suppose that does make sense.'

'Perhaps, we could do with a Churchill,' said Jake. 'And a Turing. He definitely came across as being Aspie as well as being gay. I bet he had an odd childhood.'

Concerned Robert thought he was similar to Churchill, Alice quickly said, 'I don't think we need to go as a far as comparing ourselves with any particular individuals who were involved with Bletchley. The main point is to recognise what can be achieved by people like us. The question we should now be asking ourselves is: are we going to continue as Roger Thompson Associates, whatever the outcome of the Watson & Charles project?'

'Yes,' was the resounding answer from everyone, with Robert adding, 'I call us RTA for short.'

'Does that mean you will be coming to live with us?' asked Jake, hopefully.

'I was wondering when that subject would be raised,' replied Alice. 'I haven't made my final decision but Robert and I are going to talk about it later this week. We've agreed to go to a pub together on Wednesday evening as I want to understand more about how pubs work and where Brewdat fits in.'

Alice sensed William's ears pricking up and hoped he wasn't going to make a quip about it sounding like a date, but he didn't. 'That makes a lot of sense,' he said. 'We do need to get back to concentrating on Watson & Charles so we can come to a final conclusion one way or the other. I'm conscious I've done very little with the two lots of emails I'm supposed to be looking at. Now everything has settled down after Tom's endeavours, I should have time to do more. I'll aim to form my own view as to whether it is all down to bad business decisions. Presumably, Simon and Jake can sort out what to do with Friar Tuck?'

'It's not Friar Tuck,' exclaimed Jake, 'it's Will Scarlet. Friar Tuck is different, he gobbles things up. Will just sneaks in, gains information and sneaks back out again.'

'William is only teasing,' explained Alice. 'Don't rise to it, Jake, otherwise it will only encourage him to do it more.'

'One thing I'm surprised none of you have mentioned about Bletchley,' said Simon, 'is how vitally important it was to keep everything secret. I hope you all realise without that level of secrecy, they would all have been blown up by the Germans and the war would most likely have been lost. It's just as important for us to be the same and it's why I'm constantly reminding you we need to take care. All it would have taken was a single person to say the wrong thing at the wrong time. That was the most impressive aspect for me.'

This time it was Robert's turn to tease. 'We do realise it, Simon, but we didn't want to mention it.'

'Why not?'

'Because the logical conclusion is something can be 100 per cent secure after all.' They all laughed, including Simon.

*   *   *

Three days later, Alice was still on top of the world. The Bletchley trip had gone far better than she had hoped, the forum had been very active with a mixture of humorous, positive and constructive comments, and now she was going to spend a whole evening with Robert, with the likely outcome being to move into his house. It was now eight months since he had knocked her over in Sainsbury's and the only previous occasion they had spent significant time together was when she had arranged to take him back to Sainsbury's and see Jane. She had hoped they would have been able to have time alone at Bletchley but Simon had been like a limpet, following her everywhere. Only at lunchtime had she managed to prise herself away from him just long enough to get Robert to agree to go to the pub with her. As she was driving to pick him up, she tried to remember Susan's advice. Although there were loads of things she wanted to talk to him about, she made a mental note not to ask any questions that could be considered annoying or likely to touch a nerve.

Alice had booked a table at the Dog and Duck in Outwood for two reasons. William had told her it was owned by Hall & Woodhouse, who were a family brewing company based in Dorset and similar to Watson & Charles. Secondly, it allowed her to drive through Nutfield and show Robert where she worked, although they could only just make out the outline of Lyttel Hall as they drove past in the semi-dark. They talked about non-contentious issues until they reached the pub. Robert was in a chatty mood and tried to convince Alice they would have been better going to Bletchley on the train, as there were plenty of trains on a Sunday and Bletchley station was very close to Bletchley Park. As they were sitting at their table contemplating the menu, Alice looked around the half-full restaurant area and concluded that the two of them appeared to be just like any other couple out for a meal in the evening. She decided on vegetable lasagne with orange juice to drink and noted, with interest, that Robert chose fish and chips but with garden peas rather than mushy pears, along with an apple juice. 'Did your mum tell you she showed me her cubic pea whilst we were in Kingston together?'

'No, but it doesn't surprise me. I'm amazed it has survived for so long given she carries it around with her all the time.'

'I thought it was a lovely story. It clearly means a lot to her and it did help me to understand more about you too.'

'I hope you haven't brought me here to ask more of your annoying questions.'

'No, I've brought you here because we never seem to get any time together on our own, what with Simon and Jake always being around. Also, since Watson & Charles started, William has been there much more as well. It's not that I don't like being with them all but there are some things I think it best we talk about alone. I have no intention of being annoying, far from it, but I do accept I'm still learning how not to be.' Unable to resist but trying to keep it humorous, Alice added, 'I'm sure you'll help me by letting me know if I am.'

'I will do my best,' replied Robert seriously. 'I have noticed you've been a lot better recently and you definitely try to explain things more than you used to.'

'That's your mum's influence. I suspect your elastic band is stretched just by being here. I don't want to make it any tighter for you.'

'Not really. I got used to going to pubs with my parents, although I have never liked any form of alcohol. I know you well enough now to feel as comfortable with you as I am with them. By the way,' he added with a smile on his face, 'they can still be annoying too.'

'OK, let's both do our best to make it an annoying-free evening. The two main things to discuss are me renting the room and the Watson & Charles project. Which one to you want to do first?'

'The room. That shouldn't take very long.'

'Why do you say that?'

'Well, I spoke to my mum on Monday about it and she said I must not rent the room to you.'

Alice was crestfallen. Over the previous few days and particularly since the trip to Bletchley, she had come to realise how much she wanted to live in the same house as Robert. She had been certain Susan would be on her side. Where had she gone wrong? She looked up at Robert. As usual he wasn't looking directly at her but she was aware of a glint in his eye and he hadn't lost his smile. Suspecting he was up to something, she pleaded with him, 'Please don't mess me about over this, Robert. It's really important to me. Tell me exactly what your mum said.'

'I cannot remember everything. She waffled on about how wonderful it would be and how good, not just for me but Simon and Jake as well, and then she said, "Don't you dare charge her any rent". So I will not.'

Alice was a lot happier but still confused. 'So what does that mean? Can I come or not?'

'Of course you can. I thought we all made that very clear ten days ago. In fact, Simon was concerned we'd gone on about it too much and were in danger of putting you off, so he told Jake and me not to mention it again until you did. As soon as we got home on Sunday, Simon got quite cross with Jake for asking you about it in the car.'

'Forget Simon and Jake for a minute. What I really want to know is whether you want me to come and, if so, why?'

'I have just told you the answer is yes. As to why, I would have thought that was obvious too. I like it when you come round now. I do not like it when it's time for you to leave. If you live there, you will be there all of the time so I will enjoy it more.'

'Well, it won't be all the time because I'll still be going out to work during the day but I guess that's a pretty good answer. I'm sure I'll enjoy spending more time with you as well. I still need to know how I'm going to pay. I wouldn't feel comfortable living there for nothing.'

'That is the part I didn't understand when I spoke to Mum. She said something about being sure you would pay in lots of different ways that were far more valuable than money. She also said that it was more the other way round, that I would need to work out how to reciprocate, otherwise I would be in danger of losing you.'

Feeling tears starting to form, Alice reached across the table to take his hand and felt a slight flinch. She kept a tight hold as she said, 'Don't worry. I'm sure we'll work it out between us. I know exactly what your mum means and I promise I'll do my very best to help you understand too.'

'So, does that definitely mean you are coming?'

'Yes, Robert, it does.'

Immediately, he withdrew his hand from hers, pulled his phone out of his pocket and started thumbing it. 'What are you doing?' asked Alice.

'Texting Jake and Simon. They are at their Asperger's group tonight but I promised I'd let them know as soon as there was any firm news.'

'Warn them it won't be for at least a month,' said Alice, laughing. 'I've got to give notice on my flat first. How about I aim for the beginning of December? Will you all be ready for me by then?'

'What do you mean by ready? The room is empty now. You could move in tomorrow if you wanted.'

'I think that might have been one of the things your mum meant. It's not just the bedroom. I need to understand more about how the house works as a whole. Let's say we need to have a think about it together and put a plan in place.'

'In that case, you probably ought to know that I have had the idea of changing the lounge into an operations centre. It struck me it would be far more professional for the three of us to each have a work station in the lounge than have to cram everything into our bedrooms. We are all running out of space upstairs.'

'That's exactly why we need to plan ahead together because I was planning to be able to use the lounge to relax in. Maybe I could use the snug instead, if that were changed a little as well.'

'I don't think we need to keep the snug just for meltdowns any more. I haven't had a bad one for over six months, neither has Simon. Even Jake has only had a few and, if he has a workstation downstairs, he could use his bedroom for his meltdowns.' Then as an afterthought he added, 'Unless you want to keep it like it is for when you have yours.'

'No, Robert. I don't think I'll be having a meltdown ever again.' Alice noticed a waiter approaching with their meals. 'Look, our food is here, let's each give it some thought and then we can talk again in a few days and also include Jake and Simon. This is something they do need to be involved in.'

'Good idea but, if we make it a condition of you moving in, they are bound to agree with us.'

Alice looked across at Robert's plate and couldn't help noticing quite a few of his peas were in contact with his chips. Robert didn't appear to mind and was happily eating the fish before he started on either the chips or the peas. Alice decided it was best not to raise the issue.

'Talking about Jake,' she said between mouthfuls, 'has he told you that I'm going with him to the doctor's tomorrow afternoon?'

'Yes, he said he'd managed to book online as there had been a cancellation. I don't know any more than that. Is it about his limp or something else?'

'It's about his big toe, which I believe is the cause of his limp. He spoke to me about it recently but wouldn't let me look at it. I was just happy to get him to agree to go but he only said yes if I would go with him.'

'Even I noticed he was really struggling to walk round Bletchley.'

'Your mum noticed too when she was here but he wouldn't tell her anything. He obviously doesn't like talking about it but I think he has at last realised he needs help to deal with it. Whatever the outcome tomorrow, we'll all need to be careful how we handle the situation.'

Robert, now half way through his chips, said, 'Don't you think we should start talking about Watson & Charles now?'

Not wanting the evening to come to an end, Alice replied. 'We don't need to hurry back, do we? I want to make sure we discuss Watson & Charles fully and I do feel I need to understand more about how this Brewdat system helps a pub to function. First of all, let me tell you the little bit of progress I've made myself. I'm convinced it's now a proven fact that Pauline Sharples isn't guilty of anything other than being concerned about Derek Watson. Her most recent personal emails to Debbie French, who seems to be her best friend, show she is excited about Derek Watson getting divorced but also very concerned it might lead to the collapse of the business. It's something to do with the fact that Derek's wife has to sell her shares. I didn't fully understand everything but the way she expressed her feelings left me in no doubt she's innocent.'

'I did not think it would be her in the first place but you did say right at the start, before I met Derek Watson, you thought there was more to their relationship. I am pleased to hear you were correct as it means it was the right thing to do to use it as part of the initial negotiation. The shares part makes sense as his wife cannot continue to hold shares after she is divorced, as she would no longer be considered a member of the Watson family. It ties in with some of the recent emails I have seen from Derek Watson himself. I saw one to his brother saying how worried he was after talking to his father.' Thinking aloud, he added, 'One of the problems with just having the emails is we don't get any information from face-to-face meetings or phone calls. There's still a lot going on that we miss. It's an area we need to consider for future RTA projects.'

Aiming to boost his confidence, Alice replied, 'I think you've done remarkably well from studying all the emails to build up such a detailed picture of the Watson & Charles business. The way you talk sometimes, I wonder if you now know more than Derek Watson knows himself. I bet you could run Watson & Charles just as well as him.'

'I probably could,' said Robert in a factual rather than a boastful way. 'As I said last Sunday, it does appear that not all his decisions have been good ones.'

Their conversation was interrupted by the waiter returning to clear their now empty plates and to bring dessert menus. Without consulting Robert, Alice told the waiter they wanted a break and it would be at least ten minutes before they would be ready to decide on dessert. She put the menus face down on the table so Robert would not be distracted.

'Can I check something with you? I feel a bit lost not having been in all the meetings and discussions. Am I right in thinking there are two possible explanations? The first and now most likely one is the original email was sent by someone trying to take advantage of the fact that Watson & Charles are underperforming because of poor business decisions and that same someone is now putting out falsely bad reviews as well. The second explanation is still the original one, but now a lot less likely, where someone intentionally created the poor performance by doing something fraudulent to steal from Watson & Charles and then put out the email and bad reviews to disguise the fact.'

'That's close but not quite right. There is now evidence false reviews were in place before the email was sent out. It doesn't make a lot of difference because, in either scenario, it's getting too late to improve the profits for this financial year. As we have progressed the project, probabilities have changed as more and more facts have emerged. Simon's latest calculations, based on the proven facts I've given him, show the second explanation now only has a probability of just under 10 per cent. It is highly likely Watson & Charles will be sold and we won't get any money.'

'So do you now believe your original theory was wrong? You seemed so certain. That was why you asked for so much money, wasn't it?'

'I don't think it was wrong as a theory. It was the most logical explanation based on the facts available at the time. You would probably call it an assumption. If you remember, I called it an unproven fact.'

Alice was aware Robert was starting to feel uncomfortable. As before, she reached across the table to take his hand and, again, felt him flinch.

'I do remember and, from what you've just told me, it still remains an unproven fact even if an unlikely one. My main concern is I believe you're thinking you've failed. I know you don't like failure. You think of not getting your PhD and losing your job at Crawtech as failures. They aren't. It's just life. Everyone has ups and downs. Think of it like this. We wouldn't have even thought about RTA if you'd still been at Crawtech. You and I might never have met and we certainly wouldn't be here tonight if it hadn't been for our tea parties. You just don't know what the future holds. All you can do is make the best decision possible on the information you have at the time. That's what you did when you first met Derek Watson and, I suspect, that is also what he does on a day-to-day basis. Whatever the outcome of Watson & Charles, it will have been an invaluable exercise in establishing us as RTA. It's brought all five of us so much closer than we were before. That wouldn't have happened if you hadn't pushed us. Please don't think of Watson & Charles as a failure.'

Robert didn't respond immediately. Instead, Alice felt him trying to withdraw his hand. She held on tightly. Eventually he said, 'It is not failure, it is frustration. I got frustrated over writing my thesis. It was a waste of time just repeating what I had already reported verbally on many occasions, so I didn't complete the written thesis. At Crawtech, I got frustrated with people wanting me to go on courses that had no logical purpose, so I did not go. With Watson & Charles, it is frustration because I have found out Derek Watson did not make logical decisions. Everything would be fine if people made logical decisions. It is always people.'

Alice squeezed his hand even more. 'Robert, I get that. I really do. Whatever project we take on as RTA, people are going to be involved. You yourself stressed how important it is that all five of us work as a team. The skills that you, Simon, Jake and William have are all very clear cut and obvious. You're all brilliant at what you do. I'm asking you to accept that one of the skills I bring to the team is knowing about people. So, whenever you get frustrated by someone, even if that someone is me, I can help you but only if you're prepared to tell me about it.' Noticing the waiter was hovering, Alice released Robert's hand and passed him a menu saying, 'What would you like for dessert? I'm just going to have a couple of scoops of ice-cream.'

After careful consideration, Robert said, 'I'll have the crumble with custard. It probably won't be as nice as my mum makes but I do like crumble.'

'Anyway,' said Alice, after the waiter had taken their order and left, 'we still need to decide what to do about the Watson & Charles project. It feels wrong to just give up now. We haven't robbed a bank yet.'

'What do you mean?'

'I think I mean we've got Jake all lined up and raring to go, ready to send Will Scarlet into the Watson & Charles version of Brewdat. I know I don't understand all the technicalities but I do trust Jake and Simon. I get the impression they're working much better together than when I first met them. If we don't let Jake loose now, he's going to be unhappy and disappointed. Also, I don't see why there's a risk. If there's a 90 per cent chance there's nothing to find then nobody will be watching for him. If someone is watching, they'll be doing something illegal as well, so can't cause too much harm even if they catch him.'

'I hadn't thought about it like that. Brewdat is only a relatively simple database and Watson & Charles's experts have been through it more than once without finding anything suspicious. However, I can follow your logic in allowing Jake to have a look, even if he finds nothing.'

Their desserts arrived. As they were eating them, Alice said, 'One of the main reasons for coming here was for you to explain to me how Brewdat works in a pub. How about having a pot of tea between us so you can tell me about it?'

Robert glanced towards the tills on the bar. 'I'm not certain Hall & Woodhouse has Brewdat but, even if they don't, it will be a very similar system. Think about what happened when we arrived and our order was taken, and look across to the people on the table on your right, who are paying their bill.'

Alice looked and saw the same waiter who had served them was taking a card payment at the table. 'I don't see anything unusual. That sort of payment can be made anywhere, not just in a pub.'

'Precisely. That is why it's unlikely Jake will find anything. The card reader is linked wirelessly through the internet to the bank. The actual money side doesn't touch Brewdat. Cash payments, which these days are quite rare, are taken manually from the till straight to the bank.'

'So, what you're saying is, to get at the money, you really would have to rob a bank?'

'What I am saying is it is now a proven fact money is not disappearing directly from the pubs. All of the Watson & Charles managed houses pay into the same bank account but each individual transaction is coded so it can be traced. When we get our bill, you'll see what I mean. The Watson & Charles analysts have been looking into this issue for almost a year. They've traced lots of transactions from lots of different pubs and have always found the money to have gone through correctly to the bank account. All the cash taken from the tills is also fully accounted for.'

Alice interrupted the conversation to attract the waiter's attention and order their tea. 'Where does Brewdat fit in then?'

'Brewdat holds all the data for the running of the business, pubs and brewery. When we ordered our food, our order was entered into the till. Not only does that allow our bill to be prepared, it links to the kitchen so they know what to prepare for our table and it also links to Brewdat. Brewdat is set up as a series of modules, one of which is used for stock control. So, when I ordered my fish and chips it would have decremented the pub's stock by one fish and a pre-set weight of chips and peas. Each evening, after food sales have finished, the landlord can pull up a stock report and look at the actual stock compared with the pre-set stock levels. The system will suggest ordering anything that is below the pre-set stock level. He or she can either amend or accept the order. It should be no more than a five-minute job. For most food items, pubs are on a just-in-time basis, so whatever is ordered tonight will be delivered tomorrow. Drinks are controlled in a similar way but tend to be ordered weekly rather than daily, unless it is a large pub with limited storage space. Every component item has a cost attached to it and every menu item has a selling price. All the financial information goes into the Brewdat accounting module.

'The Watson & Charles accountants can pull up reports on individual pubs or groups of pubs to look at directly, or to transfer the data to other programs, usually Excel, for further manipulation, analysis and reporting. The accountants are responsible for authorising payments against purchase orders and making sure money is received against the sales orders. All suppliers must be pre-approved and set up. People are treated in a similar manner and there is a specific payroll module. There are lots of checks and balances within and between Brewdat modules. Any errors are flagged up and can be investigated. At the end of each accounting period, everything is made to balance and management reports are prepared. Watson & Charles employees only have access to the relevant areas for their role, which may be as little as one element of one module. Members of the IT department have sys admin access to the whole system.' Robert paused for a moment. 'That is just a brief summary. There's a lot more detail to it but is that enough for you to understand the pub side of the operation?'

'That's plenty, thank you. I'm not sure I could take much more in. How come you know so much about it?'

'Just by drilling down through all the emails and attachments. I got Jake to set me up to be able to see emails from other people as well as Derek and Stephen Watson. Ian Walters and Keith Fairbrother have proved the most useful and, of course, I've had a look first hand at the Brewdat system we set up for Jake to learn on.'

Taking time to have a drink of tea, Alice thought for a moment. 'I can understand why you don't think it worthwhile for Jake to do any more. If the Watson & Charles experts can't find anything wrong and you agree with them after all you've done, then it really would seem there's nothing to find, particularly if someone would need both to rob the bank and fiddle with Brewdat to hide the fact. Given both you and Simon agree the risk is low, I still think we should let Jake do it otherwise it will be something else we are stopping him from doing. We don't want to push him into another meltdown, do we? Perhaps we give him a week and then aim to call a halt to the Watson & Charles project the weekend after next and focus instead on where RTA goes next.'

Robert wiped his mouth with his napkin. 'Maybe this Sunday we could just have another discussion over lunch and just start to think about other projects. Would you be prepared to do another roast? They're delicious.'

'Yes, of course. Would you like something different? We haven't had lamb yet or I could make a meat loaf. That goes well with all the usual roast accompaniments.'

'Lamb is not my favourite meat because of the fat but I've never had meat loaf so lamb might be the safer choice.'

'Meat loaf is a mixture of minced beef and pork sausage meat wrapped in bacon. I'm sure you'd like it.'

'Alright then, it does sound nice and you are usually right. Meat loaf it is.'

Alice realised it was getting quite late and they were the only ones left in the restaurant area. 'Have you had enough tea? We probably should pay our bill. Let me do it so I can see what you meant earlier.' Then, revealing her ulterior motive, 'You can pay next time.' She signalled to the waiter. 'Just going back to the Watson & Charles project for a minute, given what you've told me, I'm surprised there's still a 10 per cent chance of the original theory being correct. I'm going to sound like Simon now but shouldn't it be more like 100 per cent certain that nothing fraudulent has happened?' They both laughed.

'There are three reasons for it not being 100 per cent. They are not unproven facts but they are unexplained facts. All three have potential explanations and, of course, they could just be because of people behaving illogically.'

'Oh, what are they?' asked Alice, suddenly becoming interested again.

'Firstly, it is just managed houses that are performing badly. There is no sign of any similar problems in tenancies. I would have expected to see more evidence of tenancies with problems. Secondly, the timing of the email is strange. It runs the risk of creating competition for the purchase of Watson & Charles. I would have expected it to have happened in the New Year, much closer to the end of the financial year. Thirdly, the trend correlating pub performance to the position on the invest-or-divest list has only just become apparent. I would have expected to see it earlier.'

Before Robert could explain further, the waiter came with the bill. Alice paid by credit card. She looked at the receipt. 'I can see what you mean. It clearly says Dog and Duck and there is a lengthy number which is presumably the unique transaction number you mentioned.'

As soon as Alice had put the receipts away in her purse, Robert started to move. Quickly, Alice put down her purse and reached across the table to grab his hands for a third time and stop him from getting up. This time he didn't flinch. 'Robert, there's one last thing before we go. You said earlier you were learning to trust me. I want you to know that I trust you too. I don't want there to be any secrets between us, so there's something I need to tell you. It's something I haven't ever told anyone before, even my parents, and I don't want you to tell anyone else.'

'What is it?'

Taking a deep breath and making absolutely sure no-one could overhear, Alice spoke very quietly. 'When I was fourteen, I was raped.'

Robert pulled away his hands and stared past her. 'Can we go now?'

They stood up and, apart from thanking the waiter as they passed the bar, left the pub in silence. Alice couldn't help thinking about Susan and the cubic pea conversation. Had she done the same? Had she blown it when everything was going so well?

Alice broke the silence as they were driving back past her laboratory. 'You know I've still got Derek Watson's DNA. I suppose we won't be needing that now.'

She was surprised how quickly and calmly Robert replied.

'Not for the Watson & Charles project but we can use it as a test exercise for RTA. If you put the data on a memory stick I'll ask Jake to see if he can add it to the national database.' Alice thought it wasn't logical for Robert to be happy to allow Jake to hack into the national DNA database but not into the Watson & Charles Brewdat system, but she decided it was best not to ask. Instead, she asked Robert to remind Jake to be ready for his doctor's appointment.

They drove in silence until they reached Redhill but then Robert asked, in quite a strange tone, 'Alice, can you give me an example of what my mum meant by reciprocating?'

Concerned that she might again be in danger of blowing it, Alice thought carefully about her response but decided it was too good a chance to miss.

'Well, in general it means helping me in return for me helping you but without the need to keep count. A good example would be the wedding of my cousin Terry. He's getting married in April next year. The wedding is in Yorkshire. I want to go but I don't want to go alone. You would be helping me a great deal if you would go with me.'

'I see,' replied Robert thoughtfully. 'I have only ever been to one wedding a few years ago and I didn't enjoy it very much. I suppose I could try again. Can we go by train?'

'Yes, Robert, of course we can.'

They quickly arrived at Robert's house. Alice parked on the drive and started to get out of the car. 'Are you coming in?' asked Robert in a surprised manner as he too was getting out of the car.

'No, but I do want to thank you properly for tonight.'

'But it was you who paid.'

'I know but it's your company I'm thanking you for. It's been a lovely evening.'

She moved towards him and gave him a hug and a kiss on his cheek. As she was holding him, she heard him respond. 'In that case, I need to thank you twice, for your company and for paying.' To her immense surprise, she felt two very distinct kisses on her own cheek. Robert pulled away and went in the front door without another word or backward glance.

Alice drove away with the happy thought that a reciprocating relationship might work out very well indeed.

Chapter Seventeen

Jake had proved to be an extremely reluctant patient. Taking him to the Hawthorns Surgery had been an unpleasant experience for Alice. In spite of all the reminders, he had not been ready when she arrived and had to be cajoled to put his shoes on. As a result, she had felt rushed and they arrived a few minutes late for his 4 p.m. appointment. Fortunately, Dr James was also running late. Whilst they were in the waiting room, Jake moaned loudly about being kept waiting but, apart from that, he hardly said a word. Alice wasn't originally expecting to go into the consulting room with him but it became obvious Jake wouldn't go in without her. She had to do all the talking. She even had to take his shoe and sock off herself as Jake wouldn't do it, even when asked by the doctor. It struck Alice it probably didn't help that Dr James was female and quite attractive.

Even before Alice got the sock off, she was overcome by a horrific stench and when she actually saw his big toe, she nearly fainted. It was swollen to at least twice the size it should have been and covered in a mixture of blood and pus. Dr James took one look at it and said it was the worst case of an infected in-growing toenail she had ever seen. She prescribed a course of antibiotics to tackle it but stressed that if the infection had reached the bone, it might require the toe to be amputated. She called through to the nurse and then told Jake he would need to go back to the waiting room until the nurse was free, when she would clean it up and put on a protective dressing.

Dr James then asked Jake why he hadn't been to see her earlier as leaving it to get so bad was just asking for trouble. Jake remained silent, so Alice tried to explain about Asperger's syndrome but it was only when she mentioned autism that the doctor seemed to have any sympathy. However, Dr James then seemed to view Alice as Jake's carer and accused Alice of not acting sooner. Alice experienced a similar reaction from the nurse who, having washed and dressed Jake's toe, gave Alice a handful of spare dressings and instructed her in no uncertain terms to make sure the toe was bathed in a potassium permanganate bath every day and the dressing changed. By the time they left, Alice was experiencing a strong feeling of guilt and embarrassment.

When they arrived back at Robert's house, Jake shuffled, as fast as his toe would allow, upstairs and into his room, still staying silent and without a word of thanks to Alice for giving up her time to help him. Alice was quite distraught and poured out all the details to Robert and Simon over a cup of tea. Robert offered to cycle into Redhill to get the prescription and some potassium permanganate tablets. Simon said he would talk to Jake when he had calmed down about taking the antibiotics and bathing his foot. Both of them did their best to reassure her that she had done nothing wrong and, without her, Jake would never have gone. They both said they were surprised Jake hadn't screamed and shouted at everyone but had stayed silent rather than have a full meltdown. Again they put that down to Alice. Alice wasn't convinced. It had been a stark reminder that living there would not be all sweetness and light. There were bound to be many ups and downs. She wondered if that was how it had been for Susan and Tom and for all parents of Aspie children. She drove away in a much more sombre mood than the previous evening.

*   *   *

It was with more than a little trepidation that Alice arrived on the following Sunday morning with all the ingredients required to make the meat loaf. She needn't have worried. All three of them were waiting for her. Jake behaved as if the visit to the doctor's hadn't happened and even made tea without having to be asked. As they were drinking it, Alice remembered she had brought a memory stick with the DNA data on it. 'Who would like this? It's the DNA data obtained from Derek Watson's beer glass. I hope it's in the right format.'

'Jake can have it,' answered Robert. 'It needs to be put on under a different name. We already know Derek Watson isn't on the database and it would be unfair to add him when there is no good reason. This is only a test case.'

'I'll put it under Denis Watts,' said Jake, 'and then I'll search for it as an unknown to check it can be found OK. I suppose I'll have to wait until after lunch to do it.'

Alice replied. 'There will be a bit of time before lunch if you want to make a start.' Then, thinking this might be a better opportunity to ask her question from the previous evening whilst Jake was around, she said, 'I don't understand why you're so happy to let Jake play around with the DNA database but not with Brewdat.'

It was Simon who answered. 'The DNA database is on the list. Brewdat isn't.'

'What list?'

'The list of systems Jake has approval to hack into,' explained Simon. 'I thought you knew about it from our tea party discussions. It came out of your original idea to pull everything together so we could see what areas the three of us might work together on.'

'No, I know I went on about you pooling your resources but I didn't know there was a list. What else is on it?'

'DVLC,' blurted out Jake. 'I like that one. I looked up the chassis number of William's new car recently.' He then reeled off a long number to prove it. 'I also know the chassis number of your car, Miranda,' again quoting an equally long number.

'Why did you just call Alice Miranda?' asked Robert.

'It's her middle name, isn't it, Miranda? That's also in the DVLC records.'

'Yes, Jake, it is, but I don't use it very much as I'm not that fond of it, so please stick with calling me Alice.'

'I don't know why you don't like Miranda. I think it's a nice name,' said Simon. 'It's certainly better than Cedric.'

'Who's Cedric?' asked Alice.

'That's my middle name,' said Robert. 'It's carried down from my great-grandfather on my father's side. You know, the one who everyone in the family now thinks must have been an Aspie. We've had that conversation many times about my parents' being convinced that Asperger's syndrome is hereditary.'

'Yes, and I've agreed with you that a genetic connection makes sense, despite the experts not being so certain. I just didn't know he was called Cedric, that's all.'

'Cedric and Miranda,' muttered Jake.

Not sure what Jake meant but feeling it was time to get back to the original conversation, Alice said, 'So, it's because Brewdat isn't on the approved list that Jake's been held back.'

'Partly,' admitted Simon,' but also because someone could be monitoring it, the same reason we didn't want the original email pursued. We could just be giving away our intentions.'

'Even though the probability of finding anything is now so low.'

'That is irrelevant,' stated Robert. 'You are mixing up probabilities between boxes and within boxes.'

Noticing Alice was looking confused, Simon tried to explain. 'You know Robert thinks in boxes. The reason for investigating Brewdat and the likelihood of someone watching out for us doing that are in the same box, so is unchanged by whatever the probability is of the answer being in a different box.'

'Precisely,' added Robert. 'Anyway, if you wanted to know, why didn't you ask me on Wednesday evening when we talking about all this?'

'I was worried about it falling into the category of an annoying question,' admitted Alice.

'How can it be annoying when there is a perfectly logical answer? I have told you before, it is only annoying when there is no obvious logic.'

Or when you don't like the logic, thought Alice to herself, only slightly the wiser but deciding not to pursue the matter any further.

'I'm happier about Brewdat now,' said Simon. 'Hopefully, we can confirm over lunch that Jake can go ahead. By the way, did you see the message from William saying he'd be late?'

'No,' replied Alice. 'Do I need to delay lunch?'

Simon laughed. 'I don't think so. He just said he had to double check something first but he knows he'll be in big trouble if he's late for your Yorkshire pudding. You've made that very clear to us, Alice.'

'Good. I'm pleased I've got at least one message through,' responded Alice, also laughing. 'You'd better get used to listening to me and you'd all better be on your best behaviour today. I'm planning to hand in my notice on the flat tomorrow so there's still time for me to change my mind. Come on, Jake. We need to get cracking. It sounds as though I have a reputation to keep up. The first thing we need is the right-sized tin.'

As soon as the meat loaf was in the oven and everything else had been prepared, Jake went upstairs to check out the memory stick. Alice took the opportunity to join Robert and Simon in the lounge. 'What's the latest on Jake's toe?' she whispered.

'He's been taking the antibiotics willingly enough, although we have to remind him,' replied Simon. 'He's not so keen on the permanganate bath. He did it on Friday but didn't do it yesterday in spite of both Robert and me telling him to. I tried again this morning but he shouted at me that having a shower was sufficient. I was going to suggest you have a word with him.'

'I'll try.' Then, noticing a tape measure and note book, Alice asked, 'Are you measuring up?'

'Yes,' replied Robert. 'We want to get a scale plan on the computer so we can try out various layouts for the operations centre.'

'Are you going to do the same for the snug?'

'Possibly, but when I mentioned it to Jake, he didn't seem too happy,' answered Robert. 'He wasn't thrilled about working downstairs either.'

'It usually takes him time to come round to new ideas,' explained Simon. 'We thought that was something else you could talk to him about.'

'Hang on a minute. I'm not moving in here just to do your dirty work.'

'We know,' stated Robert, 'but he is much more likely to listen to you, particularly at the moment. Plus, it is mainly for you we are planning to change the snug.'

'Only because you want this as your operations centre. I'll talk to Jake but you need to let me do it in my own way. I don't want him to start seeing me as always being the villain. Also, we must include him in the discussions and make sure he understands the positive aspects. He will need a logical explanation from his perspective, just the same as you would, Robert.' Changing the subject, Alice asked, 'Any further news of William? I could do with putting the potatoes in the oven.'

'No,' said Simon, 'but I've got the front camera showing on my laptop so I'll see him when he arrives.' He turned the laptop screen to show Alice and she could see a clear image of the drive where her Fiesta was parked. 'There's also a motion sensor so it will alarm when there's any movement. I'm sure he'll be here soon. He knows it's lunch at one.'

'OK. I'll go ahead then. It's only the Yorkshire that's critical.' As she was walking out of the door, she added, 'Is it OK if I go up and have another look at what will be my room? I'll give Jake a call while I'm up there.'

'Of course it's alright,' said Robert. 'You don't have to ask, although it would probably be a good idea if Simon took you through his alarm system so you don't set anything off by mistake.'

'I can do that any time you like,' called out Simon. 'Oh, and if you want Jake you can always use the intercom by the front door to buzz up. He is number three, I'm two and Robert is one. I'll set you up as number four.'

'That would be great,' replied Alice, not certain that she wanted to be able to be buzzed at all.

Whilst they were on their own waiting for the Yorkshire to cook, Alice took the opportunity to ask Jake about his toe. 'You haven't mentioned your toe today. How are you getting on with the permanganate baths and antibiotics?'

Jake visibly tensed up. 'Everything's under control. The flucloxacillin has to be taken on an empty stomach, so it's difficult to fit in with three meals a day. I'll have to wait for at least two hours after lunch before taking the next one.'

'Good, I'm pleased you're managing OK. It's important with any antibiotics that once you start a course you finish it. I know I'm not a medical doctor but I did think Dr James made sense. She obviously wasn't happy we'd let it get so badly infected but I thought she seemed hopeful that if it was tackled internally by the flucloxacillin and externally by the permanganate baths, it would reach a point where she can do something about the toenail itself. I'm sure you want her to be pleased with you when we go to your next appointment. Have you worked out a routine for doing the permanganate baths or is there anything I can help you with?'

Thankful to have been given a way out, Jake replied, 'I like routines. Will you sort one out for me?'

'After lunch, I'll find everything you need and put it all together in the bathroom.'

'Will you write down the procedure for me as well?'

'Yes of course, as long as you promise to do it every day. There's no point in going through all that at the doctor's and then not doing what they say, is there?'

'No, I suppose not.'

Simon bounded into the kitchen. 'William's here.'

A few minutes later, exactly at one o'clock, all five of them were seated at the dining-room table, starting on their Yorkshire pudding.

'You see, Alice, Simon was correct,' said Robert. 'You needn't have worried about Bill.'

'What's this?' asked William, avoiding the usual flobbadob response. 'Have I caused a problem?'

'No, William, you haven't,' replied Alice kindly. 'It's just that I found out earlier I've built up a reputation as some sort of harridan who will dish out the most horrendous punishment if anyone dares to be even a minute late for my Yorkshires.'

'I'm sure that's not the case, Alice,' said William, trying to reassure her.

'Oh, don't worry about it. It's fine by me. My interpretation is, when I move in, these three will be so scared of me, they'll obey my every command.' Not sure how serious she was being and not knowing what else to do, everybody laughed including, after a short delay, Alice. 'Anyway, William, is everything alright? Joking apart, it isn't like you to be late.'

'Everything is fine, thank you, or at least I think it is. I was late because I've found something interesting to do with the Watson & Charles project.'

Everyone stopped eating and all eyes turned to him. 'Do tell,' said Alice excitedly.

'Don't you want to wait until the main course has been served up? I don't want to be the cause of it being spoilt. It could be a lengthy discussion because it's not clear to me what it all means.'

'Just give us the gist,' said Simon. 'Alice says it's only the Yorkshire that's critical from a timing point of view and you've got us all interested now.'

'Well, I've found two very brief emails which, to me, suggest the Finance Director of Watson & Charles could be in collusion with the Managing Director of Limberts Brewery in Newcastle.'

'Blimey,' said Simon. 'That would explain a lot.'

'I remember you saying Limberts Brewery were likely to be interested in acquiring Watson & Charles. Do you think they've done this before, used an insider?' asked Alice.

'Does that mean he's a spy? Is it industrial espionage? Will he go to jail?' asked Jake, all in a rush.

William responded calmly. 'Look, don't get over excited. It needs someone else to have a look. There may be another explanation and there may also be more to be found. I do admit to being in a hurry to get here in time for lunch so I could well have missed something.'

Sounding quite negative, Robert said, 'I agree with Bill. Let's not get too carried away until we have established all the facts. When we have finished lunch, we can have a closer look and decide what to do next.'

Realising that Robert was disappointed because it was not the answer he wanted, Alice said, 'It does make sense to have the meat loaf now. Jake, please will you help me get everything on the table. William, it just needs cutting into thickish slices, please.'

During lunch and in between mouthfuls, William explained he had spent quite a lot of time looking at the emails of both Neil Martin and Jeremy Turner, as he had promised he would.

'Until this morning, I focussed on their work emails and, as Robert had suggested, used the attachments such as minutes of board and management committee meetings to build up a picture of the difficulties facing Watson & Charles as a business. I skimmed through everything else for the last twelve months as there was so much of it but, for both men, it all looked like normal business communication. I noticed they both had a tendency to forward some of their work emails to their personal email addresses but assumed this was just to allow them to do extra work at home. To be honest, by the end of yesterday, I'd had enough and was prepared to report there was nothing to find. This morning, so I could report truthfully, I thought I'd better just have a quick look at their personal emails. I started with Neil Martin, again just skimming through, and quickly decided all looked fine. I then did the same with Jeremy Turner. I wasn't expecting to find anything and only had about five minutes before I was planning to leave to come here. However, when I was scanning his inbox, I was struck by a fairly recent one with a domain name of limbertsbrewery. On closer inspection, it was a reply from Malcolm Bickerstaff of Limberts Brewery to an email from Jeremy Turner the previous day. The wording was short and cryptic so I looked for others. I had to go back to April before I found anything. Again it was just a brief exchange of emails. I looked back further but didn't find anything else. I looked up Malcolm Bickerstaff and found out he's the Managing Director of Limberts Brewery. It made me think of Simon because the suspicious part was, in both cases, Malcolm Bickerstaff's replies effectively instructed Jeremy Turner to use the phone rather than email.'

By this stage, everyone else had almost finished eating whilst William still had a plenty of food left on his plate. He paused to try to catch up but Robert asked, 'What was in the emails from Jeremy Turner?'

Trying to keep them quiet whilst he finished his lunch before it went cold, William fished out a couple of pieces of folded paper from his pocket. 'Read them for yourselves. I printed them out before I left.' He handed one page to Simon on his right and the other to Robert on his left.

'Come on, what do they say?'

'Be patient, Jake. Give them time,' said Alice.

It was Robert who went first. 'Mine is the later one, dated 23 September. It reads, "Couldn't get though on the phone. Things hotting up and looking promising. Need to talk asap." The reply, two days later, is "Had to change phone," then gives a new mobile number and ends with "No more emails". There are no salutations or sign-offs on either.'

Simon followed. 'Mine is dated 25 April. It's more formal. "Dear Mr Bickerstaff, Cracks were starting to show at the recent AGM. I have decided I would like to follow up the conversation we had at the brewers' dinner in January after all. Please let me know if you are still interested. Yours, Jeremy Turner." The reply is dated 28 April. "Yes, I am. Call me on 07700 900234. Don't send any more emails, not secure."'

Alice commented, 'I can see why you think they seem suspicious, William. It's a shame we don't know what was said over the phone. Robert was only saying the same thing the other evening, weren't you?' Robert didn't respond.

Having finished eating, William said, 'Another thing I noticed which might be relevant is the later email was sent the day after Jeremy Turner had emailed himself the presentation Robert previously mentioned, the one about the potential impact of this year's result on the price of the shares.'

'So what does it all mean?' cried Jake. 'Has William solved the Watson & Charles project? Will we get paid? What do we need to do next?'

This time Robert did respond, although not overly enthusiastically. 'First of all we need to see if there is any further evidence to be found. Nobody has solved anything yet, although it does seem as if this might provide an explanation for some of the unproven facts we have come across. As for getting paid, I very much doubt it. It is unlikely to make much difference to the financial results for this year. If everyone has finished lunch, I suggest we move to the lounge and get these emails up and see we can find anything else of note.'

'Just a minute,' said Alice, fairly loudly. 'The clearing up needs to be done first. If we just abandon everything, it'll never get done. You three clear whilst Jake and I go and sort some things out in the bathroom. I know this does sound like a breakthrough but, if we all think about possible next steps whilst we're doing our jobs, we can then meet up in the lounge with a cup of tea to discuss the way forward.'

'Harridan,' stated William thoughtfully but with a smile on his face. 'Yes, I can now see what they mean.' Alice laughed, scrunched up her paper napkin into a ball and threw it at him across the table.

* * *

When they were all in the lounge with their tea, the mood was extremely buoyant with one exception, Robert. Alice was wishing she could have talked to him alone to try to convince him this was a success, not a failure. She decided she would just have to try to do it with everyone else present. Jake had quickly pulled up Jeremy Turner's personal email account so that it was clearly visible on the large screen. They had all moved their chairs to see and everyone was trying to talk at the same time. Robert stood up with the aim of gaining control.

'It would appear there is a consensus of opinion that these emails Bill has found are significant. The main question to be answered is how do they change our approach to the Watson & Charles project? It was my intention today to propose we close the project next weekend as we have very few outstanding actions and the probability of success had been reduced to less than 10 per cent. My personal view is the discovery of these emails only reduces the probability of success even further.'

'Surely that depends on the definition of success, Bob ... flobbadob.'

Feeling the need to re-establish her role as peacemaker, Alice leapt in. 'Can I suggest we leave discussions of successes or otherwise until we have a proper project review. There are bound to be many things we feel went well and other areas we could learn from. I agree with Robert. We should focus today on what to do about these emails but, first, I think we should all congratulate William for finding them in the first place.'

'I second that,' said Simon. 'There were hundreds to look through and it would have been very easy to miss those two.'

Even Jake chipped in, 'It's a good thing you took that job away from me. I wouldn't have recognised them as being important.'

William responded. 'Thank you. I don't feel I deserve so much credit. I'm very happy to have contributed but I strongly believe we've all played a part in getting to this point. Anything like this should be viewed as a team success. Equally, we should be very careful not to blame just one of us if something doesn't go so well.'

'Excellent point,' exclaimed Alice. 'This is the first major achievement for RTA. As Roger Thompson Associates, we've found something that may help to explain why Watson & Charles, a multi-million-pound company, is performing so badly.'

'We haven't changed the world yet though, have we?'

'Jake, changing the world can only happen little by little. It could well be the world may now change for Jeremy Turner and, hopefully, for Derek Watson too. Also,' continued Alice, looking at William and trying not to get too emotional, 'RTA has already changed my world.'

'And mine,' said William

'And ours,' said Simon. 'You made it very clear you wouldn't be coming to live here if it wasn't for RTA.'

'I hadn't thought of it like that,' said Jake happily, punching the air with his fist. 'RTA forever.'

'Let us all not get too carried away,' said Robert. 'We are supposed to be talking about what to do next.'

'Well, you're the one with the best understanding of Watson & Charles,' pointed out Alice. 'How do you think Derek Watson would feel if he knew his Finance Director had been in secret discussions with one of his main rivals?'

'I have no idea as to how Derek Watson would feel, as you well know.'

'Alright, then, let me try again. How do you think this information impacts on the Watson & Charles project?'

'It raises a key unproven fact, that Jeremy Turner may not have been acting as a Finance Director should do. If he has been taking action to undermine performance rather than enhance it, there would be a direct impact on Watson & Charles's results. If he has just been passing on information, there would be little impact.'

'How do we find out which it is and how does it help with your three outstanding concerns?' asked Alice. 'I presume we can now work on the basis the original email came from Limberts Brewery, given they were one of William's suggestions in the first place.'

'That still remains an unproven fact but with a high probability. I still cannot understand the logic behind the timing of the email. We have no additional data that relates to the managed-house-only question or the lack of any earlier trend, so these do remain as outstanding concerns. The only explanation that fits is if all three of these are due to a combination of poor business decisions and illogical behaviour by Jeremy Turner.'

Interrupting the conversation, Simon cried out, 'I've found something about the dinner. I was just having a quick look at the emails Jeremy Turner had sent to himself from work. There's one about him standing in at short notice for Derek Watson to represent Watson & Charles at a Brewers' Company Annual Livery Dinner held on January 20th 2017 at Brewers Hall in London. Look, I've put it up on the screen.'

They all looked. 'Well done, Simon,' said William. 'Clearly, I missed that one. I'm not sure it adds a lot as it's just Pauline Sharples passing on the details and thanking Jeremy for agreeing to go as Derek was unwell. It does make me wonder, though, whether I missed anything else of importance. Maybe I need to look again.'

Robert stepped in. 'We have already spent a great deal of time going through emails and investigating the Watson & Charles project in general. From a commercial viewpoint, there is little justification for doing more. I propose we stop the Watson & Charles project. It has been a useful training exercise but it would be better to consider what RTA does next.'

Realising again that Robert was using her idea to dig himself out of a hole, Alice said, 'I understand we will not be getting half a million pounds for this project, as that was dependent upon being able to turn the results around quickly. However, we don't know how valuable the information William has found will be to Derek Watson. Also, money apart, I'm sure we're all interested to find out what the impact is on Watson & Charles. As a compromise, why don't we wait a week and stick to Robert's original timescale of stopping this project next weekend. In the meantime, let's just send these emails to Derek Watson and monitor all the email accounts to see what happens. You never know, even though it's not strictly in the verbal contract, he may decide to pay us something.'

'We can always take what we think it is worth.'

Robert responded immediately. 'No, Jake, we are not going to do that. It would be against the values we agreed. Are there any objections to Alice's proposal?'

The room was quiet until Jake asked, 'I suppose there's no point in pursuing Brewdat now, even though I've now got permission. Shall I do the DNA thing instead? The data on Alice's memory stick looks to be in the right format.'

'Yes, Jake, the DNA database takes priority,' stated Robert. 'When we talk about the future for RTA, we should revisit the list of systems we can access. Also, in the light of the Watson & Charles experience, we should think about what we can do about mobile phones. Text messages should be accessible, they are just data. Tapping into conversations is likely to be a bit trickier, although the technology does exist.'

Alice was feeling a lot happier now Robert was talking positively about the future of RTA after Watson & Charles. 'Any objections to lamb for next Sunday's roast? Whatever happens between now and then, we can treat it as a celebration. RTA is clearly here to stay.'

'Lamb would be lovely,' answered Simon. 'Alice, I've been thinking. Given you will be living here, could we have an RTA Christmas dinner with roast turkey? Last year, Christmas Day was just like any other day.'

'Great idea,' added Jake. 'We could have a tree and presents as well.'

Taken by surprise, Alice answered, 'Oh, I'm not sure. I usually go to see my mum for Christmas.'

'But you have just been to see her,' pointed out Robert. 'My parents usually come to stay some time over the Christmas period but they won't be able to this year as you will be in their room.'

'To be honest,' admitted Alice, 'there's been so much going on recently I haven't given Christmas much thought. It sounds like something else we need to talk about. I'm sure we can work something out but let me think about it during the week and we can discuss it further next Sunday.'

The discussion slowly petered out. William seemed reluctant to leave and, as Alice had to wait until he moved his car, she had plenty of time to reassure Robert about Watson & Charles being a success and to convince Jake that bathing his toe was just another small step in changing his world.

Chapter Eighteen

On Monday morning, Pauline booted up her computer as usual. The very first unread email she saw had been sent just after midnight from Roger Thompson. All it said was information had been found during the course of the investigation which Derek Watson may be interested in and he would like to send it through to her at a time when Derek Watson would be available to receive it, as it was potentially sensitive. Pauline was intrigued and excited. She hoped it was good news. Derek needed it to be good news. They had been out together for evening meals another couple of times since Derek announced he was getting divorced. Pauline was delighted he was confiding in her on both a personal level and a work level but very concerned about what he had told her about the brewery situation. It was as if he had lost all fight, was accepting the brewery would end up being sold and that it was his fault. She had tried to encourage him to have further conversations with his father and with Stephen but he just reiterated that there was no more to say and nowhere else to go. He had been spending less time at work and more time on the golf course and driving range, trying to take his mind off things, but she could tell he was becoming more and more morose about the whole situation. Normally, he would have been at his desk well before she arrived but there was no sign of him yet, so she didn't know how to respond to Roger Thompson. She busied herself with doing other things until she could wait no longer. She was just about to pick up the phone to call Derek when she heard the distinctive tread of his footsteps in the corridor. She poked her head out of her office as he was unlocking the door to his.

'Morning,' she called out cheerfully, trying to stay calm. 'I've been waiting for you. There's something on my computer you need to see. It could be important.'

'I'll be there in a minute. Let me put my case down first.' Derek disappeared into his office but returned to Pauline's office a few moments later.

'What is it?' he asked in a grumpy tone of voice. Pauline showed him her screen. 'Well, get him to send over whatever it is. I'm here now.' Pauline quickly typed a reply and sent it. Derek had slumped into a chair. 'I'm sorry if I was a bit gruff. I had another go over the weekend at trying to persuade Mary to delay the sale of her shares but without any success. I even pleaded with her again this morning. She's determined to send in the official paperwork this week. That means we'll have to inform all shareholders within four weeks of receipt. The only other option would be for me to buy them myself as a private sale but that would mean finding four million pounds now, in the knowledge I would lose at least half of it when the share price changes. With the divorce settlement coming up, there's no way I can afford to do that. My own shares will be valued at the current price for the divorce calculations but will probably be only worth half as much when the divorce eventually goes through.'

As he was talking, there was a ping from Pauline's computer. 'Here we are, two more emails from Roger Thompson.' She opened them up with Derek watching over her shoulder. There was no covering note on either, just the emails exactly as William had found them. 'They are between Malcolm Bickerstaff and Jeremy Turner. How strange. Do you know what they mean?'

Derek had taken control of the mouse and was flicking from one email to the other. 'I bloody well do! That bastard Bickerstaff. He's been trying to tap me up for years, looking for a way in and trying to convince me that Limberts would pay a very good price and look after everyone's jobs as well. I'd always laughed him off. It appears he's tried the same with Jeremy and Jeremy's fallen for it, the bloody idiot. Do you remember that Livery dinner in January you made me pull out of at the last minute and got Jeremy to take my place? That'll be when it happened. All I bloody well needed now.' Derek sat back down with his head in his hands.

Pauline felt mortified and close to tears. Not only was it far from good news, Derek made it sound as if she was to blame.

'I'm sorry. I do remember. You had two days off work because you were so ill. I was convinced you would have got even worse had you gone to London. I was only trying to help.'

Realising the effect it was having on her, Derek stood up and put his arm round her shoulder. 'It's not your fault. Bickerstaff would just have found another way. Jeremy's the one to blame. He should have known better. I thought I could trust him.'

Thankful for his reassurance, Pauline asked, 'What are you going to do about it? Shall I reply to Roger Thompson?'

Derek thought for a few moments. 'Tell Tait thank you and that appropriate action will be taken. Then clear my diary for the rest of the day. Get me Bickerstaff on the phone. If you have any trouble getting through, say we might have to sell after all. That should attract his attention. After that, I'll want to see Maureen. Ask her to come to my office in half an hour. Check that Ralph's on site, and Jeremy of course, but without letting him know.'

Pauline quickly did as she had been asked. Maureen Haskill, the Human Resources Manager, and Ralph Dangerfield, the Site Security Manager, both wanted to know the issue but Pauline avoided telling them any details.

Towards the end of Derek's conversation with Malcolm Bickerstaff, Pauline could hear Derek's voice as he shouted down the telephone. After he had finished, he came back into her office. 'I was right. Bickerstaff had offered Jeremy a job in return for information on how to get his offer accepted. We're going to need an emergency board meeting. Can you line it up for noon today? Father should be able to get here for then. Also, see if he and Stephen are happy to have lunch with me. We may as well try to get some good to come out of this mess.'

'Will you want me in the meeting to take minutes?'

'Yes, but only the salient points. I don't expect it will take very long but we need to do it properly.'

* * *

Derek ensured he was the last to enter the board room. He walked straight to the head of the table. All of the muttering and supposition amongst the other directors ceased. Derek remained standing as he spoke.

'Thank you for coming at such short notice. I'm sure you are wondering why this meeting has been called but it has probably not escaped your attention that one member of the board is absent. That is because I have, this morning, summarily dismissed Jeremy Turner for gross misconduct.'

There were a few audible gasps from around the table but Derek continued.

'It has been brought to my attention that Jeremy was in collusion with Limberts Brewery with the intention of aiding them in the purchase of Watson & Charles. I spoke this morning to Malcolm Bickerstaff, Managing Director of Limberts, who confirmed this. Apparently, the current Finance Director of Limberts is due to retire next year. Bickerstaff had offered Jeremy an extremely attractive package, including share options, to take over as FD provided Watson & Charles was acquired at as low a price as possible. Jeremy confessed during the disciplinary hearing I've just held with him in the presence of Maureen Haskill. All is above board. Maureen took legal advice from our employment lawyers. Jeremy was given five minutes to clear his office of personal items and then escorted off site by Ralph Dangerfield. He has the right to appeal against his dismissal but I believe we can work on the assumption he will not be doing so.'

As Derek had paused, his father asked, 'Is there any indication that Jeremy did anything directly to undermine our performance?'

'I did try to ascertain as many details as possible. Obviously, in that sort of situation it's difficult to know whether to believe everything that is said. I can only tell you what Jeremy told me. He only made his decision to pass information to Limberts in April of this year, prompted by the mood at the AGM and the downturn in our performance since last autumn. Everything he did prior to that was in the best interests of Watson & Charles, as he saw them. He actually said he didn't need to do anything else because the results in the summer were so poor. The only thing he admitted to was not being honest about the bank situation, saying, if he had tried harder, he probably could have secured additional loans and slightly improved interest rates.

'I asked him specifically about the email that Mary had received. He was adamant the first time he knew about it was in this room.

He assumed Limberts were behind it but, when he asked, Bickerstaff denied it. I also asked Bickerstaff and got the same answer but I'm convinced it was Bickerstaff because it's exactly the sort of thing he would do. Interestingly, Bickerstaff did admit to, as he put it, "throwing out a lot of poor reviews of our pubs because every little helps", as if it was all a big game.

'The other thing you need to know is I took the opportunity to warn Bickerstaff off. I said we had plenty of evidence to take legal action against them if there was another sniff of hostile action from Limberts and I, personally, would do everything in my power to wreck their reputation within the brewing industry. The way he responded made me think there is dirty linen out there from other deals they've done in the past, so I'll be surprised if they do come back at us. He actually had the audacity to blame Jeremy and said they would need to find another target because of Jeremy's carelessness.'

Neil Martin was the next to speak. 'I understand from Pauline you wish us to brief everyone on this later today. How much do we tell them?'

'I've drafted a briefing note which Pauline will send out after this meeting. All it says about Jeremy is he has left the business with immediate effect. If questioned, you can mention misconduct but don't to give too many details. I would rather you focus on the arrangements going forward. Keith Fairbrother will be taking temporary charge of all accounting operations. Keith along with Jeremy's other managers will report directly to me until we can find a new FD. Also, it's a good opportunity to stress the importance of maximising our performance over the next few months. Results for this and the previous period have been a lot closer to budget. Summer has been a disaster, we have to accept that. Last year we had a very poor Christmas. Our goal now is to have a better Christmas this year, which would at least give us something positive to say to the shareholders.'

* * *

After the events of the morning, the atmosphere around the Watsons' lunch table at the Hare and Hounds was surprisingly relaxed. As soon as they were all sitting with a beer at Derek's favourite table, where they couldn't be overheard, Stephen said, 'I was pretty impressed with how you handled the Jeremy situation. It can't have been easy. Rather you than me.'

'There wasn't any other option. It had to be done. Maureen's excellent, so I had confidence in the process. I did lose it a bit when talking to Malcolm Bickerstaff. He's a real cocky bastard. I could picture him buttering Jeremy up. The financial package would have been very tempting. Limberts can offer shares whereas we can't and I'm very conscious that our cash bonus scheme hasn't paid out very much in recent years. I do have some sympathy for Jeremy and I believe he told me the truth. He did apologise and I even ended up shaking his hand as he left. One thing Jeremy did say that I didn't mention this morning was he really couldn't see any way forward for Watson & Charles. He criticised me personally for three things: sitting on the fence over whether to invest in the brewery, failing to get rid of John Hargreaves, and investing in pubs like this one. Given how things stand, I think he has a point.'

'But he was the one who argued vehemently against investing in the brewery. He wanted us to become just a pub company,' stated Stephen.

'True. He still holds by that. What he said this morning was that making no decision is still a decision and just letting things carry on so the unit cost of brewing remained high and the quality of the beer deteriorated was worse than either other option. Anyway, Stephen, you and I have already talked about that one and, if we get through all this, I will definitely support investment. What's your view, Father?'

Howard Watson took his time before answering. 'The brewery investment was always going to be a head versus heart decision. I wouldn't beat yourself up about it too much. It was impossible to argue against the numbers but family history dictates that Watson & Charles are brewers. Jeremy isn't family so doesn't understand that side of it. Also, there were difficult decisions to be made on the pubs and limited amounts of money to spend. Take this place. Yes, we could have sold it but look at it now. It's a good pub. It should be making more money than it is, so should most of the others. That's where the problem lies. However, as I said to you previously, I fear it's too late. This Jeremy Turner situation will not improve the results. I do want to say, though, that your performance this morning showed me I was wrong in saying you had no backbone. The trouble is, even if you have seen off Limberts, there are plenty of others out there who will come after us once they hear of our plight, which is likely to be as soon as the sale of Mary's shares gets out.'

'I suspect you're correct, Father. Malcolm Bickerstaff already knows about Mary's shares and, knowing him, it wouldn't surprise me if he finds a way to sell his knowledge about us, or just gives it away out of spite. I did think seriously about buying Mary's shares myself to avoid them becoming public knowledge. I could have stretched myself and found the money but I couldn't bring myself to do it, taking into account the likely hit when the share price drops and the impact of the divorce settlement. It made me realise, even for me, there's a price I'm not prepared to pay to keep the business alive.

'The whole issue of Mary's shares has made me see things much more from a shareholder's point of view. That's why I wanted to talk to you both now. There's no getting away from the fact that we're in a crisis. However, if so many companies are keen to buy us, there must be something about our business which is desirable. I accept the arguments about economies of scale but we know more about our own business than anyone else. For Christ's sake, we've been running it for more than two hundred years. Surely, if all three of us pull together, we can find a way to keep it going that gives a better long-term reward for the shareholders than selling it to Coors, Marston's, Greene King or whoever.

'I've spent a lot of time recently with John Hargreaves and I still can't see what he's doing wrong. However, the old adage of always doing the same thing will only bring the same results also applies so, as you suggested Father, I've decided to swap the roles of John and Neil Martin. Part of my reluctance has been, although Neil has kept tenancies chugging along, he hasn't really pushed anything new forward. John is definitely the more innovative of the two, so maybe he'll come up with some good ideas for tenancies, and it's difficult to see how managed houses can get any worse. All I'm asking is you give me until next year's AGM and, in the meantime, work with me to come up with the best plan we can. If, at the end of March, any one of us thinks it would be in the shareholders' best interest to sell, I promise I will stand up at the AGM and recommend we do so, although it might not be to the highest bidder as I would want to make sure we do whatever we can to preserve jobs and pensions.'

'I can't fault your sentiment and desire,' said Howard. 'We all know of many loyal employees who also have family history with Watson & Charles. The last thing I would want to do is put them out of work. However, everyone knows jobs are not guaranteed for life any more. We would need to wait and see what options are on the table at the time. My personal view is the end-of-year results are going to be so bad that any plan is highly unlikely to be good enough. Against that, I wouldn't like to feel that we caved in without exploring all possible options so, yes, I'll do as you ask and wait until April.'

'My view is unchanged,' added Stephen. 'I'll both support and help to develop a long-term plan as long as it includes staying in brewing.'

'Thank you,' said Derek. 'It means a lot to know we're united. It's bad enough losing my wife. I don't want to feel as if I'm losing a father or brother as well.'

'How are you coping, divorce-wise?' asked Stephen. 'It can't be easy still living together with all that going on around you.'

'It isn't much fun,' admitted Derek. 'I'll be glad when it's all over but it will be a while yet. Quickie divorces don't happen quickly when there's such a large amount of money involved. Mary and I have settled into a different way of living. We both seem to have accepted we've steadily drifted apart. The worst part for me is the realisation that money is far more important to Mary than I am. Maybe that has always been the case.'

* * *

It was Friday evening and the end of a busy week for Alice. Her laboratory technician had been on holiday all week so she felt as if she had been doing two jobs, plus the quarterly report for one of her projects had been due the previous day. She had played more squash than usual to catch up on the ladder matches she had missed by being away. In her flat, she had been tidying up and listing all her possessions so she could decide what to take with her, in preparation for her discussions with Robert.

The forum had been extremely active all week and, as much of it had not been too technical, she had found she could contribute more than usual. There had been a flurry of activity on Monday as soon as the email from Pauline had been sent out. William had posted that he felt quite guilty being responsible for someone he didn't know losing their job. Alice had tried to reassure him and was helped on Tuesday when the minutes of the emergency board meeting became visible and gave more details of Jeremy Turner's misdeeds. She also pointed out, for Jake's benefit, changing the world meant changing people's lives and that is exactly what they had done. In this case, it had led to someone being dismissed from their job, and so demonstrated how careful they needed to be, when doing it for real, to make sure they got it right.

The main theme then turned to the subject of payment. Robert had become very defensive, repeatedly stressing they were not owed anything because there was no direct impact on Watson & Charles's bottom line. Alice took the view they should wait and see, on the premise that Derek Watson would be extremely busy sorting out how to manage without a Finance Director. There was disappointment that there was no definite answer about the source of the original email, although William did his best to convince them Limberts Brewery was responsible. In between, Jake let everyone know the national DNA database now included the DNA of Dennis Watts. Alice had to remind herself that Dennis Watts was actually Derek Watson. Jake also sent Alice daily personal messages to tell her he had taken his pills and bathed his foot. However, Alice's main message back to them all was that RTA had achieved their first major success and shown what they are capable of, and everyone should be proud of their achievement.

Feeling extremely tired, she decided to a have a relaxing shower and an early night. As she was doing her final night-time checks, she noticed Jake's latest message telling everyone Will had found an extra pub. She tried to reply "well done" but soon gave up when the forum didn't appear to work. She put her phone on charge in the kitchen and went into the bedroom. In spite of her being tired, sleep didn't come easily. Her mind was racing with thoughts about what the future might hold for her and for Robert. He clearly was not happy the outcome of Watson & Charles had been an illogical one. She had tried to explain, unsuccessfully, that if you took emotions into account it was more logical. He still viewed it as a failure, especially as there had been no payment.

Alice realised this issue would need to be handled very carefully when they did have a project review. For RTA to be a successful business enterprise, they did need to make some money. She felt responsible as she had known there was a risk from Robert meeting Derek Watson on his own. Even small businesses had some form of sales and marketing function but RTA did not. They hadn't even recognised it as a significant gap when they did the SWOT analysis. In fact, when Alice had looked up SWOT analysis, she found out it was really a marketing tool, which was not the way Robert had used it. Maybe, in future, they would be better off identifying a problem, solving it and then selling the solution. She tried to force herself to think about more positive aspects. They had got a lot better at working as a team. There was no doubt about the unique skills that Robert, Simon and Jake brought to the group. The ease of accessing systems like the DNA database and understanding the intricacies of the Watson & Charles business by linking into their internal email systems had been impressive. William had played a big part in their achievement and her Sunday roasts had been a triumph. The biggest positive was moving into Robert's house. She eventually fell asleep, happy in the thought that she would be in an ideal position to slowly develop their relationship.

Chapter Nineteen

When she woke the following morning, Alice didn't want to get out of bed. She was still tired and, even in her bedroom, she could feel the chill of an early November morning. As she often did, Alice had promised herself a lazy Saturday. Normally, she would have started her day with a leisurely cup of tea but, instead, she just closed her bedroom window, redrew the curtains, made do with her bedtime water and snuggled back under her duvet. In between dozing, she thought more about Robert and RTA and the practical side of her move. She was determined to pay her way and decided the best approach was to contribute to the cost of the changes to the lounge and the snug. Until they did find a way for RTA to be a financial success, money was going to be tight. After all, that was the main reason for her new room becoming available in the first place. Eventually, she got up, showered and dressed. Feeling hungry, she went into the kitchen for a late breakfast. As she was boiling the kettle she retrieved her phone from its charger and noticed a myriad of messages and missed calls, mainly from William and Simon but also, unusually, a couple from Robert and even one from Jake. She quickly became worried that something was seriously wrong and looked through the messages to find out the cause. There was absolutely no detail on any of them, each one just asking her to phone urgently.

'So you finally decided to get up,' stated William as he answered the phone.

'What's wrong? Is there a problem?' asked Alice in a very concerned voice.

'No, only that everyone is worried about you. I tried to tell them you would just be having a lie in but they didn't believe me. According to Robert, you were always available for tea parties on a Saturday morning so it's not logical they couldn't get hold of you this morning. He seems to have translated that into something bad must have happened to you.'

'Oh, Robert is worried about me,' said Alice, thinking it was a good sign.

'Yes, in his own peculiar way. I found it quite amusing,' said William with a laugh.

'Oh, did you? I find it quite pleasing,' responded Alice, tartly. 'It feels as if I should be talking to him rather than you. You obviously weren't worried about me at all. Was there something that made you all want to contact me in the first place? There was no detail in any of the messages and the forum seems to be down.'

'Oh, yes, there definitely is. They're all extremely excited about what Jake has found. Simon has taken the forum down as a result for security reasons. Did you not see the last message on there from Jake?'

Alice racked her brains. 'I saw something last night about Will and another pub. I just assumed he was playing with Brewdat again as he had nothing else to do. Is that the one you mean?'

'Yes. He wasn't playing. He was in the Watson & Charles Brewdat system. The pub he found seems to have been hidden away. All three of them have been up all night trying to work out what it means. Simon has been holding Jake back until he's happy with the security side but they've obviously found enough to convince Robert. He's adamant it fits in with his original theory. He wants an urgent meeting this morning to talk about a way forward. My problem is I'm in the shop on my own. Nancy isn't available and I can't really be free until after one o'clock.'

'Well, it's eleven now and I'm not ready either. I'm sure it can wait a little longer. Anyway, if none of them have been to bed, what state will they be in? It sounds like a recipe for disaster. The last thing we need after such a good time last weekend is a falling-out. Surely it would be better to wait until tomorrow as we had originally planned.'

'That would suit me. Although it did sound interesting, so I'm quite keen to find out what's happened.'

'How about I suggest a compromise? Could you be there for ten thirty tomorrow? We could have a meeting before lunch. I can get there earlier to do the food prep.'

'Fine by me, but even you might find it difficult to persuade Robert to wait until tomorrow.'

'I'll call him right now. Once he knows I'm still alive, I'm sure he'll agree to whatever I say,' said Alice sarcastically. 'See you tomorrow, unless you hear otherwise.'

Before she called Robert, Alice made her tea and found two rather old digestive biscuits to go with it. 'Hello, Robert. I gather you want to talk to me. Is it anything important?' she said calmly into the phone.

'Yes, it is,' replied Robert firmly. 'Why didn't you answer your phone? I thought you might be hurt. I have been trying to contact you for hours. I am calling an emergency RTA meeting immediately.'

'I'm sorry to hear you were worried about me. I'm fine, it was just that I needed to catch up on sleep after a hectic week. If you were really concerned, you could always have cycled round to my flat. It's not very far. Hopefully, once I've moved, you won't have to worry so much.' Not wanting to admit she'd called William first, Alice added, 'Why do we need an emergency meeting? Has something changed?'

'Yes. We've discovered something important. I don't want to talk about it too much over the phone but so far it fits the first box.'

'You mean it could be fraud after all? That would be wonderful,' exclaimed Alice, 'but why do we need to meet now? We'll all be together tomorrow anyway. Can we not talk about it then?'

'We need to decide how to proceed. Simon is concerned about security. He and Jake are arguing because Jake wants to go in again and Simon won't let him. Simon has taken down the forum and is insisting we don't do any communication over the internet until we've met and agreed a way forward.'

'How much sleep have they both had?'

'None since the latest finding. Why do you ask?'

'I'm just wondering if that could be a reason why they're tetchy. Also, people tend to make bad decisions when they're tired. It would be a real shame if, having made such an interesting discovery, things go wrong now. I'm sure you wouldn't want that to happen, would you?'

'No, of course not. That is why I want a meeting before anything further is done, to make sure we take the correct action.'

Alice remained unwilling to give in. 'Can you not tell me even a little about it over the phone? I thought you said phone calls were relatively safe.'

'I will give you a brief summary,' said Robert reluctantly. 'There is a dummy managed house called the Secret Fox hidden in the Watson & Charles Brewdat system. It is designed not to show on any of the reports but a number of transactions from the real pubs are directed through it. Simon thinks whoever set up the Secret Fox will have installed enough protection to know if it has been found. That's why it is important to act quickly.'

'I agree it does sound a very significant discovery,' said Alice, trying to be supportive but still determined to talk him round. 'Realistically, the earliest William and I can get there is two o'clock. By the time we've had the meeting Jake and Simon will be even more tired but will want to implement the agreed actions straight away. It sounds like a high-risk strategy to me. What do you think?'

Robert hesitated before replying. 'I suppose an alternative would be to stop now and wait until tomorrow to have the meeting when Jake and Simon are refreshed. I would need to check with Simon but I don't think the probability of being discovered would change significantly.'

Recognising Robert was avoiding admitting he, too, had been up all night, Alice pushed home her argument. 'That sounds like a good idea. It would also mean we can still have our Sunday roast as planned. If we were to meet today, tomorrow's lunch would obviously have to be cancelled.'

'Mm, maybe you have a point,' confessed Robert. 'I will tell Jake and Simon the meeting will be tomorrow and nothing further is to be done today, apart from leaving everything as secure as possible.'

'Good and while you're at it, remind Jake about the rules, especially about his toe. If I get there and find things have slipped backwards, I'll be in a bad mood and I'm sure none of you would want that. If I hear no more from you I'll be there at half past nine to prepare the food and, providing either you or Jake are available to help, I'll let William know the meeting will start an hour later.'

Pleased with how she had handled the situation, as soon as she finished the call with Robert she sent William a text to confirm the arrangements. As she was preparing to go to Sainsbury's, Alice found herself regretting she would have to wait until the morning to find out more as even she was intrigued about the Secret Fox.

*   *   *

When she arrived on Sunday morning, Alice was surprised to find there were two willing helpers waiting for her in the kitchen. Both Robert and Jake greeted her with smiles on their faces. Robert had clearly got used to the idea of a hug and a kiss, as he walked towards her with open arms. Jake stood by watching and, although Alice heard him mutter something about Cedric and Miranda, he seemed quite happy with just a cheery 'Good morning'. They both tried to talk to her at the same time. Robert was telling her his plan to delay the meeting had worked well and Simon was carrying out extra security checks to look for signs of unusual activity. Jake was more interested in telling Alice his toe was a lot better, although he did go on to say how well Will had done and he hoped they went on to catch the bastard responsible and put him in jail for a very long time.

In spite of Alice wanting to hear more, she insisted on focussing on the lunch preparations and leaving all discussions about Watson & Charles until the meeting. They finished with plenty of time to spare. Simon came downstairs as soon as William arrived so, as everyone was ready, Robert was persuaded to start the meeting a few minutes early. Jake hurriedly made tea and they all settled in the lounge. The atmosphere was very relaxed and there was a great sense of anticipation.

Instead of Robert standing up and waving his arms around as usual, he remained seated as he said, 'As you will have gathered, it appears we have had another major breakthrough in the W & C project. There is now a significant amount of evidence to support the original unproven fact that there is a link between the loss of profit and the email sent to Mary Watson. The main question we need to answer today is how to move forward. Also, we need to consider what, when and how to tell Derek Watson.'

'Can you explain a little bit more about this Secret Fox and the security concerns?' requested Alice.

Simon answered. 'If you remember, we were told that W & C had sixty-nine managed houses. When Jake sent his mole, Will Scarlet, to look from underneath he found seventy.'

'You mean by breaking into the bank?'

'Yes, but it wasn't very difficult. A program like Brewdat doesn't have a sophisticated intrusion-prevention system,' explained Simon. 'It's more concerned with restricting access to the various users. Anyway, Jake modified his mole and had another look.'

'I don't like you talking about Will as a mole,' said Jake petulantly. 'He's much cleverer than that. I think of him as an outlaw who spies on other people's computers.'

Ignoring Jake, Simon continued. 'We found the Secret Fox had been set up just like every other pub, except it wasn't visible to users as it was flagged not to appear in any report. Also, on tracing back, we found it doesn't have any direct sales. All the sales transactions were re-routed from other pubs. These sales, therefore, didn't show up on any W & C reports, making it look like the pubs were performing worse than they actually were. There's code in the W & C version of Brewdat that allows this to happen. This code isn't present in the version we set up here even though nominally we have the same version. Whoever set this up is clearly an expert in Brewdat. They obviously don't want the Secret Fox to be known about and it's highly likely they will have put in checks and alarms to warn them if it is found. So far we've been very careful. In theory, they could trace our activity back to here but I've been monitoring our security systems very closely and am confident that hasn't happened, yet. However, if we keep going back in for more and more information, the risk of being detected will increase.'

'What are the consequences if we do get caught?' asked Alice. 'They are breaking the law as well. Presumably they can't just wipe away all of the evidence.'

'No,' replied Simon. 'They would need to update the W & C Brewdat system to wipe out all traces of the additional code. The Secret Fox is just data so could be removed, but the transactional history would remain. Their most likely action would be to stop all activities and take steps to protect their identity being traced. They might also launch some form of attack on our systems with the aim of preventing us finding them. If you think about the way they hid the source of the original email, it is clear we're dealing with a very skilful opponent.'

'It is still an unproven fact that the same person who sent the original email is also responsible for the Secret Fox fraud,' stated

Robert, 'although I do agree the probability is very high. We still need proof of a link in order to satisfy the conditions of our contract with Derek Watson.'

'It's also an unproven fact,' added William, 'the culprit is associated with Limberts Brewery. I checked and found out, not only do Limberts use Brewdat, they were one of the first breweries to do so. It made me wonder whether they've adopted this same approach with some of their previous acquisitions.'

'I don't understand what you mean. Logically, that would suggest Malcolm Bickerstaff, and possibly Jeremy Turner, lied to Derek Watson,' said Robert.

'I'm afraid that's a distinct possibility,' said Alice. 'Even from the little we know, it sounds as if Malcolm Bickerstaff is a pretty unscrupulous character.'

'Why can't everybody just tell the truth? Everything would be so much easier,' exclaimed Robert in an exasperated manner.

'Let me get this right,' said Alice, trying to summarise the situation. 'We're working on the basis that Limberts Brewery are trying to acquire W & C by devious means. They have interfered with the W & C Brewdat system to make it appear as if the profits are far less than they actually are. They sent the email to Mary Watson to create a split in the family and they used Jeremy Turner as a spy to provide inside information as to how the Watson & Charles board was reacting and when to time their bid. So, what happened to the actual money? You told me no money went through Brewdat, it went straight to the bank.'

'That does appear to be a reasonable hypothesis,' agreed Robert. 'Tracking the money is a key aspect. Looking at the managed-house bank account, the diverted transactions Jake found show up on it just as would be expected, as being from the original pubs. There must be some route for the money subsequently to leave the account, otherwise Brewdat and the bank would not be reconciled and a discrepancy would have been spotted ages ago. However, there are thousands of transactions each month on that account, all seeming to be perfectly normal. Even if we hacked into the bank instead of just accessing the account as a user, we might not find anything of note. We really need more information from Brewdat but that is where we come back to Simon's concerns over security.'

'So, what are our options?' asked Alice.

'I believe we have three options,' replied Robert. 'The first is to do nothing more except report what we have found to Derek Watson, leaving him to do the rest. The second is to continue sending in Will Scarlet to probe everything to do with the Secret Fox. The third is to send Will in just once more to set a flag so the Secret Fox can be seen in the user reports. All three have their issues.'

William responded very quickly. 'I can see the problems with the first and third suggestions. The first would be only a half done job with the risk we will still not get paid and no guarantee it would save Watson & Charles, but it would keep us safe. The third would show our hand straight away. Although it would put a stop to the fraud, if Simon is correct, it would be unlikely to provide concrete evidence of a link back to Limberts. I know, Simon, you said we're dealing with a skilful opponent but I would back you and Jake against anyone. I don't, therefore, see what's wrong with the second option. It appears to be the one with the most to gain and the least risk.'

'I know the problem with the second one,' replied Jake. 'It's time. There's a lot of data associated with the Secret Fox. Simon is only allowing Will to bring out small amounts at a time. Each time we send Will in, he has to be recoded and tested. It could take weeks to get everything out and Robert says we're running out of time.'

'That is correct,' agreed Robert. 'If we do not take action soon, it may well be too late to save Watson & Charles.'

Also,' added Simon, 'each time Will goes in there is an increased risk of detection.'

'I agree with William about option one. That would be a cop-out and we would deserve not to be paid,' stated Alice. 'If we rule out option two as well then we have no choice but to choose option three.'

Jake objected. 'But that would mean the Sheriff of Nottingham would get away with it.'

'What do you mean?' asked Alice.

'That Bickerstaff man, sitting in his castle of a brewery in Newcastle. He's like the Sheriff of Nottingham, getting his henchmen to do all the dirty work for him. I want him to go to jail as well.'

Trying to placate him, Alice responded, 'I'm not sure we can get anybody sent to jail, Jake. That would risk implicating ourselves.'

'Also, as I keep telling you,' added Robert, 'it is not yet proven it is Bickerstaff. Option three might not give us the link we are searching for.'

'I do see why it's such a dilemma and why you wanted a meeting,' admitted Alice, looking at her watch. 'How do we choose? Do we just have a vote? Maybe we should think about it over lunch. It's about time I was putting the lamb in the oven. It should be up to temperature now. Jake set the timer for me earlier this morning.' Without waiting for an answer, she stood up and went to the kitchen.

'I vote for option two,' said Jake vehemently whilst Alice was out of the room. 'I don't really care about saving Watson & Charles. I want Will to finish the job and catch the baddies.'

'I don't know which way to vote,' said Simon. 'Am I allowed to abstain?'

Robert was just about to answer but William got in first. 'Maybe there's a fourth option. I've just had a thought. Shoot me down if you think this is ridiculous but I was wondering about back-ups. Simon is always insisting we have regular back-ups of everything. That's one of the reasons you have so much kit here. As Brewdat is just a database and this fraudulent activity has been going on for around a year, will there not be enough evidence in the back-up data Watson & Charles are bound to have? Would it not be easier and safer to get hold of one of their back-ups and work with that on our Brewdat system here? If nothing else, it may help you narrow down what you want Will to look for.'

Simon looked towards Jake but, as usual, Jake was staring into space. 'That might just work. It's certainly worth a try. All we would need to do would be to copy a file from their archives rather than get data from the active system. No-one is likely to be watching out for that. What do you think, Jake?'

'It should be a doddle. We wouldn't even need Will to do that.'

'If we pretend to be Ian Walters, it should appear like a perfectly normal action,' said Simon. 'Shall we go and have a look now while lunch is cooking? We'll need to do it from upstairs.'

'You may as well,' answered Robert. 'Even I do not like any of the other options so, if Bill's suggestion is workable, it could give us a way forward without anyone else being aware of what we are doing.'

Simon leapt up with Jake hobbling along behind him. Almost immediately, Alice came back into the lounge. 'Have I missed something? Is the meeting over? I've just seen Simon and Jake heading upstairs.'

'Bill's had a good idea that might give us a fourth option. Simon and Jake have gone up to check it out,' explained Robert.

'It was only a thought, Bob ... flobbadob. I don't really understand how they do things but it's good to see them working well together. It's quite amazing what they can achieve when they put their minds to it.'

'I agree,' said Robert. 'Both of them know a lot more than I do. I only need to know something can or cannot be done, preferably with a significant degree of certainty and, yes, I know with Simon it is unlikely to be 100 per cent.'

Alice flopped into an armchair. 'I'm pleased there might be another way. I was wondering, whilst I was in the kitchen, whether Simon was being over cautious and if it might be possible to speed up option two. It would be such a shame if we can't follow it through given we've got this far. However, I don't want to give Jake the idea he can ignore Simon's advice and I certainly don't want to feel responsible for him getting caught. I feel I've got to know Jake a lot better with doing this project, as well as the business with his toe. He hasn't been quite so derogatory about women recently and I am even growing to quite like his Robin Hood analogies.'

'You know he now names all his major worms, moles, viruses and other hacking tools after outlaws,' said Robert. 'There are lots of them, even another Will, Will Stutely. The way he talks about them you would think they were his friends.'

'I think that's exactly how he views them,' said William. 'Before he knew us, he didn't have any real friends so he made some up. It's the same with his fantasy women. What he could really do with is a real girlfriend. Now there's a challenge for you, Alice. Don't you know anyone suitable?'

'No chance. In spite of what I've just said, I wouldn't wish Jake on any of my friends. In fact, I doubt there's a single female in the entire human race who would want to fill that role. You two would stand more chance than me.'

'What do you mean?' asked Robert. 'We don't know any suitable girls.'

'No, but given our past conversations about expert systems and neural networks, you could build him a robot one. A robotic girlfriend would be ideal for Jake. He could program her to be just how he wanted and, with his attitude towards women in general, she wouldn't need to be able to think very much, would she?' They all laughed, including Alice.

The three of them continued to chat in a light-hearted manner until it was time for Alice to do the final preparations towards lunch. She persuaded Robert and William to keep her company in the kitchen and it was not long before they were joined by Simon.

'It's all set up. Jake's just putting together the finishing touches. He'll be down shortly, in plenty of time for the Yorkshire pudding, and we'll do the transfer after lunch. I'll check the file is clean and then we can upload the data to our version and see what we can find out.'

'As usual,' said Alice, 'I'm not sure exactly what you're doing but it sounds promising.'

Robert did his best to explain. 'We are importing a back-up file from the W & C archives. It's unlikely our opponents will be monitoring it but Simon will make sure before we use it. The intention is that we load the data onto our version of Brewdat so we can work on it safely and find out more about how the Secret Fox is set up. There is a risk our opponents have been clever enough to prevent the Secret Fox data from being included in the back-up but that is unlikely. If it works, it will be like option three but without anyone else knowing we are doing it. The main aim will be to understand more about how the actual money is moved so we know what to look for in the bank records.'

'Well, I truly hope it works,' said Alice cheerfully. 'Wouldn't it be great if we can claim our half a million pounds? Whatever happens, I think RTA has been a success. Over lunch, I want to talk about the future. What will be our next project? It could be to do with revenge over those who have wronged us in the past, finding Aspies who are in trouble and helping them, exposing other cases of known fraud or tackling cases of hacking being used for bad purposes. Also, whether we get paid or not by W & C, I think we should go ahead with the refurbishment to create an operations centre and redo the snug. As long as it doesn't cost more than the annual rent of my flat, I would like to pay for it as my contribution in lieu of paying rent for living here.'

Chapter Twenty

Three days later, on Wednesday evening, Alice found herself back at Robert's house for another meeting. Even though she had gone straight from work having had to wait for an experiment to finish, she was late. She parked behind William's Mondeo. Everyone was in the lounge waiting for her but, instead of criticising her lack of punctuality, Robert greeted her with a hug and a kiss. Jake made her a cup of tea. Alice knew from Robert's text it was good news and she was looking forward to hearing what had been found out since Sunday. She was also pleased she didn't have to rush home to cook her own tea as Robert had also put in his text that he had made a large batch of bolognese sauce so they could all have spaghetti after the meeting. As soon as they were settled back in the lounge, Robert began.

'I am sure you will all have gathered that Bill's idea worked well. The three of us have spent the last few days finding out a lot more about how the Secret Fox is set up within the W & C Brewdat system. Most importantly, we now understand how the actual money is moved. By following the money, we believe we have found both the name of the culprit and a link to Limberts Brewery.'

'It's brilliant,' blurted out Jake eagerly. 'Simple but very clever. It would have taken Will Scarlet lots of visits to find out everything we now know. We've found the bastard.'

'Jake, I know this is very exciting but I thought we'd agreed not to use that word,' reprimanded Alice.

'Sorry, I mean we have caught the baddie.'

'We haven't caught anyone yet,' stated Robert. 'As I said, it is thanks to Bill we have been able to make such good progress in such a short time. We are again at a position where we need to decide what to do next.'

'Thanks, Bob ... flobbadob,' replied William. 'I'm pleased my idea worked but, as before, it's been a team effort to move things forward. Simon, do I take it you're happy our activities haven't been detected?'

'I'm quite happy on the Brewdat front,' replied Simon. 'Obtaining the back-up data and doing everything here was low risk. Following the money through the various bank accounts is higher risk and is one of the reasons why we've stopped. Finding Nathaniel was almost too easy. Although we've taken all our usual steps to hide our actions, if he's as good as we think he is, it's likely he'll suspect something by now.'

Alice interrupted. 'I'm afraid I'm getting lost again. We seem to be leaping about a bit. Who's Nathaniel? Is he the baddie Jake talked about? I was OK with how we left it on Sunday. Could you just talk me through the sequence of events since then, without getting too technical of course?'

Before Robert could answer, Jake leapt in. 'Yes, Nathaniel is the baddie. It's a funny name, Nathaniel Oudabade, but he's a real person and he's the one who stole all the money. He needs to be put in jail.'

Ignoring Jake, Robert said, 'Alice is correct. We cannot make a decision on what to do next unless we all understand the situation. I will explain what has happened since Sunday.' He got up from his armchair and moved across the room to where he had previously placed a small whiteboard supported on a dining-room chair.

'When we turn this room into an operations centre we will have a large whiteboard permanently in here.' Ensuring everyone could see, he wrote WHITEHOR onto the whiteboard. 'Within Brewdat, every pub is given an eight digit code to identify it. This code is attached to every transaction carried out in that pub. It is used within Brewdat for all of the various reports. It is sent via the card readers to the bank when people pay by card and is printed out on their receipt. When we obtained the back-up file of data from W & C on Sunday, we found that all of the transactions hidden away under the Secret Fox had ten digit codes, where the last two digits are always SF.' Robert added SF to make WHITEHORSF on the whiteboard and then wrote below it HARE&HOUSF and below that BLACKDOGSF. 'So, in these three examples, all transactions from the White Horse, the Hare and Hounds and the Black Dog that had the extra two digits added to their codes would automatically be sent to the Secret Fox and not, therefore, be visible through the Brewdat reports. Within the individual pubs, however, stock levels of drinks and food items would still be decremented as normal so the stock levels shown on Brewdat would still match the physical stock in each pub. When we looked in more detail, we found transactions under the Secret Fox for all sixty-nine of the W & C managed houses. Therefore, every single one of them is being reported as taking less money than they actually are.'

'But the money was still going through to the W & C bank account, wasn't it?' asked William.

'Yes,' replied Robert, 'and that's what makes it so clever. Because the card readers and the bank statements only print out the first eight digits of the code, even where the code has been modified, individual transactions can still be traced from card reader to bank without anything looking untoward.' Robert continued talking as he returned to his armchair.

'As we only imported data, we do not have sight of the programming changes that were made to the W & C Brewdat system which allows the codes to be modified. However, looking at the transactions within the Secret Fox, there is no obvious pattern to the source pubs, which suggests that some sort of random generation is involved. This would fit with the lack of trends which surprised both ourselves and the W & C analysts.'

'OK,' said Alice, 'I think I get the first bit. What you're saying is this Nathaniel person has modified the W & C Brewdat program so everyone at W & C has been fooled into thinking each one of their managed pubs is taking in less money than is actually the case. He's created this virtual pub called the Secret Fox, which no-one knows about, to hide the information about the money but not the money itself. Is it right to call the Secret Fox a virtual pub?'

'That's a very accurate description,' replied Simon. 'There's no such place as the Secret Fox. It's been set up to mimic a real pub. The main point is, from a user's point of view, nothing about the Secret Fox is visible. Nathaniel has gone to a lot of trouble to make sure it couldn't be seen. In fact, it took us quite a while to change all the settings so we could see it as a user on our system.'

'Will Scarlet still managed to find it,' stated Jake proudly. 'Will's great. He could have found out all the other stuff if we'd needed him to.'

'Maybe, Jake,' said Robert, 'but once we had got visibility of the Secret Fox as a user, it was a lot easier to get at all the information within it.'

'Is that how you managed to find out about the link to the actual money in the bank?' asked William.

'Yes,' replied Robert. 'The Secret Fox has been set up with its own unique approved suppliers and employees. All of them have their own bank accounts. When the monthly payrolls are run by Watson & Charles, payments are made to all of the accounts linked to the Secret Fox at the same time as all the other pubs. No-one at W & C would have known these Secret Fox payments were happening by just looking at Brewdat. The total amount paid each month through the Secret Fox exactly matched the total amount transferred to the Secret Fox from the other pubs. Therefore, at the end of each month, the bank account balanced with Brewdat so there would have been no reason for anyone to look in detail at the bank statement. All of the Secret Fox payments are on the bank statements but hidden amongst all the hundreds of other payments, as they look just like any valid payments to real suppliers and employees.'

'So,' asked Alice, trying to follow Robert's explanation, 'are these Secret Fox employees and suppliers fictional people and companies made up just for the purpose of channelling the money, or do they really exist?'

Simon leapt in. 'There are sixty-three accounts linked to the Secret Fox. Each account receives a payment each month of a few thousand pounds, typical amounts for real employees and suppliers. Using our tools for accessing online banking information, we've checked out all sixty-three and found, for sixty-two of them, they're not in the names of real people or companies. The exception is an account in the name of Nathaniel Oudabade. He appears to be the only real person involved. He receives a payment of five thousand pounds every month straight into his current account. Also, he is the only one with what you would call normal activity on his account. In the other sixty-two cases, as soon as the money is paid in, the majority of it is paid straight out again.'

'Nathaniel was dead easy to find,' added Jake. 'He stood out like a sore thumb.'

'The fact that Nathaniel was so easy to find is a concern,' said Robert seriously. 'Everything else fits with him being the person responsible for this fraud. It is also highly probable, although still unproven, that he was responsible for the email sent to Mary Watson. Given the steps taken to hide the source of the email and also the skill needed to set up the Secret Fox underneath Brewdat, it is surprising his personal details were not better hidden as well.'

'That's a bit of a leap to put the email down to Nathaniel as well, isn't it?' asked Alice.

'You haven't heard the whole story yet,' said Jake excitedly. 'Tell Alice and William the bit about Limberts Brewery. William, you'll like this part.'

'Once we had accessed Nathaniel's bank account,' replied Robert, 'we looked back to see when the payments from W & C started. The first one we found was just over a year ago in September 2016, which ties in with the beginning of the downturn in W & C's profits. As we were checking to make sure there was nothing earlier, we came across a payment of approximately £1500 from Limberts Brewery in June 2016. Further checks showed similar monthly payments in each of the previous twelve months. Simon then suggested using our knowledge of Brewdat to hack into the Limberts Brewdat system and get the password information for their sys admin. We did this and confirmed that Nathaniel Oudabade is 24 years old and had been employed by Limberts in their IT department from March 2015 until the end of May 2016. Interestingly, we also found another Oudabade on the system, Emmanuel Oudabade, who works for Limberts as a drayman. Both of the Oudabades live at the same address in Jesmond which is fairly close to the Limberts Brewery in Gosforth.'

'Will Scarlet had a look as well,' blurted out Jake. 'Tell them what Will found.'

'I agreed it was safe enough to send in Will Scarlet to investigate underneath the Limberts Brewery Brewdat system,' explained Simon, trying to use Alice-friendly language. 'There wasn't time for Jake to make many modifications so it was like having just a quick glance. We found there didn't appear to be a virtual pub set up like the Secret Fox but there was evidence of modifications to the Brewdat software similar to those we discovered in the W & C system.'

'It does make sense Limberts Brewery is behind all of this,' said William. 'Quite an effective strategy. Steal enough money to drive down the profits and then move in for the kill to buy the business at a low price when the shareholders are ready to sell, knowing the business is actually sound and well able to generate future profits. What about the rest of the money, though, from the other sixty-two accounts? Can any of that be traced back to Limberts or Malcolm Bickerstaff? Could he be in it for personal gain as well as company success?'

'That is where we still have a dilemma,' replied Robert. 'We are confident about the role Nathaniel Oudabade has played, so I now view it as a proven fact that he is guilty. Everything you say about Limberts and Bickerstaff, although highly probable, remains an unproven fact. We have reached an impasse with the rest of the money. I will leave the details to Simon.'

'All sixty-two accounts are with UK banks, albeit five different ones. As all five were already on Jake's list, it was quick and easy to access them all,' stated Simon. 'We were able to follow the money as it was transferred to other accounts, under other seemingly fictional names, within the same banks. However, after it had been funnelled down to just one account in each of the five banks, the next transfers were to non-UK banks, one based in Switzerland and one based in the Cayman Islands. This is where the problem lies. Neither of these banks are on Jake's list, so we haven't tried to access them before. I've looked at the security systems they use and they're different and more complex than the UK banks. Whilst I am confident we can get into them both, it would take a long time to do so. I estimate a minimum of two months to do it in a way that minimises the chances of detection. Even when we get in, there's a good chance all we'll find will be more fictitious names and accounts.'

'How much money are we talking about?' asked William.

'From September last year, we've calculated that just under 8.5 million pounds has been moved through the Secret Fox to these accounts,' replied Simon. 'Obviously, we don't know exactly where that money is now.'

'Wow,' exclaimed Alice. 'No wonder W & C are suffering if all of that would otherwise have been profit.'

'The breakdown fits as well,' Robert added. 'Just under 2 million had been taken by the end of February so would explain the dip in profits in the previous financial year, and the 6.5 million taken since

The Cubic Pea

would explain the terrible summer everyone at W & C keeps talking about. So, whilst it is good news we have an explanation that fits the financial facts, we still have to decide what to do next.'

'Surely, we've now done enough to earn our fee,' declared William. 'Even though we haven't got definite proof of Limberts' involvement, we have enough to stop the fraud and prevent more money being stolen from W & C. If we tell Derek Watson everything we know, it should be enough for him to be able to save the brewery from being sold. Once he gets the police involved, they should be able to help him trace the money.'

'Don't forget to remind Derek Watson to keep our names out of it,' said Simon worriedly. 'We can't have the police looking into what we've done otherwise we'll all end up in jail as well.'

'We could set it up so that their IT guy, Ian Walters, finds the Secret Fox and the link to Nathaniel Oudabade without anyone knowing we were involved,' said Jake.

'The problem then is, if they find it for themselves, they won't pay us,' pointed out William.

'That is why we have a dilemma,' stated Robert. 'Logic tells me this will be an issue for any other projects we undertake as RTA. How do we earn money whilst keeping our involvement a secret? If we could find the stolen money and devise a way of getting it back to W & C without involving the police, then Derek Watson would pay us and we would be safe. However, we do not have time to hack into other banking systems. If Derek Watson is going to make good use of this knowledge, he will need to know about it very soon.'

'What about coming at it from the other end?' asked William. 'Assuming we're right about Malcolm Bickerstaff, could we not dig into his finances, look for any unusually large payments and try to get proof of his involvement that way?'

Robert was starting to get agitated. 'I know you are convinced Bickerstaff is behind this but, as I said earlier, Bill, that is still an unproven fact. Even if it is him, he has been so careful to hide his involvement I doubt we would turn up anything quickly.'

'I accept it would be a long shot, Bob ... flobbadob, but we don't seem to have many alternatives.'

'I can think of a pretty obvious alternative.' All eyes turned to Alice. 'We could ask Nathaniel.'

255

'But he's the bast ... sorry, baddie. He's the one who should be in jail,' pointed out Jake vehemently.

'All I'm suggesting is we should find out more about Nathaniel before we condemn him. Also, if we were the police, knowing what we know, the next step would be to interrogate him,' argued Alice.

'What more do you need to know?' asked Robert, defensively. 'We have already told you enough to prove he is responsible for setting up this fraud and has been paid to do so.'

'I know what you've told me,' retorted Alice, looking directly at Robert. 'Now let me tell you what I've heard. All through this project we've talked about an opponent who has similar skills to Jake. We've now identified that opponent as Nathaniel Oudabade who, apparently, is a young man with exceptional IT skills, seemingly still living with his parents on the outskirts of Newcastle-on-Tyne. His surname suggests he might be different to the majority of people in Newcastle. Yes, we know he's been paid. However, if we take Jake's analogy, he's not the Sherriff of Nottingham. He is just a henchman. How often have we spoken about how lucky we are to have Jake and be able to use his skills to do good but also how easy it would have been for Jake to have ended up using his skills to do bad things? We've even talked about actively using RTA to help people with Asperger's syndrome who've got caught hacking illegally into sensitive systems. My logic tells me Nathaniel could be one of those people. What I really want to know about him, you are unlikely to be able to tell me from any database. I want know things such as does he have any friends? Was he bullied at school? Is he an Aspie?'

Silence reigned.

Recognising that no-one knew how to respond, Alice decided to change the mood. 'I don't know about the rest of you but I'm starving. How about we give this more thought and discuss it further over that spag bog you promised us all, Robert?'

* * *

The following afternoon, Alice was driving Jake back home after his latest appointment with Dr James. Everything had gone remarkably well and in complete contrast to the previous appointment. Jake had been ready on time, willing to take off his sock to show Dr James his toe and happy to talk with her about what to do next. It was only when

Dr James suggested minor surgery to remove the nail bed to prevent any recurrence that Jake baulked. Alice had got a strange look from Dr James when she intervened by telling Jake that Robin Hood would have accepted a small amount of short-term pain for longer-term gain but it had done the trick and Jake had arranged another appointment, having first made sure Alice would again go with him. Now Alice was thinking about her forthcoming conversation with Nathaniel. After complimenting Jake on his performance about his toe, she asked, 'Now you've had time to think about it, are you more comfortable about the plan to try to talk to Nathaniel?'

'I think so. I still think he's done wrong but I want to catch the person who's really responsible, the one I call the Sherriff of Nottingham. You say talking to Nathaniel is the best way of doing that, don't you?'

'I truly believe it is, Jake, but whatever happens, I don't think we'll be able to put him in jail because the risk to ourselves would be too great. I think we'll have to come up with our own way of punishing him. I have to confess, though, I'm a little nervous about being the one doing the talking to Nathaniel because I don't understand very much of the technical aspects. Also, as William pointed out, we may want to talk to him but he's not likely to want to talk to us.'

'Don't worry. It'll be fine. Me and Simon have a plan. Simon is setting everything up so it'll be ready when we get back.'

Now Alice was worried even more than before but decided not to push any further and went back to thinking about her own plan. She hoped she was right. She wanted to share her thoughts and ideas but, as only William was likely to understand her thinking, she stuck to the practicalities. 'All I need is to be able to see Nathaniel's face, be sure he can see mine and to be left alone to talk to him.'

When they arrived back, neither Robert nor Simon were interested in the progress with Jake's toe, they were too excited about contacting Nathaniel. Robert ushered Alice into the lounge and Simon started to explain the set-up. 'Whoa, slow down,' gasped Alice as she turned and walked towards the kitchen instead. 'Don't rush me. I need to compose myself first. Let's have a cup of tea. I'm sure a few minutes won't make any difference Anyway, how do you know Nathaniel will be there?'

'We sent him a message earlier this afternoon to make sure he would take your call,' replied Robert.

Somewhat surprised, Alice asked 'What do you mean you sent him a message? I thought you were certain any contact would scare him off.'

Simon intervened. 'We were concerned that as soon as we made contact he would try to implement whatever escape plan he'd put in place, so we thought we'd better do something to keep him interested. As you'd suggested Nathaniel was very much like Jake, Robert asked Jake what would grab his attention and make him want to find out more if he was faced with a similar situation. After giving it some thought, Jake came up with a good idea so we implemented it. As far as we can tell, it seems to have worked.'

Intrigued to know what message had been sent, Alice tried not to sound too sarcastic. 'That sounds like pretty good thinking, particularly as it was a people issue. I assume this is the same plan Jake mentioned to me in the car. What was the message?'

'It was to tell him we could cure his nightmares,' announced Jake proudly.

'How do you know Nathaniel has nightmares?' enquired Alice. 'That suggests you have nightmares too, Jake, whereas I thought you said you only had enjoyable dreams about all sorts of fantasy women.'

'I asked Jake that too,' said Simon, 'although I'd guessed the answer and I was correct.'

'So what is the answer?' asked Alice.

'Getting caught,' stated Jake. 'I used to have a lot of bad dreams about getting arrested but since we formed RTA, I've hardly had any. I think it's because I'm now doing things for good causes.'

'Also, I suspect, because you've got Simon as a friend who helps make sure you do things in a safe way,' pointed out Alice.

Taking everyone by surprise, Jake walked across the kitchen and held out his hand towards Simon in his awkward style, muttering, 'Thanks, mate.'

Simon ignored Jake's hand and, instead, gave Jake an enormous hug but then recoiled immediately. 'Blimey, Jake, I think you need a shower. My nose is level with your armpit.' Everybody laughed, including Jake.

'Come on, then,' said Robert. 'Nathaniel won't wait forever. Alice, all you need to do is sit in front of the computer so the camera can see you and press the A key. Simon has set it up so it will connect automatically.'

They all went into the lounge and Alice sat down as instructed. She took a deep breath. 'OK, I'm ready. You can all skedaddle and no eavesdropping.' As soon as she heard the lounge door close, Alice put on her friendliest smile and, with some trepidation, pressed the A key. Very quickly, the screen burst into life and she could see a chubby black face with a shock of dark black curly hair staring at her and looking extremely worried. 'Hello, Nathaniel. My name is Alice. Let me tell you what we do.'

Chapter Twenty-One

Derek and Stephen Watson were having lunch together at the Hare and Hounds, contemplating the management committee meeting held earlier that morning. Both were drinking a pint of Frisky Fox. 'I thought it was a very different atmosphere today,' said Stephen. 'Without Jeremy, it felt like more of a team and there was certainly no open hostility to the idea of investing in the brewery. It was a good idea of yours to invite Keith Fairbrother. He performed well and seemed to be on top of the numbers.'

'Yes,' acknowledged Derek, 'Keith knows his stuff. One day he should make a good Finance Director but not just yet. He needs more experience of the wider business aspects first. I've arranged to take him with me next week when I go to the bank. As you heard, our cash flow is getting very tight and I want to find out the true position first hand over obtaining additional loans, given Jeremy admitted he could have tried harder.'

'It's a real shame it's all going to be for nothing,' stated Stephen. 'Even if you can get more loans, it will only be a stay of execution. I suppose you've spoken to Father recently?'

'Yes, he called at the beginning of the week to tell me our secret was out, blaming Bickerstaff for opening his big mouth. I was already aware because I had a couple of calls from the big boys saying they'd heard we were struggling and would be interested in bidding if we were looking to sell. From what Father said, it seems at least one of them has been tapping up some of Father's cousins. He called to tell me if it got any worse, he would feel the need to call an extraordinary general meeting and renege on his promise to wait until the year end. In a couple of weeks, we have to come clean about Mary's shares so, if shareholders are already jittery before then, that may well be the final straw.'

'That's basically what he said to me as well,' admitted Stephen. 'In spite of trying to talk positively this morning about options for investing in the brewery, I'm resigned to the fact it will never happen. Even though the results for the last couple of months have been better, it would need a miracle to turn around our performance enough to keep both the bank and the shareholders happy. I was pleased you suggested lunch today because I wanted to tell you face to face that my view has changed. I hope you're not too angry with me but I think we need to focus our attention on how we sell. I would like to do whatever we can to help our employees rather than just accept the highest bid if it means everyone loses their jobs in the process.'

To Stephen's immense surprise, Derek rocked back in his chair and laughed. 'That makes what I wanted to say to you a damn sight easier. I think this whole business with Mary and money has made me go soft. I've also been thinking we should turn our attention to doing the best for the employees. I don't want us to become just another family brewer swallowed up by a large national or international company with all jobs lost and our heritage forgotten. Realistically, there's no way back from our current position but I believe there might be a way forward to help at least some of our staff. One of the calls I had earlier in the week was from Chris Butcher. He, too, had heard of our predicament. It wasn't quite a white-knight offer but he was very open about their own position. Apparently, they've only just been able to keep their shareholders at bay in recent years and divisions are starting to form within the Butcher family because profits have been steadily falling. They have a similar problem of an ageing brewery with spare capacity but on a potentially valuable site. Believe it or not, he says it was me asking him about that strange email to Mary that prompted him to think about making a significant strategic move. He doubts they could raise the funds to buy us outright but he did float the idea of some sort of merger. I've known Chris for a long time and Father always seemed to get on well with Chris's father, Basil Butcher. Anyway, I've accepted his invitation to stay with him next weekend to have a round of golf and explore possible options. What do you think?'

Stephen thought for a moment before replying. 'I can't see any harm in talking to Butcher's, as long as it's kept highly confidential, but I do think you need to tell Father, assuming you haven't already done so. I'm sure, in principle, he would be supportive. Whatever deal we end up doing and with whoever, I hope the three of us can agree it's for the best as I definitely don't want it to split the family.'

'I agree. I'll call Father tonight to tell him and ask his advice. The three of us should work together on this. Another benefit of going to stay with Chris Butcher is it gets me away from Mary for a night. That's also why I chose steak and ale pie for lunch so I don't need to eat with her tonight.'

'I have to say, you seem remarkably jovial given the situation with both the Company and your divorce.'

'I'm resigned to them both now. The divorce settlement is pretty much agreed. Even Mary is taking pity on me. She seems to have finally come to understand the concept of having enough. She knows I'll be taking a massive personal hit on my shares at the end of the financial year. It turns out what she really wants is to be able to maintain her current lifestyle and keep the house, only without me in it. That's the part that hurts but, between you and me, even that has been tempered by the fact I can now be more open about my feelings for Pauline, feelings which, amazingly, do seem to be reciprocated. We both know we need to be careful until the divorce is signed and sealed but Pauline has been brilliant in helping me with both issues. She's told me in no uncertain terms to stop blaming myself for the Company problems, that I made my decisions with the best of intent and whatever happens financially, I'll still have more money to live on than most people.'

'I bet she also told you to have a light lunch,' said Stephen with a smile as he tucked into his prawn baguette. 'Don't worry, brother, your secret is safe with me.'

* * *

At long last Alice was starting to feel that she was making some progress with Nathaniel. It had been very slow going. She had got very little out of her first two conversations, not helped by the fact that Nathaniel tended to mumble and stutter in a Geordie accent, making it difficult for Alice to understand him even when he did speak. She wished she could be in the same room as him. She knew she had to build up his trust in her but it was difficult at a distance. All she had been able to tell the others over the previous Sunday's lunch was Nathaniel was extremely frightened not just for himself but for his father losing his job, and because his mother was very ill and needed to be looked after. Robert, in particular, was getting frustrated and kept stressing the need to tell Derek Watson about the fraud before it was too late. Alice had managed to deflect the conversation onto other topics including arrangements for her move and Christmas. However, it was now only a couple of days before the next Sunday lunch and she had only just got to the point of mentioning the Secret Fox to Nathaniel. As he had immediately clammed up, Alice had arranged a further conversation for Saturday in the hope it would give her more to tell the others.

'Would you mind if the number on the notice board was changed from 12 to 6?' Alice asked Robert on the Sunday morning, shortly after she had emptied her shopping bag in the kitchen.

'Not a problem from my point of view,' replied Robert. 'I'm sure Simon will happily change it when he comes down. As you know, he's the one in charge of the countdown. I presume that means you want to move in next Saturday instead of a week on Friday?'

Alice was convinced there was a hint of excitement in Robert's voice. She had been taken aback when told Simon was counting down the days to her arrival, unsure as to whether to be pleased by being wanted or worried about not being able to live up to the level of expectancy.

'Yes, as I told you last week I've been trying to sort out what to do with some of the larger items of my furniture I'll no longer need. I've managed to sell my bed, dining table and chairs to a colleague who's recently bought his first house. He's arranged to borrow a van to collect them but can only do so over a weekend. As the first of December is a Friday, next Saturday was the obvious choice. He would have bought my sofa as well but I told him I wanted to keep that to replace your old purple one in the snug. Are you still OK with that plan?'

'I thought we had agreed all that with Simon and Jake a few weeks ago. We are going to change the lounge into an operations centre and the snug into a TV room. If any of us needs to escape, it will be to our bedrooms rather than the snug. Before we do any of it, we have to finish the W & C project first. How did your latest conversation with Nathaniel go yesterday? Are we able to tell Derek Watson anything yet?'

'Nice try,' responded Alice with a smile. 'I'll tell you all after lunch as I promised. I know you're frustrated because it's taking so long but I think you'll be pleased. I certainly want to hear your thoughts as I've a bit of a plan which would mean we wouldn't tell Derek Watson anything for another week.'

Robert looked deflated. 'Time is not on our side. W & C had another management committee meeting last week and, from the minutes, it is clear they are close to running out of money. Another week may be too late for Derek Watson to do anything about it.'

'Please trust me on this, Robert. The more I speak to Nathaniel, the more I'm convinced he is very similar to Jake. I'm certainly adopting the same approach I did over Jake's toe and it seems to be working. You know yourself it's a matter of planting an idea and then giving him time to consider it before pursuing the subject, so it does take a while.' As it does with you too, thought Alice to herself before changing the subject. 'Come on, take your mind off W & C for a while by helping me. It was your idea to choose meat loaf again for lunch so there's quite a lot to do and it doesn't look as though we'll have Jake to help today.'

As soon as they were all assembled ready for the Yorkshire pudding, Alice tried to pre-empt any questions about Nathaniel. 'Before any of you ask, I haven't forgotten I promised to update you about my conversations with Nathaniel. There's quite a lot to tell so I suggest we do it in the lounge after lunch over our cups of tea.'

'Do we have to clear up first?' asked Simon.

'Oh yes, of course,' replied Alice. 'Usual rules apply. The only one excused today is Robert as he helped me this morning. I'll trust William to make sure everything is cleared away properly.'

'No problem,' replied William. 'It's a small price to pay for having such lovely Sunday lunches. Dare I ask if they will continue once you have moved in?'

'I see no reason why not. Robert and I were talking about things like that earlier and we still need to finalise a few aspects, including how to balance diet and exercise for everyone.'

Jake groaned. 'I don't like exercise. It's boring.'

'The secret is to exercise for a purpose, not just for the sake of it,' stated Robert. 'That's why I have my bicycle.'

'When your toe is fully sorted, Jake, you might feel like doing more,' said Simon.

'Maybe,' replied Jake reluctantly.

The conversation fell away whilst they ate. After the main course had been served, Alice, trying to keep everyone upbeat, made an announcement. 'The other thing I was saying to Robert is I've spoken to Mum and told her I won't be going up for Christmas this year so, as far as I'm concerned, we can start planning for the RTA Christmas lunch we talked about.'

'That's great news,' said William. 'Whilst we're on the subject of Christmas, I have a suggestion about presents. Why don't we adopt a Secret Santa approach?'

'I don't know what that means,' exclaimed Jake, 'but if it means we get presents then it sounds good to me.'

'Don't forget, Jake, presents are as much about giving as receiving,' Robert pointed out. 'I believe the idea of a Secret Santa is that we would only need to give one present but, equally, we would only receive one present.'

'So how does it work, then?' asked Simon.

'We put all five names in a hat,' explained William. 'Everyone in turn draws out a name. The person whose name you draw out, you have to buy a present for. Obviously, you can't draw out your own name so, if you do, you put it back and try again. You mustn't tell anyone who you have drawn out. The names remain secret until Christmas Day, hence Secret Santa.'

'We could do the draw by computer,' stated Jake. 'Simon knows how to make it 100 per cent random.' Everyone laughed, including Simon.

'Let us not make it overly complicated,' said Robert, trying to exert his authority. 'Unless there are any objections, we will have roast turkey for Christmas Day lunch, followed by Secret Santa presents. Oh, and by the way, I've also spoken to my mum about Christmas and she has suggested they come for a couple of days between Christmas and New Year and stay in the Premier Inn. Alice, Mum suggested going with you to the sales to do some shopping.'

'That would be wonderful,' exclaimed Alice. 'I'd love to see your parents again, although I feel a bit guilty they have to stay in a hotel.'

As soon as everyone had finished eating, William leapt up. 'Come on then, Jake and Simon, let's get this lot cleared up so we can finally find out what Nathaniel has had to say.'

'By the way,' chirped Alice, by way of a teaser as she and Robert were heading for the lounge, 'he likes to be known as Nat and his father as Mani.'

'I'm pleased Christmas is sorted out,' said Robert, as he made his way towards his favourite armchair.

'Come and sit next to me on the sofa for a change. We can talk more quietly and will be less likely to be overheard.'

'I thought we weren't supposed to have any secrets from the others.'

'It's not a matter of having secrets. You asked me about what you could do to reciprocate for me being here. I have thought of a few things that would help me but I want to check that you're OK with them before I tell anyone else.'

'Oh, I see. What are they?' Robert asked cautiously.

'Don't worry,' said Alice softly, taking his hand in hers. 'They're only things that should allow us all to live together smoothly. For instance, I know rotas and routines are very important to you all. Me being here will make a difference to some of them. We'll no doubt need to introduce some new ones, particularly when this room and the snug are changed. I want to make sure you and I are aligned in our thinking. One thought I had is we could establish a new routine just for the two of us. As next Wednesday is the last of the month, I presume Simon and Jake will be going to their Asperger's group. We could go out for a meal again, just like when we went to the Dog & Duck. If we did something like that every month, it would give me a break from always cooking and the opportunity to make sure everything was under control or discuss any changes necessary. What do you think?'

'I did enjoy the Dog & Duck but we talked a lot about the W & C project. Will we have enough to talk about if we go out regularly to eat?'

Alice laughed. 'I might want you to listen more than talk but I can assure you there will be no shortage of subjects. I'm serious about balancing diet and exercise. We seem to have established Sunday roasts as a routine but Christmas Day is a Monday and we're not having two roasts in succession, so one of the things we can do is plan menus. Also, I was thinking of using a couple of my outstanding holidays for redecorating the snug, so we can talk about that, plus there's the whole subject of what's next for RTA.'

'Alright then,' agreed Robert. 'What do you have in mind for Wednesday?'

After they had decided to go to the Red Lion in Bletchingley, they turned their attention back to Christmas. Alice was so enjoying herself, conscious of the fact Robert was continuing to let her hold his hand, she failed to hear the door open. 'Oh, look, Cedric and Miranda,' announced Jake as he entered carrying a tray full of mugs of tea. Alice blushed and immediately let go of Robert's hand. Robert stood up and moved purposefully to his usual chair.

'You were very quick,' said Alice, regaining her composure.

'We're keen to hear about Nat,' stated Simon as he took Robert's place next to Alice.

'Yes we are but we've still done a good job,' reassured William, bringing up the rear.

Alice had a quick sip of her tea whilst the others were getting settled, then began. 'I'm going to tell you Nat's story from the information he's given me over the last ten days. It's not all based on fact. As Robert would say, there are still some unproven facts but it's my interpretation of everything he's said and I truly believe it's the basis upon which we should make our decision as to what to do next.'

'Are we allowed to ask questions?' enquired Jake.

'Yes, of course you are,' replied Alice, 'but it might be better if you try to let me tell the whole story first and, as I'm sure you know by now, there's no point in asking for clarification of anything technical.'

'We'll try to stay quiet,' said William encouragingly.

'We already knew Nat lives with his parents,' stated Alice. 'What we didn't know is, one of the main reasons is he has to care for his mother, who is called Simi. She was hurt in a serious car crash when Nat was nine. Her left leg had to be amputated and she suffered some permanent brain damage. Both Nat's father, Mani, who was driving, and Nat, who was strapped in the back, were unhurt apart from suffering shock. According to Nat, Mani was not at fault but still feels guilty and, as soon as Nat was old enough to be left on his own, Mani developed a tendency to drown his sorrows by regularly going to the pub. In the early days after the accident, they did have help but, by the time Nat left school, looking after Simi was essentially down to Nat and his dad. Also, as they had to have the house adapted and faced lots of other costs associated with Simi's situation, they were struggling for money even though Mani did manage to keep his job as a drayman at Limberts Brewery. The reason I'm telling you all this is because it helps to explain why Nat is as he is.'

'Did you find out if he was bullied at school or if he is Aspie?' Jake blurted out, unable to contain himself.

'No, Jake, I just tried to treat him as I found him,' replied Alice. 'However, given both his parents are Nigerian and Nat is clearly overweight, I wouldn't be surprised if he'd been bullied at some stage. He hasn't volunteered anything about Asperger's syndrome and I haven't asked him. To be honest, he just comes across as very shy and frightened. That's why it's taken so long. I do at last think he's beginning to trust me. He greeted me with a lovely smile yesterday and was the most communicative yet. He even explained in detail about the Secret Fox … but I'm in danger of getting ahead of myself. Let me focus on his involvement with Limberts Brewery. If we'd looked back further, we would've found he had a number of short-term jobs with Limberts and, before that, he did a part-time computing course. His route into computing was different to yours, Jake, but he has clearly become something of an expert, especially in Brewdat. Simon, you'll be interested to know he's installed cameras around the house so he can keep an eye on his mum whilst he's working on his computer in his bedroom.'

'That just seems like common sense to me,' stated Simon. 'I'd be more interested to know how good his security systems are around his computer.'

'Well, it's no good me asking him that,' Alice laughed. 'Hopefully, we'll reach a point where you can ask him yourself. I've tried to concentrate on how he ended up doing what he's doing now. It all started quite well for him. Limberts sounds to have been helpful to Mani after the accident, giving him a lot of flexibility and also, when Mani asked, giving Nat a chance to work in the IT department. Nat says he enjoyed the computing work but struggled to get on with the people and also felt guilty about leaving his mum. Limberts were going through a major upgrade of Brewdat so they gave Nat a role in the project and set him up with remote access so he could do a lot of the work from home. This worked really well for Nat. He learnt a lot about Brewdat and did his part of the project successfully. When the upgrade was complete and everything was running smoothly, there was little else for Nat to do but Limberts kept him on the books as they regarded him as a Brewdat expert and called on him from time to time when there were problems, so he kept his access and grew his knowledge in his own time.

'This arrangement worked well as it allowed Nat and Mani to manage the care of Simi between them. However, it all started to go wrong because one of Mani's partners on the drays, a man called Paul Jacobs, was stealing beer from the warehouse. Mani and a couple of his friends found out and told Paul Jacobs to stop or they would report him to the management. Paul Jacobs agreed but on the condition Mani got Nat to adjust the stock levels of the beers so the thefts would not be discovered, using the threat that if they were discovered he would say Mani had been involved as well.'

'Paul Jacobs doesn't sound like a nice person,' commented William.

'No,' agreed Alice, 'especially as, once he knew Nat could adjust the stock levels without being detected, he stole even more beer, increasing his threat to suck in Mani and Nat if he was caught. Nat felt trapped. They couldn't afford for Mani to lose his job so Nat continued to cover up the ever-increasing amount of theft. However, Paul Jacobs got so greedy he was caught by a different route. Apparently the brewing industry have a scheme called Kegwatch ... I think that's right, where beer containers can be traced and repatriated to their legal owners. Anyway, a number of Limberts containers were found where they shouldn't have been and were traced back to deliveries made by Paul Jacobs, who then had to face a disciplinary hearing. The manager who chaired this hearing was an area manager for Limberts' managed-house estate. For the time being, I'll call him Mr X.'

'That seems unnecessarily mysterious,' piped up Robert. 'I presume you know his name, so why not use it?'

'I think I might have guessed already,' said William with a smile.

Alice glanced across at William. 'If you're thinking it's Malcolm Bickerstaff, William, I can tell you you're wrong, although Mr X did report to Malcolm Bickerstaff at the time of the disciplinary hearing. And yes, Robert, I do know the name of Mr X but I don't want to tell you just yet because you will leap too far ahead. I want to try to convince all of you, in the same way as I am already convinced, that Nat has been exploited by both Paul Jacobs and Mr X and needs our help to get out of the pickle he is currently in. What I will say is I think Mr X fits Jake's description of the Sheriff of Nottingham and, therefore, it's Mr X we should be focussing our attention on to make sure he's caught and stopped but, at the same time, ensuring that Nat doesn't get blamed as well.'

'You say you get confused over technical issues,' stated Robert. 'Now I am getting confused over people issues. I also cannot work out how all this fits in with W & C and what we can do to help Nathaniel.'

'Sorry, I know this is difficult to follow,' apologised Alice. 'Let me go back to what happened after the disciplinary hearing. I'll try to keep it simple and straightforward. I do have a bit of a plan as to how we can help Nat but it does require that all of you really believe it's the right thing to do.'

'I do feel sorry for Nat over the beer theft,' admitted Simon. 'He does sound to have been pushed into doing something he didn't want to do.'

Holding her hand up towards Simon, Alice continued. 'The real problem, Simon, is having made that first small change to the stock levels within Brewdat, the whole thing escalated to Nat being forced into major criminal activity. Not surprisingly, Paul Jacobs was sacked by Mr X and then handed over to the police but not before he had tried to implicate Mani and Nat. When Mr X spoke to Nat, he realised how much Nat knew about Brewdat and how clever he had been to hide the missing beer. Mr X saw an opportunity to exploit Nat's talents for his own ends. As I said, Mr X was an area manager, one of four who looked after the managed pubs. All four area managers were under pressure from their boss, Malcolm Bickerstaff, to perform well. Mr X's pubs were the worst performing of the four of them and, as a result, his own job was under threat. He told Nat he would tell the police Mani wasn't involved in the theft if Nat could come up with a way to make Mr X's pubs look to be performing better than they actually were. Again, Nat felt trapped. He didn't even tell Mani about Mr X's proposal. He just wanted to do whatever he could to avoid his father losing his job because of the implications for his mother. So Nat came up with the idea of re-routing some transactions to Mr X's pubs from some of the other pubs.'

'Just like he did with the Secret Fox,' said Robert.

'Precisely,' agreed Alice, 'only the money stayed within Limberts. It was purely to make Mr X look like a better area manager and it worked. However, it gradually reached the point where the other area managers suspected something wasn't right. Mr X was worried he would be caught, so he decided to leave Limberts and he used his new position as the best-performing area manager at Limberts to boost his CV and get a job as a director of Watson & Charles, looking after their tenanted pubs.'

Quick as a flash, Robert leapt in. 'So that must mean Neil Martin is Mr X. Did we know he used to work for Limberts?'

'When Nat told me yesterday,' replied Alice, 'I was surprised. I don't think we did know about Neil Martin and, even if we had, I'm not sure it would have helped us very much. Anyway, you can probably guess the rest. Neil Martin continued his hold over Nat and got Nat to use his Brewdat knowledge to set up a similar scam on the W & C Brewdat system but this time with the Secret Fox as a fictitious pub designed to allow actual money to be embezzled. You remember, Robert, remarking on how easy it was to track down Nat from the bank account data. Well, there's an explanation for that. Neil Martin intentionally kept his own name well away from everything but insisted Nat take a payment directly from the Secret Fox so, if it was found, Nat would be the scapegoat. Once everything was set up, all Nat would get from Neil Martin was a list of sixty-nine numbers in the post every month. These were the percentage of online transactions to be moved from each pub to the Secret Fox during that month.' Alice paused and looked round the room. Everyone seemed mesmerised and deep in thought apart from William. 'You look very worried, William. What's the matter?'

'I'm aware I'd the job of going through Neil Martin's emails. I wish now that I had done it more thoroughly,' said William apologetically. 'I vaguely think I remember coming across something to do with Limberts Brewery but I can't be sure. If I'd been more vigilant, we might have made the connection much earlier.'

Simon leapt to William's defence. 'Don't beat yourself up, William. It was you who found the Jeremy Turner connection to Limberts. It's not surprising you didn't go on to look for a second link. I agree with Alice. It wouldn't have made much difference. It's only by hearing Nat's story that we really understand how it was all set up.'

'Maybe,' admitted William, 'but I can't help thinking Robert wouldn't have made the same mistake. I was so convinced Malcolm Bickerstaff was behind it all but that was just a false assumption or an unproven fact.'

In his usual to-the-point manner, Robert said, 'We can't turn the clock back. The key thing is what we do now. Alice said she has a plan. I think we should listen to that and then decide, but before we do, can we just confirm Nathaniel was also responsible for the original email?'

'Yes, he was,' stated Alice. 'According to Nat, having got away with creaming off almost two million last Christmas, Neil Martin either got too greedy or miscalculated when it came to the summer. He didn't mean to take so much money that it brought the Company down. When there was such an in-depth investigation … and remember he was in all the meetings so he could monitor the reaction, he panicked from fear of the Secret Fox being found. He instructed Nat to send the email to muddy the waters and make it look like W & C were under threat from Butcher's Brewery. It was also another way of putting Nat in the firing line and not himself. Nat was the one who extended the email chain to Stephen Watson and beyond in an attempt to hide his own involvement. Neil Martin also dropped many of the percentages to zero, which explains why the recent performance of the brewery has appeared to improve.'

'Nat hid the email pretty well,' said Jake, 'but I would've found him eventually. I had another look this morning and got close.'

'You only wanted to make sure he isn't as good as you are,' pointed out Simon.

'Jake, is that true?' asked Alice, putting two and two together. 'Is that why you didn't come to help with lunch this morning, you were trying to prove you're better than Nat?'

'I suppose so,' stuttered Jake. 'You've all been saying how much he's like me and how clever he's been. I thought he was a baddie and I wanted to beat him.'

'Do you still think he's a baddie,' asked William, 'after hearing everything Alice has just said?'

'Well … no, I suppose not,' admitted Jake. 'Neil Martin is the real baddie, the Sherriff of Nottingham. He's the one who should be put in jail.'

'At last, we have an explanation that fits all of the facts,' announced Robert, looking very pleased. 'Even I can understand how someone like Nat can be sucked into doing bad things if they're trying to protect their parents.'

'I'm pleased to hear you call him Nat rather than Nathaniel,' said Alice. 'It shows that you've softened towards him, Robert. I can assure you Neil Martin has got a stranglehold over Nat and there's nothing Nat wants more than to break free. We have a real opportunity to help him change his world for the better and rescue W & C at the same time. It needs all of you to help but this is my plan.'

Chapter Twenty-Two

It was the first Monday in December and Pauline was struggling to keep warm. She had switched on the auxiliary fan heater as soon as she had entered her office but it was failing to compete with the cold draughts coming under the door and through the ill-fitting windows. Part of her problem was nerves and she shivered as she thought of the week ahead. There was the December board meeting on Wednesday, followed by the management committee meeting on Friday. She had already sent out the board papers, which made depressing reading. The main decisions to be made surrounded the issue of Mary's shares. At Howard Watson's insistence, the letter Pauline had drafted advised shareholders not to purchase shares at this time and that an EGM was being arranged before Christmas to explain the position further.

The situation had not been helped when, after picking up the post, the first letter she opened was a stark resignation letter from Neil Martin. She had rushed through to Derek's office with it, only to find he already knew as he had received an email stating Neil had been in to clear his desk over the weekend and, for personal reasons, would not be returning. Now she had the rest of the post to deal with, most of which was corporate Christmas cards. She was tempted just to bin them all as it was obvious Watson & Charles would be having anything but a Happy Christmas. Nonetheless, she proceeded to open them prior to putting them on show in the reception hall.

Although she was only glancing at the content, she was struck by a large, almost amateurish card which had a picture of a computer on the front with the inscription "HAPPY CHRISTMAS from RTA" on the screen. When she opened it, instead of the usual Christmas wish surrounded by multiple signatures, she found a relatively large piece of typed text. She read it to herself once and then again. Surely it's good news this time, she thought as she was about to rush excitedly to Derek. Then, remembering the previous occasion with the news about Jeremy Turner, she stopped, took a few deep breaths and walked calmly into Derek's office.

'No, John,' said Derek firmly into the telephone. 'There must be an error. I've seen your results for November and they're similar to the previous two months; reasonable, but just short of budget. It doesn't make any sense at all. I strongly suggest you get the IT people to check out the Brewdat system.' He put the phone down with a thud and looked up at Pauline. 'The world is going crazy. It's not yet ten o'clock and I've already had a director resign without any explanation, and a call from Chris Butcher saying he can't raise the money we agreed. It wouldn't surprise me if whoever ends up buying us buys them as well. Now John Hargreaves is trying to tell me he's suddenly made a profit of almost a million pounds in just one weekend ... Sorry, rant over.'

Pauline just smiled and waved the Christmas card towards him. 'This may help to explain some of it. I don't want you to get too excited before you've read it, in case I've misinterpreted what it means.'

'What is it?' asked Derek, suddenly showing an interest. 'It just looks like a Christmas card.'

'It is and it's from Roger Thompson Associates. Read what it says inside. I had to read it more than once and I'm still not sure I know what it all means.'

'We should be getting used to everything from Robert Tait being anything but straightforward. You read it out and let me see what I make of it,' said Derek rocking back in his chair.

Pauline started to read.

'"Dear Mr Watson, I am pleased to inform you that the unproven facts which we discussed when we met in the Kings Arms in September are now proven. A Christmas card seemed to be the most appropriate vehicle to convey this news to you as my associates and I are confident that Watson & Charles is about to experience its best Christmas ever. In fact, we have discovered eight and a half million reasons for believing this. You should start to see proof of our findings very shortly ..."'

Before Pauline could continue, Derek had leapt up, run around his desk and swept her off her feet in a tight embrace, planting a huge kiss on her lips. She responded immediately and they hugged and kissed in silence until Derek pulled back to say, 'That's bloody brilliant. We're going to be safe. John was correct after all. I'd better tell him, and Father and Stephen and even Mary, since it was Mary who found Tait in the first place. I have to admit I'd given up on him, especially when we heard no more after the Jeremy business.'

Pauline kissed him again and then said, 'I'm so delighted it's such good news. I thought it meant something like that. But there is a bit more. Let me read you the rest.' She rescued the card which had fallen on the floor.

'"On a separate but not totally unrelated matter, I am not sorry you have lost yet another director. My advice is not to ask any questions and to focus your attention on finding a better replacement."' After thinking for a moment, she commented, 'Presumably that relates to Neil's resignation. Do you think it means Neil was responsible all the time?'

Derek pondered, still somewhat shell-shocked. 'I think it probably does and, in a way, I hope it does. Although, I'm pretty sure Neil doesn't have the technical skills to carry out a sophisticated cyber-attack. Anyway, I intend to take Tait's advice and not pursue the matter. The main thing is we get the money back and put a stop to all the talk of selling the Company. Also, maybe I should start to call him Robert instead of Tait, given he's just saved our necks.'

'You could call him Roger. I still think he wants his involvement to be kept secret so don't say anything about him when you tell the others. Also, there's another paragraph I haven't read yet and you might not like this one so much.'

'Go on then, what does it say?'

'It says,' said Pauline reading hesitantly, '"As we have fulfilled the conditions of the original contract, we have taken payment in full. On behalf of myself and my associates, I would like to thank you for your business." It's signed Roger Thompson.'

Derek returned to his desk chair and started typing on his keyboard. 'I thought as much,' he mused. 'Someone has taken half a million pounds out of my bank account without my knowledge or authorisation. The strange thing is I feel extremely pleased to see it's gone. Roger

Thompson may have his quirky ways but something tells me he's one of those rare things these days, a man of his word.' He stood up and took Pauline's hands in his. 'Changing the subject, how are you fixed this evening? We now have two reasons to celebrate.'

'Two!' exclaimed Pauline. 'The future of Watson & Charles and what else?'

'Mary signed the divorce papers on Saturday so we don't have to pretend any more.'

'That's wonderful news.' She wrapped her arms around his neck and whispered in his ear. 'We can have dinner, and you can take me home and stay the night.' Derek pulled back and roared with laughter. 'What's so funny about that?' asked Pauline, suddenly concerned.

'Nothing for you to worry about,' explained Derek, still laughing. 'I've just remembered the penalty for me breaching the confidentiality of my contract with Roger Thompson was for my DNA to be planted in your flat. Now it'll be there anyway. Don't worry, I won't tell anyone who it was that rescued us ... Come on, we've a lot to do before tonight.'

* * *

Given how early she had to get up to put the turkey in the oven, Alice crept downstairs to avoid waking the others, being careful to remember Simon's instructions about alarms. Christmas Day had come round very quickly. Although her move had gone smoothly, it had taken her longer than she had expected to settle in. Leaving for work was not a problem. Generally, no-one else was up early enough to get in her way. Occasionally, Simon would come down to make his early-morning cup of tea whilst she was having her breakfast but there was never any sign of Robert or Jake. However, when she returned after work it was a totally different story. All three of them seemed to want her attention as soon as she walked through the door. When she lived on her own, she had been used to coming home and unwinding before thinking about food or whatever she had planned for the evening. As she had not wanted to upset them, she had started by making various excuses to go up to her bedroom. However, that just delayed the problem, so she had made a point of explaining to Robert she needed some time to herself to relax after her day's work. She had been amazed how understanding he had been. He had obviously spoken to Jake and Simon because, for the last few days, she had been allowed to recover from the pressure of work without being disturbed.

Part of the problem was the euphoria that existed from having successfully completed the Watson & Charles project. William had been round a lot, particularly at the weekends, so even though she was now living in the same house as Robert, Alice still felt starved of having time with him on their own. Some of it was of her own making as she had persuaded both Simon and Jake to stop taking their main meals up to their bedrooms and eat communally instead, so as to be more sociable. She told herself she would just have to keep seeking opportunities, just like she had the previous evening when, after William had gone home and Simon and Jake had gone upstairs to call Nat, she had suggested to Robert they open the presents from their parents together. Initially, Robert had been reluctant, saying presents were not to be opened until Christmas Day, but he'd come round when Alice explained the others only had one present to open and it would be unfair if they were made to sit through watching the two of them open more. At the end of the evening it had seemed the most natural thing for her to give Robert a goodnight kiss, something else that was definitely going to become a firm routine in future.

* * *

'Well, Alice, we are facing a major problem today; you seem to have been hoist by your own petard,' said Robert with a smile on his face after he had finished his last Brussels sprout. He had only taken three to start with and left them all until the end, signifying to Alice that Brussels sprouts were not his favourite.

'I don't know what you can possibly mean,' Alice responded semi-seriously, even though she had guessed what he meant. 'Everything is going extremely well.'

'Yes,' agreed William. 'That was delicious, a real Christmas lunch and a great way to celebrate our fantastic success with the W & C project.'

'We haven't finished yet,' remarked Simon. 'There's still the Christmas pudding to come, although I'm pretty full already. I'm pleased we didn't have Yorkshires as well today.'

'So, what's the problem?' asked Jake, looking concerned. 'I hope it doesn't affect opening the presents. You promised we could open them straight after lunch if I stopped going on about them.'

'Don't worry, Jake, it's nothing too serious. I suspect Robert is referring to my rules about clearing up,' explained Alice. 'Am I right?'

'Yes,' replied Robert. 'You've made it abundantly clear anyone who helps with the preparation is excused from the clearing and washing up. We all helped this morning. Even Bill got here especially early to help.'

'I don't mind clearing up, Bob … flobbadob,' said William. 'Even if I have to do it all by myself, it would be well worth it given what my alternative Christmas lunch would have looked like.'

Even at Christmas … thought Alice to herself. I must get to the bottom of this flobbadob business.

'If you apply Robert's type of logic,' argued Simon, 'Christmas Day is special so we can have a special rule. Also, this is an RTA Christmas lunch which we all prepared together as a team so it makes sense we all clear it away as a team. It was one of the things I liked most when we had our project review, how everyone had contributed to the success. It was a real team effort.'

'There you are, Robert,' said Alice laughing, 'another new rule for Christmas. I couldn't have put it better myself.'

'Does that mean I have to wait even longer for presents, until all the washing up is done and everything put away?' asked Jake petulantly.

'Not if you don't mention them again,' stated Alice. 'I suggest we let the turkey go down then have Christmas pud, followed by presents with a cup of tea in the lounge. The rest of the clearing up can be done afterwards. Now we are RTA, I know everyone can be trusted to help.' She stood up to collect the dirty plates and took them into the kitchen.

William picked up a couple of the vegetable dishes and followed Alice so he could whisper in her ear, 'I'm concerned about how excited Jake is getting about these presents. You said not to spend too much and I've only bought him a pair of slippers. He could end up being very disappointed. I'd hate him to have a meltdown over it.'

'I know,' Alice whispered back. 'He's been like a 5-year-old all morning. I'm hoping just having one present will be enough, given he's been used to having nothing at all for years. Don't worry, I've got something lined up which I hope will help to avoid any meltdown.'

Robert, Simon and Jake trooped through with the rest of the dishes and between them they returned to the dining room with the Christmas pudding, bowls, a jug of rum sauce and a pot of brandy butter.

'I bet Nat wishes he was having a Christmas lunch like this,' said Simon, when they were all back around the table. 'All he's having is shepherd's pie.'

'It must be difficult with his mother as she is,' William responded. 'Anyway, I thought you said he was happy because we've given him the best Christmas present he could have hoped for, by getting him away from the clutches of Neil Martin.'

'That's right,' confirmed Simon. 'As we've said before, it was a great idea of Alice's to make it look like an official threat from Her Majesty's Revenue and Customs. Once Nat saw the accompanying email to Neil Martin telling him to resign from W & C, not touch the money in the off-shore bank accounts and to have no further contact with Nathaniel Oudabade, he was over the moon. I think he's getting a lot of satisfaction from giving all the money back to W & C.'

Not wanting to take all the credit, Alice leapt in. 'It might have been my original idea but it was Robert who helped to develop it into a workable solution, the night we went to the Red Lion. That's where the idea of the RTA corporate Christmas card came from too.'

'I'm pleased you only wanted one of those cards, it was harder to make than I thought,' stated William. 'I still find it strange Neil Martin gave up both his job and all the money so easily.'

'That's because you've only heard about the exploding emails,' explained Alice. 'You should see them in reality; they're quite scary.'

Jake blurted out. 'That was Little John. He usually does more damage than just destroying an email. I had to reprogram him very quickly. It took all night.'

'Yes, you've told us many times before about Little John,' pointed out Robert, 'and all your other outlaws.'

'Leave Jake alone, Robert,' reprimanded Alice. 'Without Little John, it would have been more difficult to convince Neil Martin. I'm sure it was seeing emails disappear so dramatically shortly after he'd read them that made him take the threat of twenty years in jail seriously. Also, he knows is he is guilty of fraud and embezzlement so, even though this time it wasn't an official letter from HMRC, I'm sure he believes we have the technology to generate enough evidence to make sure it is official next time. It's important to keep up the pressure but Nat understands that and, with Simon and Jake's help, will stay on top of it.'

'So how many emails has Neil Martin had now?' asked William.

'Five,' replied Robert. 'Nat's going to send one a week for a while longer and then, as long as Neil Martin remains compliant, drop the frequency to one a month. Also, more than half of the money has now been returned. The remainder will be transferred in the next two weeks because, after New Year's Day, the Christmas peak will be over. Also, we've had a second email of thanks from Pauline Sharples confirming Derek Watson is happy we took our payment.'

'I suppose it's quite ironic Nat is now going though Neil Martin's personal emails to find pieces of information he can use to prove to Mr Martin his every move is being monitored,' said William. 'As you know, I wish I'd done more with those at the time but I do accept it was a matter of limited resources. If we were to be in the same position again, Nat's assistance would be invaluable.'

'Nat would much rather work for RTA than Neil Martin, that's for sure,' said Alice.

'RTA is just the five of us,' stated Jake. 'I'm getting to like Nat but I don't want him to be one of us.'

Thinking this was a good time to introduce her latest plan, Alice announced, 'I want RTA to remain as just the five of us as well, but I do think we might consider Nat as a sub-contractor. He would need training but that would just be a continuation of the help you and Simon are giving him now, Jake. I was thinking the two of you could set up regular sessions with him in the evenings after we've eaten. Whilst you are doing that, Robert and I can concentrate on the changes to this room and the snug.'

Trying not to smirk, William said, 'It's good of Tom to offer to help with some of the DIY tasks next week. It made sense to put off the snug redecoration until he's finished. If you two want my help, you only have to ask.'

'That's very kind,' replied Alice, slightly sarcastically, 'but we'll manage fine. You've your retirement to think about, selling your shop and moving house.'

'Now you've got the Watson & Charles money, are you sure you can't afford to move close to here?' asked Simon.

No, I'm afraid not,' replied William. 'I'll try to get as close as I can but it will still need to be a cheaper area to give me the space I need for a workshop. Anyway, it'll be a little while yet before I'm ready to move.'

'Tom only does DIY tasks to avoid having to go shopping with Mum,' stated Robert. 'He told me on the phone yesterday he was very grateful Alice was going to the sales instead of him.'

'I'm very much looking forward to it,' said Alice truthfully, thinking she really did need to shop this time, in preparation for Terry's wedding. She needed a new dress for herself but, more importantly, she needed advice on how to get Robert to wear something other than chinos and trainers. 'Right, who's ready for Christmas pud?'

Without asking, Robert went into the kitchen and returned with a tub of ice-cream. 'I don't like alcohol, so I'm going to have ice-cream instead of rum sauce or brandy butter.'

When they had all finished eating and she realised Jake was about to speak, Alice beat him to it. 'Would you three mind making the tea and bringing it through? I just want to have quick word with Jake in the lounge. Come on, Jake, it's very nearly present time.'

As they brought the tea tray into the lounge to place it on the low table, which now sat in the centre of the room, William, Robert and Simon saw that the sofa and two of the armchairs had been moved to face the small artificial Christmas tree, under which were the five presents. Another chair, in which Jake was now sitting wearing a bright red Santa hat with a white fluffy trim and pompom, had been placed close to the tree, facing into the room. As soon as they were all seated, Jake rose and announced in a loud voice, 'Good afternoon, Lady and Gentlemen. Welcome to the inaugural RTA Secret Santa event. As you can see, I will be playing the part of Santa. I will ask each recipient in turn to come forward and sit on this chair to open their present, so everyone else can see clearly what it is. To demonstrate the procedure, I will open the first present myself.'

He turned and reached down under the tree to pick up a shoe box-sized gift and turned over the label. 'This one says "To Jake, Happy Christmas from William".' He sat back on the chair and quickly removed the wrapping paper and opened the box to reveal a pair of tartan slippers. Alice and William were watching very closely for signs of disappointment but Jake's face remained aglow. 'These are great. Just what I need.' Immediately, he took off his old scruffy slippers with the trodden-down heels and put on the new ones. Then, remembering his instructions, he continued. 'Don't forget to thank the giver,' as he walked over to William's chair and awkwardly held out his hand. 'Thank you, William.'

'You're very welcome, Jake,' William responded as he stood and shook Jake's hand. 'I hope they're comfortable and they don't hurt your big toe.'

'No, they feel fine. My toe doesn't hurt any more. It's now almost fully healed from having the nail removed. It's like a second Christmas present.'

'Well, you have Alice to thank for that,' stated William.

Jake turned towards Alice, holding his arm out once again. 'Thank you for helping me with my toe, Alice.'

For the first time ever, Alice felt like leaping up and giving Jake a hug and kiss but, worried it might give the wrong impression, she rose slowly, shook his hand and said, 'No problem, Jake, I was happy to be of assistance.'

Jake returned to the presents under the tree and picked out a relatively small one. 'I'm allowed to know about this one as I bought it. It says "To Simon from Jake".' He waited while Simon moved to the chair and then handed the present over. Simon found he had been given a leather wallet. Jake muttered an explanation. 'It's to help you keep your extra money from the Watson & Charles project safe.'

Simon looked more relieved than pleased, shook Jake's hand and said a quiet thank you. However, as he was heading back to the sofa to regain his seat next to Alice, William called out. 'Of course, nothing is 100 per cent secure.' Everyone laughed, including Simon.

Jake returned to the remaining presents. Everyone knew he had sneaked more than one look at them but did not let on when he feigned surprise on reading the label on the largest present. 'Oh, this one's from Alice to William. It feels quite heavy.' William ambled to the receiving chair and slowly open his gift. It turned out to be a presentation pack of a bottle of Frisky Fox and a branded celebration beer glass.

'It's not meant to be drunk, although obviously you can if you wish,' said Alice, standing up. 'I got it more as a memento of the Watson & Charles project.'

'Thank you,' said William emotionally, as he shuffled towards her and engulfed her in his arms. 'I'll definitely keep it unopened but I don't suppose any of us needs a tangible reminder of Watson & Charles. I'm sure it will stay engrained in our memories for the rest of our lives, not just because it was successful and earned us a lot of money but because it brought us closer together as a group of friends and was the first of, hopefully, many achievements for RTA.'

'Now there are only two,' stated Jake, loudly, 'both of a similar size.' He picked one up, apparently at random, looked at the label and said, '"Happy Christmas from Simon to Robert". Come on, Robert, let's see what you've got.'

Robert took his place and opened his present to find a bell for his bicycle. Showing no obvious reaction, he stood and walked towards Simon who was already waiting to shake his hand. 'Thank you, Simon. This will be very useful. I have been thinking about getting one for a while but had not got round to it.'

Simon grasped Robert's hand in both of his as he said, jokingly, 'You do realise it's not for your bike. It's for when you go to the supermarket so you can warn unsuspecting young ladies that you are approaching at speed.' Everyone laughed.

William chipped in. 'Of course, Simon, if Alice had heard Robert coming and got out of his way, she would never have been knocked over, none of us would ever have met her and there would have been no RTA. Where would we be then? I would let Robert put the bell on his bike if I were you.' Everyone laughed again.

Feeling totally relaxed and pleased everyone was enjoying themselves, Alice had totally forgotten about receiving her own present. 'You don't need to sit down just yet, Robert,' Jake was saying. 'No prizes for guessing who's next. Just one left.' He picked up the remaining present. Alice still hadn't moved from the sofa. 'Come on, Alice, your turn.'

Suddenly it all clicked. A present for her from Robert! She looked at the size and shape of what looked like a smallish box. Dare she dream? Could it possibly be what she was thinking and hoping for? She thought of Susan's words: 'You have to judge his emotions through his actions.' By the time she reached the chair and took the present from Jake, she was a bag of nerves. With trembling hands, she peeled away the wrapping paper to reveal a home-made box. She opened it slowly and YES, there it was, the tell-tale bright green plastic.

'What is it?' asked Jake, as he looked over her shoulder.

Trying to stay calm, Alice raised the object into the air. 'Isn't it obvious? It's a cubic pea in a spherical hole.' Not able to contain herself any longer and still holding her present, she rushed across the room, tears running down her cheeks, flung both her arms around Robert's neck and gave him an enormous kiss on his lips.'

'Oh, Miranda,' cried out Jake.

Alice didn't care any more that they all knew. Now, at last, she knew. Determined not to blow it this time, she stopped short of blurting out the words that had formed in her head: 'I love you, too.' Instead, she released Robert and said, in as steady a voice as she could manage, 'Thank you so very much, Robert. It's just like the one your mum has.'

Pleased to be freed, Robert sat back down in his chair as if nothing untoward had happened and replied in his usual matter-of-fact way. 'You're welcome but, actually, it isn't the same as Mum's. It is an updated version. Yours has thinner window frames. I can see a lot of things more clearly these days.'

For the first time in many years, Dr Alice Selby was truly content.

Epilogue

Six months later, Robert, Alice, Jake and Simon were all sitting in the operations centre, formerly the lounge, contemplating their next major project now they had completed the planned modifications to the house. They were surrounded by lots of computer equipment with multiple screens on the walls and Jake, as usual, was in charge of the central control console. Suddenly, there was a ping and Simon leapt up.

'Hey, Robert', he said, 'you know that email account associated with the Watson & Charles project I wanted to close but you insisted was kept alive? It's just received a message. It's from a Pauline Watson, do you know her?'

'Ah yes,' replied Robert, 'the new Mrs Derek Watson. If you recall, she was on the potential suspect list for a while until Alice realised her motivation was love and not greed. Anyway, what does she say?'

Reading aloud, Simon replied, 'It says, "On behalf of my husband and myself, I would like to inform you that Watson & Charles have recently acquired the business of Butcher's Brewery. It was a smooth and honest transaction carried out in a traditional manner, being finalised on the golf course away from prying eyes and insecure computers. Our new Finance Director is confident that, within 2–3 years and given effective management, this will result in at least a doubling of the company's profits. We believe this will stabilise both the family and the business for the foreseeable future and are certain this would not have been possible without your truly successful intervention. It is only fair, therefore, that a doubling of our profits is reflected in a doubling of your fee. Please feel free to help yourself to the other half. Derek also said to add that he knows he can trust you to spend it wisely as he finally understands. I hope you know what that means. Thank you again and kind regards, Pauline Watson.'''

'Well,' asked Alice, 'do you know what it means?'

'I think so,' said Robert smiling, 'and, if I am right, if Jake taps into Derek Watson's personal bank account, there will be half a million pounds waiting for us to collect. As far as spending wisely is concerned, I believe the house next door is still for sale and I suggest we use the money to help Bill buy it. Bill can live there now his shop is shut and he would also have plenty of space for all of his equipment, so all five of us can be close together. Would any of you object to that?'

Whilst Robert was speaking, Jake had got the bank details on the screen and, sure enough, there was the money and then, suddenly, the balance was reduced to just a few thousand. 'Got it,' said Jake, 'and as I haven't heard any objections to Robert's proposal, I'll call William straight away and tell him.'

Just as William's face was appearing on the screen, Alice said quietly to Robert, 'I think I need to have a word with you in the other room,' as she guided him by the arm to the door of the recently redecorated snug and closed it behind them. 'Robert,' she said when they were alone, 'if William is going to live next door, I really do think it's time for you to stop calling him Bill. I don't understand why you do it when it's obvious he doesn't like it.'

Robert turned to her and said, 'I don't see why it's such a big issue. It's just a bit of banter between us. I've told you before I don't want to call him William because I knew a boy at school called William, who was liked by a lot of people but was extremely horrible to me and I hated him for it. I don't want to think of that vicious bully every time I talk to Bill.'

'I can assure you, Robert,' said Alice in a firm voice, 'William does not regard it just as banter. It's far more serious to him than that. He still won't talk very much about it. You do realise, don't you, that William was called Bill at school. You've said yourself he has twice as many reasons as the rest of us for not wanting to be reminded of his schooldays.'

'No,' said Robert, trembling slightly and with tears starting to well in his eyes, 'I did not know that. Why did you not tell me before? Now you have pointed it out, I can see it does make some sort of logical sense.

How can I not see something like that for myself when I pride myself on my logical thinking in all other, non-people-related areas? It's all very well saying that being Asperger's is a positive thing but there are times when it can be incredibly frustrating.'

Alice, also fighting back the tears, put her arm gently around his shoulders and said softly, 'Robert, we know we all have different areas of difficulty. One of the reasons I want to be here is to help you with yours, if you'll let me. I know I can't teach you how to recognise people issues for yourself but, if you truly trust me, I'll try my best to explain them to you, just like I did at Terry and Juliet's wedding. Now you do understand about William, how about trying to do something positive about it? Let's go back and rejoin the others.'

She opened the door and they walked together into the operations centre to be met with three laughing, smiling faces, two in the room and one on the big screen. It was clear that the three of them had already started to plan William's move. Robert slowly made his way in front of the big screen and looked up directly at William before saying in a shaky voice, 'Hello William, I am so very sorry. I promise to never ever call you Bill again. Alice has just explained to me why you don't like it. I was called Bob at school and I hated it.'

'I know,' replied William, no longer smiling. 'You remind me of a friend, a very, very special friend I had at school. His name was Ben. He died ... Oh flobbadob.'

Nobody laughed.

Printed in Great Britain
by Amazon